I0576761

Henry C. (Henry Charles) Banister

George Alexander Macfarren

His Life, Works, and Influence

Henry C. (Henry Charles) Banister

George Alexander Macfarren
His Life, Works, and Influence

ISBN/EAN: 9783337095116

Printed in Europe, USA, Canada, Australia, Japan

Cover: Foto ©Raphael Reischuk / pixelio.de

More available books at **www.hansebooks.com**

GEORGE ALEXANDER MACFARREN

HIS LIFE, WORKS, AND INFLUENCE

BY

HENRY C. BANISTER

PROFESSOR OF HARMONY AND COMPOSITION AT THE ROYAL ACADEMY OF MUSIC,
THE GUILDHALL SCHOOL OF MUSIC, AND THE ROYAL NORMAL
COLLEGE AND ACADEMY OF MUSIC FOR THE BLIND

LONDON

GEORGE BELL AND SONS, YORK STREET

COVENT GARDEN

1891

PREFACE.

"Wenn du willst in Frieden eingehn,
Wenn du ledig willst der Pein gehn,
    Spricht Ben Kab,
So sei jeder Grössere dir ein Vater,
So sei jeder Mittlere dir ein Bruder,
So sei jeder Kleinere dir ein Kind.
Du verehre deinen Vater,
Halt'in Ehren deinen Bruder,
Zärtlich liebe du dein Kind."

THIS Arabic saying so aptly describes the spirit of
the life recorded in the following pages that it
may fitly introduce any prefatory remarks. The social
side of George Alexander Macfarren's character was
so marked by the reverence due to those around him
according to their relative ages and positions,—"every
greater one . . . a father, every equal one a brother,
every lesser one a child,"—and kept him, as an artist,
so free from petty jealousy, so ready with sympathetic
help for those struggling, as a teacher so kind and
patient, and tinged his whole life with such humility,
and such consideration for others,—that those who
knew him best, knowing his manifold attainments,
achievements, and powers, as well as these personal
and social qualities, cannot separate the two aspects
of his individuality, but delight to remember his
reverence for father, honour for brother, and tender

love for child, as having combined with his artistry to render him so revered, honoured, and loved as a friend.

Those who knew him but a little, without sympathy if without antagonism, have often judged him to be simply a somewhat hard, pedantic, even perverse theorist; and such will be little prepared for such claims on his behalf being placed in the forefront as those with which these remarks are opened. The perusal of this volume may dissipate, to some extent, the mistaken impressions that have prevailed in the minds of many.

At a dinner given by the Liverpool Musical Professors to Sir George A. Macfarren, July 28th, 1884, on occasion of his distributing the certificates to the successful candidates at the Local Examination in connection with the Royal Academy of Music, he, replying to an address, said that

"he had had a long life, and it had not been without its vicissitudes, for he could look back to the time of rejected operas sent back without the seal being broken; but he had worked hard, not for the sake of work, but for the love of the work, and if, possibly, by his example, he had been the means of encouraging others to strive in a like manner, then, indeed, he would have accomplished something tangible for music."

This long life of hard work, and of vicissitudes,— not only such as fall to the lot of earnest strivers generally, but, in addition, the terrible deprivation which would have at once dismayed and baffled an ordinary aspirant, but which drew forth from Macfarren such persistent determination, and which he never suffered to deprive him of energy, or to stay his undaunted efforts,—this life is here traced ; so that, according to his own expressed desire, his example may stimulate others who have similar aims, and their own difficulties : surely, not such difficulties as those which he so manfully overcame. The obstinacy, and dogged dogmatism, with which some have credited him, may here appear in its more admirable aspect of unswerving consistency, and high-minded perseverance. On his sixty-third birthday, March 3rd, 1876, he wrote to Mr. T. J. Dudeney: "Nine apprenticeships have taught me more and more love for art, more and more indifference to disappointment, more and more sympathy with fellow climbers up the hill whose prospect ever widens." Nearly two more apprenticeship terms did he serve without any sign appearing of these high qualities becoming less and less powerful factors in the high sustainment of his stainless artistic career. Let not the lesson be lost, the example be unobserved, by those yet in their earlier apprenticeship stage !

In his earlier days he fell into one of the Hampstead ponds : finding himself in the water, he struck out like a dog, learned to swim, and saved himself. That was his way of attacking difficulties all through life, enjoined upon others, and exemplified by himself. He would say, " the difficulty conquered, the acquisition of power abides."

Obstinate ! Well, a ground-bass is a *basso-ostinato;* but what beautiful things Purcell, Handel, Bach, could build on such a bass ! And so, a man who, unlike the crowd, thinks for himself, will act for himself, and will not easily be persuaded to move again with the throng. Macfarren was such a one: and he was branded as obstinate. It was sometimes a pity, as when, in the early days of his failing sight, not enduring to have a guide, he rushed on, and struck against a tree in the Park, a broken nose being the result. As one who knew him well writes: "Not many of his friends will forget that stooping figure, in his blindly rushing walk along the London streets, his little guide-boy straining to keep pace with the master's eagerness." The eagerness remained, though he was compelled to yield and have the guide.

Again: a friend writes:—

"One criticism he was proof against: nothing that I could say would induce him to alter. I mean, his extraordinary division of syllables in his later vocal compositions. I tried precedent, the printer's habit; I tried quizzing. No! he had never heard of Robson, and 'Villikins and his Dinah,' so it was of no use. He insisted on 'wee-ping,' 'wal-king,' till I feared to worry him more. His idea was that singers are so apt to pronounce the later consonant in a syllable before the note is over,[1] that he would do his best to prevent such an error by putting off the consonant to the end of the note, joining it to the next syllable. He had been assured by good singers and teachers that it was a wise precaution, and he would abide by it."

Enough, however, of this. The record is here given of a wonderful career of achievements for a blind man: a life of marvellous mental activity, productiveness, and influence, for any man.

A word or two as to the plan of the work.

This being a record, less of incident than of thought, utterance, and influence, no apologetic plea is needed for the somewhat copious extracts from Macfarren's

[1] See p. 369.

writings on music, by which he speaks for himself: writings, some of which are quite inaccessible, and others practically so, being buried in old numbers of periodicals, or casual numbers of those more recently issued, and almost certain to be overlooked by the majority of those desiring to know of his opinions on the multifarious subjects about which he wrote.

Moreover, for similar reasons, a strictly chronological arrangement has been discarded, it having been thought better to focus, so far as possible, the light from his clear intellect, and, therefore, to bring together utterances and writings of different times and circumstances, showing the consistency in most cases, in others the progressiveness, of his mind. A glance at the headings of the chapters will sufficiently indicate this plan.

For invaluable aid rendered to me in the preparation of this Memoir, by the loan of letters, manuscripts, programmes, etc., the furnishing of reminiscences, the verification of dates, and in various other ways, I tender my most sincere thanks to Lady Macfarren, Lady Thompson, Miss Macfarren, Miss Macirone, Miss Oliveria Prescott, Madame Lemmens-Sherrington, Mademoiselle Gabrielle Vaillant, Mr. H. O. Anderton, Mr. Edwin Barnes, Mr. J. R. Sterndale-Bennett, Mr. G. J. Bennett, Mr. Windeyer Clark, Mr. Gerard F. Cobb, Mr. J. S. Curwen, Mr. F. W. Davenport, Mr. T. J. Dudeney, Sir George Grove, Mr. Henry Holmes, Dr. E. J. Hopkins, Mr. Ernest Kiver, Mr. T. B. Knott, Mr. John Macfarren, Mr. Walter Macfarren, Mr. Charles Stewart Macpherson, Mr. Ridley Prentice, and the Rev. H. M. de St. Croix. That there are not more imperfections than I fear may be detected in the work, results largely from the hearty sympathy and ungrudging assistance so readily, and in many cases repeatedly, accorded me in this endeavour worthily to represent the unique personality and artistic course of one with whom I was more or less acquainted and personally associated for nearly half a century.

H. C. B.

LONDON, *November*, 1890.

CONTENTS.

LIFE OF SIR G. A. MACFARREN.

CHAPTER I.

EARLY LIFE. 1813—1829.

IT is not easy to realize that George Alexander Macfarren, whom so many have known in his relation to all the activities of the musical life of our day, was born only four years after the death of Haydn,—"the Father of the Symphony,"—and the birth of Mendelssohn, both of which events occurred in the year 1809. The year of Macfarren's birth, 1813, was that of the establishment of the now time-honoured Philharmonic Society, for which Salomon's Concerts, and Haydn's visits to this country in connection therewith, had prepared the way. Music, in its grandest form, the orchestral, seemed then to be making a fresh start. Though Beethoven was then forty-three years of age, many of his greatest works were not written; and of those then in existence, few, probably, were at all familiar in this country; his pianoforte works least of all. Spohr was then a young man of twenty-nine, unknown here: Weber, two years younger. Mozart's "Le Nozze di Figaro" had been heard in London for the first time in the previous year, 1812: "Don Giovanni" was not produced here

till several years later,—1817. There was musical
activity, however, of a certain kind. The Concerts of
Antient Music, whose rule was not to perform any
music composed within twenty years, were going on.
The Cæcilian Society was giving Oratorio performances in the City. The Madrigal Society and the
Catch Club pursued their several courses, devoting
themselves to the cultivation of concerted vocal music.
Muzio Clementi, termed the "Father of modern
Pianoforte Music," and Johann Baptiste Cramer, were
resident in London, exerting a wholesome influence
on pianoforte music and its performance. Dussek had
died in 1812. Among eminent musicians then living
in Europe may be mentioned Viotti, Salieri, Zingarelli,
Cherubini, Paganini, Rossini (whose opera "Tan-
credi" was produced at Venice in 1813), Méhul,
Ignace Pleyel, Steibelt, Boildieu, Onslow, Auber,
Hummel, Fétis, Schubert, Herold, Mayseder, Meyer-
beer, and many others. In England there were also
Bishop, Attwood, Shield, Crotch, etc.

Such were the musical surroundings into which the
subject of our memoir was born, at 24, Villiers Street,
Strand, on the 2nd of March, 1813, the day being
Shrove Tuesday; so that, as it is related, he would
sometimes say, playfully, that in most years he had
two birthdays.

His father was George Macfarren, described trust-
worthily as "dancing-master, dramatic author, and
journalist," a native of London, as were his immediate
progenitors, "passionately fond of music, and himself
a fair violinist." For him, his son George Alexander
ever entertained most affectionate reverence; and, as
recently as January 1877, wrote a memorial sketch of

him which is charming in its manifestation of filial feeling. It would have been most consonant with his feelings that the memory should be preserved by reference to that sketch. He begins—writing to his friend J. W. Davison, who then edited the " Musical World," in the pages of which the sketch appeared—

"MY DEAR EDITOR AND OLD FRIEND,—You ask me to write of my father, and my pride in the subject is equal to my diffidence of ability to treat it. Truly the space before me and the time to fill it are insufficient for justice to the memory of him to whom I owe, not life alone, but impetus to art, and the first and best guidance in its pursuit. Yet, however briefly, those who knew him may be pleased to be reminded of himself and his doings ; those who knew him not may still accept some words of reverence and love for one not without influence beyond his immediate circle. From 1788 to 1843 his life was of almost ceaseless activity. In early childhood he showed a talent for versification, to which a far higher definition would not be misapplied ; and some stanzas, dated on his thirteenth birthday, evince depth of thought and power of words betokening ripest years. While a schoolboy he wrote a tragedy, which was acted by his mates, with the assistance of young Edmund Kean, then known by the name of Carey, with the sanction of the afterwards famous actor, Liston, usher at that time in Archbishop Tenison's school —the scene of the performance. My father played on bowed instruments so well as to sustain either of the parts in a violin quartet. He had some facility on the pianoforte, on which and on the fiddle, he was my first instructor. Would he had had an apter pupil ! He composed songs of merit, and many country dance tunes that had great popularity. One of the latter, which may now sometimes be heard on street organs—" Off she goes "—has been claimed as a national Irish melody ; and this says more for the merit of the tune than the acumen of the editor. Music would have been his profession, had he not met with a fashionable teacher of dancing—Bishop by name—who offered to make him a 'gentleman instead of a fiddler,' and, accordingly, took him as an apprentice. Here was a disparity between name and nature, the calling and the called; and, I earnestly believe, here was a consequent loss to music. Quick in conception and sanguine in enterprise, he promptly formed the plan of a work or of an action, and eagerly pursued it. So, when eighteen, he quitted his parental home, rented a spacious room, and opened a school for dancing. The theatre was the natural home of his diverse talent and the chief arena of its varied exercise. His first public dramatic production was almost extemporized, and acted for the benefit of his then intimate friend, Harley, in 1818, at the English Opera House. Many of his other pieces were also written at a sitting, of which perhaps the most remarkable instance was the 'Emblematical Tribute' on the occasion of the Queen's marriage. He suggested the first idea of this to the management of Drury Lane Theatre on the Thursday night previous to the ceremony. The idea was applauded, but its accomplishment pronounced impossible. The pronunciation was confuted; for by a strong power of magnetism, he infused his own ardour into every functionary of the establishment. The book was written, the music composed, the scenes were painted, the dresses stitched, the whole was rehearsed, and the masque presented to the public at the free performance on the royal wedding night, the Monday next following the primary conception.[1] Then, as ever, the word impossible had no meaning for him; and to all with whom he worked, his example made 'will' and 'can' identical. Those only may be named here among his dramatic pieces which made the strongest mark at the moment. 'The Horatii and Curiatii' was written for the appearance at the Coburg Theatre—then (how times have changed!) a place of high esteem and elegant resort—of Booth, who had been a rival of Kean, and was the father of the future presidenticide. 'Sir Peter Pry,' which had great success at the same theatre, has been accredited as the foundation of a more popular comedy, whose inquisitive hero is named after another apostle. 'If the Cap fit ye, wear it,' had also good fortune, being acted throughout

---

[1] See Chapter III.

the country under the name of 'The Student,' and reproduced at the Haymarket as 'Latin, Love, and War.'
'Edward the Black Prince,' and, soon afterwards, 'Guy
Fawkes,' were talks of the town, and are still theatrical
celebrities. 'Winning a Husband,' a protean piece, was
written for the favourite actress Mrs. W. Barrymore, and
has had hundreds of representations by her and by others.
My father's first acknowledged essay—he had contributed
scenes or songs to many pieces by other authors—on the
classic boards of Drury, was the ballad opera of 'Malvina,'
the merit of which raised it into an importance far above
what was intended in the original commission. Then he
wrote 'Oberon,' which helped to familiarize the town with
the incidents of Wieland's poem, the groundwork of the
opera by Weber, at that time in preparation at Covent
Garden;[1] and the task was undertaken within a month of
the first representation. His version of 'Gil Blas,' or
rather of the first adventures of Le Sage's hero, long outlived its Drury Lane production. Elliston had acquired
great confidence in my father's power during the last year
of his Drury Lane experience, and, on abdicating the
sovereignty which had been held by Garrick and Sheridan,
sought his aid in his new enterprise at the Surrey. The
facile author being prostrated by a premonition of the
malady to which he succumbed sixteen years later, the
veteran new manager was brought to his bedside. 'I open
this day fortnight,' said Elliston, 'and must have a piece
from you;' the piece was written and acted. The most
notable of his productions at the Surrey was the 'March of
Intellect,' a protean piece for the display of the versatile
talent of little Burke, the child prodigy, who acted, and
sang, and danced, and played on the violin, and spoke
Irish with a 'brogue so rich that you might cut it with a
knife.'

*　　*　　*　　*　　*　　*

" I must hurry on to the works wherein I myself had the
priceless advantage of his co-operation. There are three

---

[1] "The year 1826 is memorable in the annals of music, for it is
that in which Carl Maria von Weber produced his last great opera,
'Oberon,' on the English stage—the deathless work of a dying
man."—*Recollections and Reflections*, J. R. Planché, p. 74.

operas that have never seen the light, one of them having been accepted at three several theatres, all of which closed in bankruptcy before the intended representation. These, with his prompting of what to think, write, and avoid, made me an apprenticeship of which I, and none but I, can feel the inestimable value. There was the ' Devil's Opera,' another case of warfare against time, waged in the bright glowing season of the Queen's Coronation, when my father used to work on his libretto till the first peep of those inspiring summer mornings, and then awaken the composer to travail on the music in the stilly hours before heat came into the day, bustle into the streets, and out-door occupation into the writer's necessities.[1]

Lastly, there was ' Don Quixote,' of which but a portion of the music came to his knowledge. This was designed for several different productions, its cast of characters changed for every such purposed occasion, and its composition only completed nearly three years after his death, when it was really to be represented.

It is now time to speak of his management of the theatre in Tottenham Street, to which, in honour of King William's consort, he gave the name of the Queen's Theatre. There he ruled from February 1831 till June 1832—or would have ruled, had not the despot, Fortune, governed him, distorted his designs, and frustrated his principles and plans. He began with Handel's ' Acis and Galatea,' to which Cipriani Potter wrote additional orchestration for him, and its performance was indeed an event in musical London. ' The legitimate drama,' a term now of the past, was then unallowed in any but the ' patent theatres,' and thus the performances at the Queen's were restricted to plays written for the purpose. In the production of these, regard was first given to the naturalness of the scene, in respect to stage arrangements, grouping of persons and objects, furniture and other accessories, all, in fact, that distinguishes the theatrical presentations of nowadays from the conventionalism of elder times, when a green baize covered the front of the stage, as if to put it in mourning, during tragedies, and when the most sump-

[1] See Chapter III.

tuously decorated chamber had but as many chairs as the
dramatic action demanded to be sat upon. Once, for the
rising of the mist, the artifice of slaked lime, which of late
has been re-appropriated with world renown, was employed
with magical effect. Elliston, one of the latest representa-
tives of the drama's so-called 'palmy days,' and himself at the
time a rival manager, declared that such perfect pictures as
he saw at the Queen's had never been put upon the stage.
My father's aptitude for painting, of which some specimens
are extant, doubtless helped him to conceive and to put in
practice these effects. His musicianship materially enhanced his literary skill in the writing of words to music,
one of the hardest tasks of authorship, one in which success
is rare as it is difficult, and one in which he was always
singularly happy—witness the poem to Henry Smart's
beautiful song of 'Estelle,' and some of those, such as a
'Legend of the Avon,' to some of the first of W. Chappell's
resuscitations of Old English Ditties. The latest thing that
occupied my father was the editorship of 'The Musical
World' journal, and you know who, at his death, succeeded him. You remember the kindly and encouraging
feeling that characterized his administration, how he
always sought for merit, and did his utmost to bring it to
the front, how he would screen defect, and how ill-will was
in him an incapacity. You remember his keen perception
of the beautiful, and the charming English in which this
was set forth. His sunny temper was vexed by many a
trouble, but never wholly darkened; and it had the power
of light as well as warmth on all who came within its
radiance, to draw out their brightest colours, as well as
to nourish their minds and hearts. Such was George
Macfarren.

G. A. M."

To the interesting sketch from which these extracts
are taken, the editor appended the following post-
script :—

" We remember all this—and more. George Macfarren
was one of those born to govern men, not by harsh
despotism, but by courtesy and kindness. Even when, as

it might happen at times, you were not entirely of his opinion, you generally found him right at the end. And then, his reasons were urged with a gentleness which, more than his logical acumen and knowledge of human nature—both remarkable—went far to convince you, even when most perverse and self-willed. We were all young then, and trust we are wiser now. It is only when our elders are gone, that we are willing to confess how much we owe to them.

J. W. D."

In some reminiscences of early family history which George Alexander sketched, he relates, in connection with the incidents at Archbishop Tenison's school :—

"At the school in Castle Street my father made the acquaintance of George Jackson, and was thus introduced to the family of my mother, George's younger sister."

Also that he became engaged to Susan Jackson, "who was by a year his elder, . . . but who died of consumption in 1806."

"That my father found consolation in the love of her sister is a psychological problem not to be discussed. He did so, and they were married in August 1808. Elizabeth Jackson was born 20th January, 1792, and it was from her, though there be no Mac in her name, that I drew my veritable Scottish descent. Her father, John, came in early manhood from Glasgow to London to seek occupation as a bookbinder. John Jackson must have been skilled in his craft, and frugal, for after a few years he purchased a house, 24, Villiers Street, wherein I was born. . . . Another friend of my father, Alexander Henning, a Scot, a navy lieutenant, and afterwards a most successful captain of an Indiaman, had promised to be my godfather, but was absent on a voyage when the christening was to be performed : the office was however filled by proxy, and I was to have been named solely after him, but that on the way to the church my grandmother insisted that her son's child should be called George, and you see the consequence. . . . My entrance on the scene expanded the little family beyond the capacity of the native home, and removal to Kemp Row, Chelsea, was the necessary consequence. There my father exercised his natural aptitude for painting, producing in oil portraits of several of his friends, and a view from the window of his study. On an evening he was playing with me before the fire, and with a spring I fell from his knee, face upward, under the grate, when he held his extended hand over my face to protect it from the falling cinders while he called for someone to draw me from under his protection; and this was one of the many instances of his presence of mind and recklessness of evil for the sake of others. . . . My own earliest recollection is of the first anniversary of the Battle of Waterloo, 18th June, 1816, the occasion of the opening of Waterloo Bridge by the Prince Regent, after which state ceremony the public was allowed to cross freely the master-piece of Rennie, and I was taken in the throng to a commemorative fair held in the fields then open between the river and the New Cut."

Macfarren relates that, in 1816, certain circumstances occasioned a visit of his father to Paris, and that

" Foreign travel was so different an affair in 1816 from what we now know it to be, that, as a preliminary to his journey, my father made his will and gave it into the keeping of my mother, together with an excellent water-colour portrait of himself, the two to ensure her welfare and his memory, should he never recross the Channel. As a point of professional duty, he took lessons of one of the chief dancing masters in the French capital, returning fresh from which, he imported into England the quadrille, a dance previously unknown here, save in its English prototype 'The Hay' with some of the concomitant figures, and the first set of quadrilles ever printed in London was music of my father's composition with detailed description of the dances.[1]

[1] See, however, Grove's Dictionary, *sub verba*.

"In the January of 1819 I was taken for the first time
to a theatre, namely the Olympic, where was played a
pantomime on the story of 'Red Riding Hood,' of which
Planché was the author; and this I regard as the foundation of my lasting love for dramatic entertainment, which
was doubtless nourished by my interest in my father's after
pursuits, but must have been to a great extent intuitive."

George Alexander was delicate in health from his
childhood, needing constant medical attention. Notwithstanding this, however, he was sent, when little
more than seven years of age, to the school kept by
Dr. Nicholas, at Ealing, in which his father had for
many years taught dancing; "a school which numbered
at different times amongst its distinguished *alumni* the
present Cardinal Newman and Professor Huxley." For
school-life, however, with its roughness and discipline,
he was little fitted with his tender constitution; and
his time at Ealing was, on his own subsequent testimony, singularly wretched. In the family record he
says :—

"In August, 1820, I was committed to the care and
culture of Ealing School, an establishment that then
numbered 365 pupils. My being there ought to have been
the most propitious fact for my comfort and education,
because my father attended the school twice weekly to
teach, and often took me forth to walk when his lessons
were over; because his singularly intimate friend Heslop
was one of the chief masters, whose very dear wife took
special care of me, and because Huxley, the philosopher's
father, was another principal master, was a familiar of our
family, and showed me many a kindness. Notwithstanding
all these seeming sources of welfare, I was more miserable
at school than words can tell. I was sickly, having, in the
course of my three years' sojourn, to be brought home on
account of inflammation of the lungs, having an exceptionally bad attack of mumps, and having much the fate

of a fag to a bigger boy in my class, though fagging was no part of the school discipline. Among other tyrannies that he exercised, one only is not to be regretted; namely, that he compelled me to tell him tales throughout the play hours, which sharpened my memory for all I had read, and my wits for all I could invent. In August 1823, after my periodical return to school, my sight began to fail, so I was taken home for medical treatment."

Those who, in his manhood, enjoyed his friendship, will readily believe that a nature so sensitive to kindness and sympathy would ill brook the lack of it which probably characterized school-life in those days, before the more humanizing influences and healthier tone, brought about by Dr. Arnold, and other educational reformers, prevailed. Of this sensitiveness and affectionate disposition, as well as of the conscientiousness which marked him through life, prompting him to a ready acknowledgment of faults and errors, there is evidence, at this early age, in his letters from school to his mother. The following is an extract from one of these.

"Sunday, *May* 19th, 1822.

"MY DEAR MOTHER,

"As I have a little time I can tell you my thoughts, and what I really have thought ever since Easter.

"I have prayed always that I might be good, both night and morning, but I could not. However, the next time I come home I will try to fulfil my promises better.

"I know how very naughty I was the two last times I was at home, and the only thing that keeps me up now is, that I know you have forgiven me and that I will try to do better another time. I will try to leave off my nasty naughty airs, my wicked ill temper and ill humour, and in fact, instead of being naughty and wicked as I was when I was at home, I will be quite the contrary a very good boy."

And in the following we get a glimpse of the methodical habit, and disposition for thoroughness in work, which were such distinguishing traits in his after years : as well, it may be said, as of his self-reliance.

"Friday, *August* 2nd, 1822.

"MY VERY DEAR MOTHER,

"You may perhaps think it odd my writing to you so soon but I write to you to inform you that I intend after this—and now I don't tell you a story when I declare upon my word and honor that I will keep my promise.

"I intend to leave off all my impudence airs ill-temper naughtiness and wickedness and be so good that you will think it is some one else and indeed I will be as good as it is possible for a boy of my age to be.

"If you please mother will you hold up your finger always after this as you promised to do last holidays but only did the first week or two, when you see me going into an ill temper and that will keep me out of it.—Now I will give you a list of what I intend to do hereafter.

"1. I keep an account of what I spend every day and when I come home to show it to you and ask you w[h]ether you think it reasonable or no.

"2. I intend to fag always as hard as ever I can and try to get my lessons perfect so as to get praise even at school.

"3. I intend always to keep the 5th commandment and always to mind what you and father say to me.

"4. To be kind and good-natured to my two sisters and my brother and try to make John a better boy.

"5. I intend to honour you and all who know me so as to make myself generally beloved by all [who] know me.

"And now mother if you will hold up your finger whenever you see me getting into an ill humour I think I shall be a very good boy indeed.

I am

My very dear Mother

Your affectionate loving and

dutiful Son

G. A. M."

The affectionate spirit which these letters breathe distinguished Macfarren all through life; though not always discerned by those but slightly acquainted with him, especially if themselves of shallow sympathies.

While yet at Ealing his sight began to fail, and it became necessary that he should use a powerful magnifying glass: also that he should be furnished with a large-type Testament, to enable him to join in class-reading. This, however, was but the prelude to his entire withdrawal from the school, in order that he might be under oculistic care and home-management. Under the advice and treatment of the then eminent oculist, Mr. Alexander, the boy was brought into such a condition of health that his very life seemed threatened; and, at the instance of the family medical attendant, the specialistic treatment was stopped, and he was removed to a school at Lancing, quite as much for his health's sake as for his education. He was accompanied by his younger brother John; and, with much enjoyment, remained at Lancing for eighteen months.

He records, in his " Family Recollections," that " the judgment of Lawrence, and afterwards that of Tyrell, were taken upon my eyes, which were both to the effect that the disease was beyond the reach of medical treatment, and that the strengthening of my general health would be the likeliest of means to restore my sight. Notably, from when my eyes first failed, the sickly weakness of my constitution was changed for the average health which, with rare and brief casual exceptions, I have since enjoyed."

During his stay at Lancing, some hope concerning

his sight seems to have arisen; as, in a letter written
in 1825, he refers to "improvement in my unfortunate
oculars." In the "Recollections" he speaks of a
"good Mrs. Blunden" of Worthing, with whom the
family had lodged, "and who lightened the hardships
of our school-life—school-life is the very hardest ship
that sails the ocean of existence—by having us both
on occasional visits."

During this period the predilection for dramatic
performance previously referred to, and afterwards so
fully developed, further manifested itself; he himself
writing little school tragedies, constructing little
stages, painting the scenes, and joining with his
schoolfellows in acting the dramas.

Another letter evinces the thoughtfulness and
reasoning habit, expressed in quaint phraseology,
which were prominent in later years.

"Lancing Academy, *May* 19th, 1825.

"My dear Father,

"I feel rather surprised at not having heard from you
before this, but, as mother says 'a letter home and an
answer back makes a good hole in one and fourpence' and
as Poor Richard says in his Almanac 'a penny saved is a
penny earnt,' so it does not matter much but that you are
all well (as I trust you are) for as 'two heads are better
than one' so one penny is better than none, but as I have
heard from you but once since my uncle left us I should
like to hear as soon as possible." . . . .

It was probably after leaving Lancing that, his
sight continuing to fail, various oculists were con-
sulted, and experimented upon him; but all in vain:
the failure was never effectually arrested, but increased until its final culmination in later years.

It will readily be understood that this imperfection of sight had hindered the lad to some extent in book studies; though he alludes, in his letters, to his geographical studies, and only mentions the want of an Atlas for himself as the hindrance to his finding the places well, not referring to any difficulty of sight. But it seems probable that at this age the eager thirst for knowledge, and desire to master any subject that he took in hand, which characterized him through life, were in operation, and led him, notwithstanding obstacles, to obtain the rudiments of a fair general education. History and biography were favourite subjects of study with him; and, besides the dramatic or theatrical amusements already mentioned, gardening was an occupation in which he took great pleasure.

But he was being appealed to by another art, not immediately necessitating sight for its enjoyment. As has already been stated, George Macfarren senior was a passionate lover of music, and a fair adept in it; and there were home performances of chamber music, vocal and instrumental, which awakened the interest of the boy. His father instructed him in the elements of the art; and his progress was such as to encourage the determination to train him for its pursuit. At the age of fourteen he was placed under the tuition of Charles Lucas, then (1827) a student in the recently instituted Royal Academy of Music. He writes: " Before quitting 1827 I may note that on its 8th of March I had my first lesson of Charles Lucas, and so formally entered my musical apprenticeship."

Lucas was about five years the senior of his pupil, having been born at Salisbury, July 28th, 1808.

After having been chorister in the cathedral, under Arthur Thomas Corfe, from his seventh to his fifteenth year, he entered the Academy, and, though he commenced his career therein by taking singing as his principal study, subsequently changed his course, and turned his attention to the violoncello, which he studied under the famous performer, Robert Lindley. He also pursued theoretical studies under Mr. Lord and Dr. Crotch. He became a distinguished musician, not only as an excellent violoncellist, but by reason of varied attainments. He was conductor of the orchestra and choir of the Academy, from 1832; organist of Hanover Chapel, Regent Street, from 1839, for a number of years, a select body of Academy students forming the choir, for full choral service; and, in 1859, succeeded Cipriani Potter as Principal of the Academy, holding that position, in conjunction with that of conductor, until his retirement in 1866. He was also composer of an opera, "The Regicide," symphonies, anthems, and other works. Under this versatile musician, then, however, only in his own pupilage, Macfarren was placed for the serious study of music; remaining with him till the teacher recommended his transference to the Royal Academy, which step was taken in 1829, one year before the termination of Lucas's studentship in the institution: therefore, the teacher and the pupil were for one year fellow-students in the Academy, of which they were both destined to be ornaments and Principals in later years. Long afterwards, Macfarren, in the "Imperial Dictionary of Biography," to which he contributed a number of articles, thus writes of his old teacher and fellow-student :—

"Lucas' qualifications for his important position as Principal of the Academy consist in his very extensive theoretical and practical knowledge of music. A sound harmonist, a good executant, having familiarity with the mechanism of almost every instrument, being greatly experienced in public performance of music of every school and style,] he is a skilful teacher and an able director."

Concerning the period of Macfarren's pupilage under Lucas, prior to his Academy studentship, he relates an early effort, made in the year 1828 :—

"In my father's wish to stimulate my exertions, he obtained the promise from Blewitt that the band of the Surrey Theatre should try an Overture of mine if I wrote one, so I made an attempt, in the absence of Lucas for the summer holiday of 1828, being . . . little fitted for so high a flight. . . . I was to some, though a very small extent, prepared for the undertaking, by a translation of the theoretical book of Friedrich Schneider that had been given me by T. Cooke, which comprised a statement of the compass of each instrument. When my master came back, I displayed, with great exultation, the score of an Overture in G, and was desperately disappointed with his condemnation of the plan, his detection of much faulty harmony, his assurance of the impracticability of many passages, though lying between the lowest and highest notes of the instruments to which they were assigned, and his declaration that the whole was entirely unfit for performance. He was certainly right, but this made the matter all the unpleasanter for me. Still I was urged to write, and to help me my father made several poems which I had to set to music."

Of Jonas Blewitt, alluded to above, Macfarren writes :—

"He was one of those so-called natural musicians, who do everything easily and nothing well, in the art to which they are supposed to have a calling. He invented musical games that sent large companies into fits of laughter; and he composed comic songs, which he sang with like result."

We have now reached that stage in the career of the subject of our memoir which concerns his public course—his first connection with the Royal Academy of Music; a connection continuing, with brief interruptions, hereafter to be recorded, till the close of his life; his last occupation, half an hour before he passed away, being the dictation of a letter concerning the business of the Institution in which he was reared, which he served so faithfully, and loved so well. His admission as a student, he himself characterizes as the fulfilment of his " highest ambition " at the time.

CHAPTER II.

WHEN Macfarren entered the Royal Academy of
Music as a student, in 1829, that Institution
had been established about seven years; if, indeed, it
may be said to have been then "established" at all,
seeing that it was undergoing much adverse criticism,
and, moreover, was by no means on a stable basis,
either financially or musically. There had been little
experience by which to profit, little to indicate the
best methods of procedure, and, moreover, the management, or direction, was bureaucratic, amateur, and,
there can be little doubt, mistaken. Founded by John
Fane, Lord Burghersh, afterwards sixth Earl of
Westmoreland, it was, at the time of which we are
speaking, under the Principalship of Dr. Crotch, who,
remarkable in his boyhood for precocious musical
capacity, seems to have well represented, in his manhood, when he was Professor of Music in the University of Oxford, the then existing state of musical
learning in England. He was fortunate in having,
as one of his professorial staff, Cipriani Potter, pianist
and composer, who, as he told me, used to have friendly
disputes with Domenico Crivelli, the singing professor,

as to which of them actually gave the first lesson in the Academy. Potter was, as he continued for years to be, abreast of the time in practical musical knowledge and attainment, having studied under Thomas Attwood, who had been Mozart's pupil, under Woelfl, and, to some extent, under Beethoven, so far as counsel and some criticism of his doings may be reckoned; and, moreover, by continental travel, and intercourse with distinguished musicians abroad, he had enlarged his acquaintance with the then modern developments of the Art, beyond the insularity which seems to have characterized and narrowed the perceptions and attainments of English musicians of the time. All this, together with his geniality of disposition, admirably fitted him for the work of guiding young musicians in their studies, which fell to his share both as teacher in, and subsequently, in succession to Dr. Crotch, as Principal of our Royal and National Institution.

Macfarren always entertained grateful and reverential remembrance of Cipriani Potter, his teachings, his compositions, and his musicianship in general: "that distinguished teacher," he termed him. Long afterwards, on January 7th, 1884, he delivered an appreciative address upon his life and work at the Musical Association. It was my wish to be present, partly because, in the conversation after the address, it would have been congenial to my feelings to offer a few reminiscences of my old master. Illness, however, prevented me from attending, and I wrote to Macfarren explaining the cause of my absence, which it would indeed have been a grief to find ascribed to any indifference to the ever green memory of one to whom

I, in common with many, owed so much. My explanatory letter drew from Macfarren the following characteristic reply :—

"MY DEAR BANISTER,—It would indeed have been a pleasure to have had the interesting additions you might have made to the too little I could say of our dear friend Potter, and I regret as much the loss of these as the illness that prevented your presence at the meeting. I deplore that the Master is at present less represented in his own works than in those of his pupils; and that persons who knew not himself have now small chance of knowing his merit, and on this account it behoves us who retain vivid recollections of his working and its worth to do all we may to impress our memory on the consciousness of others."

I am therefore acting in harmony with the injunctions of him who is the subject of this memoir, and illustrating his character, as well as doing that which is so consonant with my own pleasant recollections, when I thus dwell somewhat upon the admirable influence and notable personality of one to whom so many English musicians were indebted—Cipriani Potter.

In the address to the Musical Association, after recounting that Potter had studied under Thomas Attwood, Dr. Crotch, and Joseph Woelfl, Macfarren proceeds :—

"Potter used to speak of him [Woelfl] with profound admiration, and to ascribe to him the principles of plan of which he himself became a teacher, and to him also those principles of pianoforte playing which he himself advanced. It is important to observe that in these two particulars of pianoforte playing and composition, Potter has had a most marked influence on the musical development of the present age; and since Woelfl died before Potter was twenty years old, it must have been very largely owing to his own reflections that that style of pianoforte playing was matured, and to his own particular genius for the instrument, that we may ascribe what may, I think, fairly be designated as an English school of pianism. There must be present here, not only the chairman,[1] who, like me, may boast himself in some particulars as the pupil of our friend Cipriani Potter, but some too, who, if not his pupils, are certainly his grand-pupils, and great-grand-pupils, who represent in the second and third generation the excellence of the views which were first promulgated by him, and have been disseminated from time to time to the lasting advantage of music in England.

*　　*　　*　　*　　*　　*

"Let us now review the work of Potter as a teacher of composition. You have heard what kind of music prevailed in England before his influence changed the direction of study and the emulation of students. I believe it to have been he who first promulgated the principles of plan. 'Plan' was the word he used, a most significant and completely comprehensive word, to represent the principles of design in musical art. It is now customary to speak of the same thing under the name of 'form;' but form can only be used in a metaphoric sense, since it applies to tangible and visible objects, and unless we count the remarkable form which the waves of sound take, there is no form, truly speaking, in music; it is only metaphorically we can speak of musical form by analogy with the forms employed in other arts. But decidedly there is a plan in the arrangement of ideas, in the conduct of keys, in the juxtaposition of one musical phrase with another, the distribution of rhythm, and the whole musical structure. So I think the term 'plan,' which he was wont to use among his pupils, is the best that can be applied to what it distinctly defines; it makes music really into an art instead of an accident. As to the unrelated arrangement of thoughts which appears in the glee compositions, and in the bald writing of the previous time, whatever pleasantry of phrase, whatever momentary happiness of effect from the combination of voices or instruments, there

[1] Mr. C. E. Stephens.

is no continuity in such compositions. But Potter showed his pupils the art of continuity in the development of musical ideas—the structure of complete compositions. I believe that this was not known in England before his time, or, if known, it was certainly unpractised. His method of explaining this was so clear, so charming, so interesting to all who heard him, that the application of his principles became not only the study but the delight of those who had the advantage of hearing them; and this advantage has been disseminated by his pupils until now, when, I believe, the structure of the sonata is very generally understood, and, in many instances, very happily practised. His views on instrumentation were as important as on managing ideas. He had a great knowledge of instruments, a happy way of writing passages appropriate to each, and a very great facility, also, in arranging their combination. His scores were always clear, and he showed his pupils how to produce such clearness. He was not unused to tell us that it would take a person thirty years to learn how to fill a score, and then his education began, because it would take him thirty years more to learn to take out the surplus instruments."

In the " Imperial Dictionary of Biography " Macfarren wrote :—

" Potter's music is characterized by perspicuity of form, contrapuntal clearness, ingenious orchestration, and appropriateness to the instruments for which it is written. . . . Potter has had a most important influence on the progress of the pianoforte in England, many of the most distinguished players and teachers having been formed by him; and his excellent system being thus so widely diffused, he may truly be said to have established a school of playing. The effect of his teaching is still more valuable in the department of composition; he was the first in this country to elucidate the principles of musical construction, and since his appearance as a teacher, the productions of our composers have assumed a higher character in respect of purpose and development than ever before belonged to

English music. It will thus be seen that he has accomplished more than any other musician for the advancement of his art among us; his good influence is already felt throughout the land in the labours of the pupils of his pupils, and a large proportion of the best esteemed artists of the day have received their training personally from him."

To resume our narrative, however, and to revert to the Royal Academy of Music. During the first thirty-two years of its existence, and, therefore, when Macfarren commenced his studentship therein, students were lodged and boarded within its walls. Macfarren, however, was never an in-student, but continued to reside at home. He found, already studying in the Academy, William Sterndale Bennett, who had been brought thither three years previously, when a lad of ten, from Cambridge, where he was discovered as a chorister in King's College Chapel. Among Macfarren's fellow-students, during the seven years of his studentship, were Henry Michael Angelo (commonly called Grattan) Cooke, William Henry Holmes, etc.

Macfarren was placed under Thomas Haydon—a painstaking teacher—in the first instance, as his instructor in pianoforte playing; subsequently under William Henry Holmes, and, still later, under Potter. He was also assigned the trombone as a second study, under —— Smithies, " because "—to quote his own words in later years—" of the custom, then imperative, but now grievously disregarded, for every male student to have the valuable experience of orchestral practice." He continued for some time under his former instructor in harmony, Charles Lucas, afterwards being transferred to Potter for the study of composition.

Cipriani Potter told me that Sterndale Bennett never went through a course of contrapuntal study; and as Macfarren was his fellow-student at the Academy, perhaps he likewise did not at first study counterpoint, unless Lucas had previously commenced to teach it to him. I am led to conclude that, at that period, the importance of that branch of study was hardly recognized by the authorities of the Institution; although, subsequently, when I was a student, it was part of the regular *curriculum* for those who aspired to become composers. Even then, however, it was understood that it needed not to be included in the course of study of the female pupils. I suppose that, at the earlier time, it was not customary in England for musical students to learn much more than the nature and treatment of chords, as then classified, with just the elementary principles or rules, mainly prohibitory, of part-writing. This my impression as to the then state of theoretical musical education in this country seems borne out by the fact that when, a little earlier, Potter went to Beethoven, with the view of studying under him, the counsel of the great man to the young one was " you must study counterpoint." And yet Potter had enjoyed such opportunities as were then available in England for musical study as it was then understood and prescribed.

Some notion of the state of theoretical knowledge and education at the time of Macfarren's studentship may be formed by examination of Dr. Crotch's theoretical treatises as representing the kind of instruction given by him to Lucas and others, and passed on by them. The matter is of interest, in our present narrative, because of the wide departure afterwards made by Macfarren in his theoretical views and teachings.

Dr. Crotch's method, however, with his pupils, was to give them a theme to vary, contrapuntally, in free fashion; though there had been some course of more strict counterpoint exercises to precede that freer work. Macfarren, however, declined to be removed to Dr. Crotch's care, preferring to remain under the tuition of Lucas. Those who remember the latter will readily believe that no undisciplined freedom would be permitted to his pupils.

But, whatever the theories enunciated by Crotch, and accepted as more or less authoritative at the time, his actual class-teaching seems to have been of a somewhat free-and-easy kind. The boys would come in, with little or no work prepared, and coax him to play Handel's choruses to them instead of giving them a lesson, which he readily did.

It seems probable, however, that Cipriani Potter, after his continental experience, and the advice given him by Beethoven, would, in his position at the Royal Academy, insist on the importance of contrapuntal training. Be that as it may, there is evidence of Macfarren having submitted to such a course, either under Lucas or with Potter, or else of his own judgment, there being extant books of exercises in counterpoint written by him. Preference seems to have been divided, at that time, between the contrapuntal treatises of Cherubini and of Albrechtsberger; the latter ultimately receiving the official endorsement of the Academy authorities, and for long continuing to be the recognized class-book in the Institution. No modern English (untranslated) book on the subject seems to have been in use, though small books, such as Hamilton's " Catechisms," etc., afterwards appeared.

The difference between the teachings of all these books and those of Macfarren in his after years will come to be considered subsequently.

Under Potter's tuition he made such great advancement in composition that a Symphony in C by him was considered worthy of performance at an Academy concert in September, 1830.

In recording the performance of this, his first Symphony, Macfarren says :—

" My father's description of the event in a letter to my mother, who was at Margate, shows him to have been more anxious over and delighted at it than an ordinary man would have been at a success of which himself was the hero."

The following is an extract from the letter referred to :—

" The Duke of Cambridge and many distinguished persons were present—the Symphony went off admirably, far exceeding my sanguine foreknowledge of it. At the conclusion the Duke inquired which was Macfarren, Lord Burghersh called him forward—the Duke took his hand, and in a loud tone of approbation said, ' Macfarren, I congratulate you and your master on this performance ; it does you infinite credit and I am greatly pleased.'

" The company, consisting of about 200, seemed to join in the praise most heartily by an additional round of applause ; since then I have received so many congratulations from Mr. Attwood, Dr. Crotch, Lucas, Hamilton, Sir George Clerk, Potter, and others, that I begin to think a fond father's notions are not all illusive, that our boy is in head what we have fondly found him in heart, and that we ought to be proud of him."

Yet another Symphony, in D minor, was produced at an Academy concert, December 3rd, 1831. At another concert of the Institution, June 26th, 1833, an Overture was performed, subject not stated ; Macfarren having been awarded, two days previously, a bronze medal for improvement in pianoforte playing, as well as for composition. On May 24th, 1834, an Incantation and Elfin Chorus were produced.

In this same year, October 27th, one of his most important early works was produced as the initial piece at the first concert of a most useful society, then recently founded, the Society of British Musicians. This composition was the Symphony in F minor, and Macfarren himself directed its performance. Concerning this performance the "Athenæum" of November 2nd thus wrote :—

" We were pleased and interested with Mr. Macfarren's Symphony—both from the youth of the composer, and the enthusiasm and originality discernible throughout his work —it gives good promise of excellence ; the trio of the minuet in particular struck us as full of fine bold fancy, and the conclusion to the finale was at once clever and animating. We are not, at this instant, able to remember any work of similar length from the pen of a native writer which has given us so much pleasure."

The trio here alluded to is for horns *obbligati*, with interruptions by the full orchestra. The "conclusion to the finale " is a coda in fugal style. The whole Symphony is marked by the freshness and vigour of youth, ably and soundly trained in the study of the best models.

A further notice appeared, later on, of this same Symphony, on its publication as a pianoforte duet:—

" It bears the transformation well, and is, as it was with the full orchestra, an effective and interesting piece of music. We like the slow movement least; it is overloaded, and the melody wants freshness. We have been much pleased, in examining this composition, to find our first judgment of its merits so well borne out."

It is regrettable that even this arrangement is now difficult to obtain.

At another concert by the British Society, December 8th of the same year, a Cavatina by Macfarren was produced. More important, however, was the performance, by W. H. Holmes, at the Society's concert on November 2nd, 1835, of a Pianoforte Concerto in C minor by Macfarren, which the "Athenæum" characterized as " careful and clever writing—very neatly performed."

It is probable that the Overture performed at the Academy concert in June, 1833, was the same that was included in a concert given by Paganini, the extraordinary violinist, on the 17th of July in the same year, in Drury Lane Theatre—an inclusion which indicates that attention was already being aroused by the young composer's manifest talent, outside the Academy circle. The programme simply announces it as " Grand Overture (MS.), Macfarren." It was probably one in E, which was played more than once at Academy concerts.

To the Academy studentship period also belongs an Overture to the " Merchant of Venice," which was performed by the Society of British Musicians, and

which, in its ... ...
noticed in the "A ... ...

"The name, we fan ... ...
we find little of the ... ...
this aside, we were pl ... ...
concerts of the British ... ...
nervous style, with du ... ...
effects; and we rejoi ... ...
positions gaining gro ... ...
land. We want, how ... ...
Mr. Macfarren; ou ... ...
'Switzer's Welcome,' ... ...
who out-toils the Sun ... ...
of which were likewise ... ...
just mentioned; and ... ...
me eyes that ne'er lo ... ...
butterfly?' from the ... ...
the second of these ... ...

The farce alluded ... ...
Macfarren, as well as many other rising composers,
William Sterndale Bennett, Charles Edward Horsley,
Thomas Molleson Mudie, Henry Westrop, Edward
Perry, not forgetting Macfarren's own brother, still
among us, Mr. Walter Cecil Macfarren, owed much
to the opportunities for publicity, as well as of hearing
their orchestral works, to this excellent Society,
which, however, from causes which this is not the
place to discuss, was dissolved in 1865. At a convivial meeting of its members, November 24th, 1842,
Macfarren, called upon to respond to the toast, "the
composers of the Society," said that "whatever
position he now held in the musical world, and whatever good luck he had encountered throughout his
not unfortunate career as an artist, were wholly and

unequivocally owing to the Society of British Musicians." Making all allowance for the pardonable exaggeration stimulated by the surroundings of the moment, there is no doubt of the sincerity of his expressions of indebtedness, nor of the general truth of the statement, with regard to himself and others.

A somewhat unique product of the Academy student period of his life was the writing, in conjunction with his fellow-student, William Sterndale Bennett, a movement of a Pianoforte Concerto, the MS. score of which is now in the possession of Mr. James Sterndale-Bennett, by whose kindness I have been permitted to examine it, and am able to trace the several portions of the movement to their respective authorships.

The movement was performed by its composers at the Academy; but the difficulty of performance on the part of Macfarren, owing to his defective eyesight, probably led to the abandonment of the original design to complete the Concerto. This, moreover, was the last occasion on which he essayed even a semi-public performance on his instrument; henceforth his career was that of a composer, and—as the sequel will show—a theorist and instructor, in various ways.

In the family record several times alluded to, Macfarren thus writes concerning his distinguished fellow-student :—

" With regard to Sterndale Bennett, my father had a kind of jealousy, always considering him as a rival to me, and neither having, nor seeking, a knowledge of his remarkable power and truly exceptional merit. In 1834 Bennett lent me the manuscript of his Capriccio in D minor, which some time afterwards appeared as his first

publication. I liked the piece greatly, and practised it
assiduously on the pianoforte. One phrase prevails
throughout the whole, the accent, if not the intervals, of
which is constantly repeated; my father shared not my
admiration, and, in order to exorcise this, which he considered to be an evil spirit that possessed me, he argued
that, even were the phrase as interesting as I protested it
to be, its manifold iteration failed to constitute an attractive work, and he said further that whatever the merit of
the first line of 'Paradise Lost,' its ceaseless repetition
throughout the twelve books of the poem would have been
intolerable.   This line—

'Of man's first disobedience and the fruit'—

happens to fit the notes of Bennett's phrase, and the
derisive comparison was enhanced by his singing the
syllables and the notes again and again transposed, now
higher, now lower, till the patience of hearers was exhausted, but the judgment of his antagonist was un-
changed."

An interesting reminiscence of his earnestness as a
student, and of his determination, not only to overcome, but to turn to good account, difficulties that
would have baffled many less indefatigable workers, is
furnished by the method in which, as he himself would
relate, he studied the instrumentation of the great
masters.   Orchestral scores being rare and expensive
in those his young days, he set himself to compile
them from the band parts, beginning at the bass; and
he used to describe "the growing interest with which
he would watch the growing score, wondering what
was going to be above the last line written; and then,
as he got higher, at last the key to it all appeared,
perhaps in the 'hautboys' (as he always insisted on
calling them) or flutes."   Students nowadays, with

" Peters " and " Litolff " editions at so low a price, have undoubtedly greater facilities for learning ; but they lose the zest of curiosity which such a course as that just described would furnish. The speculation must have been delightfully exciting.

Macfarren's studentship in the Academy terminated in the year 1836, having extended over a period of more than six years. Some of his work during that period, but not connected with the Institution, as well as that following shortly afterwards, will more properly be recorded in the next chapter.

CHAPTER III.

AS has been intimated, Macfarren wrote other
works during the period of his Academy studentship besides those already referred to—works specially
called forth in connection with his father's theatrical
activities, and collateral circumstances. To these,
therefore, it is now necessary to revert. Writing
about his father, he says:—

"The desire for theatrical management became again
rampant towards the close of 1830, when J. K. Chapman
was managing the theatre in Tottenham Street, and my
father made an offer to the proprietor which seemed so far
acceptable that the tenant was dislodged in his favour.
His notion was to make opportunity to exercise his own
power as a dramatist, to give me practice as a composer,
and to form a school for my brother John as a scene-
painter when he should be old enough to enter it. So
much for private interest, while in public announcements
he professed a purpose of instituting a theatrical establishment with higher aims than those of any existing minor
theatre—the title by which those were designated which
possessed not a patent, and they were restricted to have no
performances of what was styled the legitimate drama—
and he trusted thus to attract the best of middle class
society, and indeed to raise the character of the drama,
which, then, was at a sadly low standard. He changed the

name of the place to the 'Queen's Theatre,' in honour of
William the Fourth's consort, whose accession, after a
very long period without a female by the sovereign's side,
excited great public rejoicing. A house in a back street
was added to the theatre, the auditorium was reconstructed,
having the names of the Muses in as many panels on the
box fronts, and the busts of poets displayed on brackets.
Stanfield painted an act drop and presented it 'as a
token of friendship' to the manager; Winston accepted
the post of acting manager, which was the fact that gave
great reliability to the scheme. Leitch, newly come from
Glasgow, painted a scene on probation, and on its success
was engaged as painter to the establishment. It seems to
have been a fault in the design under which the new
venture was to be conducted, that several distinct companies for opera, for melodrama, and for farce were
enlisted, which induced a heavy salary list, and, still
worse, so generalized the entertainment, that no special
attraction could ever prevail. To stamp the musical
character of the undertaking, advertisement was prominently made that the building had been formerly the
'King's Ancient Concert Room;' and to keep this in
countenance, the theatre opened with an adaptation by
my father of 'Acis and Galatea.' Its being an adaptation
was in accordance with the use of the time in regard to
musical works, which were never given on the English
stage completely. Two comic characters were accordingly
introduced, as also Ulysses, with two companions; the
part of Damon was omitted, as also the incident of the
metamorphosis of Acis, with the song that describes it, and
several pieces of music (Handel's, it is true) were inter-
polated. Spoken dialogue was inserted. Only by strong
persuasion could the adapter be induced not to re-write
the text of the songs, and he condensed the title into
'Galatea,' with the excision of her lover's name. Having
regard to Mozart's additional accompaniments to 'Messiah,' my father supposed new instrumentation indispensable for the present work; so, unaware that Mozart had
also wrought upon it, he applied to Mozart's pupil, Attwood,
to write parts for extra wind instruments, who, declining
the task, recommended Cipriani Potter, and he was there-

fore requested, and undertook to make the required additions. . . . By my father's persuasive command I wrote an Overture in D, which was played on the first night. . . . The season was, as a whole, disastrously unsuccessful: it exhausted the savings of my father's whole career. . . . The theatre was closed for the summer. His health was shaken, . . . so he went, with me as companion, to spend some weeks at a lodging . . . . in Pickering Terrace, Paddington, which was then as sequestered as if it had been 100 miles from town. King William's coronation was to be in September, and all the theatres were to be opened free at the expense of government on the night. Of great importance, therefore, was to re-organize all arrangements so as to open again the 'Queen's' timely for the festivity, in order to secure the receipts for one full house, and in hope to inaugurate better fortune. A new, less costly, and less diverse company was engaged; the band was reduced, and in every department expense was lessened; but as the expenses, so the income; and the weekly payments were impossible to meet."

After recounting the struggles that followed, he continues :—

"An offer of an engagement with certain payment at the 'Surrey' tempted [my father] to quit Tottenham Street at Christmas, where he left a pleasant memory with us all, and he was succeeded in his stage-managership by Hooper, light comedian."

It would seem, however, that the responsibility of lesseeship still burdened him.

"All England, and London not the least, being in feverish excitement about the Reform Bill, my father wrote and brought out a Christmas pantomime called 'Harlequin Reformer,' in which everything was reformed but the fortunes of the theatre. Edward Wright, the low comedian, made his first entry on the stage at the 'Queen's,' with an old stager, Mrs. Hooper, in 'The Maid of Switzerland,' a piece for which I wrote music; that I should do so having been the condition of its acceptance in January, 1832."

Later on, in 1834 probably, the father, then in Milan with his daughter Sophy, who went thither for singing study, wrote the *libretto* of an opera, " Caractacus," on purpose for George to set to music, and a large portion was set by him, but the book was rejected by T. J. Serle, censor of plays, and stage manager to S. J. Arnold, of the English Opera House (now the Lyceum), " on the ground of its historical inaccuracy."

Disappointments and vicissitudes continued to pursue the luckless manager and author, culminating in an unsuccessful attempt at managership at the Gravesend Theatre, in 1836, the year in which, as we have seen, G. A. Macfarren's studentship at the Academy terminated; and, on account of the unpromising condition of affairs, he, with characteristic and self-denying vigour and integrity of purpose, determined to become a mainstay of the family instead of a burden. In pursuance of this determination, he severed himself from his Academy associations, and other artistic and professional surroundings, with the ambitions and hopes which they might well inspire in a young and ardent nature, and accepted an engagement to teach in a large school in the Isle of Man. The principal opportunity that he there found of exercising his artistic powers was furnished by an old naval lieutenant, who used to play on the double-bass the pedal part of Bach's Organ Fugues, Macfarren playing that for the manuals on the pianoforte! Moreover, while in this voluntary exile, he received from his father the book of " Craso the Forlorn," a serious opera in one act, for him to set to music, which he began to do, in the intervals of school teaching. Of this effort, further mention will be made shortly.

As an instance of that command of resources, be they extended, limited, or unusual, which indicates thorough training, and of which, it may be mentioned, in passing, the list of Mozart's compositions affords such various examples, the closing incident in Macfarren's Isle of Man career should here be related. It illustrates, moreover, both (as happily expressed by Mdlle. Gabrielle Vaillant) his " power of adapting himself to his surroundings, and his amiability in never refusing a request made earnestly." Before leaving the island, he was asked to write an overture for his farewell concert, which would bring into requisition all the amateur performers in the place. On inquiry, he found that the available instruments with their players consisted of a few violins, one violoncello, sixteen (?) flutes, one clarinet: *voilà tout!* For this singularly ill-balanced band, nevertheless, he wrote the overture, and it was performed to the general satisfaction—probably to the special satisfaction of the performers. This was in 1837, in which year he relinquished his engagement in the island, where there was so little that could be congenial to his artistic feelings and aspirations, and returned to London. He was shortly afterwards appointed Professor of Harmony and Composition at his *Alma Mater,* the Royal Academy of Music.

It was during the latter part of his studentship at the Academy, or more probably immediately after its

termination in 1836, that he composed an Overture
which has enjoyed continued reputation, and gained
at the time, and subsequently, distinguished success,
that entitled " Chevy Chase."   It was written as the
prelude to a piece with that title by J. R. Planché,
which was produced on Easter Monday at Drury
Lane Theatre, when under the management of Alfred
Bunn, " Tom Cooke" being the director of the music.
Some incidental music being required for it, and Tom
Cooke not being ready even a week beforehand, he
asked Macfarren, who had previously written for him
a march, a chorus, and various other pieces, to write
some ; promising, moreover, that if an overture was
provided, as well as the incidental music, the young
composer's name should appear in the bills.   Notwithstanding the short notice, Macfarren, nothing
daunted, and with self-reliance as a quick worker,
undertook to provide all that was asked for.   The
incidental music consisted of a hunting chorus, a
chorus of nuns, and possibly more.   But in the Overture he determined to introduce the old English tune,
" Chevy Chase," which, however, he did not know,
or at least in connection with its name.   He employed, I believe, his younger brother John to hunt it
up for him, his own time being very fully occupied
with the other music, as well as with teaching.   On
the Friday preceding the Easter Monday, the tune
was discovered, and proved to be an old acquaintance.
Macfarren sat down and wrote the Overture in that
one night, so as to have it ready for copyists on Saturday morning.   It was ready for rehearsal; but, when
the composer went to the theatre, he found that in
the bills the music was stated to be " composed,

selected, and arranged by Mr. T. Cooke." Bunn
ignored Macfarren's claims, and simply threw all the
responsibility on Cooke ; in consequence of which the
aggrieved composer took his score away, indignant at
such a breach of faith.   The whole incident illustrates
Macfarren's determination, his capacity for quick working, and his independence of character.

Probably Tom Cooke was little, if at all, blame-
worthily responsible for this *contretemps ;* certainly
Macfarren retained no grudge against him, writing, in
after years, respecting circumstances in his father's
career :—

"Intimacy with Cooke began from this occasion, and
my father had many a pleasure in assisting his composer-
friend with verses, and experienced many a pleasantry
from him, by no means the least of which were the kind-
nesses shown to me when I was enough advanced to profit
by them."

The Overture, however, was not to be lost to the
world. Six weeks later, January 7th (?), 1838, it was
performed with success at a concert of the Society of
British Musicians, being conducted by J. W. Davison,
the composer being then in the Isle of Man.[1] And
not only did it become an accepted Concert-overture
in this country, but it was the first work by which
Macfarren was made known in Germany. In 1843,
Mendelssohn wrote to Macfarren about it ; though, by
a mistake of memory, he referred to it as " Rob Roy."
It was performed, under Mendelssohn's direction, at
one of the Gewandhaus Concerts ; and, in a letter

---

[1] It was encored on that occasion of its first performance, as well
as at its subsequent production at a Philharmonic Concert.

dated November 20th, 1843, the great composer wrote
to Macfarren :—

"I must tell you that your overture went very well, and
was most cordially and unanimously received by the public;
that the amateurs hailed it as a work which promised them
a great many treats to come, and which gave them such a
treat already in itself ; that the orchestra played it with
true delight and enthusiasm; in short, that it is sure to be
a favourite with all of them.   I rehearsed and conducted
it with the greatest care, but now I am going to Berlin,
and shall not have the pleasure of introducing some of
your other compositions to the public this winter; but I
left the whole of your music with the concert directors,
who will forward it back to you after the end of the season,
and have promised me they will bring out at least one of
your other works, if not several, in the course of this
winter ; most probably it will be the Symphony.   God
bless you, my dear Sir; yes, God bless you from all my
heart, and be as happy in your life and in your art as I
shall always wish you to be.
                "Very truly yours,
                "FELIX MENDELSSOHN BARTHOLDY."

We now revert to the year 1837, in which Macfarren returned to London from the Isle of Man.

During the twenty-four years that had elapsed
since the time when our record began, music had
made great strides, both in this country and abroad ;
and the influences at work—the musical surroundings
amid which Macfarren now fairly started a metropolitan
and public career—demand notice.

The *répertoire* of music had been enriched, during
these years, by the production of some of Beethoven's
finest works—notably, the 7th Symphony (1813), first
performed in England at a Philharmonic Concert,
1817 ; the 8th, and the 9th (Choral), expressly written

for the Philharmonic Society, and performed at the concert, March 21st, 1825 ; the Overture to " Fidelio " in E (1814), first performed in England, as well as that to "Coriolanus," by the Philharmonic Society, in 1817; Mass in D (1822, not performed in this country, however, till 1846) ; " Ruins of Athens " Overture, Op. 124; and several of his Sonatas, Quartets, and other works. Moreover, his "Eroica " Symphony had been heard for the first time in England in 1814 ; his C minor Symphony also in 1816 ; Pianoforte Concertos in 1822, 1824, 1825 ; Violin Concerto, 1832,—all for the first time in England, and at concerts by the Philharmonic Society. At these concerts, moreover, had been produced, for the first time in England, Cherubini's " Anacreon " Overture, conducted by the composer (1815); Hummel's Septet (1818) ; the Dramatic Concerto for Violin by Spohr, who made his first visit to this country in 1820, and played the Concerto himself, besides conducting his Symphony No. 2, composed for the Society, and producing his Nonet; other works of his being subsequently produced, viz., Overture in F (1821) ; Overture, " Jessonda " (1826) ; Symphony in E flat (1828) ; Double Quartet (1829) ; Overture to "Alchymist" (1831); "Weihe der Töne " (1835); also Concertos and other works by Moscheles, who made his first appearance in this country in 1821, and whose long residence exerted so healthy an influence upon pianoforte playing among us, as well as upon music generally; Concertos by Hummel, who first appeared here in 1831; many works by Mendelssohn (who first came to England in 1829, and in that year played Beethoven's Concerto in E flat, its first production here, at a concert by Drouet, the

flautist), the works first produced in this country by
the Philharmonic Society alone being his C minor
Symphony (1829) ; Overture to " Midsummer Night's
Dream " (1830) ; Overture, " Isles of Fingal," and
Concerto in G minor (1832) ; Italian Symphony and
" Trumpet " Overture (1833) ; " Melusina " Overture,
and Scena, " Infelice " (1834) ; " Calm Sea and Pros-
perous Voyage " Overture (1836). Bennett's Concertos,
in D minor (1836, when he made his first appearance
at the Philharmonic), and C minor (1836) ; and his
" Naiades " Overture (1837), had also been produced.
Such a record as this, by no means complete, will show
what a different musical atmosphere now prevailed
from that which characterized the period of Macfarren's birth.   To the enrichment of the Art by all
these great works, and the powerful influence of the
frequent visits of Spohr and Mendelssohn, not to
mention that of Weber, must be added the foundation
and growth of the Royal Academy of Music, and the
healthy teaching therein given ; and many other circumstances not to be here detailed.

Into all this full tide of musical activity and advancement, Macfarren was fully equipped to enter,
with all the eagerness of an observant and receptive
mind, well-trained, and ready for work in the diversified ways that opened out to an energetic nature and
resolute will.   He had studied well ; but his studentship did not cease with the termination of his academic
career—he was a diligent student and learner to the
very end of his life.

Of the opera commenced during his sojourn in the
Isle of Man, Macfarren writes :—

" [My father] extended 'Craso the Forlorn' into two

acts, regarding the operas of Mozart, Beethoven, and
Rossini as the standard of plan and limit of extent for
the construction of a lyrical drama, but having long
finales and other pieces of concerted music wherein the
principal action was embodied, interspersing these, according to English use, with spoken prose, instead of the
recitative of the Italian lyrical drama.   In its amplified
proportions the opera is called ' El Malechor,' and I spent
the end of the year [1837] and much of 1838 in setting it
to music.   His suggestions throughout the work as to the
laying out of the longer numbers, the declamation, and
the general expression of the words, and in the characterization of the persons, were a priceless schooling in
dramatic composition.   At the close of the two winter
theatres, some members of the company of each united in
a kind of joint-stock arrangement to open the English
Opera House [now the Lyceum Theatre] for the summer,
and to divide the receipts *pro rata*.   T. Cooke was the
musical director, and Peake was the acting manager,
treasurer, and literary arbiter.   To these two our new
opera was submitted, who respectively approved of its
music and *libretto*, and accepted it for production.   I know
not whether my joy was greater that this my third attempt
at operatic composition was to come to a hearing, or that
my father's manifold disappointments were now to be re-
versed.   The greater a joy, the severer may be its miscarriage, as was proved in this instance, for when the
company came to be practically organized, it was found to
comprise no baritone singer to whom the principal part
could be allotted, and hence our card palace fell to the
ground with all the picture sides downwards.   To trace
the history of ' El Malechor ' to its close, let me say here,
that Bunn accepted the opera for production at Drury
Lane, in 1839, but his management collapsed before the
work was put in rehearsal; in 1840, when John Barnett
and his non-relation Morris Barnett opened the St. James's
as an opera house, they accepted our piece, but their reign
ended on the first Saturday, so this third acceptance was
dishonoured; when Balfe opened the English Opera House
at Easter in the same year, he selected our piece to succeed
his own ' Keolanthe,' and now it was positively put in re-

hearsal, and foretold in the play-bills—nay, Henry Phillips,
who was to have sung the principal part, which is that of
a maniac, made an appointment to visit Bedlam to select
a subject for study among the patients, on which to found
his personation ; but now the season came to an untimely
end—the manager became bankrupt and went abroad, and
the opera had its ante-natal death, verifying too truly its
title of the ' Evil-Worker,' thus bringing disappointment
to everyone concerned with it.　Some years later, Staudigl
took a fancy to the song of ' The Wrecker's Life,' and sang
it publicly, which is the only fragment of the opera that
has ever been heard."[1]

[1] Balfe, as his biographer informs us, "actually assumed the
cares of management, and voluntarily faced the multitudinous
responsibilities of an impresario, who undertakes to satisfy the
fickle public, and a list of fashionable and exacting subscribers
into the bargain.　This piece of complicated folly Balfe perpetrated
in the year 1841, when as lessee of the English Opera House he
commenced, amidst a multitude of favourable auguries, and under
the most august patronage, the young Queen herself having engaged a box for the season, the essay of establishing a National
English Opera.　The prospectus announced a new romantic opera
by Balfe himself, entitled ' Keolanthe '; but that the field was to
be open freely and fearlessly to all comers, was abundantly apparent
by the statement that George [Alex.] Macfarren, John Barnett,
Edward [James] Loder, and others were engaged in the preparation
of works which would follow in due succession. . . . For the space
of a year or more before Balfe's attempt to establish something
permanent in the shape of a National English Opera, there had
been no inconsiderable agitation carried on through the press,
among the musical profession and a certain number of persons
who put themselves forward under various signatures as patrons
and well-wishers of musical art in this country, with the same
object in view. . . . Letters appeared signed by some of the leading names of the day in connection with the subject, supporting or
throwing cold water on the scheme.　Among the latter was ranged
the even then high-standing name of George [A.] Macfarren, whose
publicly expressed persuasion was that English musicians would
have no chance of attracting notice and patronage in their own
country, unless they formed a colony in some foreign city, and, by
publishing and performing their works there, obtained that stamp
of approval from European criticism and success, under the war-
ranty of which alone they would be accepted as deserving attention
at home.　This sounded at the time, no doubt, as a very harsh and
exaggerated satire on England's mistrust of her native talent, but
the whole history of the movement and the fate of our leading
musicians have proved, what all who knew Macfarren were fully

The opera opens with a spirited Overture in D minor, six-four time. The introduction to the first act consists firstly of a chorus and dance of villagers celebrating the conclusion of the vintage, then of various vocal pieces, with resumptions of the dance, etc. This is followed by a *duettino,* a scene and chorus, a duet termed an " Enigma," the words commencing—

> " O say, what's that which shines most bright,
> Of solid worth, yet frail and light,
> Most yielding, soft, yet hard to be controlled,
> Most dearly bought when most pursued,
> Most rarely caught, yet even then,
> Most difficult to hold ? "

the answer to which is " quicksilver ; " and the second stanza has a similar multiform inquiry, with the answer—" a donkey." Then comes the capital song alluded to by Macfarren, " The Wrecker's Life." A " Storm Scene " follows, and then the finale to the first act. The second act opens with a round and chorus, to which succeed a series of vocal pieces, and a not very long finale,—eighteen numbers in all.[1]

We now arrive at an important event in our composer's career,—one which seemed as though it would

---

aware of, that he had a very old head on young shoulders. Ungracious as the words seemed at the time, they have been fully borne out down to very recent times. Nevertheless, it was not then, nor is it now, any reason for not trying to instill a deeper interest and a stronger faith into the public mind and feeling in the cause of an English school of music. It is the business of those concerned to go on trying until they have succeeded in making a better position for themselves and their cause, etc."—Kenney's *Memoir of Balfe,* pp. 139, 143.

[1] "The cut of an English opera is certainly very different from a German one. The English is more a drama with songs, etc."—Letter of Weber to J. R. Planché.

prove the "tide . . . which, taken at the flood,"
would "lead on to fortune." This was the actual
production, not, as has been seen, of "El Malechor,"
but of an entirely new and rapidly produced opera,
bearing the infelicitous title, because of its infelicitous
subject, "The Devil's Opera," which had the result of
bringing Macfarren's name and abilities before the
public more prominently and favourably than any previous work. The circumstances of its incubation are so
graphically described by himself, that the account is
best given in his own words, following on the account
above given of "El Malechor" :—

"I will now return to 1838. Peake, [acting manager of
the English Opera Company,] knowing of my father's life-
long dramatic successes, promised that if he would submit
a plot of which the former could approve, he should be
trusted to put it into diction without further scrutiny, and
under assurance of its adoption, provided that Cooke gave
a favourable verdict of the music. On the strength of the
impracticable 'Malechor,' Cooke gave a similar guarantee
to me, with a like provision as to Peake and the plot.
Cutting to pieces had no more effect on my father's
vitality than on that of an eel, so he accepted the conditions, and undertook the construction of a piece with
parts for the persons who had positively embarked in the
scheme—Miss Rainforth, Mrs. Seguin, and Miss Poole ;
Fraser and Burnett, tenors ; Seguin and S. Jones, basses ;
and most particularly Wieland, the pantomimist, who was
notable for his diabolical and zoological impersonations.
On a radiant Sunday, June 3, my father and I walked up
and down Alfred Place for several hours, conjecturing
incidents, and welding them into a story, in all of which
the devil was necessarily conspicuous. Peake thought
highly of the program,[1] and the librettist set hopefully
to work. This was the process of gestation : he wrote at

[1] See Chap. VII.

his text from bed-time till daylight, and then betook him to rest, first awakening me, who pursued my cogitations in those early summer mornings. When life was astir in the streets, I went on my ordinary avocations, and three or four times a week John Hullah came to our lodgings to try over the music that had been written since his last visit. The English Opera House did not succeed. The company was compounded of singers and actors, each of whom regarded the unattractiveness of the other party as the cause of failure. Money was not fluent, small dividends were paid, and general anarchy was consequent. The finished *libretto* of 'The Devil's Opera' was delivered while the music was still in progress; the parts were copied and handed to the persons for whom they were designed; and each of these, ignorant of the context, took no interest in the detached speeches assigned to him, especially Wieland, who, though the principal personage, was to be mute throughout, and whose whole part, therefore, was comprised on a single leaf, came up to us one morning on the stage, protesting that he had nothing to do in the piece, and he therefore declined to do it. Ever irresistibly persuasive, my father induced him to come and hear the music. He was patiently attentive until the scene of his own entrance, and this interested him so much, that he pushed aside the table, and went through the action experimentally, in which he succeeded so well to his own satisfaction, that he admitted the eloquence of this part without words. He had to act a monkey in the afterpiece, and was therefore obliged to leave us. My father and John presently followed him, while I went to an Academy ball. When I returned at 3 o'clock, they started up to greet me; they had found the whole community of the theatre in a state of fever at Wieland's report, and it was decided with acclamations that the piece should be read on the morrow (the reading of a piece to the actors concerned was always preliminary to its otherwise preparation), and forthwith put in rehearsal. Everybody but S. Jones was pleased with his or her own part, and this worthy had a conviction as deep as his own voice that he was a neglected genius who was maliciously frustrated of every opportunity. From that occasion till the closing of the theatre, I attended a rehearsal every day, the necessity for which eternal preparation is thus explainable. Mapleson, the copyist (father of the Italian Opera adventurer), refused to continue the transcription of the music, until paid for writing the first two scenes—an impracticable event, under the state of the treasury. Practice was thus delayed till arrangements could be made with Goodwin that he should copy the parts on risk, and be paid a nightly guinea for their use throughout the run of the opera. When the study was nearly completed, the choristers, discontented with their quota, demanded payment in full, which being impossible, they deserted. New delay was until a new chorus could be enticed into the scheme, with whom the task of teaching had to begin afresh. At length, Monday, August 13th, was fixed for a first performance. On the 12th the overture was finished, and given over to the mercies of the copyist as we went down to a night rehearsal, which was the last, in order that the singers might not be fatigued on the morning before the evening of performance. I depended greatly on Cooke, (my father's friend of twelve years, and my own, on all occasions when he could serve me,) for support as leader of the band. On the morning I learned of his serious illness, by which he was confined to bed for many weeks. When I entered the orchestra to conduct the opera, the subaltern violinist who was emergently promoted to leadership, and who had primed himself with stimulants for his new and nervous position, begged me to let the overture be slow, or he would not be able to see, much less to play the notes—which prayer so moved my spleen, that I took the previously untried music at fullest speed, and the consequent spirit may have compensated for the inaccuracy of the rendering. On the next morning when all met to exchange congratulations, the Seguins announced that they had signed to start for America in a fortnight; so others had to be found to take their places. George Lejeune (the son of our Queen's Theatre friend) and Priscilla Horton were the philosopher's stones of the occasion, on whose account rehearsals had to be renewed. Scarcely were they launched in their parts, than Rainforth took a

E

country engagement for certain pay; so Horton was promoted to her part, and Mrs. Serle was her successor in
that of Mrs. Seguin. Anon Burnett was struck hoarse, so
further rehearsal was needed with his substitute, Mears
by name. On one night Wieland met with a violent hurt
that disabled him, so a deputy devil had to be practised for
the following evening; and on the very last night but one of
the season, Fraser had a quarrel with the stage manager,
who so disfigured him by a blow in the eye that he could
not show himself for a week. Should then the theatre be
closed at once? No! Shrival, a tenor still unknown to
fame, who was yearning for opportunity to woo that fickle
mistress, volunteered to fill Fraser's part, if I would teach
him the notes. We went home accordingly and practised
all night, and so on till noon, when we met the band for
the latest, last rehearsal. . . . Notwithstanding the success
of 'The Devil's Opera,' no music-seller would undertake
the publication of the music, until F. Hill, the flutist in
the band of the theatre, proposed that his father, a double-
bass player, who had a long-established music shop in
Regent Street, should print the most applauded numbers,
and pay me a royalty upon them; he, the son, deploring
that what was well received in performance should be
inaccessible in print, and the firm having no funds wherewith to pay a sum for the copyright, and he also having
the friendly feeling of a fellow-student, which he was
willing to gratify when it interfered not with his own
interest. . . . In the summer of 1839, another joint-stock
company, of which Balfe was then chairman, had possession of the English Opera House. Like their predecessors,
they failed to draw large audiences, which prompted some
of the wisest among them to propose the reproduction of
the piece which had brought success to last year's undertaking, and accordingly 'The Devil's Opera' was given
again, with as much applause as before, and played for twelve
more successive nights. The good effect of this elicited a
proposal from the management for another work from the
same hands, and accordingly 'Don Quixote' was planned
and begun, but the season collapsed while the composition
of the first *finale* was in progress. The subject was chosen
in deference to Fraser's constant complaint that tenors were

always doomed to maudlin sentimentality, and supposition was that he might distinguish himself in heroic representation as the Don. Also in the first design Balfe was to be fitted with Basilius, and Miss Rainforth with Quiteria.

"In 1840, when, as already said, Balfe managed the theatre on his own account, and when ' El Malechor' was in preparation, the composition of ' Don Quixote' was resumed, with the alteration for a contralto of what had been written for a soprano part to suit Miss Edwards, who, however, came not then forward, but appeared some years later at Her Majesty's, and was for a while notable as Mademoiselle Favanti. The work was again laid aside till 1845, when it was once more resumed, but musically quite reconstructed to fit the part of Basilius for Allen's high tenor voice, and that of Don Quixote for Leffler's baritone; and in this shape it was offered to Maddox for the Princess's, who did not accept it, and finally it was produced under Bunn at Drury Lane, February 3rd, 1846, with Miss Rainforth, for whom the original music was restored, Allen as Basilius, and Weiss as Don Quixote; it being the first dramatic piece by my father which was performed since his death."

This extract anticipates the production of " Don Quixote," which will be subsequently referred to; but it has been thought better to give the extract entire, as it is involved with the account of " The Devil's Opera."

The rapid production of " The Devil's Opera," " begun, rehearsed, and finally brought out within a month," was no solitary instance of extraordinary energy on the part of the composer, nor was it manifested under favourable circumstances of leisure, but while engaged in professional toil of uncongenial kind. An incident took place which may illustrate the unflagging industry that always characterized him. He was at this time residing in North Crescent, and had a pupil at Wimbledon Park. There were then no such facilities of transit as those which we now enjoy, nor were fares so low as to be of small consideration to a struggling young professor, whose terms were unavoidably not high. The coach fare was high, and, moreover, the coach only made the journey twice a day, at times that would not fit the appointment. On one of the days fixed for a rehearsal of the opera at noon, the conscientious teacher rose before dawn, walked to Wimbledon, and, his lesson over, started on foot to return in all haste to town. The heat of the sun was overpowering; and, as ho passed over Putney Bridge, he hailed a man in a cart which had just overtaken him, and asked if he would kindly give him "a lift." The reply was a brutal volley of oaths, and the carter drove on: the musician walked. "However," said the professor, in relating the incident, "I reached the Opera House in time for the rehearsal which I was to conduct." The fee for the lesson was seven shillings and sixpence !

At the production of "The Devil's Opera," in 1838, the resources of the establishment, both orchestral and choral, being very limited, several of Macfarren's old fellow-students, including William Dorrell, the (happily) still living and respected professor of the pianoforte, augmented those resources, during the first week of its run of fifty or sixty nights, by playing in the band gratuitously.

It was during the run of this successful opera that Macfarren's acquaintance commenced with Benedict, then recently settled in this country, who came behind the scenes to compliment the composer.

The Overture to "The Devil's Opera" is in per-

fectly regular form, almost Mozartean, indeed, with
first and second subjects, and the usual "free fantasia"
development, recapitulation, and animated coda. Prior
to the second subject, a figure is introduced indicating the entry of the malevolent being from whom
the opera takes its name, and so used, at appropriate
situations, in the course of the work. (Would that
his approach were always thus announced, to warn
tempted souls of their danger!) The introduction
to the first act is a Fair scene at St. Mark's, including
a chorus of traders, a monfrina (national dance of the
Venetian peasantry), which two, in two-four and six-
eight time respectively, are, in the climax, brought
together, etc. The trio for female voices, "Good
night!" opens in canonic (or round) form, after the
manner of the opening quartet in "Fidelio," and is
full of alternate tenderness and humour. The vocal
solos, etc., are natural and graceful, with little or nothing
to call for any criticism on the ground of *bizarrerie*.

"To recount the plot of the piece," said the "Musical
World," August 16th, 1838, "would be to go through the
juggleries of a pantomime. It is intended, we are told, to
satirize the mania, caught from mystic Germany, for the
improbable and supernatural. But the satire is either
very covert, or so transparent, as to cheat the eyes. The
same doubtful character pervades the music of the opera.
The composer seems to have hesitated as to whether he
should incline to the *buffo* or the *serio* style, in his accompaniments to the pranks of *Il Diavoletto*. Hence arise want
of unity, and defective keeping."

Later on, the same periodical wrote :—

"Mr. Macfarren appears to us to be far from an ordinary
dramatic composer. He is well versed in effects, and shows

a fondness for surprising chords, which, though they at
first appear questionable, generally yield to examination."
"There is altogether more novelty and talent in 'The
Devil's Opera' than in any native dramatic work that has
come under our notice."

"The Athenæum" of August 18th, after severely
and contemptuously condemning the *libretto*, proceeds :—

" It is useless to speak further of the book :—the music,
which is by Mr. G. A. Macfarren, offering us something
better to descant on. Though evidently requiring the cor-
rector's pen, here to prune, there to work out—it gives fair
indications of a sprightliness and vein of melody which
may be turned to account in future comic operas. Mr.
Macfarren is ambitious of success on the grandest possible
scale ; he has worked throughout, not merely as if he were
sure of finding a first-rate orchestra *corps* and chorus to
execute his compositions, but as if he possessed sufficient
grasp to find them all in due employment ; — hence,
complicated *finales*—wearisome incantation scenes—over-
scored airs, &c.—to all these we preferred the trio for the
three ladies, in which Miss Poole deserved the highest
praise for her neat and intelligible enunciation of English
words, set nearly as rapidly as the Italian ones in Fiora-
vanti's '*Amor, perche mi pizzichi ?*' It gives us pleasure
also to praise the lively drinking duet between Mr. Burnett
and Mr. Seguin, etc."

Some of this criticism may be accepted with reserve, when it is remembered that, not very long prior
to this same period, in a prominent musical periodical,
since described as " the best musical periodical ever
published in England," " The Harmonicon," the pronouncement was given that Beethoven's " Pastoral
Symphony ":—" only wants abridgment, particularly
in the *andante*, to make it welcome to all lovers

of grand orchestral performances. . . . Why, for the purpose of rendering it popular, it should not be shortened, we cannot divine." And again :—" The almost interminable Symphony of Beethoven in A has one redeeming movement, that in A minor, which cannot be too highly praised . . . it may be compared to a pleasant member of a disagreeable family, etc." " The first movement [of Beethoven's Symphony in F] is exceedingly *bizarre* and anything but agreeable " !

A jubilee performance of "The Devil's Opera " was given at Taunton by the Philharmonic Association, under the zealous direction of Mr. T. J. Dudeney, at the Taunton College of Music, on the 13th of August, 1888. The performance was successful, although the *libretto* was, as in the first instance, condemned, and some of the music was, by provincial critics, esteemed out of date.

Although not in immediate chronological sequence with that which has just been related, the following account, from Macfarren's pen, of one of his rapidly-produced compositions for the theatre may be appropriately introduced here :—

" The Queen was to be married on February 10th, 1840. On the 6th, remarkably proximate to the coming event, my father conceived the thought of celebrating the wedding, and hastened to put his conception into being by calling on Hammond, the manager of Drury Lane, with a proposal to write an appropriate Masque for performance on the occasion. The lessee applauded the proposal, but declared the impossibility of carrying it into effect within the limited time, alleging that Planché and Bishop were known to have been occupied for several weeks on a similar work for Covent Garden which was not yet ready. My father urged that the slow motion of the planets controlled not the

velocity of a comet; and straightway proved the practica-
bility of his project by having a committee called of Marshall, the scene painter, with the maker of costumes, the
property maker, and other functionaries, whose activity
would be needed were the work to be undertaken. He set
forth his design so plausibly and persuasively that each
person believed himself capable of the share in the work
proposed for him, and each one promised accordingly.
' But who will write the book?' said Hammond. ' I will,'
said the proposer. ' And who will write the music?' ' My
son.' Thereupon the idea was accepted, and at 10 on that
Thursday night my father came to tell me for the first
time of the design, and of the part in its fulfilment which
he had insured for me. Never strongly self-reliant, my
doubt of my capability was made certain to me by my
necessity to leave home at 7 a.m. on the morrow for
a day's teaching in the country, whence I should not return
till evening. I was bound, however, to go to him on my
way home, and this I did with conviction confirmed that
the task was wholly beyond me. I found him with the
libretto of ' The Emblematical Tribute' finished. He had
been to the theatre in the early morning with a working
plot for each member of the last night's committee, according to which they all entered on their duties. I went home
desperate, and very soon fell asleep over the perusal of the
verses. Saturday morning found me no more hopeful of
my powers, so I went to him, insisting that I should be
exempted from certain miscarriage. Deaf to my protest, he
took me first to Hammond, as an assurance of my readiness
and willingness, and next to my lodgings, where he remained by my side throughout that day and night, and
Sunday and its night, suggesting, encouraging, approving
and correcting, until 8 a.m. on Monday, when the last
sheet of my score was given to the copyist, who had come
every four hours in the interim for fresh relays of manuscript. If fast mean rapid, we both must have slept very
fast for the next hour; we were wakened to a hasty breakfast, and then hurried to the theatre for the 10 o'clock
rehearsal. The public were to be admitted freely to the
evening's performance, as provided by government liberality,
and tickets for the same were issued at the box office in

the morning. Many thousands of persons more than the house would hold applied for these, and the adjacent streets were thronged with clamouring crowds. At each of the approaches an emissary was appointed, who knew the looks of those who were connected with the theatre, one of whom met us and directed our way to the back of the house, where an iron railing had been withdrawn and a ladder placed, which reached by the green-room window, and through the aperture, and up the ladder everybody concerned made entrance. A roll-call ensued, to which we all answered, and then, the ladder being removed, Hammond addressed us thus: 'You cannot jump out of window, the front of the house is locked, and 20,000 persons are storming at the stage-door, so to leave the theatre is impossible, and you must therefore rehearse the piece again and again till it goes.' Under this compulsion the work began, and was continued till late in the afternoon, and when my father and John (who had been at work in the painting room) and I sallied out, I did indeed feel that the task was ended. ' Certainly not,' said my imperturbable father ; ' you must now go and sell the copyright,' and thrusting me into a cab, ordered the driver to proceed to Bond Street. All shops were closed by virtue of the holiday, and I was driven from one to another without finding its owner, till I went to that of Lavenu, a former fellow-student, a violoncello player and composer, who exceptionally dwelt on the pre-mises, and by fortunate accident was at home. He agreed to give 25 guineas for the right of printing, and fulfilled his agreement, though he only published two numbers, whereas Hammond, who had engaged to pay 50 for the acting right, became bankrupt, and paid nothing. The piece occupied 45 minutes, throughout which the music was uninterrupted, and it was played for a fortnight. The Covent Garden piece did not appear till after ours was laid to rest, and then it had no longer a career than its precursor had enjoyed."

The Overture to " Romeo and Juliet," belongs to this period of Macfarren's productive activity, having been composed, probably, about the year 1836, and performed at a Concert of the Society of British Musicians, either at the close of that year, or at the commencement of 1837. It seems not to have been so successful at its first production as it subsequently became; but it was reproduced by the same Society in 1838, and pronounced " highly honourable to the British School of instrumental music." In 1840, it appeared as a pianoforte duet, dedicated to Sterndale Bennett, and was declared to be an " exquisite composition, deserving European celebrity." It subsequently became the acknowledged precursor of the play, when put upon the stage. At the performances of "Romeo and Juliet" at the Haymarket Theatre, about forty years since, when the Misses Cushman impersonated the lovers, this Overture was so used; and those ladies took it to America and elsewhere, for a like purpose. When the Overture was performed at a concert at the Hanover Square Rooms, November 21st, 1842, it was spoken of, by a critic of the time, as " a noble piece of dramatic art . . . by . . . an Englishman, and, *though an Englishman,* one of the most accomplished musicians in Europe." The composer's synopsis of the intent and purpose of the work is as follows :—

" The following points of the play suggested this Overture :—The Montagues and Capulets—the Nurse—the Lovers and their passion—Mercutio—the Feud—the Interdiction—Mercutio wounded—the entombment of Juliet —Romeo at the Grave—the catastrophe."

The " Atlas " of November 27th, thus spoke of the same performance :—

"Mr. Macfarren's Overture is one of those deep in-spirations that cannot be unexceptionally sympathised with on a first or even a second hearing. When we heard it four or five years since, we confess it puzzled us to define our own impressions as to its merits. We had a vague feeling of grandeur, mingled with floating strains of beautiful melody, indefinite notions of startling pro-gressions, fine and novel harmonies, and noble orchestral effects—but altogether it was a semi-confusion which disturbed our brain with a sort of *olla podrida* of pleasure and pain, that for the life of us we could not make in-telligible. At each successive hearing, however, this mystic indefinity resolved itself more and more clearly, and last Monday—whether from its admirable perfor-mance, united to the co-enthusiasm of the audience and the members of the orchestra, or whether our dulness has been favoured by some unseen power with total and unsophisticated illumination—Mr. Macfarren's Overture emerged from its *quondam* obscurity, and fairly dazzled our senses with excess of light. Our present notion (now unalterable, because born of experience) is, that it is assuredly, in all respects—as a picturesque poem —as a philosophical development of profound passion —as a splendid specimen of orchestral writing—or as a simple piece of music—*one of the most remarkable productions of modern art* in any country; and we fear-lessly predict the near approach of the time when no other opinion will obtain with competent musicians in respect of it."

This verdict was so far fulfilled that, notwith-standing the withdrawal of the work from public performance by the composer, during the latter years of his life, it was included in the programme of the Philharmonic Society's Concert, April 19th, 1888.

Mention may also be made of a much earlier Shakespearian Overture, "The Merchant of Venice," which was composed, perhaps, during his Academy Student days, and performed both at Academy and British Concerts. A duet arrangement of it is " gratefully dedicated to his Master, Cipriani Potter."

CHAPTER IV.

PERSONAL ACQUAINTANCE WITH MACFARREN. SOME OF
HIS EARLY COMPOSITIONS. HIS OPINION OF DUSSEK.
HIS FIRST CRITICAL ARTICLE. INTRODUCTION TO
MENDELSSOHN. VIEWS ON RHYTHM. 1838—1842, ETC.

MY own earliest recollections of the subject of
this memoir extend to about the year 1838
or 1839, when he used frequently to visit my father,
doubtless in connection with the progress and publication of some compositions for the violoncello with
pianoforte which my father, a violoncellist in full
practice, had commissioned him to write. My father
was somewhat discerning in the matter of rising talent,
and was also conscientiously sensible of the responsibility to recognize and encourage it, so far as in him
lay, as various young artists would have testified, most
readily. I do not know what the *honorarium* was for the
works supplied by Macfarren; not large, probably. But,
many years afterwards, he related to me, when speaking of the trait in my father's character to which I
have alluded, how proudly he went home with the
thought that, at last, he had a commission to write
something for publication! This, as we have already
seen, was not the occasion of first publication of any
composition of his, but, he told me, was the first
commission that he received from a publisher, my
father, however, only publishing in a private way,

without any warehouse, but at his own residence, works adapted for use in his own particular branch of the profession.   The compositions supplied by Macfarren, were Three Rondos, "dedicated to his friend H. J. Banister," and Twelve Ariettes, with Pianoforte accompaniment—charmingly spontaneous effusions, as I used to think in my youth, when I accompanied my father in them.[1]   I find the following notice of the Ariettes in a short-lived periodical of a much later date than that of their publication.   The passage that I have italicized is amusing enough as implying that unelaborated purity and fresh simplicity are not "marks of the musician":—

" *Twelve Ariettas for the Violoncello, with an accompaniment for the Piano-forte*, by G. Alexander Macfarren, bear evidence of being an early work, though replete with the prettiest thoughts conceivable.   These twelve *ariettas* are all very short and simple melodies—as fresh as violets just gathered, and as unpretending as young girls before they have been introduced into that gallery of pictures—that receptacle for strange noises—that stronghold of hollowness and impudent pretension—thé world.   They are, indeed, very innocent, and very charming moreover ;—*few marks of the musician characterize their progress, but the feeling of the poet and enthusiast accompanies them throughout.*   For an evening's quiet amusement, between an amateur of the violoncello and an amateur of the piano, we could recommend nothing more fitting than these unobtrusive ariettas."—*Musical Examiner*, Nov. 11, 1843.

Macfarren himself, in his turn, was always ready to help on young aspirants.   Not very long after the period just referred to, he kindly offered to lend me some of Dussek's Sonatas, as being good material for reading

---

[1] These early, fresh compositions are now published by Messrs. Keith, Prowse, and Co.

at sight, as well as for regular practice; and I well remember calling for them, when he lodged in Alfred Place, Bedford Square, that he made inquiries about my musical studies, and appointed a day for me to go and play to him, which I nervously did, and received valuable suggestions from him. It is with pleasure and pardonable self-congratulation that I also think of the many occasions in after years when he esteemed me not unworthy to be his fellow-worker, in examinations, and in other departments; and in various ways recognized my professional, artistic, and literary work. Thus, for instance, when, years afterwards, I sent to him my " Lectures on Musical Analysis," and, about a month later on, my " Musical Art and Study," both published in the summer of 1887, I received from him this very friendly letter :—

"7, Hamilton Terrace, N.W.
"*June 12th.*

" MY DEAR BANISTER,
" I waited to gain some insight into your Lectures before I would thank you for the gift of the book; and now here is your ' Art and Study,' which claims also my acknowledgment. Of the first I can say that it meets what you know I consider to be an important requirement, and I think meets it in such a way as to render it clear to everybody. I am glad that you allude to me as a fellow-worker on the same subject, and I am sure that the more of us give our best energies to its exposition, the more will it gain the respect it deserves, since each of us helps to confirm what may be stated by his friends. I doubt not that the second book has a like claim to regard, but I cannot just yet make its acquaintance.
" With best wishes for their wide circulation, I am
" Yours faithfully,
"G. A. MACFARREN."
" H. C. Banister, Esq."

Though out of chronological order, I may yet be allowed to insert here another letter, bearing upon the same subject, which the Professor wrote to me soon after my reading, at the Musical Association, a paper on " Some of the Underlying Principles of Structure in Musical Composition," May 2nd, 1881 :—

"7, Hamilton Terrace, N.W.
" *9th September.*

" My dear Banister,

"The volume of 'The Musical Association' has enabled me to hear your paper from print, the public reading of which I was unable to attend. It pleases me very greatly, and I wish it may have many readers, for the sake of the good effect it is capable of producing. I concur fully in your views, and these are so happily expressed as to make them interesting even to readers who have small knowledge on the subject. Let me then thank you for casting a bright light on an important matter.

" Yours with friendly regards,
" G. A. Macfarren."

Having mentioned his recommendation, and loan to me,—a great boon I found it !—of Dussek's Sonatas, I may here quote his opinion of that neglected composer, whose title to be called a genius has even been denied by a recent critic. Macfarren's opinion is thus expressed in the " Imperial Dictionary of Biography ":—

" The immense amount of Dussek's compositions for the pianoforte have by no means equal merit ; many of them were written for the mere object of sale, still more for the purpose of tuition, and some with the design of executive display. Of those which were produced, however, in the true spirit of art, expressing the composer's feelings in his own unrestrained ideas, there exist quite enough to stamp him one of the first composers for his instrument ; and while these are indispensable in the complete library of the pianist, they are above value to the student in the development of his mechanism and the formation of his style. A strong characteristic of the composer is his almost redundant profusion of ideas ; but his rich fecundity of invention is greatly counterbalanced by diffuseness of design, resulting from the want of that power of condensation, by means of which greater interest is often given to less beautiful matter. Excess of modulation is no equivalent for contrapuntal fluency, and thus the works of this master would form a bad model for one who possessed not his exquisite sentiment and his exhaustless treasures of melody. Some of the best of his works are the Concerto in G minor, the Sonatas dedicated to Haydn, the Quintet, the Quartet, and, above all, the Sonatas entitled 'The Invocation,' 'The Farewell,' '·Plus Ultra,' and 'The Harmonic Elegy.'"

In an analysis of the above-mentioned Quintet, written for the programme of Mr. Walter Macfarren's third concert, June 11th, 1861, the Professor remarks, respecting Dussek's settlement in this country, in 1789 :—

"Here his remarkable merits found prompt appreciation. Clementi had prepared the world to comprehend a talent of the highest order, exercised, creatively and practically, in the development of the resources of the then new instrument, the pianoforte ; and Dussek's genius enabled him to surpass the utmost effect his predecessor had produced, by the melodious sweetness of his phraseology, and the mellow fulness of his tone, both of which qualities of composition, and performance, he superadded to the other charms of Clementi's music, and playing. . . . The deep feeling that characterizes his music, expressed in the tender passion of his melody, and the glowing richness of his harmony, entitles him to be ranked very high among the composers for his instrument ; and when we turn to his works from those of his best esteemed successors, we trace in them, not only the origin of many of the most beautiful effects with which later writers have been accre-

F

dited, but some of the identical ideas by which these very
writers have made their way into popularity ; and we may
thus truly consider that pianists, as well as the pianoforte,
are deeply indebted for much of the esteem they enjoy, to
the genius of Johann Ludwig Dussek."

As an instance of the identity of idea here alleged,
Macfarren compares the last movement of this Quintet
with the " beautifully impressive theme upon which "
Chopin's 15th Nocturne "is entirely constructed ; "
which comparison pianists can themselves easily in-
stitute; unless, indeed, their library lacks a copy of
Dussek's Quintet.

Mendelssohn's Symphony in A minor was first
performed in this country at the Philharmonic Concert,
June 13th, 1842 ; and in the "Musical World" of the
16th of the same month the following article by Macfarren appeared ; probably the first of the kind from
his pen, and therefore of special interest :—

" There is a sense of exultation in an artist who witnesses
the glorification of his art. From this feeling there must
have been many a one proud of being a musician who was
present at the first performance of Mendelssohn's new
symphony—a work to raise the author to the highest
pinnacle of musical repute—to raise the art which it adorns
and honours—and to raise the present generation in the
chronicles of intellectual progress, as being contemporary
with such an author, coeval with such a work. It is this
pride at being, how unworthy soever, a fellow-worshipper
with Mendelssohn of the same Goddess, that gives me
confidence to approach him, the high priest in her temple,
with a tribute to his excellence in the avowal of the feelings
which his work has given me ; and, besides the pleasure
that there is in being the voice of a manifold opinion, I feel
a satisfaction in thus breaking through our country's
custom of anonymous criticism, from supposing that, years
hence, when the present occasion shall be quite forgotten,

when this new star in the firmament of genius shall be no longer contemplated as an individual shining, but massed in men's consideration among the galaxy of splendour which illuminates the world, which quickens our purest feelings, and which gives to everyone that loves his art, or hopes to be an artist, the moth-like emulation to exalt himself into the sphere of radiance, and flutter in the light which *may* destroy him—when it shall be that this work, then no more a new one, *is*, and cannot be remembered to have *not been ;* I may look out this record of my first impressions, and feel gratified in secret to be reminded I was *one* of those who could and did at first appreciate this wondrous work ; who saw and felt the light when new and strange, which shall be then familiar. If Mendelssohn— (I cannot call a being whom Genius makes impersonal, and whom superiority to all cotemporary association raises above society, by the conventional appellatives which living men use to each other)—if Mendelssohn should see this paper, which the common course of things may easily bring before him, he will, I hope, forgive this ostentation of a capacity to feel his merit, for the sake of the sincerity which induces it.

" The symphony is, as usual, in four movements, with this peculiarity, the author means that *each* should join the next, without a stop between them, an arrangement which, in this case, has a grand effect, as giving a continuance, a oneness to the train of thought that makes us feel it to be more *a whole* than four parts disconnected ; but it is an arrangement that must not be taken as a precedent, for no music of less interest than this, and this is of the utmost possible, could hold unbroken the attention for so long a time ; and it is to be considered as an instance of the *confidence* of genius, which has an innate knowledge of its powers like the secret self-esteem of virtue, that Mendelssohn could dare to write a composition of such magnitude with the intention that his hearers should not have a breathing-place of silence to refresh their minds in the great mental task of listening to it. The movements are described as follows ; and I shall attempt, in speaking of them, to give a short analysis of their beauties, for which I claim indulgence, since, besides my own incompetence to

do such beauties justice, I have the difficulty to contend
with of the inadequacy of language to convey musical
ideas.

"INTRODUZIONE ED ALLEGRO APPASSIONATO.

"SCHERZO.

"ADAGIO CANTABILE.

"ALLEGRO GUERRIERO E FINALE.

" The introduction (in A minor, three-four time) is unlike
any other I can recollect in this respect—that it opens with
a clearly-defined, distinct, and continuous melody; whereas
the general character of such a movement is vague, abrupt,
and fragmentary. This melody, which is intensely passionate, and is, to me, beyond all things expressive of a
sense of loneliness, is heightened in its effect by the freshness of the harmony and the peculiarity of the instrumentation. The combination of two tenors with bassoons and
oboes has a strange and new effect, which is extremely
beautiful. There is in the second bar a chord of the 6th
upon G natural, which always recurs with the recurrence
of the phrase, that, though it offend a prejudice of mine
that the 7th of the scale in diatonic harmony should unexceptionably be major, I cannot but feel to be in this place
unquestionably beautiful ; and, further on, there is an
unexpected chord of C, which is to me a very heaven of
tenderness. This melody is followed by a streaming,
breathing, half watery, half airy, and all imaginative passage for the violins, which seems so excellently characteristic of the instrument, as though it had been made
alone to play this passage; and this undulates through
various modulations, accompanied occasionally by a fragment of the subject, and diversified by the *crescendo* and
diminuendo of the full orchestra, until in the key of B flat
there is a 6th on D, in which the violins and flutes remain
alone upon the F above the lines, where they seem like
a lover looking lingeringly into nothing for the eyes which
meet him not ; and the violins leave this F in an *arpeggio* of
the chord, but yet the flutes remain, as though the one
thought *would* endure, however the mind wished to wander
from it ; and then, with a heartbroken disappointment,
the original melody, in the original key, appears to say,
in its sudden recurrence, 'Yes, I have looked in vain!'

The introduction ends with a half-close on E; and the allegro (in A minor, six-eight time) begins like an assurance bursting on expectancy. The subject of this movement is a complete and satisfactory song, more lengthened, more entirely *a song*, than usually the subjects of first movements have been made; and there is no second subject, but only various modifications of this one ceaseless, burning, continual, and continuous idea—it is a thought, or, better say, a consciousness of love, for ever restless and for 'ever passionate, and, with its simplicity and yet its ardour, it takes possession of the centre of one's heart, like that intensest poetry which makes one feel it says *our* feelings, utters our own thoughts, and can create, as well as speak, those thoughts and feelings. This melody is given to the violin and clarionet in octaves—a combination of a most singularly new and beautiful effect—and here I almost use a mispression, for the two instruments do not join to make *one* sound, as in some combinations of wind instruments upon the same passage, where a new tone is formed *of* both, but *like* neither. Here is distinctly heard that two separate things express the same idea, as though one thought were sympathized by two congenial minds, but modified in each by the peculiar temperament of either; the one, perhaps, more fervent, but the other far more delicate, seeming to wish it were the other's true reflection —so the precise acuteness of the streaming violins is mirrored in the more indefinite, more gentle, and more tender breathing of the clarionet. In this melody there is a suspended 7th upon F, which skips to C, and then returns to D, its resolution, that has an effect exquisitely beautiful, which, like all the highest things in art, arises from its great simplicity. The subject is followed by a spirited *tutti*, which ends abruptly with a half-close on B, and is interrupted by a reminiscence of the subject in E minor. There then comes a sort of *ritornella*, growing from, or an appendix to, the first idea, and this finishes the first part, which is repeated. The second part begins with a most daring, powerful, and unlooked-for start in C sharp minor; and a train of modulation follows, ending in C natural minor, that is one of the most striking and original passages, as to the harmony, the phraseology, and the instrumentation, that I ever heard. The second part is full of the most masterly treatment of the subject; and immediately preceding the return to the original key, there is a sort of episode in E major, still growing out of the first thought, and built upon it, that forms a wonderful relief to the prevalence of minor keys throughout. At the repetition of the subject there is a new effect, and a new character given to it, by the addition of a counterpoint, or, rather, counter-subject, for it is not less a song than the original theme on the violoncello, that may be likened to a mutual confidante of the two separated minds of my former analogy, that gives an extra beauty to both and takes its own, although it robs not them, from either. There is a *coda*, beginning something like the second part, starting abruptly in F sharp minor, as that does in C sharp, and then having something like the same treatment of the same phrase; and there is the *ritornella*, with which the first part ended, and there is a passage of semitones, that is one of the most furious bursts of passionate excitement in the whole scope of music. Then there is a strange passage of wind instruments, partly in semitones, which has a mystical effect, almost unearthly; and then there is a short return to the slow introduction, that seems to me again to say, ' Ah, yes! I am alone!' and then, with a few broken chords, that seem to feel, but hardly say ' Alone!' this wondrous movement closes.

"The *Scherzo* (in F, two-four time) begins upon the previous movement like the inhalation, after a long-breathed sigh—the inflation and invigoration of the lungs with the pure joyous breath of life, after they have exhaled all but vitality itself. This movement is of the character we are used to call *Mendelssohnish*, because, I think, Mendelssohn first introduced it with most admirable effect in many of his works; I mean that character of restlessness displayed in the almost ceaseless motion of semiquavers, such as in his ' Midsummer Night's Dream,' the Scherzo in his Otetto, and in many other instances. It opens with a chord of F, protracted for some bars, which, from its relation to the key of A minor, in which the previous movement closed, has an effect of vagueness and anxiety that is dispelled by the determinate chord of C, which, as the unequivocal dominant of the new key, defines this beautiful uncertainty, and the movement then proceeds like regular but rapid breathing. The subject is very marked and characteristic; it is first given concisely by the clarionet, and is afterwards prolonged by various instruments until it is taken up with all the satisfaction of a joyous self-content by the full orchestra. A second subject in C major is peculiarly quaint, and has a manner of effrontery that is charming; this is continued through various relative modulations, in the course of which the chattering of the wind instruments have a very prominent and naïve effect. The first part ends in C, and the second opens with a portion of the subject in the original key, which comes out with a kingly swagger on the violoncello : after a long stop upon a fundamental 7th on F, there is a brilliant burst upon a chord of D, and then the two subjects are worked and interwoven with the utmost skill and ingenuity, and with no less character and effect. The return to F major, which is with the second subject, is very novel, is sudden and unlooked-for. The *Coda* introduces a new phrase of irresistible piquancy and simplicity, and there is a most effective example of the rising of a fundamental 7th on the tonic to a major 3rd on the dominant, which proves, by the very frequen: repetition of the passage, how Mendelssohn must like, or rather love, this beautiful but most unusual resolution of this chord. This movement closes quietly, like the natural languishing which follows preternatural excitement.

"The slow movement (in A major) opens abruptly, but still connectedly with what has just concluded, on a 6th upon F natural, which sinks into a chord of E, and sounds to me as though a sudden earthquake rent the joyous feeling which had filled a loving bosom, and in the chasm which it made, revealed the depths of fathomless despair. But then we find this momentary anguish is no other than the fear that it must cease, which is the tremulous brink of happiness, the incertitude that makes delight an ecstasy, which refines mere joy to transport; for, after what may be supposed a prelude, or what in a song we should call the symphony, there comes a stream of broad, grand flowing melody, so full of lovely tenderness, so replete with

passion, and so fervent in the heartfulness of its expression, that it seems to say all that words, or looks, or
pressure of the hand could ever signify—almost all heart
could ever feel.   This is another instance of the exquisite
use of the singing powers of the violins, which float through
the *pizzicato* accompaniment 'like the voice of one beloved
singing to you when alone.'   There is one point in this
most heavenly melody where it rises from A in a chord
of the diminished 7th on D sharp to a *sforzando* on G
sharp, in a four-two upon D natural, which is to me the
utmost possible of passionate expression.   There is then
an episode in A minor given to wind instruments, which
is, I think, the least striking subject in the symphony, and
which comes with all the cold reserve of prudence inter-
rupting the pure confidence of virgin love.   But this is
qualified by a repetition of a portion of the first subject in
E major, which breaks in on an inversion of the major
9th on B with such a lovingness as quite atones for all
the previous seeming of indifference.   There is a short
second part which leads to the return of the subject in A,
which now assumes a greater force, a deeper intensity
from the different instrumentation, the melody being
given to the most passionate of instruments, the violoncello, and from some other varieties in the treatment.
The former episode recurs now in D minor; and the
portion of the subject is repeated as before, now in A
major, and the movement finishes with all the calmness
of a satisfied desire, but such an intellectual psychean
appetite which 'grows by what it feeds on,' and is most
contented when it still desires.

   "The last movement (in A minor, common time) bursts
in convulsively on this repose, as though the self-reproach
of one who feels himself unworthily beloved, and half
despairs, half burns with the ambition to become one day
deserving.   There is a striking wildness in the subject,
another character, and not less a true one of the violins
which play it, and there is a feeling of a resolution in the
long continued accompaniment of crotchets, which seem
like the united fire of a patriot and fervour of a lover.
The second subject in E minor is more simple, and yet
not less ardent, the great excitement being still main-

tained by the reiteration of a B, which forms a sort of drone, and by keeping off the keynote in the bass until the very end of the phrase, creates a vagueness powerfully exciting. And then the basses have to play a G three times—and then—O, what a burst of powerful and grand determination!—the full orchestra has to play the six-four on that note, and to make a brief and infinitely brilliant transition into C major, with the effect of thunder. This is, like all the others, a movement in two parts, the first part ending in E minor. The second part perhaps, for those who are not carried quite beyond themselves by the strong and impulsive feeling that pervades it, may want relief, if not repose; but even for such, if they can understand, although they may not feel the music, there is a masterly musicianship in the treatment of the subject, which must be interesting. After the return to the original key, the second subject, much curtailed and without the glorious burst into the major key of the sixth of the scale, which in the first part has an effect so grand and so majestic, is repeated in A minor, and is followed by a coda, which sinks into a repose like the exhaustion of an overwrought imagination—a heart that has been stimulated by excess of passion, seeming to beat its few last broken throbs before it breaks for ever. But then a new light bursts upon the mind, new oil is poured upon the flame, a rock is shifted from its base, and a world of waters is let loose upon the cataract. A new subject with a quite new feeling in A major, and in six-eight time, bursts like an eye-beam on the darkened heart, and says, in signs unquestionable and irrevocable, ' Yes, ever yes,' to all that undefinable craving to which the wildest brain upon the pinnacle of its enthusiasm dare not, cannot give utterance. It is a joyous exultation, far beyond Hope's uttermost excitement—it is the elation of an author when he feels he has achieved a work that will immortalize him in its immortality—it is the pang of pleasure which a lover feels at knowing that his passion-dream is realized. This brief epilogue to the whole symphony remains throughout in the same key, and is mostly to be remarked upon for the breadth, clearness, energy, and passion of its phrases, and the expressive brilliancy of its instrumentation, which, seeming at first most forcible, yet gathers, gathers, gathers force until the end. A long passage of the violins in octaves is almost overpowering, and—but I scorn to dwell on technicalities in speaking of what is so great in its effects as to blind us to the means by which they are produced.

"And this is the Symphony in A minor of Felix Mendelssohn Bartholdy; at least, this is an attempt to tell the impression, which, after three times hearing it,— at the trial, the rehearsal, and the concert,—it has left on me. I am aware that there may be to some an air of ostentation, even of bombast, in this vociferation of my feelings on this subject. SOME, perhaps, *may* understand them, and all *should* take my protestation of sincerity for a guarantee of what I mean. To me the symphony is, on the whole, the most pathetic composition of the kind, and of the length, I ever heard; and by pathetic, I must not be thought to mean that morbid melancholy quality which some critics, but few poets, would set up as the essential of sublimity: by pathetic, let be understood to signify that deep, intense, and soulful feeling which dives down to the bottom of the human heart, and there enthrones itself the emperor of passion. And these are words, how vague and how inadequate to tell the thoughts which prompt them. But when the time shall come, which cannot be remote, when all the world shall own this generation has added one to the great Trinity of Genius that has stood alone in instrumental music, I shall exult to have been one who could appreciate the merit, and has, however worthless, paid his tribute of acknowledgment to the original identity of style, the grandeur of conception, and the powers of development which this symphony displays, and which, in aftermen's esteem, shall place as equals, Haydn, Mozart, Beethoven, and Mendelssohn.

"G. A. MACFARREN."

"14, North Crescent, Bedford Square,
    "14*th June*, 1842."

At the time when this was written Macfarren had not arrived at that estimate of Mendelssohn's character

which he long afterwards expressed : " The foible of
his character was his thirst for good opinion, which
led him indiscriminately to conciliate everyone whose
judgment could receive attention; thus his testi-
monials are of little credit, and his complimentary
letters are not always utterances of his true opinion." [1]
Of the disinterested sincerity of the ardent critic's
enthusiastic effusion there is no reason whatever to
doubt. The diction of the exordium may be florid or
ornate—a foreshadowing of the metaphorical style
which often characterized the writer's later style in
his literary productions; but there is nothing fulsome
in the adulation : all is the outcome of genuine artistic
perception and delight, such as many of us felt, at that
period, at the rising of the " new star in the firmament
of genius." It is pleasant—now that Macfarren's
prophetic words have been fulfilled, and that star is
" massed in the galaxy of splendour," and the Symphony can hardly " be remembered to have *not been* "
—to look back to those early performances, and to feel
some sympathetic rekindling of that early enthusiasm
and delight !

The love of analogies, which is perceptible in this
early analysis, is a prominent feature in his subsequent
writings : " like a lover looking lingeringly, etc.,"
" like an assurance bursting on expectancy," " a consciousness of love, etc.," " like that intensest poetry,
etc."; these and other comparisons one finds matched
or paralleled in such sentences as this, on a passage in
Beethoven's Seventh Symphony :—

" Can you picture one who has long lain in a hopeful

[1] " Imperial Dictionary of Universal Biography."

dream, who yearns for happiness he has never known and so cannot define, awakening to learn that his dreaming is fulfilled, and to find the fact wholly unlike, yet a thousand-fold lovelier than his expectation ?   Such a picture is realized in the remarkable passage before us; a traveller who dreams of the home he is approaching, and wakes to find caressing friends around him looking the welcome of affection ; an artist who dreams of the completion of his work, and wakes to witness its admiring reception by an appreciating public.   Fancies such as these are quickly prompted by the exquisite passage to which I refer; but no thought of tangible form can represent its loveliness, no verbal language can translate its expression."[1]

It is interesting to compare this early analysis of the A minor Symphony with that of later years, written for the Philharmonic Society's programmes. After quoting Mendelssohn's printed direction as to the " separate movements following one another imme-diately, and not being divided by the customary inter-ruptions," and commenting on similar instances, our annotator proceeds :—

"From very early in his career it seems to have been an aim of Mendelssohn to give unity to the several portions of a large instrumental work, sometimes by the connection of two or more of the movements—as in the case under notice, sometimes by the allusion in a later movement to themes which have appeared in an earlier—as in the Quartets in A minor and E flat, and in the Octet. Opinions may vary as to how this purpose may best be fulfilled, nay, as to its desirability in any form ; but it is due to an artist to respect his own purpose in the presentation of his works, and thus to play the present Symphony as he intended. There can be no question as to the grandeur of the idea of one long enchainment of thoughts that bear all upon each other and combine to make a single, though widespread impression upon the mind ; in the work of an indifferent

---

[1] " Six Lectures on Harmony," p. 148.

composer an audience may welcome the customary breaks as a relief, but in the music before us the effect of each successive movement is enhanced by its connection with the preceding, and the impression of each gathers force from the context, while we, the audience, grow more and more susceptible of its effect, and become enabled to regard the work as a whole rather than as four collected portions."

Then follow some historical and biographical details, especially bearing upon the Scottish origin of the work, and recording its first performance in London, above referred to ; eliciting from Macfarren the exclamation, " Happy are they who recollect an occasion of such infinite interest in the history of our art ! " He then relates how, at that first performance, after Beethoven's " pre-eminently beautiful " Overture to " Coriolan " had been played and encored :—

" Then came the Scottish Symphony, and this was received with acclamations, drowning in many places the music itself, the hearty delight in which these plaudits testified ; the Scherzo was especially greeted and its repetition insisted upon, in spite of the composer's fidelity to his own design, who had proceeded far into the Adagio through the deafening applause of the audience, and reluctantly broke off the unheard flow of its delicious strains to recommence the previous movement."

A graphic little bit of musical history, by an ear-witness ! The analysis proper then commences :—

" The Symphony begins with a far more clearly defined melody than is often to be found in the introductory movement of a composition of the proportions of the present. It is succeeded by a passage of rare intensity for the violins alone, which is continued through a repetition of the opening melody.

"The chief subject of the Allegro, to which the foregoing leads, derives a peculiar effect from its duplication by the clarionet in the octave below the notes of the violin, which seems like a reflection of the principal or substantial sounds in notes of more delicate or ethereal nature. A very gradual drawing together of the time prepares the hearer for the first entry of the entire orchestra, and for the 'assai agitato' which marks the exciting character of what ensues. The first theme is ingeniously appropriated as a counterpoint to the second subject, and binds it in particular unity with the general expression. This is analogous to Haydn's frequent wont to reproduce a first melody with modification in the position and in the key usually assigned to the second subject, which brings into direct comparison the musical composition with a literary essay, wherein one theme or argument is the always prevailing matter in discussion."

This is a happier exposition of the case than the bald statement in the earlier analysis that "there is no second subject." In place of the earlier account of the opening of the second part, we have :—

"The course of modulation which signalizes the beginning of the Second Part produces a most remarkable and individual effect; here is not the place to discuss the theoretical phenomena which might account for this, but attention may be directed to it and to the total revulsion of feeling wrought by it. The extraordinary orchestration conduces as much as the tonal progressions to the effect, strange almost to terrible, before us. The continuance of the Second Part loses all appearance of scholarship in its most imaginative development of the chief ideas already set forth. The recurrence of the first subject is rendered unusually interesting by the counter-melody, assigned to the violoncello, which is grafted upon it; a most happy example of a happy device, which was first applied by Mendelssohn to the enrichment of this always attractive incident in the design of a movement. A corresponding modulation to that which opens the Second Part begins the Coda; and this portion of the Allegro presents an unanticipated idea in the fiercely rushing chromatic passages that work the whole to its highest point of excitement."

It is not necessary to reproduce the whole of this more recent analysis; the above extracts sufficiently exhibiting the maturer style, if not the riper musicianship of the writer, as compared with the earlier. In the annotations on the Scherzo, instead of "kingly swagger," we find: "the rough, burly tone given to the first theme when a portion of it is allotted to the violoncellos, the weird sound it assumes when played on the low notes of the clarionet," etc. The subject of the Adagio is characterized as a "delicious song which once to have heard is a lasting delight." And the whole article terminates with the record, possibly, of a personally received testimony :—

"Mendelssohn said that he felt in this Coda [to the last movement] that the task of years was accomplished; and that he was happy, if not proud, in the completion of his labour."

It will be observed that in neither of these articles is there any attempt to indicate any connection of the ideas of the Symphony with impressions received by the composer in his visit to Scotland. At the time that the first article was written probably the work had not been named the "Scotch Symphony," and the history of the work, in its origins and promptings, was known to few.

The first of these articles was written during the period when Macfarren's father edited the "Musical World," concerning which the following occurs in the "Family Recollections" :—

"It was about this period [1840], sooner or later, that Frederick Davison, of the firm of Gray and Davison [not related to J. W. Davison], engaged my father at a small weekly stipend to succeed Henry Smart as editor of the 'Musical World,' the journal originated in 1836 by Novello and Co. Ever in earnest in what he undertook, my father threw his best energies into the fulfilment of his new office, and did all that a generous sympathy with struggling artists could suggest to make the paper popular. Some of his leading articles are delightful essays on musical generalities; his personal notices are always tender, and constantly encouraging; he forbore from distinctly technical criticism, in which indispensable department he engaged Alfred Day, until he could no longer bear with the laconical bitterness of this reviewer of new music, and he then enlisted the services of J. W. Davison, whose reckless flippancy as little satisfied him."

It appears to have been just after the appearance of the first analytical article—probably as its result—that Macfarren made personal acquaintance with Mendelssohn; the only record of his first interview being a hasty note to his family :—

"Dear everybody,
"Mendelssohn behaved to me like an Angel. G. A. M. June 27th, 1842."

The great man was ready to discern a kindred spirit; and would not fail to appreciate, as time went on, the thoroughness and purity of Macfarren's artistic nature. Although there does not seem to have been the brotherly intimacy between the two men which subsisted from very early manhood between Sterndale-Bennett and Mendelssohn, yet the artistic friendship was entire, as several letters attest. I have heard Macfarren say that no pianoforte playing ever gave him so much pleasure as that of Mendelssohn. There was no sympathy, I believe, on the part of Mendelssohn, with Macfarren's theoretical views; perhaps it would be more just to say, his theorizing habit of mind. The whole thing was distasteful to him. When I related to Macfarren the anecdote of Mendelssohn's reply to an inquirer as to the root of the first chord in the "Wedding March,"—"I don't know, and don't care,"—he said: "I never heard that story, but I can quite believe it, for Mendelssohn had such a dislike to all theorizing." Macfarren's theoretical system—to be hereafter referred to—may have led him to write unusual chords and progressions; certainly it led him to use unusual notation. Mendelssohn did not argue these matters with him, it may well be believed; but, when playing from Macfarren's manuscript, would, on coming to such cases, cry out, in that quick way which is not to be forgotten by those who once heard it: "Mac, Mac, do you mean this?" On an affirmative answer being given, he would simply say, "Very well, all right, go on," to the rest of the performers.

Owing to circumstances that cannot here be recorded in detail, Mendelssohn's Second Symphony, known as No. 4, in A major, was not published until some time after the composer's death, and then, in the first instance, only in the form of a Pianoforte Duet—the arrangement being Mendelssohn's own, however. In the "Musical World" of October 9th, 1852, Macfarren wrote an article on the Symphony as presented in this arrangement. It may be interesting, even at this period of our narrative, to insert some extracts from this article, still further rendering comparison practicable between the earlier and the more mature

G

styles of the critic.   After much preliminary matter, suggested by the late publication of the work, and some comparison with the earlier Symphony, No. 1, in C minor, he proceeds :—

"However equal may be the merits of the two Symphonies in A major and A minor, their character is widely different as the different distribution of such general characteristics as establish the identity of the composer's style can render them.   Such is the distinction that may truly be made between the bright, sunny, laughing freshness of the earlier work [in A major], and the more intense and passionate fervour that so eminently marks the later composition [in A minor], and these varieties of character involve a very important difference in the plan upon which the several movements are constructed. . . . As to the impressions of Italy embodied in the Symphony in A major, speculation may be more or less presumptuous; but as every sensitive hearer will speculate upon the expression conveyed in music of so exciting a character, . . . interpreting the intentions of the composer by the index of his own emotions while hearing the performance, it cannot be arrogant to offer what speculations suggest themselves, as an indication rather of how much than of what may be found of secondary interest in this highly poetical work of art by such as willingly seek it.

"To speak most succinctly of general impressions rather than of particular emotions, let us suppose that the first movement realizes the influence upon an ardent mind of the clear, translucent air, the genial climate, the deep, deep blue above, the endless green below, in which the golden gleam of the exhilarant sunshine is blent with the intense hue of the unfathomable heaven, the spontaneity of life around, and the restlessness of emotion within that characterize the land formed by nature for the garden of poetry, whence the spoiled child has strayed in weariness of the too great luxuriance in which it has been indulged, to wander back, how rarely, from the distant home of its adoption, and find its powers and its perceptions quickened by its native associations.

"Let us suppose that the earnest and most original Andante portrays the feelings awakened by the mighty ruins of Roman splendour, the statues, the palaces, the temples, and the colossal Colosseum, ghosts of a greatness that is gone, monuments of an immortal age, enduring witnesses in their mouldering decay of the lasting influence upon all time to come of the eternal power of mind through which at first they were, which now through them is perpetually regenerated in all who see in them and feel, who read in them and understand the sublime lesson for the sempernatal future of the never-dying past; and that the lovely· episodical melody embodies the perhaps less awful but not less solemn sentiment that must be awakened in witnessing the new life springing from the old decay, the perennial flowers and verdure, ever young, mocking while they decorate the falling ruins that have seen them bloom, and seen them fade, and seen them bloom and fade again through a long, long race of centuries, typifying the eternal identity of the spirit of good and beauty, the soul of poetry, amid the temporal variations of its manifestation which, while they seem to pass away, are born anew in the new forms they suggest by the new powers they stimulate in the mind of man."

This poetic interpretation of the movement in question is in strong contrast to the popular "Pilgrim's March" view; and, I must aver, more sympathetically expresses my own long-entertained feeling, which has always somewhat revolted from the generally accepted notion. The other movements are dealt with in similar poetical manner, and then the more technical analysis is entered upon. In the analysis of the *Andante con moto*, the following occurs, which will be of interest to those who have studied under Macfarren, been examined by him, or conversed with him on rhythm and barring :—

"Then comes the most lovely episodical melody in

A major, in which is to be noticed a curious caprice in the rhythmical arrangement—namely, that the accent of the whole is against the measure ; in explanation of this may be adduced the subsequent repetition of the same melody in the key of D major, when the barring is according to accepted rule, with the natural rhythmical division of the phrases."

This summary of the last movement is also most interesting :—

" The final Presto is certainly the most entirely individual portion of the work, albeit not one of the movements has a prototype in the writings of any other master.   It is an imitation of the Saltarello, a national dance of the south of Italy, which differs from its twin sister, the Tarantella in having a crotchet at the beginning of each bar of six-eight measure (instead of six quavers in the bar, as in the dance more familiar in this country), the marked accent of which accommodates a jumping step in the dance itself, whence it derives its name.   The ceaseless continuity of the motion, and with it the excitement of this movement, is beyond praise.   The plan of the whole is somewhat singular, and admits of longer discussion than our present space will admit.   Suffice it to state briefly that the first part is regular, like that of a first movement ; that at the close of this the subject re-commencing in the original key, after the manner of many of the last movements of Mozart and Beethoven, which very shortly diverges into the elaborations of the second part; that these are enriched, as in the first movement of the present work, by the introduction of a new episodical subject, which appears first in the key of G minor ; and finally, that the composer is so carried away by the development of this idea, in conjunction with the chief subject of the movement, that he foregoes the formality of the recapitulation of the first part, and makes no recurrence to the many admirable points which, in the key of E minor constitute the second subject, but instead, prolongs the working of the second part into a most exciting and highly wrought Coda."

It may here be stated that Macfarren preferred to

consider all the themes appearing in one key as con-
stituting the different sections of one subject—first or
second—rather than as different, or tributary, or subordinate subjects. This was evidenced in various
examination questions, prepared, or given *viva voce*,
by him.

From internal evidence, as well as from knowledge
of Macfarren's views on the subject, I judge that the
following remarks upon Rhythm, occurring in a review
of some compositions by an estimable English musician, were written by him, and will help to illustrate
the remark, in the above article, on the alleged
rhythmical " caprice " in Mendelssohn's slow movement :—

" A rule of rhythm, little understood by some musicians
and totally ignored by others, prompts a remark . . . which
must be taken as it is meant—namely, in no captious
spirit, but in the hope to elucidate, it may·be, a matter
that is of more importance than many writers suppose. A
rhythmical period should close on the first note of a bar,
unless the penultimate harmony be superseded, when the
final note is delayed till the second of the bar. There are
a very few exceptions from this otherwise universal law,
and they, rightly regarded, all tend to confirm, nay, to
illustrate, the principle involved. The works of ancient
and modern German, Italian, French, and English writers
furnish exemplifications of what is here enunciated ; there
also are many instances, it must be admitted, of the disregard of the rule by the best writers ; still, the shortcomings of a saint are no warrant for the peccadilloes of
one who has not the screen of boundless charity for his
sins, and a great man's error justifies not the wilful wan-
dering of a writer who has less claim to critical deference.
Now, as the close of a phrase is required by rule to fall on
the beginning of a bar, the opening of the same phrase
must be so placed as to accommodate the requirement, and
this seems to compel that the division of the bars through-

out the phrase be counted backwards from the final note, when the fragment of a bar which remains after such division must initiate the melody. . . . The rule applies throughout a composition, and not merely to the concluding cadence, and the extension of some period by half a bar, in order to bring about the nominally correct termination, is the worst evil of an unclear perception of the law, since one cannot hear bar lines, nor tell, by listening, where they are drawn, but one may be fully aware of a half-bar too much or too little in a phrase. The subject needs a far longer disquisition to make it thoroughly intelligible than is here offered, and which goes as far as would here be seemly. It is one of sufficient importance, however, to deserve the attention of critics and composers, and if it has not been often advanced, there is the more reason for touching on it, though lightly, at present."

I have heard Macfarren say that even Schumann is not guiltless of the device of " the extension . . . to bring about the nominally correct termination," above spoken of. At the same time, Macfarren said—" I have undergone a good deal of bullying " for insisting on this principle. He once remarked to me that, judged by this law, the whole slow movement of Mozart's wonderful C minor Sonata is wrongly barred.

And yet the final Cadence, as well as others, in Macfarren's Song, "True Love," ends at the half-bar, thus :—

CHAPTER V.

SYMPHONY IN C SHARP MINOR. MACFARREN AND DAVISON'S CONCERTS. QUINTET IN G MINOR. TRIO IN E MINOR, AND OTHER WORKS. 1842—1844.

ABOUT the year 1842, one of the finest of the instrumental works of Macfarren was completed : the Symphony in the very unusual key, for the orchestra,—C sharp minor ; which was published as a pianoforte duet, arranged by the composer, and dedicated to Mendelssohn. Concerning it, Mendelssohn wrote, in a letter to Macfarren, dated " Leipzig, 2nd April, 1843 " :—

. . . . " I tried to bring out the Symphony in one of our last [*Gewandhaus*] Concerts, but as I suspected when I first wrote to you, there was some opposition from the Directors, merely because there had been four new Symphonies in the course of the last two months, and they did so much that I was obliged to postpone it until the beginning of the next season, although it was half copied already. I am sorry you feel disappointed by the delay, but it was not in my power to help it. Meanwhile I must repeat what I said in my first letter—if you *had* an Overture I am sure it would be a better beginning for this public and these Concerts, than a Symphony. Ask Bennett, who knows the place, and will certainly concur in this opinion. And if you could accordingly let us have an Overture *before* the Symphony, I am sure the last would be much better understood and received by the public, even if there had not been such a quantity of new native Symphonies beforehand, as there has been this year."

Then follows the mistaken request for an Overture to "Rob Roy," which Mendelssohn thought he had seen, but which was that to "Chevy Chase."[1] And Mendelssohn continues :—

"As for those good friends of yours who think, as you say, that English music is a thing which cannot be endured in Germany, and that a work of yours would be here like an apparition of two moons,—pray ask them to wait a few months, before they repeat an opinion equally creditable to us and to you, or pray tell them in my name that they are sadly mistaken, and that the event will soon prove them to be so."

"The event" of the performance of "Chevy Chase" Overture may have partly proved this mistake; but the Symphony seems never to have been performed at Leipzig. Nor was it acknowledged in our own country until the year 1845, when, on the 9th of June, it was performed at a Philharmonic Concert, under the conductorship of Moscheles; when, however, the performance was discreditably indifferent, and the reception, by the more conservative portion of the (at that time) very conservative audience, worse than apathetic: ill-mannered and hostile.

In the "Musical World" of March 17th, 1842, the duet arrangement of the Symphony was thus noticed :—

"A careful perusal of this work has brought with it the conviction that, despite its occasional inequalities of style, despite the few reminiscences of the works of the

---

[1] See page 33.

great masters which it contains, it is beyond comparison
the most complete and finished composition that has proceeded from the pen of Mr. Macfarren. The first *Allegro*
is of a perverse, gloomy, and desponding character. An
abrupt and rugged phrase, or fraction of a phrase, somewhat after the manner of the C minor Symphony of Beethoven, commences and gives the prevailing feeling to the
movement. The progress of this portion of the Symphony
is unimpeded by a single weakness. Anything, however,
rather than an emotion of happiness is engendered by its
performance; a thorough sentiment of despair pervades
the whole, but since the aid of mawkishness is never once
resorted to, the judgment is unoffended, although the
heart is made to weep. It seems the prevailing custom
among the best modern composers, to exert the wonders of
their art in inciting the saddest possible current of ideas
in the mind of the hearer;—as witness the symphonies
and overtures of Spohr, Mendelssohn, and Sterndale
Bennett, after hearing any one of which we feel infinitely
more inclined to walk straight into a river and drown ourselves than to exclaim, with an ecstasy of delight, 'How
divine an art is music!' Mr. Macfarren, in most of his
works, has fallen into the same notion, and usually regales
us with a dose of the dreariest melancholy. . . . There are
so many noble points in this first *Allegro* of Mr. Macfarren's symphony that we find it impossible to enumerate
them in detail, and must therefore content ourselves with
referring our readers to the text; doubtless they will not
less vividly appreciate than ourselves the striking points to
which we have thus cursorily alluded. The *Andante Cantabile* in E major, though possessing a rich vein of melody,
and abounding in fine points, is less to our taste than the
preceding—being materially less original, and containing
constant indications of the peculiar feeling of Mendelssohn
and Beethoven. Of the *minuet* and *trio* we shall decline to
give an opinion, until a hearing of the composer's intentions, as delivered by an orchestra, shall make us enabled
to judge of them with fairness. They depend evidently so
much on instrumental aid for their proper effect, that such
a hearing is absolutely requisite for their right comprehension ;—but when that is to be—Heaven or the Philhar-

monic can alone inform us; let us hope it may be ere
long. Perhaps the triumph of the entire Symphony is
achieved by the *finale*, which is indubitably a noble piece
of impetuous daring. . The subject, however, is not altogether original, since it recalls very vividly a passage in
one of the *finales* of "Don Juan;" but the management of
the materials is masterly in the extreme, and confirms us
in an opinion which the first movement half engendered,
—viz., that this is the best Symphony we have seen from
the hands of a British composer. We have not leisure to
individualize beauties, or we could fill columns of our
journal. Suffice it to say, that as one concentrated and
single effort it is fully entitled to a place amongst the
happiest inspirations of the acknowledged great masters;
and would do honour to any existing author."

It is difficult to reconcile the appreciative intelligence that is manifested by this article with the
strange feeling expressed with regard to the sadden-
ing effect of the symphonies of Mendelssohn, Spohr
and Bennett. Moreover, Mendelssohn's symphonies
were hardly before the world at that time; and only
an early symphony or two of Bennett's had been
produced. It is not improbable, however, that a
certain influence from the reading of Shelley may
have tinged Macfarren's mind, and tended to give
some character to his writings such as that which
is here animadverted on.

In the " Musical Examiner," August 19th, 1843,
appeared this extract from a letter from H. W. Ernst,
dated Paris, August 13th, 1843 :—

" Mon cher —— [Davison?]. Voici quelques mots pour
vous dire que je suis arrivé en bonne santé et qu'à peine
un peu reposé je suis allé porter à Heller les melodies
anglaises que vous m'avez données. Le soir il a joué avec
Hallé la Symphonie de Macfarren à 4 mains, et il a été

émerveillé, et véritablement étonné de n'avoir jamais entendu parler de lui. Il met cette symphonie bien au dessus de celle de Mendelssohn. Il a voulu ajouter lui même quelques lignes pour exprimer son admiration. Hallé et moi nous avons eu beaucoup de plaisir encore à l'entendre une seconde fois ; . . . Mille choses à Macfarren et remerciments de la part de Heller, de Hallé, et de moi, de la jouissance qu'il nous a causé par sa symphonie. Heller, sans lui en faire une reproche, a regretté que le motif du premier morceau ressemble, un peu, la symphonie en Ut de Beethoven."

And in the same number of the periodical this notice occurs :—

" The Symphony of Mr. Macfarren, though by no means free from fault, is decidedly the completest, and the most striking, as well as the most ambitious work that has proceeded from his pen. The subject of the first movement reminds us, by its abrupt and unmelodic character, of Beethoven's C minor, and further on, immediately preceding the first regular *forte*, there is another reminiscence (if we may so term it) of the Symphony in F major by the same composer. The movement as a whole, is, nevertheless, in our judgment, exceedingly fine, and there are points in it of which no composer need be ashamed ; let us instance the introduction of the second subject—the *forte* immediately succeeding—the return to the original *motivo*—the happy management of the singing phrase, re-introduced in the minor tonic—and the noble diatonic passage in contrary motion towards the close. The slow movement, in E major, is full of melody, and deliciously treated, but is less original, reminding us here of Mendelssohn, there of Beethoven, and seldom of Macfarren himself—consequently it has considerably inferior interest for us. The minuet, in A flat major, is simple and imposing, and the trio as fanciful and fantastic as well may be. The grand feature of the work, however, is the *finale*, the merits of which we can scarcely exaggerate, when we place it by the side of· that of Mendelssohn's

Otetto. The subject, nevertheless, is not original, but may be found (or something very nearly resembling it) in the first *finale* of " Don Juan "—but the entire course of the movement, the headlong rushing of the incessant stream of semiquavers, the unusual key, the grand effect after grand effect coming out with unabated vigour—and the overpowering energy of the *coda*, beginning with a

masterly enharmonic modulation from the chord of the 9th on G sharp, to that of the four-two on A flat, and dashing on impetuously to the conclusion—one and all of them leave us no time for consideration; the acknowledgment that genius is at work is wrung from us whether we will or not, be we prejudiced or impartial; that genius is at work and employing *all its strength*, is mentally assented to, as the irresistible torrent of the musician's passionate eloquence is poured out, effortless and unimpeded by lack of power. This movement alone would prove Mr. Macfarren to be a composer of very high pretensions, and we care not who knows that it is our opinion, for we are not ashamed of it."

The Symphony opens as above : the musical reader can therefrom judge for himself as to the alleged suggestion of the C minor Symphony of Beethoven.

Facilities for the production of large works by English composers were not then as numerous as now ; or this work could hardly have been " shelved " and lain unrecognized, uncalled for, all these years.

The following letter from Mendelssohn to Macfarren bears date about the time of the dedication of this Symphony, though not referring immediately to it :—

"London, 10th July, 1842.

"MY DEAR SIR,

" I hoped to come to you and I hoped to see you once more here and have been disappointed in both; to-morrow I must leave England again. I wanted to thank you in person for your very, very kind letter, and for the pleasure you gave me by sending me the Album in which I could inscribe myself amongst the number of your friends. I send it back to you with these lines and hope my little song will sometimes remind you of me and ask you not to forget one who will always be with the greatest esteem and the best wishes

" Yours very truly,
" FELIX MENDELSSOHN BARTHOLDY."

And the following, of a later date, does refer to the ultimate return of the Symphony, without having been performed at Leipzig :—

" 1, Hobart Place, Eaton Square,
"20th May, 1844.

" DEAR SIR,

" I receive just now your very kind note and thank you

very much for it, and hasten to tell you that I am sure
they will send in the Leipzic parcel the score of your
Symphony as well as the other music. They asked me
when I was there last whether they could keep some of
the music for next winter, and I said that at any rate, as
they had had it now so long they were to send *everything*
back to you at present, and might make their arrangements hereafter. So I am sure you will receive everything
very soon; of all the rest of your letter I hope to speak to
you to-morrow at length."

Mention has been made of Macfarren's intimacy
with James William Davison, whose name, indeed,
was so often coupled with his own, in ordinary
parlance, during the earlier years of his professional
career. Concerning this intimacy, he writes:—

"As to Davison; my most intimate friendship with him
began . . . . through my borrowing from one to whom
he had lent it, a copy of 'Queen Mab.' From the first,
and always, my father distrusted him, and though circumstances and I brought them much together, though he
perceived, and frankly owned, the special abilities of my
loved companion, he was never without apprehension that
this friend was an evil genius to me."

How far the paternal solicitude was justified may
partly be determined by the fact that, as is hinted
above, the friendship partly originated in a common
admiration of Shelley: not, it is believed, merely an
admiration of his poetic genius, but a fervent sympathy
with,—almost worship of—his personality, his opinions
on religion, and his daring, defiant independence of
life. Probably the religious, or anti-religious, utterances and position of the poet did not so much alarm
the senior Macfarren,—though his son writes that
" though never a scoffer, he was as a boy not ortho·

dox:" and this non-orthodoxy probably characterized also his manhood,—but the extravagances, moral and otherwise, which seemed to attach to the school of Shelley-devotees may well have occasioned him some concern. G. A. Macfarren, J. W. Davison, and some other ardent young men, seem to have been drawn together by their common tastes, and to have manifested a certain amiable eccentricity, such as the forswearing of animal food, the pursuit of universal knowledge, and so on. This vegetarian diet probably injured the constitution of Macfarren, who was never robust. It has been related that he was once " the embarrassed recipient of a salmon which no one would take off his hands." What young man, with any aspiration, any romance, any inborn energy, has not formed resolutions, conceived more or less wild plans, of individuality in living, especially, moreover, when the tender passion has kindled irrepressible emotional longings, which the stern realities of life, the sobering influences of maturer life, and the reasonable gratification of natural longings, have sufficed to moderate; but which have imparted zest and interest to the period of early struggle?

Years afterwards, Macfarren wrote thus concerning his friend Davison (with whom, however, he was by no means so intimate, latterly, as in early life); after speaking of his Sonata and lighter pieces for the pianoforte:—

"His esteem as a composer more justly rests upon his songs, many of which—the series entitled 'Vocal Illustrations of Shelley," especially—are marked by an originality of thought, a command of technicalities, and a depth of feeling which attest no less his musicianship than his

poetical perception. His very extensive literary attainments and his love of music combined to induce an inclination to writing on this art, and he was for several
years an occasional contributor to various journals in
London. In 1842, and the following year, he published
the 'Musical Examiner,' a weekly periodical, of which he
was the sole author. In 1843, on the death of Mr. Macfarren [the father of G. A. M.], he became the proprietor
of the 'Musical World.' . . . In 1846 he was appointed
musical critic on the 'Times' newspaper, and it is in the
fulfilment of this office that his best claims to consideration are founded. . . . With a large amount of technical
knowledge, a considerable artistic experience, and with a
genuine love for the theme, Mr. Davison entered upon this
task in a spirit that had never before been brought to bear
upon it. The field in which he exercises his pre-eminent
qualifications is so extensive as to give him an almost
unlimited influence; his eloquent writing has not only
raised the standard of our musical literature immeasurably
above its previous level, but has formed one, by no means
the least important, of the many powerful means which
have induced the prodigious progress of music in this
country. There are certainly men who mean well to
music, and who differ from the opinions he expresses; but
this is not always a testimony against the truth of his
judgments, and never against their sincerity. There never
was a censor who was infallible, and it is one of the
specialities of art-judgment that it depends on the taste,
no less than the erudition of the critic. It is by the
general tendency of his writings and by their effect, and
not by the particular discussion of accidental works, that
their high value is to be appreciated; and this will be best
proved by a comparison of the past and present state of
music in England. During his literary avocations he has
still pursued his original profession; and in his teaching
of Miss Arabella Goddard he has evinced his rare ability
as a master of the pianoforte."—" Imperial Dictionary of
Universal Biography."

The musical public are sufficiently acquainted with

the subsequent career of this distinguished critic, to render its further record here quite unnecessary. His association with Macfarren in concert-giving will be related further on.

In the year 1843, at a concert by the Society of British Musicians, a String Quartet in A, by Macfarren, was performed by Messrs. J. H. B. Dando (still living, 1890), J. W. Thirlwall, Willy, and my father, H. J. Banister; and this was declared to be " one of the best works that have proceeded from his pen.   The first movement is sublime—the *scherzo* strikingly fanciful and original—the *andante* pretty and melodious—the *finale* irresistibly exciting.   The style is perfectly in-dividual—Macfarren all over—as any one acquainted with the music of this clever composer must imme-diately admit." [1]   It was again performed at a morning performance by the same Society, to which Spohr was invited, July 20th of the same year.

On the 4th of the same month, a song by Mac-farren, "L'ultime parole d'amour," was sung by Signor Giubilei at a matinée given in the Hanover Square Rooms by the precocious and—alas !—short-lived young pianist, Charles Filtsch.

In the same year, Macfarren joined this intimate friend, J. W. Davison, in giving a series of three Chamber Concerts, at Messrs. Chappell's Rooms, in New Bond Street, during the months of March and April; the first taking place on the 9th of March. The programmes both of this series, and a second series in 1844, were largely made up of works by the two concert-givers ; which, unreasonably enough, caused some animadversion, whereas justifiable self-

"Musical Examiner," Jan. 7th, 1843.

H

assertion, and publicity, not money-making, were, not unavowedly, the very objects in view. Macfarren's Pianoforte Sonatas in E flat and A major were performed by W. H. Holmes; and his highly intellectual and interesting series of four songs to words from Lane's translation of the " Arabian Nights' Entertainments " were also first sung, by Miss Marshall and Miss Dolby. Another most interesting incident, however, was the first performance in this country of Mendelssohn's Trio in D minor, by Sterndale Bennett, Henry G. Blagrove, and Charles Lucas. These songs, from the " Story of Alee and Shems en Nahar," are entitled respectively—"The Transport of a Bedaweeyeh," a plaintive song in A minor ; " Many a one laugheth at my tears," in G major, full of gentle pathos ; " Separation," in D minor, full of hushed passion ; and " Many a one hath invited me to love," no less interesting, with more florid accompaniment. They were termed "exquisite gushes of the misery and despondency of love,"—"nothing superior to them in the whole range of German song-writing : " " Mendelssohn himself would not have treated the burning words which the music illustrates with more intensity, pathos, and elegance." [1]

Just after the last of these concerts, Macfarren sustained the severe loss of his father, who died in Castle Street, Leicester Square, April 24th, 1843, in his fifty-fifth year. Besides the grief at the severance, on natural grounds, this was a great blow to our composer, as his father had been his valued literary *collaborateur* for years, and Macfarren had now to seek literary aid elsewhere. He was fortunate, as will be

[1] " Morning Herald."

seen, in securing that of the late John Oxenford.

The attendance at the first series of concerts being very encouraging, a second series, in the following year, was held in the concert-room in the rear of the Princess's Theatre ; the first taking place on the 26th of April, 1844, and being signalized by the first public performance of one of the most esteemed of Macfarren's Chamber compositions, the fine Quintet in G minor for pianoforte, violin, viola, violoncello, and double-bass ; the performers being Messrs. William Dorrell, Goffrie, Henry Hill, Lucas, and Charles Severn. The Quartet in A was also performed ; and H. R. Allen sang Macfarren's *aria,* " Ah ! non lasciarmi no." The Quintet was written expressly on commission for an enthusiastic amateur contrabassist, George Perkins, Esq., recently [1889] deceased. When the composer took the work to his patron, the sum agreed upon was cheerfully paid; but the remark was made that he doubted whether any double-bass player could execute the difficult part assigned to the instrument in the Quintet. Respecting the origin of this work, Mr. F. W. Davenport has written the following interesting particulars, preceding an exhaustive analysis :—

" Like many other works that have achieved distinction or popularity, the above owes its origin to an accident. During the rehearsal of another work by our composer, a gentleman was introduced to the company by a mutual friend, Mr. Brinley Richards, who, besides being an enthusiastic amateur, had acquired some skill as a player on the double-bass. The immediate business of the moment was thus interrupted, somewhat to the annoyance of those concerned in it. Shortly after taking his leave, feeling perhaps that he could gracefully make amends, and pay a compli-

ment into the bargain, the visitor commissioned Sir George
Macfarren to write a composition for the chamber, which
should include among the instruments in the score that
upon which he himself was in the habit of performing.
The present work was the result, and was written in the
course of the last three Sundays of December, 1843.   The
kindly-disposed patron of our art himself, maybe from a
feeling of modesty, never played the part that was written
for him ; but his name will be always associated with the
work, through his kindly instigation of it, and its dedication to him on the title-page.   The first performance took
place early in the following year (1844), at a concert given
by the composer and Mr. J. W. Davison, in London, and
since that date it has been frequently included in metropolitan and provincial programmes.   On one occasion,
Madame Arabella Goddard and Signor Bottesini played
the pianoforte and double bass parts, and on another, in
the rooms of the composer in Berners Street, Mendelssohn,
with his usual insight and facility, astonished the company
by his marvellous reading of it from the MS. score."

At the second concert of this series, May 17th,
1844, the new work was the "Romance and Allegro
con fuoco" in E minor, for pianoforte, violin, and
violoncello, composed expressly for Madame Dulcken,
and played by her, E. W. Thomas (known as "Taffy
Thomas"), and Lucas.   The plan of the work, consisting of only two movements, was suggested by
Madame Dulcken herself; and she had, indeed, previously played it at a Chamber Concert of her own,
earlier in this same year.   It was published in the
following year.

On this occasion also, the (at that time) somewhat
bold experiment was made of performing Beethoven's
C sharp minor posthumous Quartet, the first violin
part being taken by H. W. Ernst.   I remember the
occasion well, having sat by Dr. Day, and been some-

what astonished to hear him express his non-relish of the Quartet.

Mendelssohn was present; and the six songs just dedicated by him to Miss Dolby were sung by her and Miss Marshall, in alternation; the latter evincing considerable nervousness, partly, I believe, on account of some physical disability for the particular task assigned to her, and additionally on account of the presence of the composer.

The Trio referred to above was somewhat strangely neglected for a number of years—strangely, not only because of the interest of the music, but also because, being comparatively short, it was available for performance on occasions when a longer work was undesirable — which was Madame Dulcken's intention. The credit of reviving the work belongs to Mr. Ernest Kiver, who played it at his concert, April 27th, 1887, in presence of the composer, who sat by me on the occasion. Macfarren's account of the work is given in a letter to Mr. Kiver, March 25th:—

"The plan of the Trio was suggested by Madame Dulcken, the once deservedly popular pianiste, and the work was first played by her at one of her chamber concerts in the spring of 1844; it was printed in 1845."

It is both just and pleasurable to insert, in addition, the following letter to Mr. Kiver, furnishing, moreover, an instance of the kind appreciativeness which Macfarren was so ready to express towards rising artists, and his sense of any attention or honour paid to himself—an appreciativeness which continued to the end; for this letter was among the latest of many such which

he wrote, bearing date less than six months before his
death :—

"7, Hamilton Terrace, N.W.
"*May 17th*, 1887.

"MY DEAR KIVER,

"I have been remiss in not sooner telling you, as I have
all along wished for time to do, that I was greatly pleased
with your performance at your concert, and I now thank
you for the pains you spent upon my old Trio, and for the
capital result. I earnestly wish that this occasion may
help with others in which your merit has been evinced to
establish you in your profession, and I shall be very glad
if you will ever give me opportunity to further your
interests.

"You must not forget your promise to lend me your
copy of the Trio, for the sake of the corrections, but this
may be kept at any time most convenient to you, since the
faults that have been accepted for forty years, cannot do
much more mischief in a week or two.

"Yours with kind regards and best wishes,

"G. A. MACFARREN."

At the third concert, W. H. Holmes was to have
played Macfarren's Second Solo Sonata, "Ma Cousine,"
in A major ; but illness prevented him from doing so.
Macfarren requested Mendelssohn to play it, as he was
to play his Trio in D minor, but received the following
letter of apology :—

"4, Hobart Place, Eaton Square.
"*June 6th*, 1844.

"MY DEAR SIR,

"I need not tell you with how great a pleasure I would
have played your Sonata to-morrow, if I possibly could—
for I hope you know this. And you also know that it is
with true and sincere regret that I must say I am not
able to undertake the task which you propose me. During
the bustle of the last weeks I have not yet been able to
become acquainted with your Sonata ; the whole of this

day and of to-morrow morning is taken up with different
musical and unmusical engagements, and accordingly I
would hardly have an hour till to-morrow night to play
your Sonata over. This I cannot think sufficient, and I
would not be able to do it justice *in my own eyes.* Do not
misunderstand me and take this for false modesty ; I know
very well that I should be able to-morrow to play it
through without stopping, and perhaps without wrong
notes ; but I attach too much importance to any public
performance to believe that sufficient, and unless I am
myself thoroughly acquainted with a composition of such
importance and compass, I would never venture to play it
in public. Once more I need not tell you how much I
regret it, for you must know it very well.

"Mr. Davison told me the Concert was now to begin with
my Trio [in D minor: Op. 49] : I shall therefore be punctually
with you to-morrow evening at half-past eight. I beg you
will arrange about having a *good* piano of Erard's at the
room ; they know there already which I like best.

"Always very sincerely yours,
"Felix Mendelssohn Bartholdy."

Mendelssohn was joined, at this performance, by
Joseph Joachim and Hausmann. During this year,
Joachim, then a lad, received composition lessons from
Macfarren, to whom, as I have heard him say, he was
indebted for his first instructions in the art of writing
for an orchestra. His visit to this country, in that
year, created a great sensation ; and his performances
at Macfarren and Davison's concerts formed an attractive feature.

At this third concert, Miss Rainforth sang a
" Spinnelied " from "Faust," by Macfarren, described
as of " tristful quaintness, a melody which follows with
true sentiment the varied passion of the poetry, in all
respects worthy to be its companion."

Another fine song of Macfarren's, belonging to

this period, is the rhapsody, "O world! O life! O time!" which the "Atlas" newspaper declared to be—

"Altogether one of the most remarkable songs we have seen. From its opening amid the profoundest despondency, through all its varying shades of sentiment, down to the chilling and hopeless gloom of its close, it is filled with testimonies to the intellectuality of the true musician's art. Music must needs be metaphysical that follows up, seizes on, and incorporates itself with the thoughts of such a poet as Shelley; yet all this does this song in perfection. But few things in modern song-writing will bear comparison with the expression of the half-stifled hope in the line, 'When will return the glory of your prime?' by the grand and unexpected modulation to D major; or the rendering of the withering self-reply, 'No more! no more!' increasing in fervour with every repetition, until the climax of mental suffering seems attained in the unisonous passage that regains the tonic, and, in its course, involves that acutest of the musician's expressions of pain, the ascent of the diminished fourth. An enharmonic transition now conducts to a reposeful and lovely melody in D flat major, to the words, 'Out of the day and night a joy has taken flight.' This is interrupted by a recurrence of the poet's thoughts to their gloomy outset, and the musician, faithful to every turn of feeling he essays to depict, parallelizes this relinquishment of fancied happiness, and by a most masterly manoeuvre of harmony reverts to the stern severity of his first tonic, F sharp minor, and to his rendering of the poet's 'No more, O never more!' but, in this case, expanded over the entire surface of his last page, and wrought to its close with a chilling power of effect, of which we scarcely know a comparable instance. On the whole, we do not hesitate to pronounce this one of the most extraordinary songs in any language."

CHAPTER VI.

MACFARREN'S THEORETICAL VIEWS AND WRITINGS.
DR. DAY'S THEORY. 1838, ETC.

SOME time prior to the year 1838, Macfarren first became acquainted with Dr. Alfred Day,[1] homœopathic physician [1810-1849] : an acquaintanceship which in that year "ripened into intimacy." This intimacy had such momentous results with regard to his own theoretical views, and, by consequence, his attitude towards previous and contemporary systems of harmony, as well, it must surely be said, upon his own composition ; and moreover, his name became so identified with the system which he, against his predilections, was compelled to adopt, espouse, and defend, so as to render him its apostle and champion, that it becomes necessary to treat of the whole subject at some length. It has been customary to regard Macfarren as dogmatically obstinate, especially because of the persistency with which he enunciated and upheld his theoretical opinions. But this will ever be the fate of men who think out a subject thoroughly, and, having thought to a definite conclusion, enunciate that definite conclusion without hesitation, reserve, or concession. And especially

[2] See chapter iii. page 80.

unyielding will such a man be, when the very preci-
sion and persuadedness of his views result from his
having arrived at them by himself yielding, notwithstanding old-standing prejudices. There is, undoubtedly, a tone of finality, as of "one having
authority," about Macfarren's theoretical writings;
and that is justly to be characterized as dogmatic. But
Macfarren's contention would have been that, in in-
structing learners, it is the teacher's function to lay
down the law, to enunciate the truth, and that without wavering. Macfarren himself was "fully persuaded
in his own mind": it is not fair to characterize that
persuasion as prejudice, when it was the issue of
painstaking consideration. Prejudice is judgment that
precedes evidence. Conviction is judgment after
weighing evidence.

Macfarren himself writes, concerning Alfred Day:—

"His early predilection for music was opposed by his
father, who devoted him to the profession of medicine.
He studied in the schools of London and Paris, obtained
his diploma at Heidelberg, and practised in London as a
homœopathist. His father's hindrance of his pursuit of
music prevented his acquiring any practical facility in the
art, but could not check his interest in it, and he indulged
accordingly in theoretical investigation. His only instructor
was W. H. Kearns; but his familiar intercourse with
several of the most talented musicians of his own age gave
him constant opportunity of study. He conceived a theory
of harmony that justifies, upon fundamental principles,
many of the beautiful exceptions from conventional rules
that adorn the works of the great composers. He spent
several years in maturing his system, and gave it to the
world in his 'Treatise on Harmony,' in 1845. The lucid
distinction between the laws of the ancient, or strict, or diatonic school, and those of the modern, or free, or chromatic;
the regular and comprehensive manner in which these are

severally defined; and the original and coherent explanation of the specialities of chromatic harmony—are all novelties in this very remarkable work, which, on that account, have been barriers to its immediate acceptation. But the clearness with which this system unfolds the subject, is such as to give at once greater confidence and greater scope to the student than any theoretical work in existence; and its value is acknowledged by those who have carefully and candidly studied its principles. The peculiarity of mind which led him to reject established codes, both in medicine and in music, led him also to observe every other object from a novel aspect; and his singular genius amused itself in devising improvements in many mechanical inventions, few of which, however, with all the ingenuity they evince, have come into use." (" Imperial Dictionary of Universal Biography.")

In agreement with one remark in the above extract was an observation made by Macfarren to myself, in conversation about the theory: " Think how much you will enlarge your power and freedom in your own writing by remembering that these various resolutions are within your scope "—referring to the chromatic resolutions of the minor 9th, etc.

About the period above specified, Macfarren used to go over to Brixton to spend as many evenings as he could spare with Dr. Alfred Day, for the discussion of his views on Harmony. The history of those conferences is thus briefly related by Macfarren himself:—" He [Alfred Day] then propounded to me his theory of harmony, which I combated point by point, as each point differed from views I had hitherto learned, and every opposing argument successively fell under the convincing weight of his novel principles." Thus, Macfarren's views were revolutionized; and that, as has been already hinted, by

yielding his old prejudices or views. He goes on to
relate how he persuaded Day to commit his views to
paper, which was reluctantly, slowly, and with great
difficulty accomplished ; the amateur author reading
the chapters to his professional friend as the work
proceeded, for the benefit of such practical advice as
one actually engaged in teaching might fairly be pre-
sumed to be able to offer.   At length, in 1845, Day's
" Treatise on Harmony " was published ; and to the
preface was appended a letter of recommendation, or
rather of acquiescence, from Macfarren, in which he
makes the acknowledgment :—

"I am happy to own that in becoming acquainted with
your principles, I found my ideas of the resources of Harmony greatly to expand ; and my facility and confidence in
the practical application of them is now much greater than
I believe it could possibly be, had I not the advantage of
the peculiar view of the subject which is opened by your
new System;—above all, I am gratified by it, insomuch as
I find in it an explanation of and a rule for many of the
greatest beauties of the best masters, which formerly appeared to violate all the rules of music, and which were
sanctioned as the unaccountable aberrations of genius, but
which could only be imitated to be plagiarized.   In the
second place, since I have become familiar with your
System, feeling as I have done that it was true, and that
as Truth is single, so none but yours could be true, I have
taught upon it, and have found it most easily comprehended by pupils who had no foreknowledge of the subject;
and by those who have come to me with a small acquaintance with other works, it has been admitted to explain
many points of Harmony, which had been to them before
quite unintelligible.   It is a Theory, in my opinion, of
peculiar advantage to the student, as comprising the laws
of counterpoint with all those of the chromatic or free
style ; and, for the first time to my knowledge, distinguishing between these very dissimilar schools of harmony."

The letter from which the above is an extract is dated "73, Berners Street, July 12th, 1845," the house being at the corner of Oxford Street. Some friends wondered at a musician,—especially a composer,—choosing to reside in so crowded a thoroughfare. Macfarren's explanation was that he could sooner accustom himself to write against the wholly unmusical noise of cart-wheels, than against that of the barrel-organs and brass bands which infest so-called "quiet streets." I was a frequent visitor to that house during the residence of the Macfarren family therein.

With reference to the remark in this letter about " the peculiar view of the subject which is opened by your new System," it is curious to remember how often Macfarren would, so to speak, ignore the fact of any peculiarity or novelty about the " view" or " System" which he advocated. When he was examining one of the elementary classes at the Royal Academy of Music, the Sub-Professor who had charge of the class interposed, after one of the questions,— " Will you mind asking according to the more usual view and terminology ? "—to which the immediate rejoinder came,—" You are the first that ever intimated that there was anything unusual in my view of the subject ; " although the phraseology was undeniably the outcome of the particular theory held by the questioner. And, on another occasion, when he asked a young lady-student the notation of the chromatic scale,—one of the salient points in which the Day theory differs from ordinary usage,—she began her reply, less warily than truly, " Well, there are two different ways in which it is noted,"—and then began by giving the "Day" notation; upon which Macfarren abruptly stopped her, saying,—"I know of no other way, and advise you to keep to that": ignoring the undeniable fact that, right or wrong, another notation is (to put it mildly), frequent in the works of acknowledged composers, as well as in books of instruction.

In saying "Truth is single, so none but [your system] could be true," Macfarren perhaps hardly attached sufficient weight to the axiom—"Truth is many-sided;" although that axiom may often be used to cover laxity, neology, or latitudinarianism. But he held by that principle, commencing the preface to his "Rudiments" with the sentence, "This book presents the truth, and nothing but the truth, though not the whole truth, on the boundless subject of which it treats." And again, in the concluding lecture of his "Six Lectures on Harmony," he re-asseverates:—

"Truth is single. This Spenser has pointedly symbolized in naming his heroine, who is the personification of verity. A notable evidence, then, of the truth of Alfred Day's theory of harmony, is that perfect unity prevails throughout it; and in this respect it differs from every other of the many I have studied."

And, in the introductory lecture:—

"I am indeed so thoroughly convinced of the truth of Day's theory, and I have derived such infinite advantage from its knowledge in my own practical musicianship, that I should be dishonest to myself and to my hearers were I to pretend to teach any other."

And in his "Musical History," page 136, he states:—

"As a summary of all the precept and example that has

been cited in the survey of the centuries, let the writer
state his convictions on musical theory, which are, that the
"Treatise on Harmony" by Alfred Day comprehends
whatever is practically available, and reconciles the previously apparent discrepancies between principle and use.
. . . . . The author now cited was the first to classify the
ancient, strict, uniform, diatonic, contrapuntal style, apart
from the modern, free, exceptive, chromatic, massive style,
to separate the principles that guide the one, from the laws
that control the other, and to place a subject that is at
once sublime and beautiful in a light of unfailing clearness. He showed that one or another beautiful chord and
the progressions thence were not capricious violations of
rule, permissible to genius though unallowable to ordinary
writers ; he showed that such things were acceptable, not
only because great masters had written them, and so small
writers might repeat the trespass ; he proved this by
demonstrating the self-perfection of the ancient canon, and
the also perfect modern system that rests on a basis totally
distinct from that of the other."

Yet once more, Macfarren concludes the Introduction to his " Eighty Musical Sentences " thus :—

" The author is happy to issue this publication as a con-
fession of musical faith, avowing implicit belief in the
harmonic theory on which it is based, and thorough conviction that the theory accounts for everything that is
beautiful, and guards against what is unsatisfactory in
musical combination and progression."

These last extracts, moreover, re-assert and em-
phasize his averment in the above letter to Day concerning the light thrown by the theory on the practice
of the best masters ; always a strong contention in its
favour, urged by its upholders. An incident may
here be related, however, illustrating Macfarren's
" singular openness to conviction," so justly acknowledged by the pupil who furnishes it, and in whose

words I give it.   " Owing to his refusal to accept as
valid the explanation I offered according to Day of
certain chromatic chords which I contended were in
the key, and *his admission of a chord which he frankly
admitted he could not account for by Day's theory,
saying, ' Here I must own Day breaks down,'* I, in conjunction with another, prepared an extremely revolutionary ' extension ' of Day's theory, which I took an
opportunity of submitting to him privately. He heard
me with the utmost patience, and refused to give an
opinion on the matter, but, reserving judgment, took
more than a week to consider it; and when he found
himself compelled to dissent, did so with the utmost
courtesy and consideration; and that, though he had
been wedded to a theory for half a century."

It must have been soon after the publication, in
1845, of Day's " Treatise," which was " received
worse than coldly by the heads of the musical profession "—" was denounced by the chief musicians in
London, and a single believer [Macfarren himself]
for some time alone maintained and taught its
enlightened views," — that the attention of the
" authorities " at the Royal Academy was inevitably
directed to the fact that Macfarren was teaching his
classes " new-fangled notions,"—unorthodox here-
sies, and using a new book. Quite justifiably, the
matter was duly inquired into: nothing peremptory,
inconsiderate, or disregardful of one whose musicianship was so deservedly recognised, and who was so
highly esteemed personally, was to be looked for from
such men as the then Principal, Cipriani Potter; but
Macfarren was invited to discuss the questions in
dispute, with the other harmony professors of the insti-

tution. A meeting was held — a " round-table " conference—at which, besides the Principal, Sterndale Bennett, Sir Henry R. Bishop, John Goss, and Charles Lucas were present; and a lively discussion ensued. Macfarren was probably better equipped for dialectics than his opponents, from his own experience in his original antagonism to Day. He was outweighed, outnumbered, but not, as he believed, outwitted; and, refusing to succumb by teaching contrary to his convictions, felt bound in honesty to resign his appointment—much to the regret, doubtless, of his colleagues. But he never wavered—was no time-server, but bided his time, which came later on. Before long, better counsels prevailed; not the acceptance of Day's theory, but the wise persuasion that it was better to have a musician of unquestioned competence and power to teach that which he believed from his own out-thinking, than that any old traditions should be so stereotyped in an educational system or *curriculum* as to bar all free thought, and to alienate from the institution one whose worth was so fully recognized. In 1851 Macfarren resumed his professional work at the Royal Academy at the instance of Cipriani Potter, his own old teacher, who said to him, " Come back and teach anything you please."

In the " Musical World," March 10th, 1849, an article on Day's theory, expository and defensive, appeared, signed " M.," and bearing internal evidence of being written by Macfarren.

As time went on the system gained adherents, even amidst the strenuous opposition which it still encountered. One of its most determined opponents even said to me, concerning Day's book, " If you read it,

I

you will find that it will set you thinking about combinations and progressions which you have not been
accustomed to consider, and will be suggestive, and
enlarge your views," or words to that effect. At all
events, Macfarren continued to gain respect for his
sturdy independence; and the numerous pupils indoc-
trinated by him were an attached band of devotees.
But an impression prevailed, I think, that the new
doctrines were as obscure and difficult of apprehension as they were doubtful; at all events, Day's own
book was so considered. Accordingly, Macfarren was
urged to embody the principles that he was teaching
in such a form as to render them available for tuition.
Day's book was a " treatise "—an exposition, and that,
moreover, in apologetic or even polemic manner, of
an unfamiliar theory, and, not including any exercises, was wholly unadapted for teaching purposes.
Therefore, in compliance with the desire so expressed,
Macfarren prepared his " Rudiments of Harmony,"
which was published in 1860. His aim was to provide " a book of less extent and smaller price than
Day's 'Treatise,' wherein rules should be stated, but no
arguments given for their support, wherein the points
of least frequent application should be omitted, and
wherein a series of illustrative exercises should be
included for practical service to the student." This
book, therefore, instead of being a treatise, is a class-
book or lesson-book. And this should in fairness
be borne in mind as accounting for the uncompro-
misingly dogmatic tone of the book, which appears in
the already-quoted first sentence of its preface. Macfarren's purpose was didactic, not polemic. He was,
at the time of its preparation, reinstated as a professor

at the Royal Academy; the weight of his opinions was acknowledged, even though those opinions were dissented from; he was tacitly regarded as one who had a right to be an epoch-maker, and there was now no doubt that his book, and the system on which it was founded, had to be reckoned with in theoretical education.

In the "Rudiments," however, Macfarren departed from the new method introduced by Day of figuring basses, "for the sake of avoiding a possible, if only imaginary, obstacle to the acceptance of" his theory of harmony. This departure, however, was not to be "interpreted as an admission of its impracticability, but as a concession to established habit, if not to prejudice." Macfarren was accustomed to designate as "misleading" the method of figuring ordinarily adopted in "Thorough-bass." That which he advocated was the figuring from the root of the chord, with alphabetical indications as to which position or inversion was used.

The disciplinarian character of his mind was evinced in this book by the framing of rules and exceptions in abundance, requiring considerable exercise of discerning memory on the part of the student, little discretionary latitude being allowed him. This method of teaching was characteristic of Macfarren, I think, all along his professional course. Pupils of a restive, erratic, or independent temperament chafed somewhat under the almost numberless restrictions which, as it seemed to them, curbed them on every hand. Some pupils, indeed, did more than chafe; or rather, escaped from the chafing by defiance, not disrespectful or mutinous, but self-assertive; they struck for liberty. This was especially the case when they began to compose, or, perhaps, later on than at the beginning, saying, "I like this, and mean to have it so." All teachers are familiar with this class of "free-lances;" perhaps Macfarren's rigidity was somewhat likely to rouse a little of such a spirit where it was latent. But it is impossible not to admire the ingenuity with which Macfarren's rules, and even more his exceptions, were devised and framed to meet, as it would seem, every case likely to arise. In a subsequent edition of the "Rudiments," a fresh batch of exceptions was added in the form of an appendix.

A further opportunity was accorded to Macfarren of enunciating and enforcing his theoretical views by the invitation given him, in 1867, to deliver a course of "Six Lectures on Harmony" at the Royal Institution of Great Britain—an invitation which was mainly due to the good offices of his "early friend," the esteemed professor, Mr. G. A. Osborne.

Macfarren was waiting in a music-warehouse in Bond Street, when Mr. Osborne came in; and, conversation turning upon these theoretical matters, Macfarren expressed his desire to lecture, in exposition of his views, at the Royal Institution. He was unaware that his old friend had any influence in the matter; but such was the case, and Mr. Osborne, finding that Macfarren was remaining some time in that meeting-place, asked him not to leave till his return, and hastened to the Royal Institution and had an interview with Dr. Bence Jones, the secretary. Returning to Bond Street, he was able to say, "Macfarren, your lectures will be welcome; terms will be satisfactory, and there will be prospect of the lectures being published." Macfarren

told me that he would never again go through the
anxiety of bringing lectures within exact compass of
time, to be indicated relentlessly by a clock-bell, at the
sound of which the audience were all to rise and
depart, regardless of the finish or non-finish of the
lecture.

These lectures when published were characterized
by a writer who was opposed to the theory therein
expounded, as forming, nevertheless, "one of the most
interesting volumes ever written on musical theory."
In them Macfarren was not the rule-maker, but the
expounder and the illustrator, and was apologetic by
means of exposition and illustration. He availed himself of the opportunity to justify his contention that,
all along, the works of the great Masters exemplified
the principles of which he had been the unflinching
advocate; that however "new in theory," as Day had
observed, these principles were "old in practice;"
that by them "many discrepancies of principle and
practice were reconciled between the writings of profound teachers and the works of the great Masters."

One great Master, indeed, Dr. Day sought to enlist
as an adherent—Felix Mendelssohn Bartholdy. He
prevailed on Macfarren to arrange a meeting with the
Master, that he might have an opportunity of expounding the theory, and indoctrinating Mendelssohn
therewith. The meeting took place at Macfarren's
residence; but, he told me, before Dr. Day had proceeded far with his argumentative exposition, the face
of Mendelssohn assumed an expression so suggestive
of his having taken a dose of nauseous medicine, that,
to avoid a scene, Macfarren was compelled to bring
the discussion to an abrupt, if not untimely, end. His

explanation was that Mendelssohn was so opposed to theorizing about the beautiful art which he so enriched by his productions, not that he rejected Dr. Day's theories in themselves. Anyhow, Day had evidently reckoned—not, indeed, without his host—but without calculating the temper of his host's distinguished guest. As Macfarren remarks, in his biographical sketch in the "Imperial Dictionary of Biography" : " [Mendelssohn] had the strongest aversion to pedantry, and detested theoretical discussions, as being the cause, if not the result, of pedantic feeling."

In 1885, Day's original " Treatise " being out of print,—forty years after its publication !—it was deemed desirable to issue a new edition. Naturally, Macfarren was engaged to supervise this re-issue ; and the second edition was published with an interesting preface by the editor, giving an account of its original production, a summary of the theory itself, some reply to objections, and a statement as to wherein the second edition was different from the first, and on what authority the alterations were made. With one exception, these alterations might be said to be made on Day's own authority, inasmuch as he had given Macfarren an interleaved copy of the original book, with the request that he would make memoranda of such modifications, in phraseology or otherwise, as " daily observation of the working of the system," in actual teaching, might suggest as desirable. This Macfarren did, and discussed all his suggestions with Day, with the result that they were all accepted fully by him, till his death in 1849. Such modifications as occurred to Macfarren subsequently, as the result of, or during, thirty-six years' experience, were given in an appendix; those approved by Day were incorporated in the text. The one exception above referred to consisted in the omission of an intermediate chapter between the first and second parts of Day's book, on " Diatonic Free Music," which Macfarren considered " redundant if not confusing." While he fully endorsed, and considered an important speciality, as one of the foundations of Day's system—

" the very broad, but not universally recognized distinctions between the ancient, strict, uniform, diatonic, artificial, or contrapuntal style of harmony, comprised in what may be called archaic art in music; and the modern, free, exceptive, chromatic, natural, massive, or harmonic style of harmony, comprised in the living art of our own times;" yet he acknowledged that " the twilight between the prevalence of the ancient and modern styles in music has so many examples of each, the strict and the free so continually overlap each other in the music produced throughout what may be assumed as the transition period, that to date the dawning of the one or the setting of the other is impossible."

The present being a biographical, not a theoretical or polemical work, any full exposition of, or argument concerning, the system of harmony espoused by the subject of this memoir, and so staunchly and ably advocated by him, so that his name has become inseparably identified with it, would be out of place. The broad distinction between the diatonic and chromatic styles, just adverted to, lay at its threshold; and with that distinction, a separate set of rules for each style. In connection with the chromatic style, the initial novelty was that which was termed by Macfarren " Alfred Day's beautiful theory, which identifies with every key the twelve notes of its chromatic scale, and proves that, as concords or as discords, they are all essential to the tonality." And, as a corollary of this theory, the notation of the chromatic scale referred to above, founded on the combined major and minor scales on the tonic. And, still further, in connection with this recognition of the notes of the chromatic scale as integral to the key, was the recognition of fundamental chromatic chords—the roots assigned for fundamental discords being the dominant, the tonic, and the supertonic. Many and various additional collateral differences of view, usage, and notation were connected with and resultant from these essential points, to illustrate which would require much music type and much space for explanation. Even the summary given, without music type, in Macfarren's "Six Lectures" (p. 214 *et seq.*), occupies a few pages; as does a similar summary in his "Musical History" (p. 136 *et seq.*). Another summary, with music type, is given in my "Text-book of Music," Appendix I. (later editions). Some of the salient practical issues, patent to observation, either in progression or in expression, notational or verbal, are sketched in some remarks which I made when addressing the students of the Royal Academy of Music, in November, 1887, shortly after they had been bereaved of their Principal, which I venture, therefore, to insert in this place, as bearing on the subject in hand.

"I think it only right and fair, both for your own sakes, and for his memory's sake, to try briefly to summarize the points in theory, and theoretical explanation and nomenclature, for which you are indebted to him, or to the so-called 'Day theory,' as expounded by him; in other words, what changes or differences, in the way of looking at matters theoretical, and expressing them, have been brought about by the diffusion of, and insistence on, the teaching in question. To some of you, probably to most of you, it has been a surprise, an astonishment, to hear that there ever was a time in the history of this, our valued Academy, when such an incident could occur as the almost compulsory resignation of your revered theoretical guide, Professor —but then plain Mr. Macfarren—on account of alleged errors in his views of harmony and methods of teaching. But so it was ; in Music, as in other things, all along the line, it has been that the radicalism of yesterday becomes the conservatism of to-day, the heresy of the past the orthodoxy of the present. Only so recently as about twenty years ago, when Sterndale Bennett was appointed Principal of this Institution, he, talking with me about my own teaching here, expressed virtually his hope that I should not be adopting the very terminology which is now familiar to you as household words. Had you, at that time, and from that time further back, studied here, you would have been taught that the inter-diatonic notes of the Chromatic Scale were simply ornamental inflexions of the diatonic notes ; whereas now, with a different notation, you learn to regard them as integers of the key. You owe that to Macfarren, or to Dr. Day through him. Therefore to him you also owe it that you include, under the general heading of Chromatic Chords, all those chords which, while having accidentals, do not effect modulation, and are regarded, therefore, as appertaining to the key; part of its furniture, the resources which it furnishes. You owe it, therefore, to him, that instead of regarding these chords as chromatic alterations of diatonic chords—which you would have been taught twenty years ago—you refer them all to certain fundamentals, as, so to speak, chords in their own right; dissonant chords being referred either to the Dominant, the Tonic, or the Supertonic, as the root. Even in the case of a chord of, as was thought, such a decidedly chromatic-alteration aspect as the Augmented 6th, in either of its three forms, Italian, French, or German, instead of so regarding it, as would have been taught of old, you owe it to Macfarren that you account for it as proceeding from two roots: the supertonic and the dominant, if occurring on the minor 6th of the scale; the dominant and tonic, if upon the minor 2nd of the scale. You owe it to him that the chord of the minor 6th on the subdominant, instead of being regarded as a fancy softening of the diatonic chord, with the fancy name of the Neapolitan 6th, is regarded as the inversion of the legitimate chord on the minor 2nd of the chromatic scale. You owe it to him that the chords of the 11th and of the 13th are to be regarded as fundamental discords; and that as a corollary, for example, the chord of the $\frac{6}{4}$ on the subdominant is not, as formerly, to be most unsatisfactorily accounted for, if account it can be called, as the *added 6th*, but as the 2nd available inversion of the chord of the 11th. All this, and much more, is entirely the outcome of his teaching, together with various *terms* which are not by any means inseparable from the theories. I have thought it instructive for you thus to know the extent of the metamorphosis which has been effected in this department, through the authoritative inculcation by our late Principal of those theories which alone, as it seemed to him, were satisfactorily consistent."

To this enumeration may be added the adoption of the terms, " 1st inversion," " 2nd inversion," " last inversion," respectively ; of the suspended 9th, or of the suspended 4th, according to whether the 3rd or 5th of the chord, or the suspension itself, be in the bass; whereas it is only when in the bass that the *suspension* is inverted, if the term " invert " is to be used in its proper sense of change of position, or " turning upside down." The principle involved in Macfarren's (or Day's) phraseology—namely, that the suspension is the same whichever position of the chord be taken— is of course not only sound, but most important and simple, and no exception can be taken to his remarks on that head in Appendix M to Day's " Treatise." But it remains true, nevertheless, that the suspension itself is not inverted when it remains in an upper part. Another peculiarity of terminology is that of the application of the term "Passing-note" to a note which, though a tone or a semitone below or above an essential note, is approached by skip—such a note as is usually known as an *auxiliary* note, or *appoggiatura*, or *acciaccatura*.   I once spoke to Macfarren about this point, urging that "*Passing-note*" meant a note taken *in passing* from one note to another, and, therefore, was an inappropriate term for a note taken by skip.   His reply was, "You are quite right, logically; but is it not desirable, as much as possible, to avoid multiplication of technicalities, and, therefore, to bring all these unessential notes under one general term?" In the same conversation, I instanced my elucidation of that exceptional treatment of *Passing-notes* (known as *Changing-notes*) by skip of a 3rd, in my "Textbook of Music" (p. 108), taken from Chopin's Study in C sharp minor, to wich he replied, "Yes, that is excellent."   Indeed, he was always most ready to accord praise, and, it may be added, to acknowledge indebtedness.   Again and again did he disclaim all credit for the theories which he so chivalrously defended.   "My late friend, Alfred Day, communicated to me his very original and very perspicuous theory of Harmony, by means of which many obscurities in the subject were cleared that my previous anxious study had vainly sought to penetrate," &c. ("Six Lectures," p. 2).   "Emphatically I disclaim any merit of authorship, but I trust that I am doing the best I may to disseminate a system which, if true, as I believe it to be, must in course of time supersede all other theories of harmony" (Preface to second edition of Day's "Treatise"). In telling the Academy students that they owed the various changes enumerated to Macfarren, I by no means lost sight of the advocacy by Sir F. Gore Ouseley of some at least of the same theories—an advocacy, however, subsequent to that maintained by Macfarren in the face of so much opposition. Macfarren once said to me, "This double-root theory of the Augmented 6th Ouseley has obtained so much credit for, he got it all from Day."

Yet one more book in illustration and "wider exemplification of the views in" the "Lectures" than they could contain, did Macfarren prepare, at the suggestion of the Rev. John Curwen, a highly-esteemed dissenting minister, who was honoured as the "founder" of the "Tonic Sol-fa" system of teaching music, but who "professed to have derived it from Sarah Glover of Norwich, whose method he but modified and expanded."[1] The system itself Macfarren opposed, as will be subsequently related; although, in his preface to the second edition of Day's "Treatise," he gives credit for the adoption, though incompletely, in its notation, of Day's "method of figuring the bass to denote the chords that accompany it." But he complied with Mr. Curwen's request, and in 1867 wrote (though they were not issued till 1875), "Eighty Musical Sentences to illustrate Chromatic Chords," acknowledging the "happy definition" of the "concise strains" therein contained to be due to Mr. Curwen. In the preface, while he asserts that it would have been easy to cite, from the works of the great Masters, "instances of every chord and every progression herein exemplified," yet, as these cita-

[1] Macfarren's "Musical History," p. 135.

tions would have been "so surrounded by other matter that their distinction would have been troublesome for a learner," he states that it was considered best to frame "these original Sentences, which, in systematic order, display the entire subject."

Apart from the light which these "Sentences" ostensibly throw on the theory advocated, and the confirmation which it is alleged that they afford to it, they are in themselves interesting, although one critic affirmed that some of them " will, in the notation he has employed, present the theory of Alfred Day in its most repulsive aspect to the great majority of musical theorists and musicians in this country and abroad."[1]   But this *dictum* did not apply to the music, but, as it would seem, to the notation.   With regard to this very matter of notation, however, Macfarren did make concessions, both to expediency —in order to avoid contradiction of accidentals—and to popular usage.   Even this, however, not being a necessity in Tonic Sol-fa notation, in which, as well as in the Staff notation, these " Sentences" were printed, and the Tonic Sol-fa edition having the Staff notation on the opposite page, we find the letter to Mr. Curwen, from which the following is an extract :—

"Calais, August 11, 1878.

" My dear Mr. Curwen,

*   *   *   *   *   *

" It occurs to me that, in the Sol-fa version of the ' Sentences' (where no accidentals are used, and contradiction signs are therefore unneeded), it may be well to write the true names of the supertonic minor 9th and the dominant minor 13th (Mi flat in both cases), rather than

---

[1] "Musical Standard," Jan. 1, 1876.

disguise them in the false notation expediently employed by many composers. The side by side appearance of the two notations will show the student how expediency trifles with truth, and I think prove an useful lesson. If you approve of this, I will insert a paragraph on the subject in the preface.

"Yours, with kind regards,
"G. A. MACFARREN."

This suggestion was acted upon. Indeed, Macfarren acknowledged the *expediency* — mainly with reference to economy of accidentals—of occasional false notation in some cases, and the *fact* of its frequent use, whether from expediency, real or supposed, or from carelessness, or from mistaken theory, in the writings of acknowledged composers. But, while enunciating that "the chromatic scale of any major or minor key consists of the seven notes of its major diatonic scale, with the three that are altered from these in the signature of the minor form of the key; and the minor 2nd between the tonic and supertonic, and the augmented 4th between the subdominant and dominant" (Preface to "Eighty Sentences"), he also, in the "Rudiments," says, "Composers of all schools agree in writing the augmented 4th from the key-note" (not the diminished 5th), and the minor 7th from the key-note (not the augmented 6th).

I once pointed out to him, however, that, besides other musicians, two whose musicianship he would not dispute did, as a matter of fact, rightly or wrongly, write the chromatic scale, in ascending, with the chromatically raised 6th, and, in descending, with the lowered 5th—namely, Sterndale Bennett, in his "Scales and Intervals for Pianoforte Students," and John Goss, in his "Introduction to Harmony and

Thorough Bass." His reply was, "Well, you surprise me! It only shows how careful one must be in making general statements of that kind."

The following short letter to the Rev. John Curwen concerning the system of figuring basses, may fitly be inserted here :—

"7, Hamilton Terrace, N.W.
"*July 8th* [1868 ?].

" MY DEAR SIR,
"Many thanks for the copy of your journal with the kind notice of my 'Lectures.' Should you again write about figured basses, you may perhaps like to allude to Day's system, which, so far as I can gather, accords with your own views, and which I found practically excellent, though I was compelled to discontinue its use.
"I am yours faithfully,
"G. A. MACFARREN."

Macfarren could say smart—not to call them severe —things concerning opponents and their arguments ; such, for instance, as this, anent the chord of the 13th :—

" Some opponents of these views have thought to over- turn them by humorously defining the chord of the 13th as a combination of the entire seven notes of the scale—an incongruous abomination such as no ear could tolerate. The joke is well sounding ; it is so probably because of its hollowness. The stringent rule against the simultaneous striking of a dissonance with the note of its resolution precludes .... either the 5th or 7th when the 13th is superadded. ... For all that may be said by scoffers, however, there are instances of the effective employment of the chord in its entirety." [1]

More in the way of banter, to avert an inopportune argument, was his answer to Dr. Gauntlett, who, meet-

[1] "Six Lectures," p. 174.

ing him in a music-warehouse, accosted him with—
" Ah ! Macfarren, I have read your book, and I don't
agree with you at all." " Indeed ! " was the reply ;
" no more does Christmas pudding ! "

He was not solicitous of controversy ; partly, perhaps, from estimating some of his antagonists as not
wholly " worthy of his steel," not having pondered
the whole subject as he had ; partly because it took
him some little time to formulate his rebutting arguments.

When, however, Mr. Gerard F. Cobb, at the Musical
Association, read, June 2nd, 1884, a most elaborately
argued paper " On Certain Principles of Musical Exposition," in which, among other matters, he opposed
the views held by Macfarren, the chairman (Major
Crawford), in inviting discussion, said, " I hope Sir
George Macfarren will favour us with his views ; "
whereupon the Professor commenced by saying :—

" Am I to suppose, by this invitation, that I am put
upon my trial, and that I am to be confronted in disputa-
tion with a lecturer whose eloquence, whose learning, whose
reading of all the writers for and against the subject he
has discussed is manifest, and who has shown authority
for everything he has said ? If that is to be the case, I
feel myself at a serious disadvantage in having no immediate preparation, either to receive the attack or rebut it.
I most thoroughly respect the care which has been bestowed, and the argument which has been brought forward,
but yet I am unable to accept it."

He proceeded to deal, unpreparedly and partially, with
some of the arguments advanced by Mr. Cobb, which
it would be necessary to reproduce here, in order to
render the reply appreciable.   One or two sentences,

however, are worthy of being quoted, apart from their immediate occasion :—

" As to the effect of beats [in nature], and whether we listen to them or count them, I believe we no more do so than the person who contemplates a picture counts the rays that combine to make a single colour ; but that the more or less distinctness of beats has an important effect on musical sound is manifest in the particular force that is given to a discordant harmony when two instruments of the same quality, such as two horns, two clarinets, or two hautboys, have to sound the interval of a second. The amount of tone that reaches the audience in that case is far greater than when one horn sounds one note, and one clarinet sounds the other, in this conjunct relationship.[1] I think the effect of this great discordance, springing from beats or otherwise, is important to the composer as direct- ing him to lay out the position of the notes so as to produce the greatest power. . . .

"The theory which my late friend Alfred Day enunciated to the world [is] that . . . . the tonic, the dominant, and the supertonic yield combinations [in harmonics] which are available in musical composition ; and that accounts for the progressions which some composers had, with beau- tiful effect, employed, as directed by their own intuition of beauty, before theory traced a line by which they might proceed. I think Day's view is so far satisfactory that it explains many passages previously inexplicable by the theories at that time in credit, and includes in its explana- tion everything with which my musical reading has yet made me acquainted."

The argument of Mr. Cobb's paper having tended to the basis of music being psychical rather than physical, the Professor immediately proceeds :—

" However, the discussion is not as to the merit of this one theorist, but as to the whole principle of music resting

---

[1] See page 69.

K

upon any theory, of its springing from natural laws, or of its being empirically originated at the caprice of human fancy. We are to refer to psychic principles rather than to physics for our art; that is, to make art arbitrary, accidental, and wilful ; and the artist is to plunge into a vast ocean of experiment, with no chart to direct his course, and nothing to aid him to distinguish between the proprieties or the improprieties of his proceedings. Surely, upon these grounds, nothing could be too gross for acceptance : nothing could justify objection if we were to be guided by impressions. It would thus depend wholly and only upon the amount of cultivation in a particular state of society as to what is to be tolerated and admired, and what is to be excluded. I believe that it is essential to musical art, as much as to the other artistic applications of natural principles, that we should work upon a grammar, that we should believe in propriety and impropriety. The fact that music has differed in different ages and in different nations seems to me to accord with ethnology ; that the whole habits of different populations and different times vary from those of other times, and that each race has its own moral code, as much as it has its own art code. We experiment forward and forward until we find the explanation of the principles upon which art is founded, and by which it is to be guided. I think it would be dangerous to art of any kind to trust it wholly to impression and to habit, unless the habit itself were to be directed by some ruling principle."

He concluded this striking example of his powers of rapid formulating and unpremeditated speaking by saying :—

"I believe, had I been able to take notes of what has been said, and had time for deliberation, I might meet some of Mr. Cobb's eloquent arguments. If I say so little, you must not attribute it to the want of material, but to the impossibility I have had of preparing what might be to say, and of arranging it categorically in order of reply. I must offer my tribute of sincere admiration to the speaker for the paper he has given us, and for the grounds he lays open ; and I shall most certainly in private, if not at this meeting, when I have had the opportunity of inspecting the arguments in the printed records, discuss more fully than I have now the points in question."

The promise of these concluding words, however, was never fulfilled, either in private or in public. Indeed, I believe that this was the last public utterance of an apologetic or polemical kind that proceeded from the distinguished theorist.

Not only was he somewhat averse to controversy— some would say, because of dictatorial dogmatism, but not those who knew him best — he was averse to theoretical writing, even of an educational kind. This accounts for his not having enriched the student's library with any treatise on Fugue or on Instrumentation ; on both of which subjects, the latter especially, his teaching, in permanent and accessible form, would have been invaluable. He was repeatedly urged to write such treatises, but either declined or postponed the tasks ; and musical literature is, therefore, the poorer.

It is not to be urged that Macfarren's own compositions owed their originality, style, individuality, or whatever else it may be termed, to the theoretical views which he advocated so strongly and unwaveringly ; but it is at once interesting to trace, and undeniable, that those views had their influence in shaping his manner of thought and methods of harmonic procedure. With some composers, the effort to avoid the commonplace, as the substitute for and semblance of being original—the result generally being eccentricity, *bizarrerie*—is very observable. In Macfarren no such absurdity, or pettiness, or unnaturalness can be traced; far too really thoughtful, earnest, and solid was he to have recourse to, or to have need of, such superficiality. But there is a very observable indication, in many—in most, perhaps—of his larger works, of a consciousness of having a mission to demonstratively and practically defend and illustrate, by persistent presentation, combinations, progressions, and, it may be added, notations, which, as it seemed to him, he had, if not rescued from oblivion, far less invented, yet shown in their right light as normal rather than exceptional. He disclaimed any credit for originality in the views that he propounded with so much vigour, assigning all such credit to Dr. Day. But he emphatically contended that any seeming novelty was not in the musical practice, but in the theoretical assignment and explanation of that which seemed new, and that his " endeavour [was] to . . . . remove discrepancies between the laws of early theorists and the practice of modern composers " (Preface to " Rudiments "). Nevertheless, as has just been advanced, there is evident in his compositions a tendency to bring to the front that which had been in the background, and to erect the exceptional into a precedent. And this, moreover, not only in these less familiar combinations. For instance, taking as his precedent the rare progression in the opening of Mozart's " Jupiter " Symphony, bars 7 and 8—one of those flashes of genius which cannot be reproduced—Macfarren based upon it, though not avowedly, the axiom that two $\frac{6}{4}$ chords in succession are of good effect, when the first chord is the second inversion of the dominant chord, and the second that of the sub-dominant (" Rudiments," chap. iv. 31).

And it was surely an inverted logic by which Macfarren sometimes sought to establish a theory: the deducing the theory from a rule, instead of founding the rule upon the theory. But this seemed the process by which, for example, he accounted the chord of the 7th on the 5th of the scale, when followed by a common chord on the submediant, as a first inversion (without the root) of the chord of the 9th on the mediant, not as a true dominant 7th; because, forsooth, of a rule previously laid down, that "a diatonic chord of the 7th must be resolved upon a chord the root of which is a 4th above the root of the discord;" although exceptions were allowed even to this rule— seemingly, however, as afterthoughts. (Compare "Rudiments of Harmony," sect. 2, chap. xi.; sect. 11, Appendix M.)

In conversation on disputed points, I have more than once known him tell some funny story, ostensibly to illustrate the point that he was seeking to enforce; but I observed on these occasions that the argument was by no means the strongest, though I will not insinuate that his intention knowingly was thus to cover a vulnerable point.

But, after all abatement has been made, it remains impossible to exaggerate the important service rendered to musical studentship by the persistence of Macfarren in endeavouring to establish a definite and a founded theory of harmony, instead of leaving the whole matter a mere collection of arbitrary or empirical rules. Consideration has been rendered compulsory in this country, and the very diversity of views propounded in this, which some consider a transition era, result not a little from the activity of thought quickened by his resolute contention for that which seemed to him logical. No man who has helped to bring this about must be considered a pedant or an obstructive; whatever difference of opinion may prevail with regard to his theories, the student world, and the musical community generally, owe much to his labours in the cause of consistency and reason in the region of musical theory.

CHAPTER VII.

IN the year 1838 the late Mr. William Chappell,
F.S.A., published the first part of a work which
he had been preparing, entitled, "A Collection of
National English Airs, consisting of Ancient Songs,
Ballads, and Dance Tunes, interspersed with Remarks
and Anecdote, and preceded by an Essay on English
Minstrelsy. The Airs harmonized for the Pianoforte,
by W. Crotch, Mus. Doc., G. Alex. Macfarren, and J.
Augustine Wade. Edited by W. Chappell." The
songs in this collection were assigned to Macfarren.
Of the other arrangements, those of Dr. Crotch were
found incongruously scholastic, and those of Wade
as much too trivial; and ultimately the whole of the
musical portion of the succeeding parts of the work
was entrusted to Macfarren. An enlarged edition of
this work was published, after about fourteen years
had exhausted the first issue, under the title of
"Popular Music of the Olden Time," with "the whole
of the Airs harmonized by G. A. Macfarren;" and, in

a subsequent edition, the title was: "The Ballad
Literature and Popular Music of the Olden Time;"
Mr. Chappell, in referring to the first edition, in the
Introduction, recording his obligation to Macfarren
" for having volunteered to rearrange the airs which
were to be taken from my former collection, as well as
to harmonize the new upon a simple and consistent
plan throughout.   In my former work, some had too
much harmony, and others even too little, or such as
was not in accordance with the spirit of the words.
The musician will best understand the amount of
thought required to find characteristic harmonies to
melodies of irregular construction, and how much a
simple air will sometimes gain by being well fitted."

Concerning these labours of Mr. Chappell, Macfarren writes, in his " Family Recollections ":—

" For a year or two before and after 1840 William Chappell was busy in collecting and publishing his first edition
of ' Ancient English Ballads,' and directly afterwards the
separate collection of some of these with pianoforte accompaniment, and, to the tunes of which the original poems
were lost or unavailable, new verses had to be written, the
task being entrusted to my father at the remuneration of
a guinea apiece.   True to our family motto, ' Libertas et
natute solum,' he was a thorough patriot, and this character had impelled him to some of his early poems during the
war with Bonaparte, had given enthusiasm to his writing
of ' Edward the Black Prince ' and ' Guy Fawkes,' and had
prompted the subject of the never-acted opera of ' Caractacus.'   Hence he took particular interest in this nationalis-
tic task, which he accomplished with proportionate felicity.
Chappell's researches had been induced by the taunts of a
Scottish shopman of his father, who, exulting in the
popularity of many spurious and some real Scottish melodies, asserted that England possessed no tunes of her own.
This taunt, and Chappell's action upon it, gave a bias to

his whole career, the main pleasure of his life having been to seek for vindication of the tuneful ability of our southern compatriots."

No less than to his father must such a task as this have been eminently consonant with G. A. Macfarren's English proclivities. All through his life he mani-fested a liking for English subjects, a desire to uphold the claims of English music, to defend it from asper-sion, and rescue it from neglect; not only writing, later on than the period at which we have arrived, on the evil effects of the Italian language, but also, in the " Cornhill Magazine," of September, 1868, on the almost proverbial saying among English people, " The English are not a musical people." Commencing with the remark—" One of our humourists has said that a quotation is never so apt as when it is misap-plied; so I trust to prove the perfect aptitude of the quotation from common prejudice which heads these remarks, by showing its utter misapplication "—he proceeds to reprehend the pandering, by English musicians,—

"to the prevalent folly, by assuming foreign names or affecting foreign titles. It is their fashion, indeed, as if they would wholly expatriate music from the land, to give a foreign termination to words used in connection with music; thus the list of pieces to be performed in a concert is styled by them a programme; whereas good writers of our language, who apply the term to other than musical uses, spell it as they spell all words derived from the same Greek root."

After referring to the analogous words, " anagram," " diagram," " epigram," " monogram," " telegram," he continues :—

"I am told, however, that we have taken the idea of concert bills, and, consequently, the word which defines them, from the French; and that is why we spell it not, as we spell all like derivatives, program. Granting, for courtesy's sake, the questionable proposition, I cannot admit the consequence. We took India, or a large part of it, from the French, but we call it not L'Inde. The same is the case with other British possessions, territorial and technical; but it is rarely, save in matters musical, that the Gallican orthography marks the English adoption. We take, indeed, *ennui* from the French, literally and constitutionally; but it will be well if in print, as in person, we avail ourselves as little as possible of this French quality. The prejudice against which English musicianship has to contend springs from domestic mistrust, more than from foreign depreciation, of our native capacity to love and practise the art. It dates, at earliest, within these last hundred and fifty years, to prove which I will adduce some pertinent facts from all periods of English history."

In some MS. fragments labelled "Cuts from Cornhill" there are some additional remarks upon the subject of English terminology, reference being made to—

"Men of letters, whose erudition, if not their nationalism, should have kept them aloof from such popular error, have ignored the genuine English origin of some of our most truly English words in connection with music, and sought to trace them to foreign derivation. For instance, John Wilson Croker, De Quincey, and even Dr. Trench, whose high authority gives weight to the fallacy, drew the name of our old English *Country Dance* from the French *Contredanse*, whereas Framery, in the 'Encyclopédie Méthodique,' reverses the etymology, and refers the dance as well as its name to English origin. Moreover, the earliest French dictionaries wherein the term *Contredanse* occurs are of centuries later date than the practice of the dance, among gentle and simple, in this country; what is now called *Quadrille* being our old *Square dance for eight*, as distinguished from a *round dance*, and that (still in favourite use) danced *long ways for as many as will*, and the figure defined of yore as *dancing the hay*."[1]

In pursuance of his contention, he gives anecdotal quotation from an old chronicle of the eleventh century, of singing "in harmony of three parts," which latter—

"the chronicle especially states, was according to the custom of the race that then peopled our eastern counties. Here is distinct evidence, which might easily be developed into far greater amplitude, that harmony, the art of musical combination, which is the basis of all musical construction, was known and practised and enjoyed here some hundreds of years before the greatly vaunted Roman School appropriated the art of descant or counterpoint, which art the Church indeed derived from the unschooled practice of our Northern Italy. In the latter part of the twelfth century, this practice of polyphony was certainly current as much among the people of Wales as among those of the north-east of our island; and there is good ground to assume that harmony must have been commonly familiar in England when those stalwart Danes, the Vikings of the sea and lords of the shell, masters alike of sword and song, first set foot upon our shores."

In refutation of the pretence that "all historical allusions to the musical proclivities of our countrymen refer at best to their relish for simple tunes and their preference for the vulgarest," Macfarren contends not only that "by intuition and by cultivation the English were for long in advance of Continental nations in the province of harmony," but also that they were "before the rest of the world in contrapuntal elaborations;" in support of which contention he adduces—

[1] See p. 9.

"the Six-men's Song—'Sumer is icumen in'—as a testimony of the state of music here at a period when there is no sign of its equal advancement in any other land.   The date of the MS. of this remarkable specimen of scholarship, and, I will aver, of such melodious fluency as critics call inspiration, was long disputed; but I believe that the best judges now agree in assigning it, from internal and collateral evidence, to 1250.[1] Now, to speak technically—and I must be technical to be true—this piece is a canon for four in one in the unison, with a foot or burden, also of canonic construction, for yet two more voices; and as such, while some grammatical irregularities cannot be denied in it, it presents an amount of twofold complication that is wonderful for its age, and remarkable for any age."

Hazarding the conjecture that, as—

"It is not to be supposed that in those remote times, any more than at present, six singers were always at hand for the performance of a piece of such extensive requirements, ... the likelihood of the case would furnish ample evidence of this canon having been sung, as very frequently were the catches of more recent days, by a single voice, either with or without instrumental accompaniment; and thus it is to be classed among our national melodies;"[2]—

Macfarren proceeds—

"Every city had, of old, its band of musicians.   We moderns have still our Waits, whose assumed denomination is their excuse for disturbing our sleep on winter nights, and appealing for Christmas-boxes on St. Stephen's morning.   Their braying upon cornets and ophicleides of Italian opera airs and Christy Minstrel melodies is the melancholy remnant—alas, how tattered and woebegone! —of the ancient city custom for the waites, or watch, to

---

[1] This is a somewhat later date than that assigned by Sir F. Madden and other authorities.—H. C. B.
[2] In Chappell's "Ballad Literature and Popular Music," etc., p. 24, the tune is printed, with accompaniment for pianoforte by Macfarren.

pass on their rounds with harmonious piping, or with the
sweet sound of song breathing a benison on the sleepers.
Not only in the royal court, but in the house of every
nobleman and gentleman, there was, down to the Stuart
times, an appointed band of musicians, whose functions
were to compose and to perform for the diversion of their
lord and his guests. The small potentates of Germany
have adopted this practice, each of whom maintains his
Kapellmeister with an ample artist band; and it is not the
only practice of our forefathers for the honour and promotion of music which has been adopted in the Father-
land from the precedent of the Mother-country. Finan-
cialists represent that the pecuniary means of our present
nobility surpass those of their ancestors, and exceed those
of the small German potentates; thus it seems that, in
respect to the support of musical art, the more the means
the less the meaning."

He draws further illustrations and evidences of the
indigenous love and early practice of music in England from the part-music in the Fairfax MS.; the publication in separate vocal parts of a collection of concerted pieces by various composers as early as 1560;
the dialogue plan of Thomas Morley's " Plain and
Easy Introduction to Practical Music," 1597; the
record of Round and Catch singing among "the
people,"—

" when Sir John Norman, in 1453, first broke through the
primal custom of a land procession along the strand of the
river and through the village of Charing to take his oaths
at Westminster as Lord Mayor of London, the Thames
watermen [having] their roundel to celebrate his honouring
their element with his civic pageant,—' Row the boat,
Norman,' [being] sung on stream and on shore by any
three men of the water, or of the land, who met in good
fellowship from that time forward;"—

from the existence, " in chivalric times," of " the

order of minstrels," with "its *Rex Minstrallorum*," the "institutions for the care and culture of the art in England," the recognition in England only of "the culture of music in its universities of learning, Alfred [having] instituted a musical professorship in his foundation of the University of Oxford in 866," and from other facts. He deals with the false allegation "that the decadence of music in this country is due to the Puritan influence," urging that "it is under the Commonwealth that several facts have date which bear strongly upon the development at least of the secular branch of the art;" the first fact that he adduces being the publication by Playford, in 1651, of—

"the 'Dancing Master,' which is the earliest printed collection of our dance tunes, with descriptions of the figures; a work of infinite importance, since we owe to it the preservation of many of the most beautiful airs of our songs in those of the dances that are named after them. Hence it is clear that there was dancing to very pretty tunes in the days of the Roundheads."

He also mentions the issue by the same publisher, in 1652, of

"'Select Ayres and Dialogues,' which collection of vocal music, by various composers, comprises the first two pieces to which the definition 'Glee' was ever applied."

Another fact adduced is that "In 1656, at Rutland House, in Aldersgate Street, Sir William Davenant gave the first public performance of an English opera," it being—

"equally remarkable, since quite as important, that the character of Ianthe in this opera ['The Siege of Rhodes'] was sustained by Mrs. Henry Colman, who was the first female that ever performed in public in this country. We owe, then, to Puritan times the perpetuation of our oldest national melodies, and the origination of our glee, our opera, and our pleasurable privilege of hearing female singers."

He then passes in rapid review the musical tendencies of the Protector himself, the institution by Charles II. of "four-and-twenty fiddlers," the eminent native musicians of the period, such as

"Henry Lawes, whose exquisite powers of musical expression and declamation are eulogized by Milton and Waller;" . . . "Matthew Locke, who, though the music be lost which he composed for 'Macbeth,' and though the music in "Macbeth' be not his which is commonly accredited to him, wrote the opera of 'Psyche' prior to Lully's of the same name, wrote other works for the stage, wrote for the Romanist Church as organist to the Queen, wrote vocal and instrumental music for the Chamber, and wrote glees for the people;" . . . "Pelham Humphreys, whom Pepys describes as 'keeping time to the music' (or, in modern phrase, conducting) at Whitehall in the year when, at the age of nineteen, he wrote the music for Dryden's spoliation of the 'Tempest,' and therein proved that the lyrical art of the age was superior to the poetical;" . . . "Henry Purcell, who was the greatest musician of his own age, and who, in his wonderful insight into the latest modern resources of harmony, and his delicate application of the powers of melodic expression, as far exceeded the past as he anticipated the future of his art." [1]

---

[1] "Purcell and his two colossal successors, Handel and J. S. Bach, wrote every combination of musical notes that down to our latest times has ever been employed with good effect; and the more the works of these masters are studied the more they are found to foreshadow the supposed novelties in harmony employed by subsequent artists. . . . Purcell's voluminous and superb works for the church, his many compositions for the theatre, his countless convivial pieces, and his far less numerous instrumental writings are now but little known, and the ignorance of the age is its loss. They have a wealth of expression that cannot be too highly esteemed, and a fluency of melody that proves the perfect ease of their production. The idiom of the age in which they were written is perhaps a partial barrier to their present acceptance," etc.—Macfarren's "Musical History," pp. 73, 74.

And then Macfarren proceeds to inveigh against
that which he considered to be the "first shock"
which "the musical faith of England" received—a
faith "which the asperity of the Protectorate could
not crush, and the frivolity of the Restoration could
not dissipate." This was ":in Queen Anne's reign" :—

> "It was during her sovereignty that the first experiment
> of Italian opera was made in this country; and it is to its
> subsequent establishment as one of the institutions of the
> metropolis, and the gross affectation which this bred and
> nourished, that the degradation of art is wholly to be
> ascribed."

This is urged and illustrated with considerable elaboration and persuasive eloquence. The founding and proceedings of the Madrigal Society, the Noblemen and
Gentlemen's Catch Club, the Glee Club, and the Concen-
tores Sodales, are chronicled; animadversion upon the
glee is incidentally made ; musicians "whose talent
brightened the early years of the present century"—
notably Sir H. R. Bishop—are referred to. The
Philharmonic Society, the Society of British Musicians,
the labours of John Hullah, and the Tonic Sol-Fa
Association, receive their meed of acknowledgment,
and this interesting paper concludes with the expression of hope that, obstacles being removed,—

> "the people will become regenerate, when the love and
> the talent natural to them will find free scope, when we
> shall no longer allow, and foreigners will no longer acquiesce
> in, the prejudice that 'the English are not a musical
> people.'"

This copious, but yet insufficient, summary of the
article in which Macfarren's pronouncements upon the
subject are so emphatically given, makes a long digres-

sion; but it has its fit place here, as affording evidence of his power of marshalling facts and arguments, of his incisive mode of utterance, and of the deep interest that he took in the patriotic aspects of his art : an interest, doubtless, intensified by the researches with which he became acquainted, and in which he engaged, during his collaboration with Mr. William Chappell. Much of the lore connected with that work may have been brought to the surface by Mr. Chappell ; but the musical discrimination evinced in the above-summarized paper, and found also, together with much technical information, in Mr. Chappell's pages, are doubtless Macfarren's own.

In connection with this same subject of our national music, Macfarren delivered a course of four lectures on the " National Music of Ireland, Scotland, Wales, and England," at the London Institution, in January and February, 1870. The Syllabus of this course indicates the thoroughness of research, thought, and arrangement with which the lectures were prepared, and is therefore here inserted.

.." LECTURE I.—THURSDAY, *January 6th.*
" IRELAND.
"Illustrated by
"Miss ANNIE SINCLAIR and Miss EMMA FORBES,
" Mr. WILBYE COOPER and Mr. J. G. PATEY.

"NATIONAL MUSIC.—Its more permanent nature in Northern than in Southern countries. Is it an index of the character of the people ? Is it a clue to their ethnology? The Scoti invaded Ireland and conquered the Hibernii in the third century, and they called the land Scotia, which name it retained till the eleventh century. Migrating from the North East, they probably came originally through Scythia

from the south. Sculpture of a harp constructed like those
of Egypt and Assyria, on a monument of the eighth century, at Ullard, in Kilkenny. Importation of the Irish
harp into Italy mentioned by Dante in the thirteenth and
referred to by Vincenzo Galileo in the sixteenth century.
The so-called 'Scotch scale' of five notes (the pentatonic
scale of C. Engel), probably in use among ancient, and
certainly among modern, oriental nations, as also in Mexico
and Peru at the time of their discovery. Antiquity and
universality of the bagpipe; representation of one found
in the ruins of Tarsus, dating two centuries B.C. The scale
of this instrument. Appropriation of the Gregorian scales
to secular melody. The English practice of singing songs
with a foot, undersong, or burden, possibly imported into
Northumberland in the sixth century by the monks of
Bangor, or Benchor, in Down. The Hindoo 'bárdáhi' or
'bhát,' perhaps the origin of the title and function of the
Bard. Irish bards. Spenser's account of their character
and habits. Their race continued in the harpers of later
date. John and Harry Scott, famous in the time of Queen
Elizabeth. Turlogh O'Carolan, famous in the time of Queen
Anne. His reception by Irish gentry. Endeavours to pre-
serve the use of the Irish harp. Last meeting of harpers,
in 1792, at Belfast. Preservation of the Irish melodies.
Bunting's publications in 1796, 1809, and 1840. Moore's
Poems—1st series, from 1807 to 1815; 2nd series, 1834.
Irish society and Dr. Petrie. The Flaxsaraidh or Planxty.
The Clan March corrupted into the Jig. Appropriation of
English dance tunes by Irish editors. Appropriation of
English tunes to Irish party songs."

"LECTURE II.—Thursday, *January 13th.*
"SCOTLAND.
"Illustrated by
"Miss Annie Sinclair and Miss Julia Elton,
"Mr. Wilbye Cooper and Mr. Theodore Distin.

"Dr. Johnson's estimate of the modern Scotchmen. Cairbar
Riada led a colony of Scots from Ireland into Argyleshire,

which was named Dalraida after him, A.D. 503. These were called the 'Scots in Briton.' They imported their music, musical instruments, and musical officers or bards. Their constant warfare with the northern or southern Picts, or Pechs, until their amalgamation with this people under Kenneth II. in 843. The Saxon race first settled in Scotland under Malcolm Canmore, 1058. Engagement of English pipers and other musicians to play at the Scotch court in the fifteenth century. Evil influence of the Reformation upon music in Scotland. Magisterial prohibitions. Scotch music not known in England until the time of Charles II. The Scotch songs in Playford's Choice Ayres are by English poets and composers. Forbes' Cantus Caledoniensis, 1662, the first publication of secular music in Scotland, consists of English compositions. Allan Ramsay's Tea-Table Miscellany, 1724, W. Thompson's Orpheus Caledonius, 1725, and Oswald's collection, all printed in London, contain English songs. Burns wrote poems for Johnson's Museum, 1787, and G. Thompson's collection, 1793. Engagement of distinguished German musicians to write accompaniments to the tunes for the latter work. Forgeries of Ossianic poems by McPherson, and of Nithsdale ballads by Cunningham. Jacobite relics. Great fashion for Scotch tunes in England. Consequent imitation of their style by James Hook and other composers. Appropriation of English tunes, and alteration of English poems into the Scotch dialect. The so-called 'Scotch snap,' introduced into Scotland by Gipsy fiddlers. The reel (hreol or reol) of Danish, if not Anglo-Saxon origin. The strathspey."

"LECTURE III.—Thursday, *January 27th.*

"WALES.

"Illustrated by

"Miss Robertine Henderson and Miss Emma Forbes.

"Mr. Wilbye Cooper and Mr. Winn.

"Duties, privileges, and indemnifications of the Welsh Bards. Gryffydd engaged Irish bards to improve and regulate the music in Wales, 1078. Ordinances then established, and specimens of music of the period, are preserved in a MS. of the time of Charles I., the notation in which cannot now be deciphered. Institution of the Eisteddfod, 'Allm-harach' (foreign strain), the second of the twenty-four Welsh musical terms. No remnant of the pentatonic scale, the scale of the bagpipe, the Gregorian scales, the predominance of the sixth note of the key, the minor seventh of the key, or any other tonal peculiarity in popular tunes now claimed as Welsh. The harp and bagpipe were common to Wales and the three sister nations; the crwth resembles in name the Irish word 'cruit,' for a harp, and the instrument is a supposed link between that and the Anglo-Saxon fithl, fiddle, viol, or violin. Skill in performance upon the harp, and the possession of one, essential to a Welsh gentleman. Tradition an uncertain authority. Tunes of English origin. Honourable pride of the Welsh in the nationality and antiquity of their music, and their estimable endeavours of the last century and a-half to collect and preserve it. 'Ancient British Music,' collected by Parry and Williams, 1742; 'British Harmony,' collected by Parry, of Ruabon, 1781; 'Welsh Bards,' collected by Jones, 1784; collections by John Parry, Miss M. J. Williams, and John Thomas, in the present century. Lady Greenly's prize for a collection of Welsh tunes, 1838. Brinley Richards' efforts to revive the use of the triple harp, Lady Llanover's prize for performance upon it, 1869.''

"LECTURE IV.—THURSDAY, *February 3rd.*

"ENGLAND.

" Illustrated by

"Miss ANNIE SINCLAIR and Madame PATEY-WHYTOCK,
" Mr. WILBYE COOPER and Mr. J. G. PATEY.

" ALL the national elements compounded in the present Englishman, save perhaps the Norman, have been musically notable. Love of secular music by the early clergy. Aldhelm's politic use of it in the seventh century. Edgar's law against priestly indulgence in it, A.D. 960. Constant appropriation of secular tunes to church use, from the days of William I. to our own. The many instruments in early use in England. Caxton's edition of Chaucer, with picture of the miller playing on a bagpipe. This instrument common to many countries. The recorder, or English flute. The 'corno inglese' or 'cor anglais' of present use. The 'chaine anglaise,' identical with the 'hay,' as is the 'contre danse' with the 'country dance.' Rounds, hornpipes, and other popular dance tunes. Common practice of singing catches. Narrative ballads of the minstrels; the extended application of this form by the people. Evil influence of Puritanism upon music counteracted by the steadfast feeling of the opposite party. Music declined in England from the permanent establishment of the Italian Opera under George I. Indifference of the modern English to their own music. Popular music of the olden time collected by Chappell. 'God save the Queen,' originally English, now the national tune of many countries; its contended authorship."

In the pages of the "Musical Times" for July and following months of the same year, appeared a series of articles with the same title as that of these lectures, and evidently being substantially identical with them. Some extracts may be given here.

Commencing with the ejaculation, "Alas! for the cosmopolite, whose citizenship is so universal, that he has no special affection for the soil that gave him birth," Macfarren proceeds :—

"The term 'national music' needs definition, and needs this all the more because it has been often and variously defined. It is not here to increase its vagueness by adding to its limitation; but it may be as well to state what it is here meant to signify, in order that its use may be here understood. A melody is national when it has been commonly sung by a people through several generations, and sung because it naturally expressed the people's feelings, not because of its artistic merit. Every melody must have had a composer, and that composer must have been a technically trained musician. Let me not take from Mr. Chappell the merit of first putting forward this view, but do what I may to confirm the view and support its upholder. . . . . . . Whether this musician was taught in modern schools, whether a harper—of the race now dying out in Wales, and dead for seventy years at least in Ireland—whether as a minstrel, whether as a bard, matters not or matters little; he must have learned the rules of art according to some principle, or he can never have produced anything original, if even he can have reconstructed into good shape anything familiar. . . . . . In almost all instances, the name of a true composer of a national tune is forgotten; exceptionally it may be preserved, if not generally remembered. The tune is not divested of its characteristics, loses not hold upon popular feeling, ceases not to be national, if its composer's name be brought to light after people, from mother to babe, from father to son, have sung or whistled it by the life-long. Thus Dibdin, or Cary, or Carolan, or Purcell, or John or Harry Scott, or who you will, may have made a tune; it is the people who, by finding in it the idiom which gives truest utterance to their own emotions, by adopting and handing it from one generation to another, ... have made it national."[1]

He considers that "musical evidence," in addition to that derived from other sources, points to the migration of the Irish "from very far in the southeast." The fact that the pentatonic scale — "the diatonic scale of modern music with its 4th and 7th degrees omitted—having, that is, no interval of a semitone, but that of a minor third below its 1st and above its 3rd degree"—which is proved "to have been the scale of the ancient Egyptians and Assyrians," and "is now in theoretical and practical use among Eastern nations, especially the Chinese,"—

" point to the source of the scale, and of the people who brought it into Ireland," and indicate that " the Irish seem to be the eldest in musical claims to consideration " of " the members of our national family." He thinks this to be further indicated by " a sculptured monument at Ullard, in Kilkenny, which cannot have been erected later than the eighth century," and which " comprises a representation of a man playing on a harp, identical in form with those painted in the temples of Egyptian Thebes, and differing from the modern harp in having no fore-pillar." Further evidence in the same direction, " feeble, taken alone," but still worth consideration, is the use by the Irish of the bagpipes, which are of proved antiquity.

After alluding to the importation of the Gregorian scales into Ireland, he continues :—

" It is probably to one of these Church modes, the Æolian, that we may refer the frequent prominence of the 6th degree of the scale, and sometimes the conclusion on this note, in one class of Irish tunes. Possibly the bagpipes may have been constructed with regard to this very mode ; but it is more credible that their peculiar scale originated in the same source as the Gregorian system itself."

This source, in Macfarren's opinion, was pagan. He continues :—

" Last of all, when the principles of modern music took root in Ireland, the diatonic scale flourished as their natural blossom. It seems to have been rather as a settler than as a native, however ; since, for very long, the conservative spirit, and the desire to perpetuate their nationality, seem to have prompted musicians to adhere to the pentatonic, the bagpipe, or the Gregorian scales in the composition of their melodies ; nay, even now, when a writer wishes to be characteristic of the Irish—to put, as it were, a brogue into his song—he has recourse to one of these scales, and his music has of consequence the true national savour."

After reference to " the practice in Ireland, as well as in Wales, and in the North and East of England, of accompanying a song with a foot, or under-song, or burden, that was sustained by another singer," and the fact, therefore, vouched for by Giraldus, " that harmony was an essential element of our national music seven hundred years ago,"—even six centuries earlier, according to Bunting;—the practice of singing in parts by monks, at the place " named after the singers, Benchor, *Anglice* White Choir, now corrupted into Bangor—and other interesting facts, " the Bardic institution " is treated of; and then, the collection and transcription of the harpers' melodies by " Bunting, a professional musician trained on modern principles."

"At three wide intervals he printed the result of his researches. The merit of Irish melodies as a class was perceived, and fashion adopted what then came forth as a discovery. An Irish music-seller, in London, projected the publication of a series of his native airs with new English poetry. He hesitated for some time as to who should share the responsibility of interpreting in verse the passion of the tunes: and he determined to confide it solely to Moore, who was thus associated with Irish melodies, and who is consequently believed by many uninquiring persons, who are misled by equivocal title-pages, to be the composer of the tunes. Moore's collection is by no means exhaustive, though it contains several airs, some avowedly and some not, that are of unquestionably English origin. Its success, however, more than its incompleteness, has induced other writers to follow in his steps, and the name of Irish melody has become an almost certain passport to popular favour.

" A vast majority, if not the total of the best-esteemed

tunes can be fairly proved to be of modern origin in comparison with the early date to which the foregoing remarks might
suggest their ascription. It may be more than doubted
whether any true favourites can be older than a couple of
hundred years; and it cannot be denied that, in many, if
not all cases, what sounds old and Irish in them is due, as
has already been hinted, to imitation."

People do not care to have their favourite predilections or prejudices disturbed; and it is probable that
the belief in "Irish melodies" will continue to be
cherished, notwithstanding these ruthless facts and
arguments.

An arrangement by Macfarren of "Moore's Irish
Melodies" was published in 1859.

Proceeding to the consideration of Scotch music,
it is shown that, whereas—

"The Scots themselves are immigrants in the land of
their pride, having migrated from the north-east early in
the third century, 'invaded Ireland, conquered the early
settlers, made themselves masters of the soil, and called
the land Scotia . . . they [subsequently] carried into Britain their language, their pentatonic scale, their harp, and
their bagpipes; and hence the difficult distinction between
the music of the original nation and that of her offshoot.
Herein is the explanation . . . of how the scale of five
notes comes to be called the 'Scotch scale.'"

The repressive tendency of the Reformation in
North Britain, as most pernicious to music, is dwelt
upon.

" Art withers without cultivation, and it could not but
be that, under the circumstances, music fell soundly to
sleep, if not died out in the North; and by natural consequence, the Scotch appear to have been indifferent to their
own tuneful wealth, if not unaware of its existence, until

advised of it from England, which advice was of questionable authenticity."

The undoubted English origin of many so-called Scotch melodies is shown; the inexplicableness of "the strong Southern predilection for the name (observe it is but the name) of Scotch music." The term "Scottish" was in the time of Charles II.—

"Substituted for Northern as a definition of rustic ditties: the Scots in Britain afterwards took a hint from their brethren of the south, and accepted the term whenever it was offered them; but they regarded the word less as the distinction of a particular class of poetry and music than as an assertion of nationality, and they assumed every piece that was described as Scottish to have been produced in the Land of Cakes, and they claimed it accordingly as national property."

Macfarren adduces various considerations "to show that the broad assertion is not unauthorized" of "the Southern, if not London origin of many of the so-called Scotch tunes now in highest favour."

"One peculiarity in Scotch music had no origin in Ireland, and is to be found in no tunes of English origin save those written in imitation of the supposed Scotch character. This is what we call the snap, the lengthening the time of a second note at the cost of the one before it, the placing a semiquaver before a dotted quaver. This is, to say the best of it, a vulgarism in vocal music which leads to the undue prolongation of unaccented syllables; and such prolongation would warrant the assumption that English is a bad language for singing, if the language were at fault because it was mispronounced. The snap, however, gives emphasis and consequent spirit to dance tunes, and is an element of good effect when well applied. The snap appears not in any tunes that make any pretension to antiquity."

After some remarks upon the Clan Marches — "some of the most genuine products of our Northern soil," he continues :—

"Lastly, it is to speak of the Reel. Well, this owes nothing to Scotland but its preservation. When folks here used to dance 'The Hay,' in the days of good Queen Bess, they performed the identical figure of the Reel. . . . An earlier form of the word is ·Rhay, which brings us back to Anglo-Saxon days. A Danish form of the word—Hreol or Reol—belongs to the same period. . . . A like dance is now practised by the peasantry in Denmark, and one favourite Danish tune for it—research is not easy on the subject—is all but identical with a Scotch tune for a Scotch Reel."

In the same cogent manner, giving evidence of no little research and thought, doubtless in connection with his work in association with Mr. Chappell, Macfarren discusses Welsh music, asserting that "the assumed Welsh melodies "—for he does not deny their national origin, though it may be questionable—

"That are best known have none of the tonal characteristics that distinguish those of other districts. The structure of some shows them to have been composed for the harp. . . . . These have not the wild and fervid passion of the best of those of Ireland, nor the strongly-defined rhythm and accent marked almost to vulgarity of those given to Scotland and readily enough claimed by her, but they have a sweetly tender grace that is undeniably charming, and evinces a beautiful musical feeling in those who made them, whether in times remote from or near to our own."

Passing to the general subject of our national music, Macfarren avers that—

"It is now manifest that the Anglo-Saxons cultivated

music to a very high degree; that the Anglo-Danes, who commingled with them, fed their stream of song with kindred waters; and that this country was immensely in advance of the South of Europe in the popular disposition for, and the scholastic development of the art.   The Normans set their foot upon everything that was national when they took possession here; but though they trampled upon, they could not crush the love of music that was innate in the race.   This was left for the House of Hanover to accomplish with the Italian Opera for its Nasmyth Hammer; but though this destructive engine bruised, and contused, and dislocated, and fractured, and mangled in every way the body, the spirit is immortal, and begins again to take corporate shape among us. . . . Independently of those [tunes] which may have been wafted hence into Ireland, Scotland, and Wales, the tunes of unequivocal Anglican origin are more numerous, and are more various in character, than are those of other districts, while their merit entitles them to a proud place beside the others. As an united nation, we subjects of British rule are singularly wealthy in native melodies ; and it should give confidence to artists of the highest aspirations, that they have been born where such tunes as ours have been produced and loved."

Three lectures on the " Secular Music of England " were given by Macfarren before the Literary and Philosophical Society, Newcastle-upon-Tyne, in January, 1871, which seem to have embraced similar material to that just recorded.

In the article, alluded to above, in the " Musical Times " of March 1st, 1869, on " The Italian Language : its evil influence upon Music," Macfarren's contention is that " the Italian language has been, and is, a most baneful influence to music, affecting its production, its performance, and its effect."   This threefold contention he seeks to sustain, firstly, by—

"The notable case of Handel's operas. These are cast in a form that limited the workings of the mighty genius of the master, and allowed no play to its higher attributes: ... being without choruses, ... and, therefore, presenting ... no field for the exercise of his boundless contrapuntal resources: ... consisting exclusively, or nearly so, of airs that embody no dramatic action, and in many instances, constructed with the object rather of executive display than of poetical expression, his operas gave the rarest opportunity for that wonderful power of characterization, and that unsurpassable felicity of verbal declaration which particularly make his personages and the words they utter to live before the hearers. Based upon subjects that are entirely unsympathetic to our times, and constructed upon principles that are totally uncongenial to our stage, his operas will never, and can never, be performed again: ... and a large mass of the labours of one of the greatest, and, perhaps, the very grandest of musicians, wrought at a period of life when men's abilities are at the strongest, are obsolete and virtually lost to the world for ever. ... Now, Handel wrote his operas in subservience to a fashion which set in but two or three years before his first coming to this country: a fashion for affecting to believe that the Italian language was better fitted than any other for the purposes of music, and for affecting to admire performances in the Italian tongue above any in the vernacular of the nation. This fashion was founded, as many fashions are, upon falsehood. To wit: the first and highest element in vocal music is the general expression and minute declamation of the words. This element is a nullity with an audience by whom the words to which music is set are not familiarly and habitually spoken, and thus, and only thus, fully understood; and no language is, therefore, so good for the most important of all musical purposes as the native language of the people before whom it is performed. It was, then, to this gross falsehood of fashion, this lie against all sense and reason, this perfidy against pure art and undistorted nature, Handel sacrificed the best years of his manhood."

After noting how Handel, at the solicitation of

Aaron Hill, whose letter is given, dated December 5th, 1732, "first produced before the public his compositions to English words, 'Esther' and 'Acis and Galatea,'" Macfarren concludes this portion of his argument by saying :—

"The practical answer to this letter is the series of English oratorios and secular cantatas through which the name and the genius of Handel are universally known."

The next instance cited is that of Mozart, as—

"Most anxiously desiring to set music to his own German language. . . . Had his natural wish more frequently been gratified, had his more important and more regularly formed works been set to the words of his native speech, they perhaps could not have been better—it is impossible to suppose that the music of Mozart could have been better than it is—but they certainly would have been better understood, and might, doubtless, have been produced with greater pleasure to their author."

After instancing Weber, whose "best efforts were sorely hindered, if they could not be frustrated, by the ever poisonous working of the Italian predilections of his time," Macfarren proceeds to consider "the influence of this language upon the performance of works which have been written in spite and through the midst of its antagonism":—

"First, then, as regards the singers. The majority of those who now-a-days present themselves at the Italian theatres in London are Germans, or Swedish, or French, or American, or English, or in some other way foreign to the manner born of the text they have to enunciate. . . . The greater number of the vocalists, and nearly all of the best of them, who sing in Italian to London hearers, have the embarrassment, and make the consequent shortcomings

of contending with an acquired, and therefore to them un-
natural, language. To judge from the practice of a large
number of these, and of nearly all the private singers who
study under the best esteemed Italian teachers, it would
be fair and right to denounce the Italian language as
eminently, nay, pre-eminently, bad for music; and this
because it appears to induce a habit of false musical
phrasing, and of violating one of the most obvious and
simple laws of musical expression. Every one knows, for
instance, that the note following an *appoggiatura* should
be unaccented, and that the whole stress of the phrase
should be thrown upon the leading [leaning?] note itself;
but English vocalists, who sing Italian, commonly give
emphasis to a final, instead of a penultimate note, and
strongly accentuate the second instead of the first syllable
of such words as ' mio,' ' padre,' ' core ; ' if, in cases like
the last, they do not substitute an ' a ' for the ' e,' in order,
apparently, to give extra force to their false rendering of
the musical requirements."

Macfarren proceeds with "grounds of complaint, in
operatic Italianization, still more cogent than have yet
been set forth ; " these being the blunders of " the
wordmongers—higher definition may not be applied to
them—to whom the most delicate and most difficult
task of translation is for the most part confided,"
e.g. :—

" They not only place syllables of different vowel sounds
to emphatic notes from those to which these notes were
set, and so materially affect the mechanism of vocal production, but they vary the construction of their sentences
so as to distort either the verbal sense or the musical
phrasing, and they not rarely substitute other and even
contrary meaning for those to which music of pointed significance and careful expression has been written."

Examples of such perversities are given, from
Beethoven's " Fidelio." And the paper concludes
with a—

" Proposition that rising vocalists waste not their best years and their best energies in the study of music and words that can be of no possible avail to them for technical training or popular advancement, but that they devote themselves to the practice of works in the language which it is their duty to ennoble, by freeing it from the vulgarisms of mispronunciation, and which they will find, and may prove to be, better susceptible of musical expression than any which is not next to intuitive in themselves and their hearers."

In agreement with the opinions so trenchantly enunciated, he elsewhere speaks of Italian operas composed for England as " that apparent hotbed of non-success," after having traced the succession of a number of such works which have failed to retain any hold upon public estimation, notwithstanding the exceptionally adventitious circumstances under which they have been produced. Macfarren lived to witness the reaction set in which he probably anticipated, though not in the form which he would have expected or desired : the fashion —who will yet say whether it is more?—of acceptance of, and admiration for, the newer school of music-drama brought into vogue, so far as modern usage is concerned, by Wagner. Not—be it observed—opera in our vernacular; though even of that there have been notable symptoms of revival, both in production and in public interest.

It may not be out of place to insert here some observations occurring in an article on " Choral Singing," contributed by Macfarren to the first number of the " Part-Song Magazine " (May, 1868), in which, after enumerating " faults most common to untutored singers, and most needful to be overcome," he concludes as follows :—

" It is needful to ignore utterly the foolish fallacy that the English language is not good for music. This is disproved by the example of our best solo singers, who show our vernacular to be as apt as any for vocalization, and a better medium than some languages for expressive decla- mation. English is only unmusical when it is mispro- nounced. When the language escapes this ill-treatment, every unprejudiced person must feel that we need not to sing in a tongue which is unintelligible to our hearers in order to make our performance interesting."

In conversation with myself, Macfarren animad- verted on the practice of accenting the final syllable in " toward," even when separated from the first syllable, as in the locution " to-us-ward."

In the " Cornhill" article, reference is made to Orlando Gibbons and Purcell. It may be interesting here to quote his remarks on the former of these from Chappell's " Popular Music of the Olden Time ":—

" The fantasies of Orlando Gibbons are most admirable specimens of pure part-writing in the strict contrapuntal style; the announcement of the several points, and the suc- cessive answers and close elaboration of these, the freedom of the melody of each part, and the independence of each other, are the manifest result of great scholastic acquire- ment, and consequent technical facility. Their form, like that of the madrigals and other vocal compositions of the period, consists of the successive introduction of several points or subjects, each of which is fully developed before the entry of that which succeeds it. The earlier fantasies in the set are more closely and extensively elaborated, and written in stricter accordance with the Gregorian modes than those towards the close of the collection, which, from their comparatively rhythmical character and greater freedom of modulation, may even be supposed to have been aimed at popular effect. They would, it is true, be little congenial to modern ears, but this is because of the strangeness to us of the crude tonal system that prevailed

at the time, and upon which they are constructed. The
peculiarities that result from it are the peculiarities of the
age, and were common to all the best writers of the school
in this and every other country. Judged by the only true
standard of criticism—judged merely as what they were
designed to be—they must be pronounced excellent proofs
of the musical erudition, the ingenious contrivance, and
the fluent invention of the composer."[1]

In the discussion that ensued after the reading of an
admirable paper on " Henry Purcell and his Family,"
by Mr. W. H. Cummings, at the Musical Association,
December 4th, 1876, Macfarren said that—

" he considered it a matter of very great consequence that
Purcell's merits should be known and acknowledged.
English music had long been under a stigma from which
he believed the present time was freeing it, for people
were now beginning to admit that Englishmen could not
only admire the music of others, but that there had been
some amongst them who could add to the treasures of
musical art. If one could suppose a person to be born at
Christmas at the North Pole who never saw the sun, it
would be to him a vain expectation that there could ever
be daylight, and if we were born in this country with the
idea that there never had been good English musicians,
it would be almost a hopeless aspiration to dream of becoming so. But now that it could be proved that before
the darkness set in there was such a light as Purcell, it
might perhaps be an encouragement to aim at the new
dawning. He was convinced that Purcell was a very
remarkable genius, and the more remarkable because of
the hard circumstances by which he was surrounded. Mr.
Cummings had perhaps done one little injustice to English
music, at and before Purcell's time, when he said that the
faculty of melody was not possessed by previous musicians.
He could not but think of the beautiful songs of Henry
Lawes, which were gems of melody, and of those of his

---

[1] " Popular Music of the Olden Time," p. 470.

brother William. Henry Lawes might have known
Purcell, but he was his elder; and going still farther back,
there were part-songs to be sung by a solo voice when the
other three were not there, some of which were more
remarkable for the melody than for the harmony. One in
particular was scarcely known in its original form, namely,
Ford's 'Since first I saw your face,' which was tuneful
enough for any country. Then, again, there were the
songs of John Dowland, which contain most acceptable
melodies, and many of them had had great popularity, as,
for instance, 'Now, oh, now, we needs must part.' Reference might also be made to the long string of national
melodies, which in number and variety would hold their
own with the national music of any other country; however, the great merit of Purcell was not in being the first
of our countrymen to write tunes, because others had done
that before him, but in his harmonies, many of which the
speaker considered prodigious, as being really in anticipation of the harmonic progressions of modern times, and
showed him to have had a complete insight into the beautiful, and to have felt the principles of harmonic construction and harmonic derivation in a manner which he could
only have done by possessing the most keen sensitiveness
to musical propriety. It was a great glory, not to our
country only, but to the art of music, that at this early
period, preceding the works of Handel and Bach, there
was a man writing music which amazed one even now with
its beauty and its likeness to modern compositions. Many
instances of what seemed to be deep research into the
acoustical derivation of chords appear in Purcell, and
showed him to be a most original thinker; and although
he made some experiments which were not so successful,
there was a character of beauty in his music which justified
the highest admiration. There was, however, one quality
in Purcell more remarkable than his beautiful melodies or
his wonderful anticipation of modern harmony, and that
was his very grand power of musical declamation and
strong dramatic feeling. The form of operas in his days
very narrowly restricted his dramatic powers, it being then
the habit to construct dramas for speaking, in accordance
with the prejudice set forth by Dryden, that it was incom-

patible with dramatic action to have persons sing their words, and that the music of the stage should for the most part be restricted either to supernatural beings or to madmen. Purcell had such strong dramatic feeling as would have made him a great master in this kind of music, had dramas then been constructed to give him such an opportunity. Nothing could be more picturesque than the frost scene in 'King Arthur,' and nothing could be more expressive than the pathetic music in several of his pieces. For instance, in the two great scenes in his opera of 'Don Quixote,' one the song of Cardenio when he is mad, and thinks of Lucinda's eyes as the only light that can warm him in his coldness, and the other the soprano scene, 'From rosy bowers.' It was very pleasing to think that there had been such a great, pre-eminent English musician, and they could not be too grateful to Mr. Cummings for having given them so much information about him."

In the year 1840, the Musical Antiquarian Society was instituted, with the laudable object of rescuing from oblivion English music of the highest character, either existing in manuscript only, or very scarce, and therefore costly; by printing and publishing such works under competent editorship. At that time, Purcell's "King Arthur," "Dido and Æneas," "The Libertine," "Timon of Athens," and several of his "Odes" existed only in manuscript. Only six of the "Madrigals" by Wilbye were purchasable. Many other valuable works were out of all ordinary reach, such as many by Tallis, Orlando Gibbons, Dowland, William Byrde, Weelkes, Henry Lawes, etc. The Council of the Society, on its formation, consisted of W. Sterndale Bennett, Henry R. Bishop, W. Chappell, George Hogarth, E. J. Hopkins, W. Horsley, G. A. Macfarren, T. Oliphant, E. F. Rimbault (Secretary), Sir G. Smart, Professor Edward Taylor, and James Turle.

To Macfarren was allotted the editorship of Purcell's "Dido and Æneas." In the introduction (or preface) to this edition, he writes, with characteristic evincement of his interest in dramatic performance :—

"Considering it essential to the full appreciation of the dramatic feeling which pervades the music of 'Dido and Æneas,' that the reader should be able to comprehend at one view the incidents and conduct of the story, I have thought it desirable to prefix the drama. Unable to meet with any copy separate from the music, and the MS. scores to which I have had access presenting but the mere words and the names of the characters who sing them, I have ventured to make such divisions of the acts as were suggested to me by apparent musical climaxes and by the progress of the plot; also to introduce the descriptions of the scenes and other stage directions which seemed to be needful for the right understanding of the whole."

He added marks of expression, of which there were very few in the MS. He also compressed the score for the pianoforte, both of " Dido " and of Purcell's " Bonduca," filling up also the figured bass. It is now known, however, that the copy of " Dido and Æneas " which he used was imperfect: additional pieces have since been discovered, and are included in Mr. W. H. Cummings' beautiful edition issued by the Purcell Society. Still, Macfarren's edition is a standing evidence of his industrious research.

The Council of the Musical Antiquarian Society decided that no pianoforte compression should accompany the works issued by them; but the publishers, Messrs. Chappell and Co., determined on a separate issue of such compression, the preparation of which was undertaken by Macfarren—the works so arranged by him being the " Fantasies in three parts, composed for Viols by Orlando Gibbons " (previously alluded to) ; the whole Book of Psalms with their wonted tunes in four parts, as published by Thomas Este, 1592; the first set of songs by John Dowland; "King Arthur " and " Bonduca," by Purcell, etc.

The Musical Antiquarian Society had, unhappily, a too brief career of only seven years.

As has been said, Macfarren in his " Cornhill " article animadverted upon the Glee, saying :—

" Upon the whole, although the Glee be admitted as a class of composition essentially English, it is a class in which we poor, self-denying English have not great occasion for pride, since, as a class, the excellent pieces which form the minority of its instances are too exceptional to give it specific dignity."

Similarly, in his lecture on Cipriani Potter, before the Musical Association [1] :—

" We must, in order to judge of the merit of Potter as a teacher of composition, consider what was the state of music at the time when he came upon the world. The music in England then of the highest esteem was that which has the merit of being peculiarly English—namely, the Glee; and Webbe and Dr. Callcott were the most highly honoured classicists of this school, a species of composition in which there is no development at all, in which an idea is presented, and before it is entirely complete, there is some change of *tempo*, some change of measure, and a new idea is started. The grand masterpiece, as it is generally considered, of Glee writing—' When winds breathe soft '—is cut up into as many fragments as entitle it to be called a musical mosaic. Continuity seems to have been outside the thoughts, as well as outside the capability of the writers of the period."

[1] See page 21.

This animadversion has, in its turn, been animadverted upon by an intelligent and enthusiastic writer,
who says :—

"One of the worthiest native musicians of the present
day has asserted that the best of the English Glees are
only 'musical mosaics,' and he has singled this work
['When winds breathe soft'] for his special animadversion. He quotes it as an example to prove his statement
that continuity of treatment was not only outside the
power, but was also outside the thought, of the English
musicians of the last century. This is unfortunately an
ill-advised statement, which must have been made in an
unhappy mood. The whole glee is constructed upon one
continuous idea, and is no more a piece of 'musical mosaic'
than the statue of the Apollo Belvidere can be said to be
the true effigy of Darwin's progenitor of the human race.
Mr. David Baptie is right when . . . he calls this glee
'the noblest production of its composer, a truly grand
conception.' "

Then follows an analysis of the Glee, terminating
with the statement that—

"the unity of the whole design, the relation each part or
movement bears to the other, is a most striking instance
of the continuity of the idea entered upon in the opening
phrase, and developed to the greatest possible extent in a
work of its character. It therefore offers a complete
refutation of the mistake made by the learned musician
alluded to." [1]

Whether the refutation be so complete as this writer
alleges, may be left to competent judgment ; but
assuredly Macfarren did not "mistake" by overlook-
ing the points of design indicated. He was speaking

---

[1] *English Glees and Part-Songs. An Inquiry into their Historical
Development.* W. A. Barrett. London, 1886. Pp. 226-228.

of a different order of plan : that of *one movement*, with contrasted subjects, conjointly or otherwise worked ; and he did not recognize this element of continuity in the Glees to which he alluded.   Much more might now be advanced, were this a controversial work. Enough that Macfarren's *dicta* upon this, as well as upon other subjects, did not pass unchallenged ; the very formidableness of his opposition being so far recognized as to arouse, not unfrequently, something almost approaching to rancour in the contention to which it gave rise.   It must not be supposed that the characterization is intended to apply to the very respectful antagonism above cited.

Notwithstanding his strictures on English Glees, or at least on the weak style and structure characterizing them, Macfarren himself wrote several such compositions.   There is a set of Six Convivial Glees, illustrative of the history of England, for three men's voices, published in 1842, the words by his father, viz.— "King Canute" (also published as a song), "William Rufus," "Fair Rosamond," "Queen Bess," "Oliver Cromwell," "Sir Hugh Middleton." With the exception of "William Rufus," the words of all have some reference to conviviality, being designed for the use of Glee Clubs, and such gatherings, in which habit of that kind was associated with music.   Another Glee, for the same voices, was "Hail to the Chief!" words also being by George Macfarren, sen.   All of these are fresh, and with defined structure, principally of episodical kind. The "Musical World" of January 6th, 1842, reviewing "Oliver Cromwell," says :— "Since the glees of Mr. Bishop, none have afforded us so much pleasure as those of Mr. Macfarren. There

is a humour in them which sorts mightily with our
temperament." Concerning these Glees, Macfarren
thus writes, after recording the publication of the
" Devil's Opera " by Hill [1] :—

" Thus brought into close connection with the house, I
was soon asked to write a Glee that would be available for
singing at the supper houses which were numerous in the
vicinity of the theatres; and for this my father furnished
me with the verses of ' King Canute.' I was lucky in my
setting of them, and the notes with the words were
so successful as well to have reimbursed the publishers
for the three guineas they had paid for the twofold copyright. The sale of this Glee, however, led to our engagement for five others to constitute a series, on the same
terms, which, as times went, we felt to be a miniature
fortune. They are all humorous relations of English historical incidents, and the verses of some of them are at
least as full of point as are those of the first; but, by a
caprice of luck as unaccountable as are most of the freaks
of that wayward deity, no one but ' King Canute' has ever
had acceptance."

Besides these, Macfarren produced " Shakespeare
Songs for four voices " (1860-64), and a host of
similar compositions, both for mixed and for equal
voices, which are for the most part sufficiently well
known to render their enumeration here unnecessary.

[1] See page 50.

CHAPTER VIII.

PRIOR to the death of George Macfarren, sen., in April, 1843, he had made a suggestion to his son which was willingly acted on: that of the formation of a society for the publication of a complete edition of Handel's works, under competent editorship—a scheme which it was supposed would be hailed with acclamation and meet with abundant support in the land of Handel's adoption, and in which those works were held in such high esteem. As was the case with the Musical Antiquarian Society, however, the expectations of its promoters were not fully realized; the Handel Society, instituted in 1843, having an existence of only a few years. Macfarren, however, acted upon his father's suggestion—the father, indeed, being present at the first meeting convened for the formation of the Society, and with the co-operation of R. Addison (Treasurer), W. Sterndale Bennett, Sir

H. R. Bishop, Dr. Crotch, J. W. Davison, E. J.
Hopkins, I. Moscheles, T. M. Mudie, G. F. Rimbault,
Sir George Smart, and Henry Smart, G. A. Macfarren
as Secretary, issued the Prospectus, from 73, Berners
Street, June 16, 1843. Into the work of the Society,
which commenced with 1,000 members, but was dissolved in January, 1848, through lack of support, this
is not the place to enter, beyond recording that for it
Macfarren edited " Belshazzar," " Judas Maccabeus,"
and " Jephtha." With his sadly imperfect eyesight,
such work must have been exacting and laborious.
He had very conscientious ideas as to the nature,
responsibility, and duties of editorship, and it was
indicative of the artistic aims which always animated
him, that he entered with painstaking energy into
comparatively unprofitable work of this or any other
kind, which tended towards the highest advancement
of the art to which he had devoted himself.

His sight continuing to fail increasingly, he was
allured by the accounts which he received of the skill
and success of an oculist in New York; and, in the
fond hope of obtaining some benefit from the much-
vaunted treatment, was induced in 1847 to proceed
to that city and place himself under the lauded prac-
titioner. The hope was vain : although the oculist
from time to time pronounced, as the result of diag-
nosis, that there was improvement, the poor patient
had to reply,—" I only know that I can't see any
better." Even at this time, however, Macfarren was
able to write, with the help of a powerful magnifying
glass, the use of which, indeed, he did not relinquish
until about twelve years later. The blindness did
not become total till about 1865. It is hardly to be

wondered at that, under the depressing circumstances
of his visit to America, the period of eighteen months'
sojourn there was not remarkable or prolific in an
artistic way.   He found the sea-voyages insufferably
tedious, although he seems not to have been wholly
idle even with his pen while on his way to the United
States.   A Vocal Duet, words by W. A. Hammond,
bears date "British Channel, 10 August, 47."   The
stanzas commence :—

> "Let us haste to the river, whose tremulous breast
> Is a bed where the calm face of heaven might rest;
> As we float o'er the stream in its mantle of blue,
> We fancy it heaven it mirrors so true."

At the end of the manuscript, Macfarren writes :—

"Dear Mr. Hammond, had you had half so much of the
water when you wrote these words as I have had now, you
would have told a very different story.   However poetical,
they are strictly romantic, in Dr. Johnson's full meaning of
the word.—Yours very truly, G. A. Macfarren."

During his stay in New York, however, he completed another opera, " Charles the Second "(of which
more anon), forwarding the numbers to England, sheet
by sheet.   He corresponded about musical matters
with his intimate friend, the late Henry Gattie,
violinist, a man of great intelligence beyond the
domain of his art, with whom at that time I was in
very frequent intercourse, and from whom I received
intelligence when he heard from Macfarren.   One
matter of his solicitude, about which he begged intelligence from Gattie, was the progress, artistically, of
his youngest brother, Walter Cecil, now so well

known, but then in the early days of his professional
career.

Another incident of his sojourn in New York was a
performance, at a concert given by Henri Herz and
Camillo Sivori, of Macfarren's "Chevy Chase" overture, the composer conducting, Sivori playing first
violin, Bottesini the double-bass, Herz the drums,
and J. L. Hatton the triangle! All this was so
announced!

This digression respecting the visit to New York
will explain the dating thence of the preface to "Belshazzar," to Macfarren's edition of which we now
revert.

In that preface to the first part of "Belshazzar,"
dated November 1, 1847—after giving various historical particulars concerning the Oratorio—he states
that it was his

"object to follow the manuscript of Hande as closely as
possible ;" upon which authority he was "enabled to make
many important corrections of the score, as it has appeared
in the old printed copies, sometimes in single notes, sometimes in the accentuation of words, and sometimes in the
restoration of passages, which have hitherto been always
omitted."

He further states that the

"edition contains several entire pieces which have never
before been printed, ... and several resettings of pieces
already known ;"

all these being derived from Handel's manuscript in
the Library of Buckingham Palace. These are pointed
out in detail; and it is also stated that, in certain
places,—

"there are [in the MS.] several erasures, sometimes of
single bars, sometimes of two, three, or four bars together,
and these furnish a most interesting illustration of Handel's
method of composition, in the circumstance of the voice
and the bass-parts being written continuously throughout
the whole movement, and the violin and viola-parts not
being filled up in the erased bars, thus showing that it was
the custom of the composer to make first a skeleton of his
score, which he corrected and completed afterwards, etc."

And Macfarren goes on to speak of one place in
which he has seen it fit and necessary, for the sake of
performance, to fill in this " skeleton," as he believed
Handel would have done.   Various minor corrections, also, he specifies; and then speaks of the organ
part which he supplied, following the example of
Mendelssohn in his edition of " Israel in Egypt " for
the same society.

These few particulars give some indication of the
painstaking care with which Macfarren performed his
task ; and the same care is manifested in his edition of
" Judas Maccabeus," in the preface to which, dated
London, March, 1855, occur the following characteristic remarks :—

"It is important to notice that in all Handel's manuscripts the figuring of the bass is extremely incomplete.
In the old printed copies this deficiency, if deficiency it be,
is most profusely made up, though not unexceptionably
in accordance with the harmony. The very unsatisfactory
system of musical shorthand, that goes by the most inex-
pressive name of 'thorough bass,' is now for practical
purposes as good as obsolete, and any one who can comprehend a figured bass, can as easily read the notes of the
score, and where these complete not the harmony, supply
from the indication they afford what others may be necessary."

To this edition of " Judas Maccabeus " Macfarren did not supply an organ part, nor to " Jephtha," published in 1858. The reason of this is not stated ; it was probably by direction of the council. Macfarren, in the preface to " Judas," deplores

" the custom . . . that prevailed in Handel's time, of leaving the organ part to the discretion of the performer, with the indefinite guide only of the figured bass. It is not alone that the effect of the chords greatly depends upon the position in which they may be distributed ; but in the solo pieces, not merely the filling up of the harmony was left to the knowledge and invention of the organist, even the form or figure of the accompaniment, in fact, the construction of an independent counterpoint, rested entirely upon the ability of this most responsible interpreter of the composer's meaning."

In the preface to " Jephtha," Macfarren again refers to this subject ; as also to " the extremely scarce, and, so to speak, fitful figuring in the composer's score," as " characteristic of him, and of his mode of writing."

In the concluding paper of a series on the " Messiah," in the " Musical World," March and April, 1849, he also remarks on the same subject :—

" It is always a matter of lament that it was Handel's custom, as that of his age, to leave the organ part, which sustained the chief accompaniment of his solo pieces, to the improvisation of the performer, giving only the vague indication of a figured bass to direct the organist as to the harmony—without implying in any manner the position in which the chords are to be dispersed, upon which very much, if not the whole of their effect depends, nor, what is still more important, suggesting the form or figure of the accompaniment. The traditional mode of performing these organ accompaniments having been, to a great extent, lost, and the organists of our day having, for the most part, a discreet hesitation to venture their extemporaneities upon such everlasting themes, the custom generally prevails now of omitting the organ in such pieces altogether; and hence the miserably weak and meagre effect of those many songs, of which we hear nothing but the outline in the voice and the bass parts, with an occasional point of imitation, and sometimes a symphony for the violin. In the case of the 'Messiah,' the great composer has a powerful advantage in the effect of his creation on a modern audience, from the labours of an equally great commentator, in the additional parts Mozart has added to the original score, the purport of which is to fill up the blank places, and to supply in the orchestra such effects as Handel himself would have produced in accompanying his own work on the organ.   Without Mozart's masterly additions, a performance of this oratorio must then always be regarded as incomplete."

I remember Macfarren conversing with me about the admirable way in which Henry Smart, for the Handel Society, edited Handel's " Chamber Duets," filling up the figured bass part for the pianoforte— "counterpointing" the accompaniment; saying how much his opinion of Smart's musicianship was thereby raised.

Macfarren's views on editing, to which allusion has been made, are presented in an article by him of much later date, in which he specifies " three orders of editorship" :—

" One takes upon himself the duty of purifying the text of an inaccessible author. . . . An editor of this class needs to exercise his discretion, when there is the choice of two authorities of nearly equal value; for instance, there may be the autograph of a work and a printed copy of the first edition of the same.   In many cases the reliability of the former is indisputable; but in others, it may often happen that a composer has improved upon his first intentions, either from the experience of performance, from a reconsideration of a phrase, or from any other cause. He will then naturally alter the parts from which his piece is to be played, or he will alter the proof sheets if it is to be printed; but he will rarely run home from a rehearsal or a printing-office to correct his original MS. When this happens, of necessity a copy of the first edition is a better guide for the editor, than is even the handwriting of the composer."

Macfarren cites an instance from "Israel in Egypt," which Mendelssohn edited for the Handel Society :—

"Throughout the Chorus, 'And with the blast of thy nostrils,' Handel wrote the often repeated phrase, 'the waters were gathered,' with the word 'we-re' in two syllables, having four separate quavers for 'wa-ters we-re;' but printed it, as we all know, with two joined quavers for the first syllable, and one quaver each for the other two."

The Council of the Society, in opposition to Mendelssohn, determined to adhere to the printed version.

"Another order of editorship engages itself with expounding, so to speak, the original, and by the substitution perhaps of one word or note for another, or by the change of punctuation, to make clear the sense of phrases which has been left doubtful by the author. To this order belong the countless array of Shakespearian commentators. . . . The punctuation of music consists in the slurs to indicate the phrasing, which supply the place of the commas, semicolons, and the like, of literature, which are almost as essential to the sense as the very words they divide and congregate. It is in this matter of slurring or phrasing that the works of many musicians, even among the most eminent, are sadly defective. . . . Some editors, of the order in present consideration, stretch their duty to its very verge, if not break it by excess of tension; which are they who not only indicate how many notes are to be given

N

in one breath, or in one bow, or without raising the fingers
from the key-board, but mark what notes are to be played
loudly and what softly, what are to be detached and what
conjoined, and thus give often a meaning to a phrase
which is apart from the composer's intention, and is sometimes opposed to the natural tendency of the phrase itself.
This kind of thing is admissible in performance, where the
personality of the player may give interest to his erratic
construction of a composer's meaning; but it should not
be perpetuated in print, unless accompanied with a complete description of what was originally written, and of
what has been altered from, and what added to the author's
text. . . . An edition of the pianoforte works of Beethoven,
now in the course of issue in Germany, carries this assumed
prerogative of an editor to an extent happily extraordinary,
and extraordinary let us hope it may long continue. In
this, with most reckless disregard of evidence, the editors,
and one in particular, assume to have a kind of second
sight of the author's meaning, and by the guidance of this
preternatural light, they take upon themselves to set aside
what Beethoven wrote and printed, and they supersede
this in many passages by substitutions of their own, which
materially change the character and alter the effect of what
commonplace folks blindly believe must have been intended by the master—poor commonplace folks! who
have but the indisputable notes of the original, the general
manner of the author, a comprehension of the theoretical
and practical state of art in his time, and a reverence for a
great man's meaning, and his individual way of expressing
it, to guide them. . . . The German edition must be a
curiosity from which reason and feeling will revolt.

    *   *   *   *   *

" Our third order of editorship assumes the right and
presumes the capability to add to the works of great
musicians in order to fit them for present use. In letters
the same was done by John Dryden, by Nahum Tate, and
by David Garrick, with regard to the plays of Shakespeare,
and a pretty business they made of their changements.
. . . Perhaps one of the greatest evils that have ever been
done in music, is the reinstrumentation by Mozart of
Handel's ' Messiah ; ' and the evil lies in the fact that the

score is written with such consummate artistry as to rival
the beauty of the original matter, that it is hence inseparable (save in those pieces in which, from the first,
Mozart's additions have been unused) from Handel's
groundwork, in public performances. Because of its infinite merit, Mozart's orchestration is now indispensable ;
and because of its indispensability, any one now regards it
as a precedent, and takes licence from its example, to invest
other works of Handel with 'additional accompaniments.'
Unhappily, or happily, as the case may be, everybody who
paints Handel with the vivid colours of the modern
orchestra is not Mozart. If he were, and were always at
his best, then should we become strangers to the effects
intended by the mighty one of Halle, the stern grandeur
and the special sweetness of the Saxon giant would have
no existence, and the delicious haze of sunset glories, that
hangs as a kind of veil between the ancient style of music
and the modern, would hide from view the most salient
features of the master's individuality."

In the four articles on Handel's " Messiah," in the
" Musical World," to which allusion has been made,
Macfarren contends that—

"Handel, by reason of his greatness, must be esteemed
an original genius ; but his originality is to be regarded in
respect to the excellence of his works, which had never
previously been approached and can never be surpassed,
rather than with reference to the unlikeness of his style to
that of his predecessors, and more especially of his cotem-
poraries."

After some reasons for this verdict, he continues
that—

"The originality, the true dignity of Handel's genius, is
to be seen in the exquisite beauty of many of his melodies,
. . . . that beauty which proves the true consanguinity of
genius in all schools ; that beauty which, indeed, is not of an
age, but for all time, and which makes it seem possible that
' Love in her eyes sits playing,' ' When I seek from Love's

sickness to fly,' 'Nel cor più,' 'My mother bids me bind my hair,' 'Voi che sapete,' 'Kennst du das Land,' 'Rose softly blooming,' 'Assisa a piè d'un salice,' and many of the 'Songs without words' for the pianoforte, might all have been thought by one mind, and written by one person. It is to be seen in the wonderful points of harmony which he somewhat rarely, but never inappropriately, and never without prodigious effect, employs, that quite transcend his age, and but for their perfect fitness to the situations where he introduces them, might seem to be taken from the most ultra-modern compositions of the present day; such, to give a single but most striking example, as the great point on the words, 'Still as a stone,' in 'Israel in Egypt,' where the bass descends to G sharp, and the first inversion of the chord of the major ninth on E has an effect that no words can describe; it is to be seen in the truly beautiful, because beautifully truthful, and therefore also intensely poetical expression, not of words, but of sentiments, feelings, passions, with which his works abound; it is to be seen in his wonderful command over all the resources of counterpoint, his complete mastery over which intricate art makes his most elaborate and complicated fugues appear to have been written with as much ease and fluency as they are grand and natural in their effect; it is to be seen in his lofty, noble, almost divine conceptions of the greatest and grandest subjects, and it is this last, perhaps, more than all the other evidences of his greatness, but decidedly in conjunction with them all, that marks him unapproachable in what is his own peculiar excellence, and has made, in the minds of all who know and appreciate his power, the word Handelian to be a synonym for sublimity."

With characteristic courage, Macfarren, in the course of these analytical articles, animadverts most vehemently upon the song "The Trumpet shall sound," one of the most "popular" in the Oratorio, on account of those very qualities about it which he considers incongruous with the solemnity of the subject.

" The recitative, 'For behold I tell you a mystery,' is a broad ¡piece of declamation; but the air which it intro-duces we cannot—with all the reverence with which the composer everywhere, and especially in this work, im-presses us—we cannot—after the most careful study of the piece we are presuming to censure—we cannot but consider to be a complete misconception. 'The Trumpet shall sound, and the dead shall be raised,' appears to be a passage as suggestive as any in the oratorio, and one peculiarly likely to have called out the noblest powers of Handel's genius. What a truly sublime image does it raise, even without the strong aid of musical enforcement, of the awful sounding of an overwhelming tone that bursts the bonds of death, and calls together from the widest range of space, from the remotest depths of time, all that have lived to live again!—tearing the till then impene-trable curtain from eternity, it discloses the everlasting Now, the vast understanding of Divinity, the last sense new created, and merges is, and was, and is to be, in the mighty consciousness of the infinite and the true; and how particularly does it strike us, first, that such an image, even one so superhuman, was quite within the province, and possibly within the power of the composer of the ' Messiah' to embody; and secondly, that it was for him, and for none other, to essay the human expression of so divine a subject. This is a rude presentation of the rude pre-sentiment we feel of what was the glorious scope open to the musician who should exercise his art and his genius upon the composition of this passage; and we cannot but feel, and feeling cannot but regret, that the trivial—for so, com-pared with the theme, we must regard it—the trivial song before us, and the trifling conventionalities of the common-place trumpet accompaniment must wholly disappoint all those who know the powers of Handel, and appreciate the unequalled susceptibility of the subject, of what they have a right to expect from his treatment of it. The tremendous summons of the last trumpet is reduced to the display of the executive excellence of a tolerably skilled solo player, and the thrilling annunciation of the destiny of all mor-tality rendered by the unmeaning divisions of an expres-sionless *bravura*. Yes, indeed, this song must be felt to be a misconception, and it is the more conspicuous, and the more to be regretted, because, as such, it is the only failure in a work that would otherwise defy all question of its propriety."

On September 27, 1844, Macfarren was married at Marylebone Church to Clarina Thalia Andrae, a native of Lübeck, well known as Natalia Macfarren, by her translations and adaptations of opera *libretti*, words of Mendelssohn's songs, etc., as well as for her ability as a teacher of singing. I believe it is an open secret that certain musical souvenirs known as "Six Romances," were written for her, being originally superscribed, "To Thalia." As issue of this marriage, a daughter survives him, now Mrs. F. W. Davenport, for whom, I believe it is also an open secret, he wrote the quaint little instruction-book for the pianoforte, entitled, "Little Clarina's Lesson Book," which, though published, has not, so far as I am aware, obtained general acceptance.

In the year 1845, when Laurent was manager of Covent Garden Theatre, he determined to bring out the "Antigone" of Sophocles, with Mendelssohn's music; and Macfarren having been engaged as musical director to the theatre, it became his onerous, responsible, and difficult duty to conduct it; difficult, because of the structure of the work, consisting not merely of choruses, some of them double choruses, but also of spoken recitation accompanied by the orchestra, necessitating on Macfarren's part complete familiarity with the words as well as the music. For, on account of his greatly impaired sight, he was under the necessity of committing the whole to memory, and of conducting from memory; a marvellous feat, but not by any means the only feat of memory which has to be recounted concerning him. Mendelssohn was much gratified on hearing of the arrangement, and wrote to Macfarren as follows:—

"Frankfurt, 8 *December*, 1844.

"MY DEAR SIR,

..... "Have many thanks for the interest you take in bringing out my music to the 'Antigone' choruses; I am very glad it is in your hands, because it wants a musician like you to make it go as intended—quite as a subordinate part of the whole, as a mere link in the chain of the poem, and yet perfectly clear and independent in itself."

Then follow minute directions respecting the choruses, especially the choral recitatives, the action, etc., followed by, " Pray excuse this long analysis; but you would have it!"

Yes, Macfarren " would have it;" he always would have everything accessible that tended towards the thoroughness of performance of any task undertaken by him. No wonder that the enterprise was perfectly successful, and the piece ran thirty nights, only stopping with the termination of the season—as is recorded by Karl Mendelssohn Bartholdy, son of the great composer, who speaks of Sterndale Bennett and Macfarren as " English artists of congenial mind with [his father's] own."

As illustrating Macfarren's presence of mind and promptitude, an incident may be here related which he told to a pupil years afterwards. At one of the performances of the " Antigone," there was a point where the chorus were to walk on to the stage singing. The orchestra were playing their part in front, and the chorus marched in from the back, having begun their song out of time. Macfarren detected what was wrong—shouted to his band behind him, "Cut out half a bar!" and thus a *fiasco* was averted, without the audience being aware of its imminence.

In connection with these performances of "Antigone," there is a charming little letter to that accomplished musician Miss Kate Loder, now Lady Thompson, which, though having no bearing on music, is so characteristic at once of Macfarren's affectionate feelings towards his artistic associates, and of his graceful dexterity in delicate expression, that it may be given here :—

" Wednesday.

"MY OWN THALIA'S DEAR KITTY,

"We shall get a box to-morrow night for 'Antigone' in hopes that you will go with Thalia; and we shall ask my mother to take care of you—please be here AT 6.

"My wife sends her best love; and as all her love is mine, you may conclude if you please that in hers she sends mine also.

" Sincerely yours,
"G. A. MACFARREN."

Lady Thompson retains a pleasant memory of the occasion, which young enthusiasm for Mendelssohn's music, enjoyed under such auspices, rendered specially delightful.

In a series of articles upon Mendelssohn's subsequently composed music to the " Œdipus in Colonos," in the " Musical World," January 7th, 1854, and following numbers, Macfarren advances the opinion that :—

" The element of the Chorus, which, in spite of the advocacy of Schiller, remains to the present appreciation an incongruity in the Greek drama, is here much more essential to the whole than in the tragedy of ' Antigone;'

since, besides the several Odes which carry on the progress of the action, eulogizing the state, and moralizing upon such conditions of humanity as the incidents present, this impersonal personality sustains a very considerable portion of the dialogue with the principal characters, and thus becomes a party in many of the most impassioned scenes of the play."

Concerning these two works, Macfarren wrote, in the "Imperial Dictionary of Biography" :—

"Some English classical scholars [1] have violently depreciated this remarkable composition ['Antigone'], regarding it from a totally false point of view; it outlives their undiscerning censure, and, with its companion work, the 'Œdipus in Colonos,' written under the same circumstances in 1845, proves the poetical vigour of Mendelssohn's power of conception in a wholly untrodden field, and his capability of appropriating the resources of his art to a previously untried subject."

Referring to the fact that Mendelssohn composed this music, as well as that for "Antigone," etc., at the command of the King of Prussia, he rejoices both "in the genius that could elicit and so worthily obey such a command," and in "the enlightened liberality of the monarch."

"Prussia proved herself worthy of a great artist by the confidence reposed in Mendelssohn, and the homage paid to his talent. Of what is England worthy? . . . *Possibly* we have no Mendelssohn—*certainly* we have no King of Prussia. . . . So long as it is the policy of our government, personally and officially, to furnish themes for the writers of leading articles in newspapers, and inflammatory excitement to their readers, while it neglects that most important medium of moral discipline, intellectual cultivation—so long will politics be the amusement of the people, art their handiwork, their furniture, their hard livelihood in pursuit, and, at best, their paper-hanging in its attainment. So

[1] De Quincey, etc.

long as the beautiful is but a business, and the stimulant
of genius but a shop account of loss and profit, and the
inconsequent example of the great works that have been
produced under other auspices, must we bear the stigma
the rest of the world has placed upon us, of being an unmusical nation.   In Prussia, it is otherwise ; and of that
state of things Mendelssohn's 'Œdipus' is among the
results of which we share the advantage."

Macfarren said in my hearing— " I cannot understand politics."   Continuing the article, he says :—

" The form of the Greek drama affords a novel and a
very wide scope for the exercise of the musician's art; but,
at the same time, the details of its construction fetter him
with uncommon and embarrassing difficulties.

" It was not new in the revival of the tragedies of
Sophocles upon the German stage, to blend spoken declamation with instrumental accompaniment. The biographers
of Mozart describe, as one of his first important dramatic
successes, his music to 'Mithridates,' which consisted
entirely of orchestral accompaniments to the dialogue, in
the style of recitative ; and this, it seems, was a form of
composition much esteemed at that period.   The choral
responses to the speeches of the characters constitute a new
element, in the treatment of which 'Antigone' has proved
the greatness of Mendelssohn's power ; and the present
work, as it contains more of such scenes, and of a more
complicated and extensive character, has more severely
tested this power, and thus still more successfully established it.   The difficulty of execution presented by the
intermixture of speaking and singing, and by the reduc-
tion of spoken declamation to the restrictions of musical
rhythm, while impeding the realization of the composer's
effects, detracts nothing from his merit in producing it ;
and the feeling of every one who has witnessed the competent performance of 'Antigone' is, that the effect thus
attained is of the most powerfully exciting character that
the dramatic musical art can attain.

" The first difficulty, I may say danger, of this class of
writing exists in the necessity of reaching the pinnacle

which lies between dulness on its more cautious and gradual
ascent, and absurdity on the precipitous and sunny side of
its declivity, and thus to elevate without exaggerating
the dramatic situation. This demands the profoundest
artistry, and the highest natural qualifications in the composer. The next difficulty or danger belongs to the fascination of continuous action, which impels the embodiment
of line after line, phrase after phrase, in fresh ideas; in
which uninterrupted succession, so attractive to the musician, he is liable to abandon that unity which is indispensable
to the gratification of the hearer.

"It is especially to be admired in the work under consideration, that in these declamatory scenes, while the
expression of the general sentiment and the enunciation of
particular words form the chief purport of the musician,
and the chief medium of his impression upon an audience,
the principles of construction are so ingeniously, and so
successfully brought to bear upon the treatment, even of
the most impetuous, broken, and seemingly irregular
passages, as to render each scene a model of symmetry.
Thus we have all the excitement of an unpremeditated
passionate impulse, refined and beautified by the agency of
artistic design. Such a handling of the subject is especially
appropriate in a composition illustrative of a work of Greek
art, the elements of which in all its branches of manifestation were artificial, refinement being the necessity, and
nature the germ from which her inventions had to be
ripened. It is eminently to the purpose that the unities
of our own art should be scrupulously maintained, when it
is brought into connection with another in which the laws
of unity were despotic.

"We must now consider another department of the work,
and the difficulties that beset its treatment—viz., the
adaptation of music to the Odes. The obvious purpose of
this important feature in the design of the Greek drama
was to afford intervals of repose during the progress of the
action, which would else have been too violent and exciting
to come within the rule of gradual undulation, which, as
the principle of ideal beauty, was imperative in ancient
art. . . . Further; the absence of metaphor is a studied
characteristic of the dialogue of the Greek drama; and the

employment of this graceful figure of rhetoric, and charming poetical medium, was confined to the Odes, which, by
contrast no less than by sympathy, were made to soften
while they heightened the effect, and promoted the development of the action. As, then, the musical treatment
of the dialogue is intended to enforce the excitement of the
dramatic action, so the musical rendering of the episodes
is designed to soften the reliefs of the points of repose with
which it is interspersed. Again, as in the accompanied
dialogue there is little or no scope for rhythmical regu-
larity, so in the Odes we have the contrast of continuous
movement and unbroken melody, which is the metaphor
of music. The composer's obstacle in treating these has
been the enormous number of words, and the necessity of
comprising them within such limits as the exigencies of
the stage and the impatience, most natural to their situation, of a theatrical audience impose. Each Ode has words
enough to form the text of an Oratorio; and yet the
minutes, the seconds, of the duration of each must be
counted. The difficulty of constructing rhythmical melodies
and symmetrical compositions, without repeating words and
recurring to passages, may be easily conceived; and it is
obvious that such repetitions and recurrences would
lengthen the music far beyond all practical availability.
This difficulty having been mastered completely and successfully by Mendelssohn betokens the most consummate
judgment and the greatest fluency; and a musical interest
is produced which eminently fulfils the requirements of the
situation."

The thorough comprehension of the artistic requirements—the *rationale*—of such compositions, here
evinced, amply accounts for the successful accomplishment by Macfarren of his task in directing the
" Antigone " performances, although, from causes
beyond his immediate control, there were casualties at
first which afforded opportunity for cynical criticism
in certain quarters.

CHAPTER IX.

OPERAS, CANTATAS, ETC. "DON QUIXOTE," 1846; "KING CHARLES II.," 1849; "THE SLEEPER AWAKENED," 1850; "ALLAN OF ABERFELDY," 1851; "QUARTET IN G MINOR," 1852; "LENORA," 1853; "HAMLET OVERTURE," 1856; "MAY DAY," 1857; "CHRISTMAS," "ROBIN HOOD;" ENTIRE FAILURE OF SIGHT, AND COMMENCEMENT OF DICTATION, 1860; "FREYA'S GIFT," "JESSY LEA," 1863; "THE SOLDIER'S LEGACY," "SHE STOOPS TO CONQUER," "HELVELLYN," 1864; "SONGS IN A CORNFIELD," 1868; "OUTWARD BOUND," 1872; "THE LADY OF THE LAKE," 1877; "KENILWORTH," 1880.

THE first inception of Macfarren's opera, "Don Quixote," the resumption of its composition, its reconstruction, and its subsequent rejection by Maddox, have been recorded in Chapter III. With respect to the resumption of the composition, with a view to its production under Balfe's management, it was related by Macfarren's intimate friend, Mr. G. A. Osborne, in an entertaining paper of "Musical Coincidences and Reminiscences," read by him at the Musical Association, April 2nd, 1883, that:—

"Balfe was always anxious for the establishment of a permanent English Opera in London, and, among other composers, he invited the co-operation of Macfarren, the present Principal of the Royal Academy of Music. He was anxious to show that British musicians deserved some of the patronage lavished on foreign artists. 'Don Quixote,' by Macfarren, was put in rehearsal; but owing to the theatre being closed for want of funds, it was not produced till five years later. On this subject I will read you a letter from Macfarren :—

> "'15, Hanover Cottages.
>
> "'MY DEAR OSBORNE,
>
> "'Let me give you the first intelligence that the attempt to establish the National Opera Company has failed. You will in a few days receive the report of the Committee.
>
> "'Sincerely yours,
>
> "'G. A. MACFARREN.'"

One of Balfe's biographers, more at length, records that in 1841, engaging the English Opera House— now the Lyceum Theatre—

> "Balfe thought to create a national opera by inviting all the known English opera writers to compose works, and thus to show the public that there were as good musicians among the natives of the country worthy of support as the foreigner, upon whom was lavished all the praise, and who also obtained the greater share of recognition. Barnett, Rooke, Lover, and Macfarren were invited to co-operate. Lover had written a comic operetta called 'Paddy Whack in Italia,' which Balfe produced. Macfarren had been invited by Balfe to compose an opera on the subject of 'Don Quixote.' This was placed in rehearsal, and would have been brought out but for the untimely end of the scheme,"

through the defection of certain members of the company.

> "Five years later, Balfe, knowing the excellent qualities of the work, recommended it for production at Drury Lane, which recommendation was accepted, and the opera was performed successfully. . . .
>
> "Balfe thought when he started his ill-fated venture

that he had the help of enough composers to enable him
to continue his scheme. The only one who had foresight
and wisdom enough to help and actively to encourage it
was George Alexander Macfarren. The other composers
of the period gave only a' half-hearted assistance. The
time for the recognition of English art as an actuality was
not come." [1]

The work was not, however, to be lost to the musical
world. As has been already briefly recorded in Macfarren's own words (p. 51), the opera was brought out
at Drury Lane, under Bunn's management, February
3rd, 1846; and "Balfe . . . was present at the first
performance" of the "fine opera . . . the theme of
which he had suggested." [2] The cast was as follows,
Edward J. Loder conducting :—

Quiteria	Miss Rainforth.
Camacho.	Mr. D. W. King.
Sancho	Mr. Stretton.
Don Quixote . . .	Mr. W. H. Weiss.
Rovedos	Mr. S. Jones.
Basilius	Mr. Allen.

The *libretto*, by the composer's father, was founded
on the same "adventure," or episode, as that which
furnished the text of Mendelssohn's early opera, "The
Marriage of Camacho." Just before its production,
Mendelssohn wrote to Macfarren, in 1845 :—"Many
good wishes for your opera; may it succeed and give
you and your friends many happy hours in '46, '56, and
so on." Indeed, it is stated that Mendelssohn, when
in England, once said: "Your best composer is un-

---

[1] "Balfe; his Life and Work: by W. A. Barrett. London.
1882."
[2] *Ibid.*, p. 176.

known—Macfarren ;"—not said, however, in any way to imply the ignoring of Sterndale Bennett.

One of the songs in " Don Quixote " was more or less known several years before the completion and production of the entire opera, viz., " Ah, why do we love ? " which has for long been a favourite in our concert-rooms; and concerning which the " Musical World " of March 26th, 1840, wrote:—

"It is one of the most perfect songs of its class we have ever seen. It sparkles all over with freshness and beauty — from the beginning to the end it would be difficult to point out a bar which does not contain some racy piece of thought, or some unlooked-for turn of expression."

A chorus in the opera, " The rights of hospitality," is in the form of the Spanish dance, the *Seguidilla*.

The " Atlas " contained the following summary of the work :—

"From Mr. Macfarren's known independence of thought, and inflexible adhesion to his own standard of excellence, it was at once to be predicated that no vision of popularity would tempt him to wilfully indite rubbish for *encore's* sake, to descend to a maudlin prettiness at the expense of dramatic truth,—in fine, to lend his pen to a single bar not authorized by his judgment. If the public was to have music light, airy, and captivating at first sight, it must spring naturally from the situations of his *libretto*—where these led him, thither and nowhere else, would he go. And exactly thus has it proved with his ' Don Quixote.' It has been the experiment of a thoroughly right thinker —novel from seven years' disuse—but, we rejoice to say, it has completely succeeded. The public not only listened attentively, but received with delight the volume of beautiful things this opera contains, and the result must have been as gratifying to the composer, as it undoubtedly was to every musician of true and liberal feeling in the theatre.

" Never was success more thoroughly deserved, because
never has it been more honestly and artistically achieved.
To speak of ' Don Quixote' as a ' fine opera,' conveys no
impression of its peculiar excellences, nor of the almost
innumerable points of musicianship by which it is so widely
distinguished from the merely, and designedly, *popular*
works of the day. The exquisite unity, consistence, and
purity of its style, its perfect dramatic expression, its great
development of fresh and unworn thought, its masterly
instances of constructive power—of which we may quote,
by way of example, the first *finale*, as quite equal in symmetrical form and continuity of interest to any similar
achievement of modern times—and the vigour and musician-
like certainty with which all its materials are vitalized in
the orchestra, are all matters that substantiate it as the
work of a greatly accomplished artist. And this not the
less that it makes no pretension to what is ordinarily and
vulgarly deemed ' grandeur.' The drama demands precisely that length and breadth of style adopted for it, and no
other; and this truthfulness and consistency of musical rendering is one of its most notable charms. Not only is this
life-like integrity of manner at once apparent on the general
aspect of the work, but it even grows brighter and more vivid
as we question it in detail. Take, for example, the quaint
and admirable conception of Don Quixote's isolated posture
among the other characters of the drama—the enthusiastic
dreamer of bygone ages surrounded by the bustling denizens
of the living world of fact—how simply and forcibly expressed by assigning to the pseudo-knight a style of music
as far separated by its antiquity from that pervading all
the other portions of the score, as were the chivalrous pro-
vocatives of the Don's madness from the age in which
Cervantes made him live! In this general estimation of
the opera we may seem to have been speaking very big
words about what may, to some, appear a small matter.
Nevertheless we have a stout faith in our perfect ability to
justify them when we come to discuss ' Don Quixote' in
detail—which, as it may lead us into considerable length,
we must defer until next week. Meanwhile we earnestly
counsel all music-loving people who have not heard ' Don
Quixote' to hear it; and those who have heard it we as

strenuously advise to hear it again—it will improve wonderfully with acquaintance."

In a touching and appreciative obituary notice of W. H. Weiss, who died, greatly regretted, in 1867, Macfarren, after recounting various operatic parts in which Weiss had distinguished himself, in operas by Balfe, Benedict, etc., continues:—

"For my own part, I shall not forget the thankful pleasure I felt in witnessing Weiss's chivalric magniloquence in Don Quixote; his seamanly roughness, authoritative loyalty, and burly embarrassment in Captain Copp; nor his jovial impersonation of a thorough old English gentleman in Squire Hardcastle. And I shall ever acknowledge that, in these capital assumptions, he gave to my airy nothings truly a local habitation and a name." [1]

The second and third characters referred to are in subsequent operas of Macfarren's. It is pleasant to insert the above, as illustrative of his generous and grateful disposition.

The published pianoforte score of the opera is inscribed :—

To the memory of

MY FATHER

This Opera is dedicated as a

Tribute of Affection.

In the year 1859—thirteen years after the successful production of this opera—the "New York Musical Review and Gazette" amusingly and patronizingly said : "Mr. Macfarren, an excellent English musician, has written an overture, 'Don Quixote.' We should

---

[1] "Choir," Nov. 30th, 1867.

think the subject rather too much for Mr. Macfarren"!
To which the "Musical World" replied :—

"Whether the subject be 'too much' or too little for
Mr. Macfarren, our contemporary may, perhaps, not object
to be informed that the overture in question is the prelude
to an opera of the same name, produced at Drury Lane
Theatre in 1846, and justly regarded as one of the best
English dramatic compositions extant."

Although Maddox rejected "Don Quixote" in
1845, yet, such was its success, that Macfarren's next
operatic production, "King Charles II.," was brought
out by him at the Princess's Theatre, October 27th,
1849 ; the work having been composed during Macfarren's disappointing sojourn in New York, during
the years 1847 and 1848, and sent over to this country,
in portions, as it progressed. The *libretto* was by
Desmond Ryan. The success of this opera was unequivocal : it had a run of the greater part of two
seasons. The cast included Miss Louisa Pyne (now
Madame Bodda), Madame (now Lady) Macfarren,
Madame Weiss, Messrs. W. Harrison, Weiss, and
H. Corri. It was the occasion of Madame Macfarren's
début on the stage, she taking the part of the Page ;
and her modest intelligence was the subject of favourable remark. The composer, through infirmity of
sight, was not able to conduct the performances; but
this responsible task was ably accomplished by his
sympathetic brother-musician, the late Edward James
Loder.

Of "King Charles II." such opinions were expressed
as that it was—

"the best that Mr. Macfarren has written. The melodies

are more varied and plentiful, the design of the concerted pieces larger, their development more masterly, and the general tone of the work more dramatic and effective than in his previous essays. There is also (as in 'Don Quixote,' but even still more remarkably,) a fine individuality preserved in each of the separate characters, amidst an evident unity of purpose. The style, moreover, is so decided, that not one of the pieces, long or short, but would, by anyone acquainted with Mr. Macfarren's manner of writing, be at once laid to his account." " In all there were nine encores, more than half the pieces in the opera." " It is the finest and most complete operatic work of a native musician ever produced on the stage." "Mr. Macfarren's greatest, and most simple and unaffected music is comprised in 'K. Charles II.'" "The madrigal, 'Maidens, would ye 'scape undoing,' is worthy of a place beside the finest madrigals of Wilbye and the other worthies of the Elizabethan age." " As regards the completeness of the work, we do not recollect anything comparable to it on the English stage for a long time; there is in it no crudeness of style—no vagueness of purpose. You perceive in every passage the mind of the master directing itself to a definite point, and achieving its object with the greatest possible ease."

The first of a notable series of Cantatas by Macfarren, " The Sleeper Awakened," termed a Serenata, words by John Oxenford, was performed at the National Concerts, Her Majesty's Theatre, in 1850, the parts being sustained by Mr. F. Bodda (Haroon Alraschid), Mr. Sims Reeves (Abou Hassan), and Madlle. Angri (Zuleika). It contains, among other noteworthy numbers, a Canon for three voices, "Good Night"; a Vocal Rondo (Zuleika), "Gone, he's gone"; a Ballet, consisting of (a) Arab War-Dance, (b) Shawl Dance, (c) Ballabile; a Finale, including a March, a Vocal Rondo (Zuleika), "The cloud that o'er our peaceful days." Even the "Athenæum," at that time not too favourably inclined;

declared that the "Stage Music" was "very cleverly constructed;" and that, in the Turkish March and Chorus, the local colour "so happily used by Weber in 'Oberon' is fairly matched in its pure and clear nationality": adding, however, that there were "some instances of *discord* which the most defying disciple of Dr. Day's system could hardly defend or recommend,— with such intolerable and gratuitous harshness do they strike the ear."

The published vocal score is dedicated to Mr. Walter Broadwood.

Amidst the labours of these large works, more-over, Macfarren found time and energy to write, in 1852, a Quartet in G minor for stringed instruments, expressly for the Quartet Association, at whose second concert, in May of that year, it was performed by Messrs. Sainton, Cooper, Hill, and Piatti, and, accord-ing to the "Times," exhibited "throughout the hand of an experienced master." Notwithstanding the number of such works in the department of Chamber Music that emanated from him, however, yet when, years afterwards, I asked him, on behalf of the Musical Artists' Society, to allow some such work to be performed at one of their concerts, he at first hesitated, then said that he would consider which work to send, and ultimately wrote saying that he found that he had nothing that he would like to be played. This was certainly from no ill-will to the Society, of which he was a Vice-President, and in which he evinced considerable interest.

In 1851, when Drury Lane Theatre was under the management of Bunn, Macfarren wrote for produc-tion there an opera to a *libretto* by John Oxenford,

which was intended to follow Balfe's " Sicilian Bride."
The title was " Allan of Aberfeldy ; " and there were
strong parts for tenor, soprano, and contralto, which
were to be sung respectively by Mr. Sims Reeves,
Miss Rainforth, and Miss Priscilla Horton (now Mrs.
German Reed). The opera was on the point of being
put in rehearsal, when, from causes not here to be
entered into, Bunn became a bankrupt, and the season
was brought to an abrupt close. " Allan of Aberfeldy " never saw the light.

Another opera which has never been produced is
to an Italian *libretto*, on the subject of Kenilworth,
composed many years later, probably in 1880, expressly for the eminent vocalist Madame Albani ; but,
from some unavoidable circumstances, it was not produced on the occasion for which it was intended, and
never performed, with the exception of the overture,
which was played at a concert of the Philharmonic
Society in 1887, and supposed by some to be an early
work, or else the prelude to an unfinished opera.
" Kenilworth " contained a ballet of four contrasted
dances, instead of a Scotch masque, originally planned.

Macfarren's cantata " Lenora," a musical setting
of Bürger's ballad, the English version by John Oxenford, was produced at the sixth concert of the Harmonic Union, Exeter Hall, April 25th, 1853, only
having once previously been publicly performed at a
concert by the students of the Royal Academy of
Music (which I remember), not very well, and, therefore, with but small success. Though the performance
by the Harmonic Union appears to have been by no
means efficient, it was so far adequate as to enable a
more distinct judgment to be formed of it, and it

was declared to indicate "a very high order of dramatic feeling." The principal solo singers were Miss Louisa Pyne, Madame Macfarren, and Herr Staudigl; the conductor, Mr. Benedict. The work consists of an orchestral introduction, leading into a contralto recitative, nine other vocal numbers, and a Notturno.

In 1856, his Overture to "Hamlet" was produced at the New Philharmonic Society's Concert, April 23rd. The analysis, presumably by the composer himself, in the programme is as follows :—

"This Overture was suggested by the following points in the tragedy:—Hamlet's melancholy—aggravated by the frivolities of the court—yielding to his love of Ophelia—his foreboding of the purpose of the ghost's visitation—the ghost's appearance to him—he addresses it—the spirit of the murdered king reveals the secret of his death and exhorts his son to avenge him—he adjures his companions not to relate what they have seen, and the ghost, invisible, calls upon them to swear—this awful scene is opposed by the revelry of the court—in the midst of this, the ghost's revelation is ever present to Hamlet—it distracts him from his love of Ophelia—the scene with her in the gallery—the play-scene, where his melancholy is disguised under the pretence of riotous gaiety—the scene with the queen in the closet, where, urged by the same intention that prepared him for the ghost's disclosure, he presses upon her the subject of his melancholy—the frivolity of the court again obtrudes itself upon him—he leaves for England, thinking of Ophelia and of the ghost—he returns, remembering her love, to learn of her madness and her death—this excites him for the present time to action—in the midst of his phrensy he remembers the ghost's exhortation—the cause of his melancholy, which has always made him a passive reflector, is now his motive for desperate action—the last scene, where he dies, knowing the ghost's admonition to be fulfilled."

One of the most popular of Macfarren's works, the cantata " May Day," was brought out at the Bradford Festival, 1857, under the conductorship of Costa, Madame Lemmens-Sherrington being the principal vocalist.   In that portion of it termed "The Revels," the old English dance-tune, the " Staines Morris," is introduced, for the Ottavino.   The whole work is most exhilarating, and is one of the few works of Macfarren's of which the full score is published (by Novello, Ewer, and Co.).

In the year 1860, May 9th, the fine cantata, again on a characteristically English subject, " Christmas," was first produced by the Musical Society of London, under the conductorship of Alfred Mellon, the soloists being Mesdames Lemmens-Sherrington and Sainton-Dolby.   Having been present on the occasion, I remember that, with some excellent musicians, the work obtained rather a *succès d'estime*, though no one could resist the speaking effect of the beautiful song with chorus concerning King Alfred, or the pretty duet, " Little Children ; " and there has, subsequently, been no backwardness in awarding the whole cantata high praise.   The " Musical World," at the time, declared that " on the whole it may be unhesitatingly stated that no English musician, from the time of Purcell to the present epoch, has written anything in its way more genuine and masterly."

" Robin Hood " was produced at Her Majesty's Theatre, when under the management of E. T. Smith, October 11th, 1860; the cast including Madame Lemmens-Sherrington, Madame Lemaire, Mr. Sims Reeves, Mr. Santley, Mr. George Honey, Mr. Bartleman, Mr. J. E. Patey, and Mr. Parkinson ; conduc-

tor, Mr. Charles Hallé. The overture was encored.
It was declared that " Mr. Macfarren has done his
very best : . . . the championship of the English
School, until a better opera than ' Robin Hood' is
produced, must remain in possession of its composer."
It was pronounced " the greatest work that has been
produced for the English musical stage since the days
of Purcell."

Mr. Sims Reeves, in his life of himself, says :
" Macfarren composed the principal part in what is
now generally recognized as that master's best opera
for myself." The "Musical World" recorded that:—

" As regards Mr. Macfarren's new opera, a greater and
more legitimate success than that achieved by the work
we never witnessed. The crowd was immense, the excitement unusual, and expectation on tiptoe. . . . The cast of
the parts presented an unusual attraction in itself. Mr.
Sims Reeves . . . was to play the principal character; and
Madame Lemmens-Sherrington, who has never appeared
on the stage at all, was to make her *début*. Mr. Santley,
too, and Mr. George Honey, from the Royal English Opera.
were both included in the cast."

Among the popular pieces in this opera were the
well-known songs, " My own, my guiding star," and
" True love." The delivery by Mr. Sims Reeves of
" Thy gentle voice would lead me on," " The grasp-
ing, rasping Norman race," and the patriotic song,
"Englishmen by birth are free," are said to have been
" the talk of the town." " The first Act is more or
less introductory, the second contains the greenwood
revel and the scene at Nottingham fair, and the third
the prison scene and the outlaw's pardon." The
success was so great that a punster said " it was less

Robin Hood than robbin' Harrison," who, with Miss Pyne, was then performing opera at Covent Garden.

During the composition of this opera, Macfarren's sight so completely failed that he was compelled finally to relinquish the use of the pen, and, thenceforth, to depend wholly on the services of amanuenses, to whom he dictated every note : a very simple statement, and as pathetic as it is simple. But it marks almost a new era, almost a turning-point, as some would think, in his career of mental activity. It was no turning-point, however, with him : he still went right on. An obstacle, a difficulty, was not a stumbling-block to him; not the occasion for giving up, or turning aside ; but for the calling into exercise renewed determination, energy, contrivance. Those who have any knowledge of the process of musical composition, and of the complications of a full-score, for orchestra and voices, will best appreciate the Herculean achievements of Macfarren in producing, subsequently to this period, such a succession of large, elaborate works ; and those who know the lighter effusions of his imagination may well wonder that such freshness should characterize compositions dictated under conditions that would seem so depressing, even paralyzing, to the artistic faculties. But Macfarren seems never, from this time, to have abated "one jot of heart or hope, but steered right onward." Among those who loyally and intelligently served him in the capacity of musical amanuenses, may be mentioned the now well-known professor, Miss Clara A. Macirone;[1] that highly promising young

---

[1] For an interesting and touching sketch of Macfarren, and his method of working, see an admirable paper, by this excellent musician, in the "Argosy" for January, 1888.

musician (for some time my own pupil), Frederick Barnes, whose early death was so much deplored ; Miss Oliveria Prescott, who assisted her revered professor with an affection only equalled by its efficiency, and Mr. Windeyer Clark, who was acting in this capacity, faithfully, during the later years of Macfarren's life. When, later on, Macfarren's duties were, so to speak, threefold, having to do with the University of Cambridge, the Royal Academy of Music, and his own productions (or private correspondence), the papers concerning these were separately "pigeon-holed," and, colloquially if not by inscription, playfully labelled respectively, "Cam.," "R. A. M.," and "G. A. M.;" and he would say to young Barnes, on his entry, "Well, I think we will take ' C. A. M.' (or whichever budget he selected) this morning."

"Robin Hood" was reproduced by Pyne and Harrison at Covent Garden in 1861, with Madame Guerrabella, Messrs. Henry Haigh, Santley, Patey, George Honey, in the cast, and Mellon as conductor. The opera was revived in the year 1889 at the Princess's Theatre, under the management of Mr. Turner.

"Freya's Gift, an Allegorical Masque, in honour of the marriage of His Royal Highness the Prince of Wales," was composed by Macfarren, and performed at the Royal English Opera, Covent Garden, March 10th, 1863 ; the words being by John Oxenford. After a short introduction, a Chorus in B flat, "By a heavy mist is the land oppress'd," is sung behind the scenes. This is immediately followed by an entire change of key, the "catch phrase," if it may be so termed, of the termination of the chorus forming the opening of a *Scena* in E major, "Freya the harbinger of bliss is here." After a ballad, "When those you love," *Revels* follow: chorus, "Arouse thee, merrie England"; Hymn—(Danish National Tune) "With shouts of welcome"—Freya interpolating *our* national anthem, and the two melodies being afterwards brought together.

In this same year, Mr. and Mrs. German Reed started a series of performances under the designation of "Opera di Camera;" and for these, Macfarren, being commissioned to write, supplied a charming little work, "Jessy Lea," which was produced in October, and in which Miss Edith Wynne made her first appearance on the lyric stage. So decided was the success of this operetta that another was commissioned for the following year; and "The Soldier's Legacy," *libretto* by John Oxenford, was the result. The scheme does not appear to have proved a success, notwithstanding the merit and favourable reception of these, and works by other composers written for the purpose.

In the year 1863, during the management of the Royal English Opera at Covent Garden by Pyne and Harrison, Macfarren was commissioned by them to compose an opera; and the work produced, February 11th, 1864, was "She Stoops to Conquer," the *libretto* being furnished by Edward Fitzball. The conductor was Alfred Mellon; the cast included the two lessees, Weiss, Corri, and George Perren. This opera, which contains, according to competent judgment, some of Macfarren's most tuneful music, was very successful. As Harrison's vocal powers were, by that time, on the wane, but his acting powers had greatly improved, the principal singing part was assigned to Perren (as Hastings), and the acting part to Harrison (as Marlow), with little sustained music, and that rarely going above D; but this part he represented admirably.

Later, in 1864, when Covent Garden Theatre was in the hands of the English Opera Company, in succession to Pyne and Harrison, a grand opera of Macfarren's, in four acts, " Helvellyn," was produced, the *libretto* being by his almost constant collaborator, John Oxenford. The cast included Mesdames Lemmens-Sherrington and Parepa, Messrs. Henry Haigh and Alberto Lawrence, etc. A very fine orchestra was led by Mr. Carrodus, and conducted by Alfred Mellon. The introductory prelude was termed an " Illustrated Overture," the chorus singing behind the scenes, during its continuance, a maledictory theme, recurring in the opera, " Curse on the head that the evil planned." An important feature was to have been the lime-lighted *tableau* shown in the course of this overture, illustrating the progress of the story. This, for reasons of economy and convenience, was, however, abandoned for a drop-scene, which had in its centre a scenic representation of the murder by fire referred to in the malediction. This opera ran about eighteen or twenty nights.

The next work of the series that we are now considering is "The Lady of the Lake," concerning which Macfarren himself, in the programme of the Glasgow Choral Union, wrote :—

" The cantata of ' The Lady of the Lake ' was composed, at the request of the Glasgow Musical Festival Executive Committee, expressly for performance at the opening of the New Halls in Glasgow. The commission was proposed at the beginning of 1874; much time was spent in the selection of the subject, more in the adaptation of the poem to lyrical purposes, and the composition was completed in

January, 1876, timely for the proposed Festival of that year.

"Oct., 1877.   "G. A. MACFARREN."

The adaptation of the text was the work of Natalia Macfarren; and the published vocal score is " dedicated in friendly remembrance to Thomas Logan Stillie," at whose suggestion the work was undertaken.

On the production of this cantata, a critic wrote:—

"The amount of work which Dr. Macfarren has got through lately is simply amazing. Three oratorios and a cantata, in four years, would not have been thought much of in Handel's time, when the old Halle master could manufacture a grand oratorio in less than a month, and never seemed so happy as when composing—inventing or borrowing his materials as the occasion demanded. But the scores of Handel's oratorios are in a very skeleton condition; and even if we were to accept as a fact that in three weeks or a month the old musician could have filled in the score completely, we have to confront the altered state of the orchestra since then, with the immense importance that now attaches to instrumentation. It is double difficulty, as well as double labour, when every single note has to be dictated—not written in *manu propriâ*—it will be easily seen how the progress of composition is retarded. Hence we consider that, in having brought out three oratorios and a cantata in four years, at the same time attending to his manifold duties in Tenterden Street and at Cambridge University, Dr. Macfarren has achieved a notable feat. Another thing to take into consideration, if excusing circumstances are needed, is, that Dr. Macfarren is now working hard at an age when most men consider themselves entitled to retire from worldly labours, and enjoy in seclusion the short span which mortality permits them upon this sublunary sphere. Your true artist, however, never grows old and never wearies of his task; and never was there truer artist than George Alexander Macfarren."

This extract, though appropriately introduced here, anticipates certain events to be subsequently chronicled.

A little cantata for female voices, with pianoforte accompaniment, "Songs in a Cornfield," the words by Christina Rossetti, performed for the first time in 1868, by Mr. Henry Leslie's Choir; and a cantata, "Outward Bound," the words by John Oxenford, composed for, and performed at the Norwich Festival, 1872, are, with one addition to be mentioned later on, the only works remaining to complete this enumeration of Macfarren's works of this class — operas and cantatas—besides those specified in a previous chapter. The larger cantatas are characterized, as much as the operas, by the dramatic element, and the local colour associated therewith.

It is worthy of record that Macfarren, in a biographical notice of John Barnett, gave his opinion with characteristic generosity and non-jealousy, that " The Mountain Sylph," by that composer, " opened a new era for music in this country "—doubtless meaning, specially, dramatic music. This clever musician has died while these pages have been passing through the press.

CHAPTER X.

Macfarren's Critical Opinions. Articles on Mendelssohn, Mozart, Beethoven's Symphonies, "Ruins
of Athens," "Fidelio," and "Mass in D." Remarks on Pedal-points. Opinions concerning
Haydn, Chopin, Cherubini, Auber. Airs with
Variations. 1849—1854, etc.

DURING the whole of the long period of his pro-
ductivity as a composer, Macfarren was keenly
observant, and, it may truly be added, constantly
studious of all that was passing in the domain of music,
and of the tendencies of thought and feeling therein ;
staunchly conservative of all sound principles ; eagerly
receptive of all that was new and good. He was
"ever learning;" but, unlike those who were reproached for their lack of earnestness, was *always*
"coming to the knowledge of the truth,"—more
truth,—expanding his grasp of the past and present
of the beautiful art which absorbed his attention;
and being possessed of unquestionable literary ability—
although his diction was sometimes involved, and, as
some would judge, disfigured by certain peculiarities
of form and expression—he gave forth the results of
his thinking and learning, from time to time, in
lectures and papers, of great interest, on music and

musical matters from some of which copious extracts have already been made. Notwithstanding the involvement to which reference has been made, there was such unmistakable decision of opinion, the outcome of such clearly reasoned thought and thoroughness of investigation, that even those who were not able to coincide with all his conclusions and pronouncements were unable to entirely evade their force. He was felt to be a power in our midst, doing much towards the shaping and directing of critical thought concerning music, especially among the rising generation of musical students; this thought being, as may reasonably be concluded, not a little tinctured by his special theoretical views.

In January, 1849, when the whole musical world were still mourning the irreparable loss they had sustained by the death of Mendelssohn in November, 1847, a series of articles on that great composer, from Macfarren's pen, appeared in the "Musical World." The opening sentence of the first article, January 20th, somewhat involved, it must be confessed, or, at all events, long-drawn, may be given entire :—

"FELIX MENDELSSOHN BARTHOLDY may justly be regarded as one of those very few among mankind whose genius at once separates them from, by its exalting them above the world around them, and unites them to, by its sympathizing with, that world which it extends from the limited circle of private personal knowledge to the boundless inclusion of· all educated men, in all places and in all time; as one of those men, whose intellectual superiority, while it distinguishes them from the narrow sphere of their own social connections, identifies them with that broad universe of all human intelligence which ever and everywhere acknowledges the impersonal presence of a master mind, in the influence it produces."

After alluding to the then recent death of the great Master, he proceeds :—

" We own in him the true associate of Bach, Handel, Haydn, Mozart, and Beethoven. His claims to this eminence lie in the purely classical character of all his writing, by which is to be understood not merely cold correctness, but irresistible beauty in the highest style of musical expression ; and in the striking originality that so obviously manifests itself in all his works as to give them an individuality which, it is not too much to say, is not to be found in the music of any of the great composers with whose names he is here classed, and which, devoid of mannerism, can hardly be attributed to the collected works of any other musician."

This *dictum* is somewhat startling, especially in these later days when it is the fashion to decry Mendelssohn ; and, moreover, considering that even those who entertain the highest estimation of his works hardly care to deny that the individuality is not wholly unmarked by mannerism. Macfarren admits that—

" this assertion is so strong, and includes so much beyond the immediate subject of the present remarks, that it may require some explanation to justify it; and as this individuality forms a most important characteristic of Mendelssohn's genius, it may not be superfluous to enter somewhat at length into its discussion. Let it, then, be first understood what is here meant by originality in music. This will be best proved by a negative: namely, that a composer is by no means to be charged with a want of originality who may have written a phrase that is more or less like, or even identical with, some phrase that has been written by another. Of such accidental coincidences examples are innumerable in the works of the most esteemed masters."

Many examples are adduced from various composers.

" Style may be said to consist rather in general characteristics than in particular ideas ; in a composer's habits of thought, and the forms of construction and elaboration in which such thought is developed, than in any peculiar, perhaps exceptional, passage. It is the unlikeness of the style of an author to any archetype that constitutes his originality, and not the resemblance of any one or more of his phrases, however originally treated, to some phrase previously known, that constitutes his want of it. There may not exist a parallel passage in the works of two authors ; and yet what is seen to constitute the style of both may be so similar as to deprive him who wrote second of a claim to originality, at least to such originality as will distinguish his music from all that preceded it. Thus we find the colossal masses of elaboration, in which the genius of Bach declares itself to the wondering student of the present day, are composed in the form, and made up of the passages which were conventional in his time. The same thing is noticeable in the works of Handel. . . . In Haydn, again, we find the phraseology of his age . . . by degrees he modified his form, until in his later quartets and symphonies he produced what the adoption of all his great successors, and the opinion of all the world, prove to be the perfect model of instrumental composition, which, as there will always be the example, not only of his own orchestral and chamber works, but also of those no less imperishable of Mozart, Beethoven, Spohr, and Mendelssohn, cannot but remain, like the division into five acts, and the other accepted rules of construction in dramatic poetry, the approved form and classical model of instrumental music. Mozart, with all his excelling beauty, walked but in the footsteps of Haydn ; he may indeed be said to have overtaken his illustrious friend, who was both his predecessor and his follower ; for though Haydn founded the form of instrumental composition that is now universally recognized as the classical, and so set Mozart the great example, he himself wrote all his best works after Mozart had shown him of what extreme beauty that form was capable. . . . Beethoven . . . so completely adopted the style of Mozart, that his compositions for the first third of his career may be mistaken for productions of that great original. . . . In what critics designate the second and third periods of the expansion of Beethoven's genius, there is a striking breaking away from this style of his predecessors and of his early self. . . . After enlarging so much upon the want of originality, in a certain sense, of these great masters—a proposition offered, however, with the most enthusiastic admiration for the genius of each, and the most unqualified delight, in the creations of all—it is necessary, for the entire explanation of what is meant by the rare characteristic here attributed to Mendelssohn, to adduce some instances of musical composers that have also possessed it. Before all, then, must be mentioned Purcell, who, as being the first to break through the purely scholastic trammels of the ancient diatonic school, to enter upon the exhaustless field of the beautiful that lies open to the modern musician in the inexhaustible resources of chromatic harmony, and as the first to apply musical sounds to the poetical expression of words, and to the delineation of the wildest and the gentlest of the passions, is to be considered the most truly original composer the world has known. It must be granted, indeed, that his speculations, as they must be esteemed, in the previously unattempted combinations of chromatic harmony, are occasionally failures, producing effects equally harsh, unsatisfactory, and inexplicable; and that his expression sometimes degenerates into word-painting; but with all the experience that has intervened, the same things are to be remarked in the most approved writers that have succeeded him; and that his genius was not always at its happiest, detracts not from the infinite honour that is due to him for the many exquisite beauties he has left us, and for the incalculable services he rendered to his art by the new direction he gave to its cultivation. Let us next instance Weber, whose peculiarity of phraseology, singular application of certain harmonies, and novel conduct of his dramatic, pieces, decidedly constitute a style—one that cannot be imitated (since all who have attempted its

adoption have fallen into the most vapid musical bathos),
and one that was in no respect anticipated. Most fascinating has proved this Weberish style, no less to the
public than to the host of composers who have failed in
the attempt to write in it; but, in spite of its irresistible
charms, an investigation of all its peculiarities could lead
only to the conclusion, that however teeming with originality, it is greatly wanting in what may purely be termed
classicality.

"This long digression is important to the subject, insomuch as it goes to explain the application of a term which
is meant to convey the chief idea of Mendelssohn's excellence, and as it may serve to illustrate the position that
this composer takes in relation to those who have preceded him."

The interest of these remarks fully condones the
length of the "digression." But the writer proceeds
to expatiate upon the originality of Mendelssohn, as
evinced (*a*) in his phraseology; (*b*) his "frequent introduction of the combinations, or, more particularly,
the progressions, of Bach and his era, as the basis and
accompaniment of his own original phraseology, or of
less individual modern passages"—which characteristic
might by some be thought rather to resemble the
use made of existing idioms attributed to other writers
in the earlier part of the paper; and (*c*)—

"More striking in itself, and far more important to the
art, is his resolution of certain chromatic discords upon a
principle occasionally hinted at in the middle and later
works of Beethoven, but never carried to such an extent
as it is by Mendelssohn in his earlier works; such, for
instance, as the chord of the minor ninth on the tonic to
the chord of the seventh on the dominant, with the progressions of the intervals of the seventh and ninth of the
first chord to the third and fifth of the second, and many
others which it would be here tedious to describe. There

is the more merit in these innovations—discoveries they would be better named—on account of their being in direct violation of all pre-existing rules of harmony; and they evince the greatness of his genius as a philosopher no less than as a musician, by showing him capable of penetrating, through the obscurity and prejudice of the schools, to the truth of nature, and by his most successful practice to lay the foundation of a theory, which in intelligence, in usefulness, in comprehension, and in what constitutes true philosophy, surpasses all that had ever before been advanced in musical and (so far as connected with music) acoustical science—a theory which translates the province of music from art to nature, and so dignifies its investigation, in the scale of human study and research, from the learning by rote of the arbitrary trammels of bygone times and schools, to the examination and comprehension of a subject, the principles of which are as deeply rooted as those of perspective or light itself."

It need hardly be said that Macfarren has here seized an opportunity to vaunt the "Day theory." Mendelssohn's " great originality of construction " is the next characteristic dealt with, which—

"while he preserves the general outline, or certainly its chief features, to which . . . allusion has already been made, manifests itself in the novelty of detail, with which this classical outline is filled up."

The originality of his *scherzi*, of his poetical overtures, of his oratorios, "in the generally more dramatic character they possess than the previous works of that class," etc., are then enlarged upon. Also, the condensation of the conventional form, in his Concertos. And the " Midsummer Night's Dream " overture is characterized as "an example of originality " which " must always be a perfect marvel of the human mind."

"A careful examination of all its features, and a comparison of them with all that had previously existed in the writings of other composers, must establish the conviction that there is more that is new in this one work than in any other one that has ever been produced."

This is dilated upon, with reference to—

"idea, character, phrase, harmony, construction, instrumentation, and every particular of outline and detail for which his style is remarkable."

It is well to remember that these opinions were formed when the novelty and originality were truly fresh, before the style had become familiar, and before that familiarity had induced depreciation by shallow critics.   Mendelssohn's works are afterwards grouped and characterized; and, in conclusion, it is admitted that—

"his melodies are often more fragmentary than continuous—that his compositions abound more in detached, though beautiful, phrases, than in streaming, unbroken, and unquestionable tune; and it is no less true that he is generally less successful in the composition of slow movements than in those of a more exciting and animated character; but, true as are both these propositions, there are so many brilliant exceptions to each as to make it a matter of question with his enthusiastic admirers whether the peculiarities referred to, were not points of design with him, rather than evidence of inability to avoid them."

I remember that when the Purcell Society was formed, for the purpose of issuing a complete edition of that master's works, Macfarren said to me, "You must expect to find in them many things quite opposed to all our present views of harmony."

Macfarren was no mere impressionist: the verdicts

that he pronounced were opinions thought out, and the result of conviction. It was no Mendelssohn "fever," such as was epidemic in musical circles during the few years succeeding the great man's death, that prompted him to write as he did in this article, and in others later on. In 1851, December 6th, he wrote an interesting review of Mendelssohn's pianoforte duet, "Allegro Brillante." In the "Musical World," August 28th, 1852, he wrote a highly appreciative article on the then just published fragment of "Lorely," Mendelssohn's projected opera. In the same periodical, October 23rd of the same year, he also wrote on the fragments from "Christus." His analysis, October 9th, of the "Italian Symphony" has already been referred to (page 81). In January, 1853, appeared in the same periodical an earnest appeal, signed by him, to the trustees of Mendelssohn's unpublished works, urging their immediate publication. On April 30th appeared an analysis of Mendelssohn's posthumous Quartet in F minor: enthusiastic, but reasoned out. In that same periodical, in January, 1854, as has been already recorded in Chapter VIII., he wrote elaborately on the music to "Œdipus in Colonos"; and, again, a brief review of one book of the "Songs without Words," December 16th of the same year. A much later article on Mendelssohn's Prelude and Fugue in F minor will be noticed in another connection. An analysis of "St. Paul" proceeded from Macfarren's pen, and appeared in the "Musical World," July 30th and following numbers; and, in the "Musical Times," January, 1873, an article entitled "St. Paul at St. Paul's," to which, also, reference will be made later on.

The effect upon many of the glitter, or highly-wrought effectiveness—shall the term "many-notedness" be used?—and the more varied harmonies and demonstrativeness of a certain kind—one must avoid the term "sensationalism"—of modern music, especially from Mendelssohn till the present time, expressing as it does that indefinable sentiment which goes by the name of "the spirit of the age," is to cast into the shade, as puerile, effete, "periwiggish," the works of the older masters, such as Haydn and Mozart. There was, during the early years of Macfarren's career, a Spohr "craze" among the younger musicians, which, in its turn, made way for a Mendelssohn craze; which, again, gave place to a Schumann craze; and so on. Young musicians cannot resist the fascinations of novelty; nor need they, if they will only separate accidents from essentials, and recognize the true and beautiful in its old as well as in its newer garb. But this requires balance of mind, thoughtful discrimination, possessed by few in the student-stage of their career. Even Macfarren, while under Cipriani Potter's care, said to him, "Don't you think, Sir, that Mozart is sometimes a little puerile?" But then he had that discriminating balance of mind which soon righted him; and, as time went on, his practical recantation was entire, and, in his later days particularly, he never tired of expatiating upon Mozart's greatness. But it was not only in his later days; in the very same year, 1849, in which the enthusiastic articles upon his friend Mendelssohn appeared, he also wrote, during the month of February, a series of articles upon Mozart and his works. It may be opportune and interesting to quote the following remarks concerning certain neglected masterpieces :—

" To Mozart's Concertos for the pianoforte too high praise cannot be awarded. They were an immense advance upon all that had been written or were written about the same period ; and the best of them, for they are very numerous, and of various degrees of merit, rank with the noblest works of the class that have been since produced. . . . The Concerto in D minor of Mozart, and that in C major, have never been surpassed for symmetry of design and beauty of phraseology ; they abound also in most effective combinations of the orchestra with the principal instrument ; but this merit, it must be admitted, has been greatly extended in some more recent compositions of the same class, since the resources of the orchestra, from the increased excellence of the performers, have been more at the command of the composer ; still, though less frequent, Mozart's mixture of the pianoforte with the orchestra is, in many instances, in these concertos, not less beautiful and ingenious than the happiest results of modern research.

" The pianist must, however, bear in mind one curious, it may be justly said unfortunate, evidence of the custom of the time in which they were written ; viz., that the pianoforte part, as handed down to us, presents a mere skeleton of the composer's intentions, to be filled up throughout, according to the discretion and ability of the performer, leaving to him the opportunity of the cadence for the greatest display of his inventive ingenuity and executive agility.   Unhappily for the worthy rendering of these great works before a modern audience, some excellent players of our time have little discretion, and some less ability, to dilate upon and embody the outline which such music presents ; it must, therefore, be always matter of regret in reference to these works—as to the songs and choruses of Handel and his contemporaries, of which the organ or cembalo part was always left to the improvisation of the accompanist—that the author did not make a definite record of the effects and passages he intended.   Certainly, when Mozart himself played these concertos, it must have been a matter of great interest to compare the different readings of the same work which he would give at different performances."[1]

Macfarren might well have included the C *minor* Concerto of Mozart in his special mention. Would that, by any means, the attention of pianists might be drawn to all these beautiful works!

He remarked to me once how much he disliked the conventional "cut" of a concerto on, for instance, the plan of Hummel, who was Mozart's pupil; in which, at certain understood places, one always felt inclined to say, "Now for the Solo!" The feeling is one which all who have listened to many compositions of that class and period will readily recognize. Those who have watched the progress of matters are aware that this form has become pretty well obsolete; especially since Mendelssohn compressed the concerto first-movement. Concertos of the old type—three solos in the first movement, with introductory and intervening *tuttis*—are not now written. Weber, however, seems to have initiated the reform by his "Concert-Stück."

Of "Idomeneo," Macfarren remarks:—

"This Opera is interesting in the history of the art as being the earliest example of what may be esteemed the modern school of instrumentation, distinguished from that which preceded it by the general difference in the relative treatment of the wind and stringed instruments—employing the former, not merely to contrast or to strengthen the latter, but to relieve, and colour, and qualify their effect, by occasionally sustaining the harmony while they move

[1] Mozart never played these concertos twice alike. This fact I had, and so had Macfarren, from our teacher, Cipriani Potter, on the authority of Attwood, who was Mozart's pupil.—H. C. B.

in some figure or passage, and to produce all the varieties which they who are accustomed to hear and analyze orchestral combinations will understand better from their own recollection than from any verbal description, and which they who are not so accustomed will not be likely to understand from any description whatever.

"It must be granted that similar effects of orchestration are to be occasionally found in the works of earlier masters —as in the chorus, ' He sent a thick darkness,' in Handel's ' Israel in Egypt ; ' in the second part of the song, ' Revenge, Timotheus cries,' in the ' Alexander's Feast' of the same composer ; in the chorus of Furies with Orestes in prison, and in the grand declamatory scene in which Orestes adjures Pylades to leave him to the sacrifice, in the ' Iphigenie en Tauride' of Gluck ; and in many other isolated instances which it would be superfluous here to adduce. Enough has been cited to prove that Mozart did not originate what everyone must allow he systematized and brought to a perfection, which, however it may be varied, all the ingenuity and research of modern times cannot surpass."

After remarks upon "Die Entführung aus dem Serail " and "Le Nozze di Figaro," there follows a lengthy analysis of " Don Giovanni," " the opera which is received by all the world as the greatest production of the lyric stage, the work which gives the brightest lustre to its author's crown of glory." " Cosi fan Tutte," "La Clemenza di Tito," and "Die Zauberflöte " are passed in rapid review ; and " the chief characteristics of Mozart's style " are thus enumerated :—

"First, his frequent peculiarity of rhythm, a trait more observable in his music than in that of any other composer, and which makes his metre—often unusual, though always quite regular—unquestionably his own ;[1] second, the particular form of his melodic phrases, and the infinite

---

[1] See, however, the closing remarks of Chapter IV.

continuousness of his melodies; third, his familiar fluency in all the resources of contrapuntal contrivance; fourth, his wonderful symmetry and perfection of construction, which, cultivated in his instrumental works, has had the most valuable and manifest influence upon his vocal compositions, even in situations where the dramatic action would have seduced other composers into the fantasia style of writing, and which makes every movement he has written a model for the musical student; and, last, the wonderful truthfulness of his dramatic delineations."

The conclusion which Macfarren thinks justified by the summary is " that the greatest musician who has delighted and enriched the world is WOLFGANG AMADEUS MOZART."

Concerning this enthusiasm for Mozart, one of his esteemed amanuenses writes :—

" Mozart was his idol in a musical way. Some friend sent him a postcard, begging him to say whether of the two, Mozart or Beethoven, he thought the greater composer. 'Mozart,' he wrote, without the slightest hesitation —saying afterwards to me : ' Beethoven was sometimes weak, Mozart never.' You know how chary he was of admitting a doubtful passage to be good, *because so and so wrote it.* Bach, Handel, all were admitted to be human and liable to error—or, perhaps it was ' the strong feeling for the individual parts, in the older writers, made them overlook the ill effect of the combination ; ' perhaps it was ' we love his music, notwithstanding the ill effect of some passages, but that does not make us like what is not good.' ' Follow his good example, but not his bad.' But when Mozart was in question it was another thing. I remember a pair of 4ths from the bass in a symphony coming to notice. ' I have always bid you guard against the ill effect of such, but when I come across it here, I frankly must confess I like it—Mozart must have known how to introduce it.' The rugged nature would bend before no man but Mozart, and to him he gave implicit trust."

But let no one think that this high estimation of Mozart implied any depreciation of other composers. Although he admitted that "Beethoven was sometimes weak"—and who shall gainsay it ?—although, perhaps, it will not be so general to add, " Mozart—never ! "—yet no one could hold Beethoven in higher *absolute* estimation than Macfarren, though the *comparative* estimate might be questioned ; especially by the less thoughtful, who do not consider the historical or chronological bearings of the matter, and the indebtedness of the later to the earlier composer, as affecting the question of orig'inality. In the analytical programme of the Philharmonic Society's Concert, July 11th, 1870, "in honour of " the centenary of Beethoven's birth, Macfarren wrote :—

" Who shall say how much of the vast changes in the inward constitution and outward acceptance of musical art, which have been wrought within this period [of a hundred years], are due to the creations and influence of his wonderful genius ! "

And, in the comments upon the first Symphony, with which the concert opened, he wrote :—

" The present work shows the composer still under the influence of Mozart, who was nine years dead, and of Haydn, who was living and writing; but he was influenced as a plant is by the sunshine, to display its own virtues rather than to mirror the light which quickens them. His strength was his own, the example of those two earlier maturities was its nourishment. The style is masterly in its freedom and clearness, in breadth of thought and boldness of statement; and the orchestration proves a knowledge of the capabilities and characters of instruments, and a judgment in their combination, that could only result from strong intuition directed by careful observance,

in one who had Beethoven's small experience—two Concertos are the only pieces for the orchestra he had then
[1800] written."

In the same year, 1849, as that in which the articles
on Mendelssohn and those on Mozart appeared, Macfarren also commenced a series on Beethoven's Symphonies. And here it may be remarked that, so far
as this country was concerned, he was, so to speak,
first in the field in this analytical work. There were
no models on which to construct such analyses, nor
did he need any. They are the products of his own
thoughtful and cultured appreciativeness, informed
by ample theoretical knowledge, and expressed with
great felicity of language, and often aptness of metaphor. As an illustration of his discrimination and
courage in the expression of his critical opinions,
take the following concerning the *Adagio* of the
fourth Symphony :—

" This *Adagio* is in the form of a two-part movement;
but instead of the free fantasia, consisting in the working
of the principal subjects, such as usually opens the Second
Part of a movement thus constructed, we have an immediate return to the chief subject in the original key ; and,
after this, a short digression, previous to the recapitulation
of the rest of the First Part."

After an interesting analysis of the movement up to
the end of the First Part, he proceeds :—

" The dominant 7th on B flat brings us at once back
to the original key, and thus, introduced by the one bar
that always precedes it, we have an immediate return to
the subject. The original beautiful melody is this time
no less beautifully varied ; and here is one of the very,
very rare instances in all music where the variation of a

melody is indeed an embellishment ; such truly is this, every excellence of the original being now excelled, the colouring of the whole heightened, intensified, but not exaggerated. We now come to the digression to which I have alluded, as forming so important a feature in the plan of the movement. Our introductory bar, instead of bringing in a repetition of the subject with varied instrumentation, introduces a portion only of the subject for the whole orchestra, in the key of E flat minor.   There is something, to me, extremely unsatisfactory in this passage, as our great author has given it to us ; the alternate tonic and dominant pedal assigned to the horns, trumpets, and drums, identifies the whole with the key of E flat minor, while the harmony assigned to the rest of the orchestra is, after the first chord, unquestionably in the key of G flat major, and we have thus an effect of false relation, that, to my sense, is the remotest from beautiful."

The theoretical student will perceive that the objection here urged lies against the "arbitrary" minor scale over the two pedal notes.   Macfarren follows up his particular animadversion by the enunciation of a general principle ; respecting which, it is only fair to state that it has been objected to by some musicians *since* his pronouncement :—

"There is one law with respect to pedals that is universally received, in so far as no theorist has ever disputed it and no composer of recognized merit has ever disregarded it ; this is, that the pedal note must be either the tonic or the dominant of whatever key may prevail at the time such pedal is employed. It is here confidently stated that no eminent composer has ever disregarded this law, because, although there may perhaps be found . . . instances of its partial violation, in all such cases, . . . though there may occur harmonies that are foreign to the key, and therefore harsh from their inaccordance with the pedal note, such pedal note has always that relationship to what precedes or follows the passage as must make it either the tonic or the dominant of the key that principally prevails. This may well be coupled with another important rule in music, namely, that the test of whether a chromatic harmony belong to any particular key is the possibility of its being taken upon a pedal note which is either the tonic or the dominant of such key, to make which test unequivocally satisfactory, it is necessary to play the root of the chromatic chord below the pedal note, which can be borne with any combination, chromatic or diatonic, that is proper to the key of the said pedal, but which is intolerable with any chord that is not deducible from and assignable to such tonic. I know of but one exception to this general principle, which is that, upon a dominant pedal, the fundamental chromatic harmonies derivable from the major sixth of the key can be employed, provided such be followed by the common chord of the second of the scale : . . . the grounds of this single exception are, I think, wholly satisfactory, and, rather than otherwise, corroborative of the principle, if not of the law."

Macfarren " would often quote Beethoven's habit to write what came into his mind, and then cut out what was not wanted ": a process of excision and self-discipline to which student-composers are often sub-jected by judicious teachers; and maturer composers not infrequently determine on similar " cutting." Macfarren was no exception with himself and with his pupils. In some cases, however, he was more con-demnatory still : banning a whole work, even by a great man. Thus, in the " Musical World," Novem-ber 13th and 20th, 1852, appeared two articles by him on Beethoven's music to the drama or masque, " The

Ruins of Athens," then just issued with an English version for the first time. He pronounces " tho merit of the music " to be " very unequal."

" There are some pieces in the work that add a radiance to the brightest glory with which the immortal composer is crowned ; there are others that bear no indication of the hand of Beethoven, but only his name on the title page. . . . It is little to be wondered at that our Philharmonic Society [as previously related in the article] esteemed the Overture unworthy the name of Beethoven, and therefore unavailable for performance at their concerts, since the most impartial examination of the composition must always lead to a confirmation of this decision. . . . It is, on the other hand, matter of very considerable marvel that Beethoven, who was most jealous of his reputation, should at three different periods have submitted so weak a production to the public. The inequality of the works of a great master is the fact that proves him to be such, or at least, that distinguishes what, for want of another term, must still be called by the conventional name of divine inspiration from what we know to be mere mechanical facility. The satisfaction of an author with his work at the period of its composition, when his imagination is still glowing with the ardour of intention, which is at the time impossible to distinguish from the fervour of the creative power, is a circumstance so natural that there can scarcely exist one who has written, much or little, but must have proved it in his proper experience. . . . Hence it is quite accountable that Beethoven should have given this over-ture out for performance on the occasion for which it was composed. . . . The intoxication of mental procreation is, however, but an ephemeral rapture, and the glow of our whole being that illuminates the birth of a new idea, is itself extinguished in the moment of our giving such idea to the world, then enthusiasm, the butterfly, that has sprung from study, the chrysalis, flies into the flame of which her bright colours and her flickering wings are the incarnation, the mind renews itself, and judgment, the worm, rises from the ashes of the faded fantasy to toil, and travail, and foredo the futile fabrications whereof its parent was the vain glory. Hence, we must always wonder that Beethoven, whose tempered judgment should have been profound as his excited genius was brilliant, should on reviewing his overture after the lapse of years, have so little seen that it was so little worth as to have again sent it forth into the world, and again hazarded his reputation, and so have abrogated his self-respect, upon its merits. Beethoven, than whom no one can have been more scrupulously jealous of the dignity of art, and of his own true rank as an artist."

Proceeding with the other pieces, Macfarren says of the opening " very beautiful duet," that it—

" Gives scope for the warmest, the sincerest expressions of unqualified admiration. . . . Every phrase of this exquisite little movement calls forth an exclamation of delight."

Of the Chorus of Dervishes :—

" Music presents nothing more strikingly characteristic than the uncouth melody that marks this truly extraordinary composition, and even this is more powerfully coloured by the perfectly original and quite individual accompaniment that is maintained throughout."

The other movements are then commented on : the Turkish March, " vividly picturesque and truly dramatic : "—

" A technical point that will always be prominent in its effect is the anticipation of the key of B flat, with the full force of the orchestra, at each recurrence to the subject after the momentary digression to G major ; and whoever hears the movement with attention, or examines it with care, will find still much more matter to repay his pains."

The Triumphal March and Chorus, " Twine ye a

Garland," " becomes mouthy, inflated, and bathetic,"
because :—

"Here we pass from the true poetry of life to the bombast of allegory. . . . The Chorus, 'Susceptible Hearts,'
is a most lovely stream of song. . . . The remaining
pieces . . . . carry out the feeling, or if you will, the want
of it, that is embodied in the overture and the opening
chorus. . . . Such is the 'Ruins of Athens,' a work
written to be ephemeral, but presenting, (besides those
four pieces, . . . which will live so long as the name of
Beethoven is known,) this lasting moral to the world,
namely, that no greatness is immaculate, since even Beethoven, at a period when his imagination was in the exercise
of its utmost vigour, was capable of the production of such
music, as, but for his name, would now be utterly unworthy of the pains that may be spent in censuring it."

Macfarren also wrote an exhautive series of articles
on " Fidelio," in the " Musical World," May 24th,
et seq., 1851, which, in substance, formed the Preface
to an edition of that Opera. Also, an analysis of
Beethoven's Mass in D, for the Sacred Harmonic
Society, in 1854.

It would hardly be fair to say that Macfarren depreciated " Papa " Haydn; but he often referred to
the obligations of the patriarch to Mozart, whom he
both preceded and outlived. Perhaps the following
extract from the analytical programme of the Sixth
Concert of the Quartet Association, June 30th,
1852, will exhibit his views with regard to the old
Master :—

"Somewhat too much credit is given to Haydn for
having founded the form of composition which universally
prevails in the classical style of music, and until the innovations of the ultra-modern school, was adopted also in the

lighter class of writing. The form to which I allude, consisting, namely, of a first part that comprises a leading
idea in one key, and a secondary idea in the fifth or some
other close relative of such key, and a second part that
comprises the development of the ideas already announced,
and the recapitulation of the first part with the second
idea now in the original key of the movement. This form,
I say, is to be traced in many of the instrumental compositions of Bach, and of Handel, and of Scarlatti, and
other writers of the same epoch, and it is therefore
obviously not to be ascribed to Haydn as its originator.
The chief quality of this great master that entitles him to
be reverenced as the Father of the Symphony, is his
employment of a more definite, because more rhythmical,
style of melody to fill up this form, than appears in the
works of earlier writers, and giving to it thus an interest
and indeed an expression that it never before possessed.
Among the first Quartets of Haydn there are several
entire compositions in which this form does not appear,
and we find only a large number of small movements,
Minuets, and other dances, and the like, containing some
graceful thoughts, it is true, but written in the most
puerile style of simplicity. We are to observe from this,
that our composer was at the commencement of his career,
behind the age in which he wrote, and that gradually, as
his powers developed themselves, and as probably, the executants and the audience for whom he wrote, advanced
in capacity and comprehension, his style assumed more
dignity, his ideas more importance, and his character as a
musician, that stamp which no change of fashion can
efface. It was then that Haydn reduced the Symphony (I
speak of the class of composition under the general title of
the most important work that belongs to it) to its present
generally average complement of four movements, from
which complement there are very many exceptions, in a
few cases to increase, and more frequently to diminish it,
but which is established as affording scope to the composer for the necessary and sufficient variety of ideas and
treatment. It appears that the style of Haydn was greatly
modified by the stimulant, if not the genius of Mozart;
since his best works, and most especially his best instru-

mental works, were produced after that most brilliant
glory had dawned and even set upon the earth, for it will
be remembered that, though following in the footsteps of
Haydn as a composer, Mozart preceded him to the grave
by many years, having in the course of his brief career
produced those masterpieces which, as they have never
yet been equalled, we may fairly presume, are not likely to
be surpassed. Hence, then, though in the works of Haydn
we see the Symphony in all its various stages of development (saving only some especial modifications that Beethoven and later writers have introduced) he neither originated it, nor perfected it to that degree which it attained
in his own time ; and yet the lasting thanks of the world
of art are due to him, for having produced so many works
of real interest in this class, as to make it the true standard
of classical composition, and the consequent subject of
emulation to all who follow."

These remarks may supplement those above quoted
earlier in the chapter, p. 211.

Macfarren, like some other musicians who, possessing sound knowledge, and definite theoretical principles, rightly bring these to bear upon their judgments concerning music, and are therefore credited
with pedantic prejudice, and dry insensibility to
natural charm and spontaneous freshness, if it bear
not the test of grammatical examination, was nevertheless as susceptible of impression by genuinely inspired, if not soundly constructed music, as those who
vaunt their unprejudiced openness to such influence.
He has, indeed, said to me, that it were well if much,
if not all, that Chopin wrote, had never been produced. He then spoke as a theorist, with due solicitude for the healthy current of thought and feeling
among the younger generation of musicians. But
yet, concerning the same composer, he has written :—

"With no command of the principles of construction, he made his lengthened pieces incoherent, and even his lightest productions give occasion to question the soundness of his grammatical knowledge. The singular beauty, and the constant individuality of his ideas, however; his exquisite feeling for harmonic combination and progression, which led to his habitual employment of resources most rarely used by others; his unreserved application of exceptional forms of passing-notes, and his perfect and peculiar gracefulness of phraseology—give a charm to his music which is irresistibly fascinating. His mazurkas are unique in the range of musical composition, and they are as full of character, national colouring, sentiment, humour, and technical peculiarity, as they are insusceptible of imitation."

On the other hand, of a widely different composer, most rigid in style, he wrote:—

"Clementi was a master of all the resources of counterpoint, with a complete grasp of the powers of modern harmony; and, besides the depth of character resulting from this knowledge, his music is distinguished by energy, fire, and intense passion; tenderness and melodious grace, however, the qualities one would most expect in the writings for his instrument, of an artist whose playing was especially signalized by these points of style, are rarely to be found in his compositions."

Years after the above was written, Macfarren said to me: "There is one composer I cannot stand—that is Clementi: queer counterpoint, awkward modulation, etc.," making exception in favour of the Sonata in B minor, however—which, Gattie once (previously) told me, Macfarren considered one of the finest Sonatas ever written. Another expression of his opinion concerning Clementi has been quoted, p. 65.

Of Cherubini he wrote in laudatory terms, in the "Imperial Dictionary of Biography" (from which the

last two extracts are taken) ; as, for instance, in the
following :—

"' Les Deux Journées ':—though forgotten in France,
this beautiful opera is still, like several others of its author,
a standard work at the principal German theatres, where,
under the name of 'Der Wasserträger,' it ranks high in
popular esteem and critical approval. In England, little
is known of it besides the overture; but this, by the power
of its ideas, their admirable development, the peculiarity of
its form and the vigour and brilliancy of its orchestration,
gives Cherubini a foremost rank among musicians, in the
estimation of all who set the highest value on the greatest
order of artistic productions."

Macfarren's breadth of appreciative power may be
illustrated by yet another critical estimate concerning
a composer with whom it might have been supposed
that one so severe, even (as some thought) to pedantry,
would have little sympathy. Speaking of Auber's
" La Muette de Portici," which Macfarren characterizes as " his unquestionable masterpiece," which
" met with the brilliant success it eminently merits,"
he goes on to say :—

" Critics have in vain sought to detract from the credit
of this success, by ascribing it to the dramatic interest of
the *libretto*, and to the sympathy with the story of the
political feeling of the time; but the eminently dramatic
music, which certainly could only have been written to
illustrate powerful dramatic situations, gives vitality to
these situations, such as no form of words could impart;
and the revolutionary spirit of the time could neither have
made a bad opera successful, nor maintained the entire
work upon the stage of every country, and its countless
melodies in universal popularity all over the world, for all
these years after the political agitation that was then
ripening had come to its crisis, subsided, and been followed

by another, still more violent, which also now belongs to the past."

But, later on, the discriminating critic thus proceeds :—

"Auber, with all his success and with all his merit, cannot be classed as a great musician, which is because of a want of profundity in all his works that must result from his temperament as a man, not from his defective qualification as an artist. His genius is especially dramatic, and it is in the most exciting situations, . . . that it asserts itself to the best advantage; but he has also an infinite power of vivacity, as is amply proved in 'Fra Diavolo,' 'Le Domino Noir,' and many other of his comic operas. His melodies, of which he has produced more than perhaps any composer that ever existed, are irresistibly striking, essentially individual, piquant, pretty, tender, but rarely, if ever, pathetic, and never grand; the feeling they embody is intense, but never deep. His habit of making repeated rhythmical closes, instead of giving continuous development to an idea, imparts an air of triviality to his longer pieces, that nothing but their ceaseless fluency and constant animation could counterbalance. His instrumentation, the colouring of music, is perhaps that branch of the art in which he is most consummately a master; brilliant, sparkling, rich, and clear to transparency; his method of treating the orchestra alone is sufficient to make him a valuable study."

Macfarren had little liking for "Variations" on a Theme. He was, of course, quite sensible and appreciative of the ingenuity, contrapuntal resource, and fancy, which might be, and often are, evinced in their construction; and spoke to me of the attractiveness of Haydn's "Variations" in F minor, and Schubert's "Impromptu" in B flat, which, as musicians know, is simply an air with variations. But he said to me that,

while he could understand the interest to a composer
of writing variations, and to a performer of playing
them, it was, to him, so tiresome to know that, all
along, the same progressions, and the same closes, at
the same places, were always to be expected. These
remarks were made to me during performances of the
two pieces above-mentioned. I venture to think that
the attractiveness of that by Haydn lies in the *naïve*
beauty of the Theme; and that the "Impromptu" by
Schubert would hardly have been selected by Macfarren as a specially notable specimen of variation
writing, though he seemed to rate it more highly than
I did.   Macfarren himself wrote a set of "Variations" on a Dutch melody; being the number entitled
"Holland," in a series of Pianoforte pieces bearing
the general title "Le Voyageur," which were published by Duff and Hodgson.   But this set of variations was doubtless written to order, for a consideration;
not from artistic promptings.

    This series of quotations will help to give a compre-
hensive view of Macfarren's principles and methods of
judgment, and susceptibility of impression, which are
further illustrated in other contexts.   It may be left
to the reader to estimate the soundness or otherwise
of an opinion once expressed in my hearing by one
who knew him well:—" Macfarren is an uncommonly
bad judge of music !"

CHAPTER XI.

MACFARREN AS A LECTURER. LECTURES ON SONATA
STRUCTURE, THE LYRICAL DRAMA, SACRED AND SECULAR
ART, AND CHURCH MUSIC. PAPERS ON RECITATIVE,
CHURCH OF ENGLAND MUSIC, GREGORIANISM, ORATORIO
IN CHURCH, ROSSINI'S MASS, MOZART'S REQUIEM,
WAGNER, ORGAN, PITCH. COMPOSITIONS: OVERTURE
TO "DON CARLOS," FESTIVAL OVERTURE, SYMPHONIES
IN D MAJOR AND E MINOR, FLUTE CONCERTO, VIOLIN
CONCERTO, ORGAN WORKS, CHURCH MUSIC, SONATAS
FOR PIANOFORTE, AND PIANOFORTE AND VIOLIN, CON-
CERTINA, ETC. 1854—1879.

MUCH allusion has been made to Macfarren's
lectures. He became prominent as a lecturer
and public speaker during the last twenty-five years
of his life. His first lecture, or one of the first given
by him, was delivered to the students of the Royal
Academy of Music, about the year 1860, during the
Principalship of Charles Lucas, who invited several
professors of the institution to lecture on subjects
germane to the branches of musical study which they
had in charge: one on the Violin being delivered by
Mr. H. G. Blagrove, one on Singing by Mr. F. R.
Cox, another on Notation by Mr. H. C. Lunn, one on
Harmonics by Mr. Lucas. Macfarren's was on the
Structure of a Sonata, though that may not have

been its precise title.   The substance of it doubtless
appears in the little *brochure* on that subject published
by Messrs. Rudall, Rose, and Carte ; originally as an
appendix to a sonata by him for flute and pianoforte,
in No. 5 of the " Journal of the London Society of
Amateur Flute Players."

At about the same period, when Macfarren was on
a visit at Radley College, together with his brother,
Mr. Walter Macfarren, the suggestion was made that
it would be very interesting if he would address the
students ; and he at once assented, and with little premeditation delivered an analytical lecture to the
assembled students and teachers, the late Sir F. A. Gore-
Ouseley being also present, upon Beethoven's Sonaia,
Op. 22, with illustration on the pianoforte by his
brother.

Shortly afterwards, he delivered a similar lecture at
Blackheath, on three of Beethoven's Sonatas for Pianoforte and Violin, the illustrations being performed by
Mr. Walter Macfarren and Monsieur Sainton.   From
that time to the close of his career, his appearances as
a lecturer were somewhat frequent.   Not only did he
deliver the course on Harmony, already recorded, at
the Royal Institution, and later on, his various courses,
in his Professorial capacity, in the University of Cambridge, and as Principal of the Royal Academy of
Music, re-delivering his Cambridge lectures to the
students, besides addressing the students and professors at the commencement of each academical year ;
but also several courses at the London Institution,
and the College of Organists, and single lectures in
various localities, metropolitan and provincial.   Some
of these lectures were prepared at considerable length,

and with verbal detail, by dictation, and must have been
more or less fully and accurately committed to memory
—*his* memory, so minute and so comprehensive. This
may partly account for his frequent hesitancy, as though
endeavouring to recall an expression with exactitude;
although it may also be surmised that the inability, at
the moment, to determine upon a word—the most
fitting for the purpose—might equally account for
this hesitancy, which was occasionally somewhat painful. But many of the lectures—probably most of
them — were dictated in the form of more or less
copious notes, so as to get the subject in order before
his own mind, and to serve for reference in case of re-
delivery. When it is remembered that it was a blind
man lecturing,—not haranguing, but setting forth
facts, dates, names on the one hand; or theoretical
principles, analyses, illustrated by examples, on the
other,—it is all the more to wonder that his fluency
and accuracy—this latter, indeed, seldom if ever failing—were such as they were. In later years, at all
events, it was his custom to sit while lecturing ; and
he would rest his face on one hand, thus sometimes
slightly intercepting the outflow of his voice, in itself
not strong, latterly ; and, forgetting that he was
speaking in a comparatively large room, would " chat "
rather than "orate ; " these habits interfering much
with his audibility. But, at his best, it was interesting to listen to him, beyond the interest of the matter
itself, because of the emotional sincerity with which
he delivered himself of his views of the Art that he
loved so well, especially, also, when he was addressing
sympathetic and reverential students, whom he also
loved so well. He said to me that he liked address-

ing the academicians annually, because it seemed the
one way open to him—that of sight being denied to
him—of being brought into personal intercourse with
them : he might have said " en rapport ; " but he did
not use a French term when one in English was available : he believed in his own language, like a true
Englishman, as we have already seen.   And no small
command of it had he, and extensive acquaintance
with its resources : sometimes peculiarly felicitous
in his choice of terms ; though addicted much to
rather involved, inverted, not to say long-winded,
structure of his sentences, as well as some mannerisms,
such as beginning fresh divisions with—" It is now
to speak of," etc.

In the year 1867, in which the six lectures on
Harmony were delivered, he also gave, during March,
an important course of four lectures on the " Origin
and Development of the Lyrical Drama," at the
London Institution, of which the syllabus, as in a
former instance, will give the best account.

" LECTURE I.

" Illustrated by

" Miss ROBERTINE HENDERSON and Mr WILBYE COOPER.

" The Greek Drama.—Chanted declamation, engrafted
upon the Dithyrambic and other Hymns, was essentially
lyrical. It was a religious institution, and therefore opposed
by the Christians.   The mediæval drama was also a religious institution, being a form of instruction in morals and
in sacred history employed by the Church ; and the drama
of the first Reformers, especially that instituted by Calvin
at Geneva, had the same tendency.   The songs or ballads
of the people, the music of which was identical with that
of their dances, were always distinct from the music of the

Church, although they were only appropriated, as a basis of contrapuntal elaboration, to ecclesiastical use. The first secular dramas were interspersed with music; ' Le jeu de Robin et de Marion,' by Adam de la Hale, 1240—1287, and ' Orfeo,' by Angelo Poliziano, 1483. The foundation of the Oratorio by Animuccia, 1556, analogous to that of the Greek drama. Many of the plays of Shakespeare and his predecessors and contemporaries include songs that were popular before the plays were written. The immediate effect of the Rénaissance upon music was the invention of recitative, to emulate the declamation of the Greeks. This was applied to dramatic purposes in the Oratorio of Emilio del Cavaliere, 1600, and in the Operas of this composer, Giulio Caccini, Jacopo Peri, and Claudio Monteverde, 1590 — 1607. These were the first dramas set throughout to music. Signification of the term ' Opera.'— The court masques of James I. and Charles I. were set to recitative by Laniere and Ferabosco. The court ballets of Louis the XIV. were composed in the same style by Lully. Milton's ' Comus,' with incidental music by Henry Lawes, 1634; Aria parlante or arioso. Lully followed Mailly and Cambert in the composition of French Operas, which consisted of recitative, airs, and choruses, and always included dancing; 'Psyche,' 1678; couplets. The ' Siege of Rhodes,' the first English Opera, with Mrs. Colman, the first female that appeared on the English stage, was brought out under the sanction of Cromwell, 1646. Henry Purcell's first Opera, ' Dido and Æneas,' 1680, consisted of recitative, songs, and choruses; subsequently he wrote incidental music for spoken dramas. Appropriation of scholastic forms to dramatic use. Cantata, an alternation of recitative and air."

"LECTURE II.

" Illustrated by

" Madame LOUISA VINNING, Mr. WILBYE COOPER, and Mr. J. G. PATEY.

" Advance of the Opera in Italy.—It was imported into Germany, with ' Daphne,' by Schultz, 1627 ; but scarcely

adopted there until the time of Keiser, 1692. — Male
Sopranos.—Formal character of the aria.—Accompanied
recitative first written by Vinci.—Conventional construction of the Opera.—The same *libretti* repeatedly set to
music by different, and even by the same Composers.—The
Italian Operas of Handel, consisting of recitative and airs,
represent the smaller forms of the Lyrical Drama of the
day ; his English Oratorios (except those set to Scriptural
texts) having the addition of choruses to the other two
elements, represent the grander form.—Distinction between
the Grand Opera, the Opéra Comique, and the Vaudeville.
—' The Beggar's Opera,' and the many pieces produced in
consequence of its popularity.—Arne's English imitation
of the Italian Operas of his time, 1762.—Piccini abandoned the prescribed form of the aria ; success of ' La
buona Figliuola,' 1760.—Gluck's design to reform Dramatic
Music by making it a vehicle for declamation instead of
for vocal display, 1764, was a renewal of the purpose of
the inventors of recitative.—His appropriation of dancing,
that was indispensable in French Grand Operas.—Rivalry
of the Italian and German styles."

" LECTURE III.

" Illustrated by

" Miss BANKS, Mdlle. CHARLIER, and Miss JULIA ELTON,

" Mr. WILBYE COOPER, Mr. R. WILKINSON, and

Mr. J. G. PATEY.

" The embodiment of dramatic action in concerted music
originated by Logroscino, 1747; advanced by Piccini; perfected by Mozart in his great finales.—This exalts the
Opera, insomuch as music is an expression of character
and sentiment, above every other form of vocal composition.—Melo-drama or accompanied speaking.—Beethoven's
' Fidelio ' the completest Opera.—Rossini's innovations ;
his influence on the music of his day ; ' Otello ' the first
Italian Opera accompanied throughout by the orchestra.—
Bishop's Operas, spoken dramas with incidental music ;
English dramatic music in his time; the glee.—The appro-

priation of national character to dramatic purposes by Mozart, extended by Weber in 'Preciosa,' ' Der Freischütz,' and 'Oberon.'—He first incorporated the aria in the action of the scene, this being an expansion of Gluck's principle. —The romantic Opera.—The Overture originated by Lully; perfected by Mozart; idealised by Beethoven; popularised by Weber.—Spohr's 'Jessonda' the first German Opera set throughout to music."

"LECTURE IV.

"Illustrated by

" Miss EDITH WYNNE and Miss JULIA ELTON.

" Mr. T. WHIFFIN and Mr. J. G. PATEY.

" The illustration of Pantomime by music, first essayeu by Mouret for the 'nuits blanches' of the Duchesse du Maine in 'Les Horaces,' in 1680, was incorporated in the Opera by Weber in 'Sylvana,' and by Auber in 'Masaniello.' This work was the first of the class of historico-romantic Operas.—Resumption of the composition of Operas, properly so-called, in English, 1834; E. J. Loder; John Barnett; Balfe and the ballad; Benedict; Wallace.— Mendelssohn's music for the revived tragedies of Sophocles no restoration of the character of Greek music, but a new form of composition which had been incompletely anticipated in the tragedies of Racine.—Paramount importance of a good dramatic story for operatic purposes.—All the best opera books, save those written for the French stage, have been adaptations of previously successful dramatic pieces.—Secondary, but yet high importance of the poetry of an Opera.—Consideration of the views of Richard Wagner.—Pernicious influence of the Italian language on the development of dramatic music; first shaken off in France, next in Germany, and now in Russia; but England still suffers from its bane, and suffers worse than any other country has suffered, since the fashion for hearing Operas in a tongue that cannot be pronounced by the majority of the singers, nor understood by the majority of the audience, not only impedes the progress of indigenous productive

R

and executive talent. but compels the distortion of the German and French works which constitute the staple performances of our lyrical theatres."

In the year 1880 Macfarren gave a lecture on the same subject before the Musical Association.

On one subject touched on in the first of these lectures, he wrote at length, in the " Musical Times," of December, 1872, that of " The Accompaniment of Recitative," advancing the statement that :—

" The broad distinction between ancient and modern in music dates from the invention of recitative in the last decade of the sixteenth century. Then, an association of Florentine nobles and gentlemen undertook the interesting experiment of restoring to the art of song the character-istics that had marked it in the Grecian age, as opposed to the qualities to which the music of the period was limited. These qualities were rhythmical tune, exemplified in the songs and dances of the people, and the imitations of these by schooled artists ; and contrapuntal elaboration, exem-plified in the motets or moving parts, and anthems or counter-themes, constructed upon ecclesiastical or secular melodies for church use, and in the madrigals of the musi-cians. In neither of these was there scope for free decla-mation, nor for any but the most general expression of words, which, in classic times, had been the main if not the sole object of vocal music. The idea was then conceived of recitative. . . . . The experiment was so entirely successful that the new style of declamatory music not only took a place beside the rigidly ruled art of the period, but has, to a great extent, superseded it, and importantly modified the materials and the structure of subsequent composition.

" To secure the perfect freedom of the singer in his declamation, to hasten or retard the words as he might be impelled by the passion they embodied, it was essential that the accompaniment should be of such a nature as might in no respect restrict his performance in the matter of mea-sure, while it might fully guide and support him in the matter of intonation. Accordingly, it was confined usually to a single instrument, in most cases the theorbo or large lute ; and this, in the earliest instances, was played by the singer himself, whose fingers were moved by the same impulse that directed his vocal utterance."

After tracing the custom of sustaining the harmony " by the band during the vocal declamation : " that of accompanying the recitative " on some equivalent to the pianoforte," " with also a bowed instrument . . . to support the bass notes, because of the little resonance of the keyed string instruments of the time ;" he goes on to record that :—

"Near the end of the seventeenth century Vinci was the first to write what in England is called 'Accompanied Recitative'. . . reserved for dramatic passages, while he retained for ordinary colloquy and narration what the Italians name 'Recitativo Parlante.' The distinction is, that in the latter the instruments just named were used, and in the former the full orchestra.

"Let it not be supposed that the practice ever was, in colloquial recitative, to sustain the chords on any instrument from semibreve to semibreve, as they were habitually written . . . ; these extensive notes imply the prevalence but not the sustenance of the same harmony, which harmony was and is to be repeated according to the punctuation of the words, whenever their sense indicates a breathing place for the singer."

After various historical details concerning the growth of recitative, he goes on to trace the rise and prevalence of the custom of accompanying colloquial recitative mainly by the violoncello, to the displacement of the pianoforte ; animadverts upon the undesirableness of that method, and urges that—

"According to the size and uses of the building, and the gaiety or gravity of the subject, the pianoforte or the organ ought to be the accompanying instrument in colloquial re-

citative. Let it be hoped that before long its restitution
may be universal, when the richer tone and the fuller resonance of the Pianoforte than of the ancient Harpsi-
chord, especially in the lower range of its compass, will
render the bowed basses entirely dispensable."

He instances occasions, then recent, of the experiment (if such it may be termed) being successfully
made under Herr Otto Goldschmidt, Sir Sterndale
Bennett, and Mr. Joseph Barnby, in Handel's
" L'Allegro " and Bach's " Passion."

It will not be inopportune to insert here some remarks on this same subject occurring in the Preface to
Macfarren's "Analysis of Haydn's ' Creation,' " written
for the Sacred Harmonic Society, dated February,
1854 : —

" One might discuss at some length the setting of most
of the Scriptural passages, surely the most important portions of the text, in the unimportant form of unaccompanied Recitative ; but that the present purpose is to consider how the subject is, not how it might have been,
treated. As, however, there is so much of this form of Recitative without orchestra in the Oratorio, it is desirable to
offer some remarks upon the manner in which it is in
England, and on that in which it should be accompanied.
The custom was, I am told, introduced by Mr. Lindley, and
confirmed by Signor Dragonetti, of accompanying this style
of Recitative with the solo violoncello and double bass ;
and, to those who play the violoncello and double bass, this
custom may be sufficiently amusing; to those, however, who
require the fulfilment of a composer's intention, and to
those, less scrupulous, who look for musical effect, the said
custom has nothing to recommend, nor even to justify it—
it is peculiar to this country, and it is a peculiarity upon
which we have no cause to plume ourselves. The proper way
of performing this style of Recitative—the way that is still
practised out of England—is for the harmony to be played
upon the organ or upon the pianoforte ; in witness whereof,

let me recur to the occasional direction, *Senza Cembalo,*
that we find in composers' scores (since there could be no
occasion to direct that a particular passage should be played
without the pianoforte, if it were not the general custom
for the pianoforte to be played) ; the constant announcement in our old programmes that he, who is now called the
Conductor, would preside ' at the organ or pianoforte ; '
the recollection of every one of some forty or fifty years'
familiarity with musical performances ; and the daily experience of any one who hears the execution of these Recitatives in Italy or Germany. I can only suggest to an
audience, that they imagine the effect of complete and sustained harmony in these accompaniments, and, if their
imagination be lively, they may form some idea of the effect
intended.'

In the Preface to the " Performing Edition of the
Messiah," an important work undertaken by Macfarren, he remarks :—

" Composers of this class of music, till far later than
Handel's time, meant not that the harmony should be sustained as semibreves or minims, though they wrote such
notes for the bass, but intended that a chord should prevail
for the length of the written notes, and be repeated or not,
according to the punctuation of the voice part, or according to the singer's need of support. Neither meant they
that the chord should be struck with the final note of a
phrase whereon the harmony changes, as is often the habit
of inexperienced accompanists to do, by which the enunciation of the last word is rendered indistinct ; the chords
should be played after, rather than with, the voice at the
conclusion, and before the voice at the commencement of
a sentence."

This is exemplified in the notation in the edition
itself, as well as in a similar edition of Haydn's " Creation," in the Preface to which he remarks to the same
effect :—

" The chords were to be played after the vocal closes, excepting only if the harmony changed in the course of a phrase, and the singer was to recommence after the chord had been sounded, and thus the edges of the enunciation were not to be blunted by the striking of the instruments together with the vocal utterance."

With reference to one item in the syllabus of the Fourth Lecture, some remarks of Macfarren's may be relevantly quoted from the programme of Mr. Walter Macfarren's Third Concert of Pianoforte Music, June 11th, 1861, which may be taken in connection with those on John Barnett, at the close of Chapter X.

" Mr. Loder's Opera of 'Nourjahad,' produced in 1834, was the inaugural work of the institution of modern English Opera ; and is therefore remembered with gratification by all who take interest in the progress among us of dramatic music. His 'Francis the First' was brought out in 1838, and his 'Night Dancers,' the most successful, and therefore the best known, and in many respects the best of his operas, was first played in 1846. 'Puck' and 'Raymond and Agnes' are further examples of his labours in the same branch of art."

Macfarren's non-acceptance of the theories of Richard Wagner, and of much of his Music-Drama composition, is well-known ; and was, at times, so vehemently asserted as to lay him open to charges of prejudice, non-progressiveness, and even inability to comprehend the advanced thought of the time. He remarked to me:— " I know that they think me a rabid old Tory." But he was not insensible to excellence or beauty of any kind, and discriminated in his judgment even of that which he could not wholly accept. Thus, in a notice of the Prelude to " Lohengrin," in the Programme of the British Orchestral Society's second Concert, December 19, 1872, he remarks :—

"It may be regarded rather as a study of orchestral effect than as a composition. Its entire plan consists of three presentations of this one theme, [quoted] . . . . Every recurrence of the theme introduces it with some novelty of treatment, consisting not merely in a varied distribution of the instruments, but in the engrafting of new passages upon the original, which are remarkable for their skilful contrivance as much as for their good effect. In its orchestration, this piece commands respect for the knowledge of the capabilities and the relative qualities of the several instruments, and for the careful thoughts in its appliance, that are evinced in every combination; just as a painting is to be esteemed for its colouring, apart from its drawing and its composition, is this Prelude to be considered for its instrumental effect, wherein a special but unquestionable quality of imagination is displayed."

Macfarren delivered four lectures on " Sacred and Secular Art, as exemplified in Music," at the London Institution, in February and March, 1869. " Taking his stand on the principle that all the fine arts have a twofold application to Sacred and Secular subjects, he proceeded to define and exemplify these distinctions under the several heads of music for worship—music for illustrating characters and incidents in sacred story, and moral and religious sentiments—music for depicting the passions and personalities of men—and music for stimulating our emotions and developing our faculties in the circle of home." In the first lecture, on Church Music, he contended that:—

"The first music employed in our Reformed Church was an adaptation, or in some instances, perhaps, an imitation of the Plain Song of Roman use to the text of the English Liturgy, by John Merbeck. The people's love of musical combination prompted the construction of more or less florid counterpoint upon these ancient Church tunes, and many musicians won distinction by their ingenious efforts in this class of composition, whose names are now known only to the antiquary, because the style in which they wrote, with the themes they elaborated, has become obsolete."

Tallis, Byrd, and others, being instanced, who :—

"Made original settings of the Canticles, Creed, and other invariable portions of the service, which have the technical peculiarities of their age, but are equally remarkable for the solemn simplicity of their treatment of the text. The fugitives from Mary's persecution imported, on their return from Frankfort and Geneva the practice of Hymn-singing, which spread so rapidly among their countrymen, that it was authoritatively 'permitted' in public worship by Elizabeth's Injunction of 1559. A collection of tunes, fitted to the entire book of Psalms, was consequently printed in 1563, the custom having been at first for congregations to sing these without harmony ; but in the next year, the same were reprinted in harmony of four parts by several composers. In this and all elaborations of Psalmody for congregational use, of this period, the tune, or Plain Song, or Church Part, is set for the tenor voice. It is only assigned to the *cantus*, or highest part in the harmony, in arrangements for domestic use. The substitution of the word 'Anthem' for 'Hymn,' and its definition as 'a little thing in metre,' in a later Prayer Book of Elizabeth, imply that the first Anthems were harmonized Psalm-tunes, and the earliest original compositions described as Anthems are so simple in form as almost to belong to the same class. . . . Church Music, after the Restoration, gives noble signs of the advance of art, and of the illustrious brightness of English genius, [but] all branches of Church music, like every other department of the art in England, degenerated under the influence of our German rulers, or at least, from the date of their accession."

The second lecture was on "The Opera ; " and the Lecturer contended that :—

"In the boundless range it affords for the portrayal of every phase of character, and the opportunity for bringing these into contrast and combination, the Opera may be regarded as the highest class of composition."

"Il Don Giovanni" was selected for illustrative analysis.

The third lecture was on "The Oratorio." After historical allusion to its origin, he advanced that "the Oratorio is of two kinds—the didactic or narrative, and the dramatic;" the former being exemplified in the periodical recitation of the story of the Passion in the Roman Church, in Bach's setting of the account by Matthew of the Passion—that of John not being alluded to, apparently being then unknown to the lecturer—in Handel's "Messiah," and in Mendelssohn's "St. Paul:" the latter (the dramatic) being exemplified firstly by "La Rappresentazione di Anima e di Corpo," by Cavalieri (1600), and, subsequently, by nearly all the Oratorios of Handel and the Italian composers of his and a far later time. Handel's "Jephtha" was selected as an instance of the dramatic Oratorio; and Mendelssohn's "Lobgesang" of the didactic. Macfarren admits that "Mendelssohn, in a letter, denies the classification of this work as an Oratorio because it is not dramatic;" but contends that he "must have done so without considering the wide use of the term."

The concluding lecture was on Chamber music; the Fugue, the Suite de Pièces, the Symphony or Sonata: conciser forms employed in instrumental music of the present day, the Song without words, being discussed; compositions exclusively for the Orchestra being described by analogy with their corresponding types in music for the Chamber.

He prefaced the first lecture by saying that :—

"The people of this country are more interested in the
art appliances of the English Church than in those of any
other devotional institution ; " and, therefore, the lecture
was "limited to the classification of our national ecclesiastical music, and a brief sketch of its historical development."

In pursuance of this purpose, he took much the
same line as in an earlier lecture, on "the Music of
the Church of England," delivered at the Royal
Institution, April 20th, 1866, in which he premised
that :—

"The objects of Church music are : 1st, passively to
stimulate the hearer to the highest emotions : 2nd, actively
to engage the worshipper in the most powerful expression
of such emotions : "

and then proceeded :—

"A secondary, and not unworthy object of Church
music has been, from the days of S. Aldhelm, Abbot of
Malmesbury, A.D., 700, or earlier, to the present time, to
form an attraction for the laity to enter the sacred
building, etc."

After a historical glance at "the importation of
music into the Western Church by St. Ambrose," he
contends that "certainly the music that was sung was
that of the Greek Theatre ; " the proofs being :—

"First, that the musical scale was divided, by the ancient
Jews, and the nations among whom they sojourned, into
smaller intervals than those of the Greek diatonic genus,
whereas the Ambrosian Chant exactly accords with this
genus ; second, that the four modes employed by St.

Ambrose—the Dorian, the Phrygian, the Lydian, and the Mixo-Lydian—are identical with the Greek modes so named, and are applied, in ecclesiastical use, each to the expression of the same sentiment as in the Greek Theatre. St. Ambrose was an innovator in incorporating music in the service of the Church; and he appropriated the pagan music which was accessible to his congregation, and indeed familiar."

Macfarren incurred some obloquy in certain circles for his outspoken views on this matter; but he never flinched from the position here taken up.

He next notices the labours of St. Gregory in "adding four additional modes of the Greeks to those of Ambrose, and perpetuating his revised and extended system by inventing a method of notation;" and the introduction, several centuries later, of harmony, "in the form of extempore descant upon the Gregorian Chant; and long after this, the rules of written Counterpoint were instituted."

Following upon this introductory survey, "the adoption of music in the English Church at the Reformation, in the first instance, direct from the Church of Rome," is recorded, the labours of John Merbeck, Tallis, and others, being referred to; then the singing of Hymns, of the metrical versions of the Psalms, etc. Of the various derivations of the word :—

" 'Anthem,'—substituted for *Hymn* in the later Prayer Book of Elizabeth, that is to be preferred which assigns its origin to *Antithema*, implying that it first denoted free counterpoint against a given theme—the harmony to the Psalm-tune—analogous to *Motet*, the *Motettus* or moving part against the *Cantus Fermus* of the Roman Church. Several illustrations of this definition prove the concise character originally purposed for the Anthem, and point

to the dereliction from this in the lengthy and complicated compositions of later times."

This latter pronouncement may be recommended to
all whom it may concern : as may also that which
succeeds :—though the persons herewith concerned
are not those concerned in the last.

"The corruption of English Church Music has its root
in the retention of the precentorship as a priestly office at
the time of the Reformation, the period at which the study
of Music, like all other civil studies, first became common
among the laity. The effect of this first great fundamental evil was not felt till much later ; but there can be now
no question of the impropriety of committing the entire
control of the singers, the choice of the music, and every
arrangement and responsibility of this highly important
element of the Church Service to an officer who is not com-
pulsorily acquainted with music. That some few precen-
tors have a knowledge of the subject which it is their duty
to direct only aggravates the ill-working of the system,
since it gives countenance to the very many more who are
equally ignorant, and either indifferent or prejudiced.
The contributions to Psalmody by persons of little musical
education, or with none, began early in the last century,
and have tended seriously to vulgarise and emasculate this
noble branch of Church Music. The misappropriation of
the Glee style of writing to church composition has done
equally much to deteriorate the music special to the cathedral. The admission of Solo Anthems has tended to make
the church an arena for the display of the singers, and for
the indulgence of the audience, who have attended service
more for the amusement of criticism than for the edification of prayer. The adaptation of irrelevant words to
music from the florid Masses of composers of later times,
from Oratorios, and from instrumental works, has perverted
the composer's designed expression, which is the highest
quality in music, and has thus degraded the Art and its
influences. The introduction of compositions by clerical
amateurs or their friends, whose social position has com-

manded attention to their productions, has often made the
church a medium for the gratification of vanity, at the expense of genuine artistry. The attempt to revive the use
in the church of the Greek system of music, (which Ambrose introduced and Gregory continued, because there
was then none other accessible), produces, if not an affectation of sanctity, at least a pedantic assumption of anti-
quarianism that is as remote from devotion."

This distribution of censure pretty well all round
derives its severity from its justice; and it is easier
to evade its hard hits by asking whether Macfarren
was specially qualified to pronounce judgment in this
matter, seeing that he was not an habitual church
attendant,—or by some other *tu quoque* retorts,—than
to rebut the terse sentences by denial or argument.
Much of that which has been quoted applies equally
to Noncomformist practices in the matter of Psalmody
and congregational anthem-singing. But the criticisms and principles themselves are sound, and worthy
of consideration by very many concerned, whether in
the Established Church or in the Free Churches.

In a review which bears internal evidence of being
Macfarren's, he makes some observations which were
very timely when written, and, even now, are not untimely in their reproduction :—

"A choral is, to the best of our belief, a hymn-tune sung by
the people in chorus in the service of the Lutheran Church.
Chorals are for the most part, old, and they are also, for
the most part, each associated with its own poem. It has
been common for the musicians of North Germany, almost
from the date of the Reformation, to employ the choral
tunes as themes for elaboration in their vocal, as much as
instrumental works. Some of the oldest and best of them
are thus introduced by Mendelssohn in his ' St. Paul,' and
their insertion is justified, and their interest induced in

the situation of their occurrence, by the German people's intimacy with them in connection with the words to which they have habitually sung them, every man from childhood onwards. When this oratorio was imported into England, folks thought it necessary to preserve the definition of the Chorals, since they were unlike in character, form, and extent, to any pieces in oratorios with which the English public was familiar; and to secure the German pronunciation of the word with the accent on the final syllable, an ' e ' was added at the end, which must have been meant to be mute. The public, however, misunderstood the orthoepic intention of the English editors, read the extended word, Chorale, as a tri-syllable, and took to pronouncing its new and peculiarly English addition as they do in ' Charley.' Since Mendelssohn's first oratorio, his ' Hymn of Praise ' and his Organ Sonatas, in which some specimens of the old Choral appear to have helped to make their definition in its English three-syllable form familiar, and this familiarity is strongly confirmed by the knowledge, recently becoming general, of Bach's ' Music of the Passion,' wherein examples abound of the ancient Lutheran Choral tune. Respect for these works, and for others from the same source, has, we may suppose, been the prompting to some of our best English composers to emulate the precedent of the great Germans; and they have incorporated in like manner, in some of their extensive works, pieces that might serve for hymn-tunes, and these they anomalously entitle ' Chorale(y)s,' unmindful that they are not venerable tunes of Lutheran use, that they are not old hymn-tunes at all, that they can never call to remembrance particular poems, since they have never been associated with any words whatever, and seeming to forget that the said melodies are their own, the said composers' original productions. Now, if such misuse of the term chorale(y) is not an affectation, it is surely a mistake; since the word so applied is a misnomer. We earnestly suggest, then, to our native musicians of experience and credit to discontinue the example to their younger brethren of a misuse which savours so strongly of affectation as to imbue those who practise it with its odour. Hymn-tune is a good enough term, and hymn, without tune, is a better; moreover they

have both been English since further back than it is easy
to trace their use; and we urge that either of these would
be appropriate to the pieces that writers of latest times
have taken to calling Chorale(y)s."

In reply to an inquiry, the nature of which may be
surmised, Macfarren addressed the following to Mr.
Gilbert Scott, in the year 1879:—

"On the question proposed to me, I think that if the
object be to lead congregational singing, or, more properly
expressed, to drown the inaccuracies of unskilled vocalists,
a large, coarse-toned organ may be highly desirable. If
the object be to produce the effect of musical beauty, by
judicious accompaniment of a trained choir, then an organ
of moderate power, but of good tone, and with full pedal
compass, is very greatly to be preferred to a larger and
louder instrument, which no player with a real feeling for
his task would use at the full for such a purpose. If a
sum of money be contributed for musical ends in any
church, I believe it would be far better applied in some
investment that would yield an annual fund to be spent
upon choir-training than on the increase of an organ, inasmuch as it would lead to the efficient performance of
admirable compositions, and the taste of hearers as well as
executants would thereby be exalted. This opinion, being
framed more upon general principles than upon experience
in church music, is offered with diffidence, but I believe it
would have the concurrence of persons better versed in this
particular branch of the subject than myself."

Macfarren's account of, and views about the Ecclesiastical Modes are succinctly stated in his analysis,
written in the programme of the second performance
of the Quartet Association, May 12th, 1852, of the
third movement of Beethoven's Quartet in A minor,
Op. 132; the movement in question being indicated
by Beethoven as '*in modo Lidico*'—in the Lydian

Mode. The analyst avails himself of the opportunity to say :—

" It is now-a-days no novelty to speak of the Gregorian Tones and the Ecclesiastical Modes. Many, however, who may have been in the very midst of the contest that has for some while prevailed upon this subject, may be unaware of the musical grounds upon which all persons of cultivated taste, or even of common sense, must, when they become acquainted with the principle, denounce the restoration of Gregorianism as an act of the most absurd, and either wilful or ignorant barbarity. It would, of course, be wholly out of place to enter here upon any lengthened discussion of this curious point of musical antiquity. But it is indispensable to the understanding of the present Adagio, that I should advance a few of the principles of the style of music which it emulates; and this I shall do as succinctly as possible.

St. Gregory, and St. Ambrose before him, knew nothing of the inflection of notes by sharps and flats. They had the notes of our present scale of C and none other. They found, however, that from many causes, of which, probably, monotony was not the least important, it was impossible to restrict themselves exclusively to the key of C, as we now understand it, and therefore employed the several Modes of the more ancient Greek diatonic music, rejecting the chromatic and the enharmonic systems that were in use with the heathen musicians. These Modes, bearing still the original Greek names, are on the six first notes of our scale of C, each being treated as a tonic or key-note, in so far as that a composition begins and ends upon it; but having, as I have said, no sharps and flats—this Lydian Mode, in which this movement is written—said to be the most gentle and plaintive in character, whence the line of the poet—

"Softly sweet in Lydian measure "—

answers to what would be our key of F without a B flat, the unsatisfactory, not to say disagreeable, effect of which savage artifice is, at least, strange and uncouth, and irreconcilable to ears accustomed to the modern scale of nature. It is not to be wondered that the fashionable dilettanti, and the astute critics of the Olympic Games, thought so favourably of the sweetness of the Lydian Mode, as we find expressed by Milton, who in this is the representative of a host of classic authorities, since, whatever be the effect of this upon us, who have very different associations to direct our judgment, it is the very perfection of propriety, when compared to that of the keys of D and A and E without sharps, which were, to express different sentiments, equally in use, not only among the Greeks, but, until some two or three centuries ago, in the Christian Church, from which they have been gradually banished—as from secular music also—by the gradual advance of the art, and indeed of the science of music."

The views of Macfarren on Church Music, as thus enunciated, were by no means unchallenged, however; but were the occasion of a correspondence, perhaps not wholly free from acrimony, in the " Choir " of September 21st, October 5th, 19th, and November 2nd, 1867 ;—the discussion being opened by Rev. S. S. Greatheed, calling forth a reply from Macfarren, a rejoinder from Rev. S. S. Greatheed, with an article by James Finn on the " Origin of Gregorian Music," and a final reply from Macfarren.

With reference to the introduction of *Oratorios in Church*, is to be recorded that Macfarren wrote an article in the "Musical Times" for March 1872; commencing :—

" What is an oratorio? Originally, a musical composition to be performed in the oratory.

" What is an oratory? A place set apart for prayer in a private dwelling; a portion of a church appropriated to special uses—such as that of the meetings instituted in Rome by S. Philippo Neri, where oratorios were performed, which took their defining title from that of the place wherein they were heard.

" What is a church ? 'The Lord's house;' a building dedicated to public worship and to religious edification.

Since some churches include an oratory, and since the oratory gave rise and definition to the oratorio, it is at least anomalous that certain well-meaning and thoughtful persons should publicly protest against the performance of oratorios in ecclesiastical buildings. The history of the development of this grand class of musical composition, and of its influence, furnishes argument against the protest; let me glance at the history and hint at the argument."

The historical sketch is copious, including not only the origination of the Oratorio, and its two forms, but passing in review its secularizing in Italy, till it became distinctly an Opera upon a Biblical subject : its introduction into Germany in the time of Luther, who

" Aimed to conserve and perpetuate all that he deemed good and pure in Roman use; hence many choral tunes of Roman origin are associated with his name; hence, too, the recital of the story of the Passion at Eastertide, with all possible earnestness, solemnity, and vitality of effect :"

The music for these recitals by Handel " the name dearest to us all," and by other composers: " the culmination of this gradual ascent in character and in importance of the Oratorio for Holy Week . . . in Bach's setting of two, if not three, of the Biblical versions of the Passion,"—the " Matthew Passion " of Bach being pronounced " the Author's masterpiece " : the introduction of the Oratorio into England by Handel, in 1720, by the performance of his " Esther ": the Lent performances in Covent Garden Theatre : the performance of the " Messiah," first in Dublin, then in London, March 23rd, 1743 : and he continues :—

" This oratorio has done and still does far more than any other, more even than any work of other arts, more I believe than any literary essays or spoken discourses, to popularise throughout England the Scripture texts which most strongly bear upon the Christian story ; and it has thus been of infinite consequence in the dissemination of Christian lore, in making familiar to every one, of every rank and station, of every sect, of every degree of education and ignorance, the revered words whereon is based the whole of the Church's teaching. Aversion was so strong, however, from the supposed profanation of this holiest of themes, that it was deemed indecorous to announce the work by the title to which it had been written, ... and it was accordingly advertised as 'A Sacred Oratorio,' a name that Handel reserved for this one work alone. In spite of this evasion, the repugnance of the London world was so strong against the public presentation of the 'Messiah,' that though its name was withheld, its success was indifferent. It was heard but thrice, and that coldly, in the year of its production, and once in 1745 ; then it lay by for four years, and was brought forward again as the 'Messiah,' in 1749, but with no happier result. In 1750, when the composer opened the organ he had presented to the chapel of the Foundling Hospital, the 'Messiah' was reproduced in that building, when, for the first time, it was felt to be in its natural and legitimate home. All prejudice against it was dispelled, crowds thronged to witness its performance, and from that notable 1st of May, all England has acknowledged the equal importance to Christianity and to art of this glorious monument to its author's genius. Now, when we hear the 'Messiah' texts, as they occur incidentally in the Daily Service, they fall upon our ear as quotations from the oratorio ; for all that is most significant has been so happily chosen, and has been so effectively brought together in this work, that it is a complete epitome of the subject, and we hear the sacred words in association with notes of Handel so frequently, that it is all but impossible to part either from other, in our recollection, or in the impression they make."

This is all eloquently stated, as is much more in
this paper: for instance, at the "Festival of the
three Choirs"—Worcester, Hereford, and Gloucester,
in the cathedrals of which cities,—alternately,—

"Thousands of persons are yearly brought together to
witness the performance of the noblest works in sacred
art, on a grander scale, and with a nearer approach to
perfection, than is elsewhere to be heard, save under exceptional, and somewhat analogous circumstances. The
grandeur of the works themselves, and of their presentation is enormously enhanced by the site where they take
place ; the gorgeous effect of sound within those superb
buildings, the associations wherewith they are invested,
and the scene they present, all swell the solemnity of the
occasion and aid in the impression of the hour, and its
lasting influence. People receive thus the highest moral
education in the refinement of their taste, and the nurture
of their intellect, and the highest religious education in the
implanting in their hearts of the Church's principles with
such healthful adjuncts that they may not easily be eradi-
cated. I have met with devout men and trivial, learned
and uninstructed, some who have sought edification and
some mere amusement, who have all concurred in the
admission that they have been far more deeply impressed
by oratorios when they have heard them in these holy
piles than on any other occasion, and a deep impression is
the seed of an ever-green memory."

The beauty of this last axiomatic clause will at
once strike the reader.

After alluding to the Commemoration of Handel in
Westminster Abbey, and the Festival in the same
building in 1834, he proceeds to the then recent performance therein, on Maunday Thursday, of Bach's
Matthew Passion-Music, which he reverts to "with
an intense feeling of gratitude."

"The 'Passion' of Sebastian Bach has no element of

popular effect, makes no appeal to vulgar appreciation, but aims ever at the most exalted expression of the purest ideas, and aims not in vain. In that vast area, one felt by sympathy—and sympathy's language is the universal silent speech that can never be misinterpreted—that a single emotion conjoined the thousands of hearts which beat there as with one pulse, and that all were for the time translated out of their ordinary selves into a nobler state of being."

There is much more to the same purpose ; and the paper concludes with an earnest peroration :—

" I believe in a great future for English Music ; I think that the Church may be its field ; and I know that, except the opportunities be greatly widened for oratorio performances, there can be no use for the grandest class of musical works, nor fair scope for the exercise of musical genius in their composition. It would be a mighty and a glorious task for those who are to come, were they to be called upon to supplement the repertory of masterpieces to which allusion has been made, and to be assured that kindred excellence to these would be a guarantee for the presentation of such newly created works on the occasions to which they were appropriate. These works would have a preference over productions of elder times in their being written in the technical idiom of the age in which they were produced, and in the expressing the feelings of that age, and of the generation to which they were addressed. To men who love their art, to men who love their religion, to men who love their country, this should not be a trifling argument ; let me hope at least that it may weigh with others which have been adduced in the consideration of persons who examine the important question as to the propriety of the presentation of Oratorios in Church."

It is impossible, or at all events would be out of place here to discuss the questions, ecclesiastical, religious, and other, which are involved in the subject of this paper. It is here quoted copiously in order to supplement the views advanced by Macfarren in his

Lecture on the Music of the Church of England ; and
the concluding paragraph may, in some sense, supplement his views, elsewhere presented in this volume,
as to English Music generally, and its prospects.   He
again urged his views on the subject of Oratorios in
Church, in an article in the "Musical Times," January,
1873, forecasting the performance of Mendelssohn's
" St. Paul," or a selection therefrom, in St. Paul's
Cathedral, on the 25th of that month.

Mention may appropriately be made here of an
elaborate criticism which Macfarren wrote, in the
" Musical Times," of May and June, 1869, of Rossini's
then recently published " Messe Solennelle :" concerning which, among other depreciatory comments,
he says :—

"Among audiences, they who make the boarding-school
distinction between singing and music, loving sound for
its physical beauty, rather than for its intellectual influence, for its effect upon the senses more than for its
embodiment of sense, will be enraptured with this composition, which is from end to end a course of vocalization—
pure singing for the sake of vocal display ; devoid entirely
of the encumbrance of declamation and expression ; interrupted only with such demonstrations of supposed learning
as will afford convenient moments of repose to the hearers
who may talk, during which, of the exquisite performance
of the last solo piece, and think the chorus then proceeding
too profound for their comprehension."

Reference has been made to Macfarren's incidental
animadversion upon the Glee,—a specially English
form of composition.   More general assent will be
given to his animadversion upon the importation of
the Glee style into the music of the Church.   Perhaps
it would now be more exact to characterize such im-

portation as the *Part-song* style. But, as we have
already seen, Macfarren has elsewhere expressed himself strongly upon the fragmentary character of English
Glees, even those which were at one time in great
vogue.

Although Macfarren was not a church-goer, he
himself contributed not a little to Church Music;
Services, Anthems, Introits (a complete series, adapted
to the Festivals of the Church of England, the words
selected by Dr. E. G. Monk), Psalm-tunes, and Chants.
His Oratorios will be subsequently spoken of.

Indeed, in conjunction with his work as an analyst
and critic, his work as a producer of music continued
with little or no intermission. During the period of
lecturing and article-writing, dealt with in this and
the preceding chapters, Macfarren produced not only,
as we have seen, several dramatic works, but also the
Quartet in G minor, which was so favourably received
at its first performance,[1] that it was repeated during
the same season, " by particular desire." The slow
movement is described by one who has heard it as "a
lovely little song." The programme gives the subjects
of this movement as follows :—

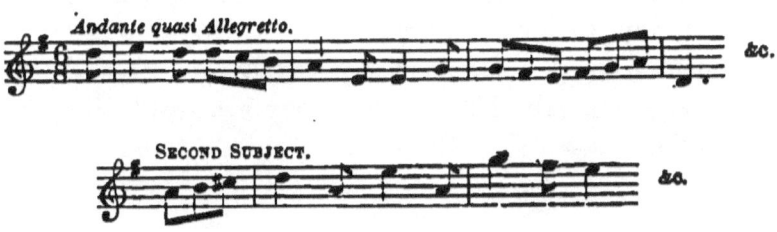

---

[1] See p. 197.

The programme in which the first performance forms an item contains also the above-quoted remarks on the Gregorian modes.

. In 1856, when Sterndale Bennett was appointed Conductor of the Philharmonic Society's Concerts, he expressed a wish that, at the first performance directed by him, a work by his old fellow-student should be played ; and Macfarren selected an overture written by him some years previously, that to Schiller's " Don Carlos ; " which, indeed, had been tried by the Society of British Musicians, under the conductorship of Mr. Walter Macfarren, during the composer's absence in America, and subsequently performed at one of John Hullah's concerts at St. Martin's Hall, and again at a New Philharmonic concert.

A " Festival Overture " was composed for and performed at the Liverpool Festival, 1874 ; but, according to contemporary account, that performance was not satisfactory, the audience were inattentive, and success consequently not great, although Macfarren's name was in the ascendant, as a result of the recent production of " St. John the Baptist." The " Festival Overture " was, however, repeated, with better success, at one of the Novello Concerts at the Royal Albert Hall, under the directorship of Mr. Barnby ; at one of Mr. Henry Leslie's Concerts ; at a Royal Academy Concert ; and at a Concert by the British Orchestral Society, April 7th, 1875. One very agreeable subject is as follows :—

At the British Orchestral Society, also, in 1874, March 26th, under the conductorship of Mr. George Mount, was produced Macfarren's Symphony in E minor, composed for the occasion; the sixth or seventh of his Symphonies; which was again performed by the Philharmonic Society in 1879. A Symphony in D was composed at an earlier period for the Amateur Musical Society, conducted by Mr. Henry Leslie. Nor must a Flute Concerto, composed for Mr. Radcliffe, and a Violin Concerto, in G minor, composed for Herr Ludwig Straus, be overlooked: the latter was first played by Herr Straus, at a Philharmonic Concert, May 12th, 1873; and again, May 28th, 1877.

Concerning the E minor Symphony, a critic wrote:—

"Our distinguished musician earns his greatest triumphs at a period in life when mental activity might be considered to be on the wane. . . . Mr. Macfarren's Symphony is ambitious and imposing; it possesses undoubted grandeur, both in the original conception and the method of its treatment; it is elaborated, as only a master hand could have worked it out, and it possesses those abstract principles which bespeak the nature of its ideas as not lying merely upon the surface, but penetrating to 'stilly depths' unfathomable save by the expert. . . . There is something in the conception of Mr. Macfarren's work which is almost terrible in its intensity; the opening phrase, like the curse in 'Rigoletto,' interrupts the serenity of the lighter portions, and interposes a direful obstacle which nothing can surmount. Throughout the Symphony this haunting phrase occurs, like the ever-active sword of Damocles, 'Swift to strike, if not to kill.' Any such element as 'prettiness' in such a work as this would be out of place: the first movement is restless, agitated, and mournful; the second (serenade, *andante*), though melodious in character, cannot escape the influence of destiny as embodied in the phrase to which we have alluded; the third, *Gavotte : musette : Gavotte . da capo*, with *coda* (in place of the usual scherzo), is perhaps the lightest section of a serious work; but the final *allegro* is, despite the flowing nature of its themes, as sorrowful and as agitated as the opening movement. Taken all in all the Symphony in E minor represents the nature of a 'man of sorrow, and acquainted with grief' more than anything else; its episodes are futile to contend against the overwhelming mournfulness of the subjects, and the Symphony runs its course in an atmosphere of sadness and regret. The quiet and meditative beauties of various isolated portions we cannot here deal with."

The Serenade was pronounced by another critic " a charming song throughout."

The " direful obstacle " theme of the opening movement is :—

Among smaller works, of which Macfarren was continually issuing examples, may be mentioned two

Romances, not published together, for Concertina and Pianoforte, written for Mr. Richard Blagrove, about 1856 and 1859 respectively. Also two songs with Pianoforte and Clarinet (or Harmonium) *obbligato* accompaniment. That admirable artist, Mr. Henry Lazarus, asked him to write a song with accompaniment for his instrument: " A widow bird," to words by Shelley, was the result. But the eminent clarinettist was not satisfied without a more gay song to follow; and "Pack clouds away," words by Thomas Heywood, followed. To this mention of some of the compositions of this period must be added two Sonatas for Pianoforte and Violin, in A and C respectively; one being dedicated to his brother Walter. And, further, he contributed a Sonata for the Organ to the " Organist's Quarterly Journal of Original Compositions; " concerning which a critic wrote :—

" Mr. Macfarren's Sonata is a piece of some pretension, and by no means easy to play. We must say that we think it a very grand and striking composition. It is surprising that the composer, who is no performer himself, should have so completely hit off the character and capabilities of the instrument for which he was writing. But true genius can accomplish anything."

Other works written for the Organ were a " Religious March " in E flat, with a *Trio* (or *Alternativo*) in which the Old Hundredth is treated contrapuntally, the Pedal part being partly in Canon with the Melody: an " Andante in G : " " Secular March " in A : and " Variations on the tune ' Windsor,'" the last variation being fugal.

He also lent his name as editor,—doubtless doing more than this, however,—to " The Mother's Book of Song : two-part Songs for little singers, on the Kindergarten School system. Music by Lady Baker."

Macfarren himself published "Three Madrigals" to the words of Nursery Rhymes :—"Sing a Song of Sixpence : " "Girls and Boys come out to play : " "The Man of Edmonton : " the first having been written for Hullah's "Part-Music : " but these were by no means for "Kindergarten," or even for juvenile use.

And, ever interested in all musical questions, and especially any concerning Mozart, he wrote a somewhat detailed letter to Dr. Pole, in connection with that gentleman's interesting and exhaustive researches about the matter, giving emphatic expression of his opinion that the Requiem was entirely the composition of Mozart, though the orchestration indicates another hand in some places; giving this opinion on intrinsic, not extrinsic evidence.

In June, 1859, the Council of the Society of Arts appointed a Committee " to consider the present state of musical pitch in England : " the musical profession being represented by Professor W. Sterndale Bennett, Sir George Smart, Benedict, H. G. Blagrove, Godfrey, Otto Goldschmidt, Goss, J. H. Griesbach, Hallé, Harper, W. Hawes, Hobbs, E. J. Hopkins, C. E. Horsley, Hullah, H. C. Lunn, G. A. Macfarren, Alfred Mellon, A. Nicholson, Cipriani Potter, J. Turle, J. R. Tutton, and Waddell, besides many scientific authorities, and others. After the presentation of the report of this Committee, Macfarren wrote in the "Choir," March 29th, April 3rd, and April 17th, 1869, a short series of articles on the subject, commencing :—

"Acuteness is brilliancy! Altitude is brightness!! There never was a greater fallacy in the whole history of error. The heavens have forbidden it ever since the creation, and have made their protest manifest to man ever since he was inspired to calculate the distances and to analyse the composition of the stars. Yet, while astronomers and other men of science reverentially profess the opposite conviction, it is possible, strangely possible, and not only possible, but true, that some musicians assert the mistake and maintain it as steadfastly as if it were Gospel. Unhappily, some of them stand in high and authoritative places, and have thus the power of enforcing their false creed, to the destruction of voices, to the deterioration of instruments, and to the injury of music. Hence the present superiority of the musical pitch of England over that of all other countries—most inferior superiority, when sound is higher than sense, and intonation is higher than reason.

"The analogy is perfect between sound and light in respect to quality, and nothing but quality being the cause of its more or less brightness of character. This same quality results wholly from the peculiar constitution of the sound-giving or light-giving body. Thus it is not the proximity or remoteness of the orbs of heaven, not even their relative magnitude, that induces the greater or less intensity of their light, which is entirely a consequence of the proportions and combinations of their chemical elements. Thus also, it is not the acuteness or gravity of a musical sound, nor even its loudness or softness, that induces the greater or less brilliancy of tone, which in like manner is entirely a consequence of the peculiar structure of the natural or artificial organ by which it is produced. Every one knows that the tone of a Straduarius violin is more brilliant and that of an Amati sweeter than the other; that the tone of an oboe is more piercing than that of a clarionet; that the tone of a trumpet, when played pianissimo, is brighter than that of a flute; etc."

The whole matter is then cogently argued, with regard to instruments and voices.

For the first volume of the late Mr. W. Chappell's "History of Music," Macfarren harmonized two Greek melodies, with reference to which the "Musical World," August 22nd, 1874, remarked :—

"To the question whether the Greeks were acquainted with harmony, Mr. Chappell answers positively in the affirmative; while to Dr. Burney's assertion that such Greek melodies as have come down to us cannot be harmonized, he replies by handing the said melodies to Mr. G. A. Macfarren, who forthwith harmonizes them."

The "Musical Times," October, 1874, said:

"It may, however, be fairly questioned whether the result is Greek Music. . . . . . By making such tunes form part of a modern tissue of harmonies, they become an essentially modern piece of music."

Some idea may be formed, even from the record given in this chapter, of the intense, unwearied and diversified activity of Macfarren's mind, always clear and thorough, whatever the subject of its energies.

CHAPTER XII.

A NOTEWORTHY chapter in Macfarren's attitude, opinions and utterances, is that concerning the Tonic Sol-Fa method of teaching music (especially singing), with its special nomenclature and notation, together with the theory of music and tonality upon which it is founded. That his antagonism thereto was entirely conscientious, against his personal feelings, but in the interests of truth as he conceived it, cannot be questioned; inasmuch as, judging by results,—surely no mean test—he, in the first instance, gave a favourable verdict respecting the system; and, all along, he was on most friendly terms with its promoters, Rev. John Curwen and his son, Mr. J. Spencer Curwen, the latter of whom studied with the Professor at the Academy, and was, most deservedly, held in high esteem by him. That Macfarren should, like many professors, oppose any system which, using new terms and adopting new methods, seemed to reflect on the established notation, and to delay, instead of facilitating, its acquisition, was not surprising. Such opposition has been encountered by all reforms, alleged or fallacious, when first advanced : whether from inertness or from prejudice. But Macfarren's opposition was distinctly theoretical, which was, to some, all the more surprising, as it seemed to many of the advocates of Tonic Sol-Fa that it had a theoretical basis very much in agreement with the views of tonality espoused by Macfarren himself; and that he might rather have been expected to give it his consistent support. But I have heard him say—not, as it seemed to me, with his usual acuteness—" Tonic Sol-Fa is a singular misnomer for the system, inasmuch as the Tonic is movable : and instead of *Sol* they say *Soh,* and *Fah* instead of *Fa.*" If this utterance were to be taken as the almost epigrammatic summing up of the objections to the system, its designation, or its nomenclature, the matter might well be left unnoticed : so little force does there seem in such a presentation of the case. But it was not so : Macfarren objected on harmonic grounds. In a letter to the Rev. John Curwen, dated October 25th, 1868, the following remarks occur :—

"I earnestly wish . . . . . all possible success to any system that may extend the practical knowledge of music.

" I wish I could communicate to you my conviction of the identity of the key of C in its major and minor forms; and of its total distinction from the key of E flat, for which I will offer you some new arguments when you come. I am certain that this modification of your system would immensely augment its usefulness by facilitating the perception of true tone relationship. Remember that F flat, G flat, and C flat, which are peculiar to the key of E flat, can have no existence in the key of C ; while E, F sharp, and B, are totally foreign to the key of E flat. Besides which, the temperament is different of every chord in the two keys."

It would be beyond our province to expound the acoustical principles here referred to, or to uphold or combat the inferences therefrom deduced.

His first acquaintance with the practical results of the system appears to have been made at a Concert by the Paris Prize Choir, July 26th, 1867, when his own Part-Song, "Harvest Home," was sung, and, by its admirable rendering, aroused such enthusiastic applause that Macfarren was compelled to address the company, and delivered the following characteristic speech, which, dealing with other matters than the merits of the system, is here given *in extenso :*—

" Pray allow me to thank you for the very high gratification you have given me in this most flattering performance of one of my songs. Allow me to offer my congratulations on the success of the choir on another ground. It has long been the custom to ignore abroad and at home the musical capacities of the English people. I am very proud to find that our musicality has been so ably vindicated, and that not by practised artists of great repute, but by members of the community at large, who have not shown mere individual talent, but the general talent of the English people. I feel sure that the singing to-night must have satisfied everybody of English capability. It is, of course, very gratifying to me that one of the pieces selected by the choir in the recent competition was one of my own; but while I have a personal pride in this, it is also with national pride that I congratulate them upon their success. I feel certain that, whatever the merits of the Tonic Sol-fa system—and until to-night I have had no opportunity of judging—a system which can produce such good results must be a good system."

And in the " Cornhill Magazine " for September of the following year, 1868,[1] he wrote as follows :—

----

[1] See pp. 137-144.

T

…de mention because it begins
…rt. This is … Tonic Sol-fa
…ul… its instr… dona… means,
…isseminating …usical know-
…lect mainly d… to the zealous
…ad…uce, with …mankful plea-
…a year old in evidence of the
…s of art. At … …ultitudinous
…is singular system, …plece of
…sed for the occasion, and had
…ay human eye save those of
…as handed for… h to the mem-
…t, and then, bef…e an audience
…th copies to …el the accuracy
…hundred si…gers sang it at
…the highest …equirements of

…however, and the fact that
…son…ren him…elf as a sight-
…— though …ree Anthems
…e was easy enough for the
…e purpose,—he ultimately assumed …n att…
…etermined hostility to the system, s …uch s…
…in March, 1882, he addressed the follow …g lette…
to the Right Hon. A. J. Mundella, M.P., V…-Pres…
dent of the Council, with reference to the p… …osal t…
recognize the system :—

"7, Hamilton Ter… …N.W.

"SIR,
"I am told it is contemplated by the Counci… …Educa…
tion to authorize the use of the so-called Tonic So… …Syste…
of musical notation in elementary schools thro… …hout th…
country; and as I think strongly on this subj… …I tru…
you will allow me to offer my carefully-formed …ion f…
your consideration. I think the system to be b… …becau…
it hinders the acquisition of a sense of pitch, …hich is…
most valuable quality for musicians; because it …onfoun…

the characteristics of keys, which have distinctly different harmonic derivation; and because many of its signs are so vague that persons familiar with the system often mistake them. I think it to be inconvenient, because it can only apply to music up to a very definite limit; because persons who have learnt from this system have greater difficulty to acquire the ordinary technicalities of music than those who begin to study the art from the standard notation; and because persons who read only from this system are unable to participate in musical performances with those who read from the usual alphabet. I think the adoption of the system unjust, since imposing on the poor an expenditure of time and money which they can never turn to any practical account, and placing them at a disadvantage with the rich, who are able to read musical publications of all countries, whereas the use of this exceptional notation is confined to a sect in England and some of its colonies alone.

" I have the honour to be, Sir,
" Faithfully yours,
" G. A. MACFARREN."

It is only fair to record—and Macfarren would have cheerfully accorded such fairness—that these objections were met by the counterpleas that, not only would "the vast majority of those who have been reached by the Tonic Sol-fa System have had no instruction at all but for the efforts of its missionaries," but that " the ear-training, which is so distinctive a feature of Tonic Sol-fa teaching, must and does sharpen the perception of absolute pitch when attention is particularly directed to it ; " that Macfarren himself had testified to the admirable success in reading and singing at sight by Tonic Sol-faists in his " Cornhill Magazine " article ; that such authority as that of Mr. Sedley Taylor, member of the Board of Musical Studies in Cambridge University was to be quoted on the opposite side, and so on. This is not the place to pursue the controversy, especially as the opposition to the system is no longer so formidable. Mr. A. J. Ellis, F.R.S., translator of Helmholtz's " Sensations of Tone," wrote:—

" Professor Macfarren has deserved so well of music that everyone must regret his having placed himself in such pronounced antagonism to a method of teaching which has done and is doing so much to diffuse a practical knowledge of the art of singing, and a more than merely elementary scientific knowledge of music among classes who were never reached by any other method. . . . . The glory of the Tonic Sol-fa method is that it does its utmost to give the sense of relative pitch, which, with due deference to Professor Macfarren, I consider a much more " valuable quality for musicians" than a sense of absolute pitch, which can only exist in relation to a tempered scale, etc. . . . I submit that the first assertion of Professor Macfarren falls to the ground."

And by the same writer, and others, not specially identified with the Tonic Sol-fa movement, the other contentions were rebutted. The following remarks appeared in the " Tonic Sol-fa Reporter," January, 1888, and are interesting in other ways than as referring to the controversy :—

" What was the reason for Macfarren's hostility to the Tonic Sol-fa system ? In his harmonic thought he was a strong Tonicist, if we may coin a word. He stood alone among harmony teachers in requiring pupils to mark the roots of all the chords they wrote in two-part harmony. His system of chord derivation is based on key; he considered the whence and where of a combination, not merely its intervals. We have heard him speak of figured bass as an 'exploded fallacy'; he was constantly falling foul of it in his teaching, because of its tendency to mislead pupils. Yet he never adopted any other system, even though his friend Day had left a tonic nomenclature of chords ready to his hand. For the reform of that bundle of inconsistencies, an orchestral score, he cared not at all. We have heard him laugh over the curious usage by which the horns, when they pass down into the bass clef, are written an octave lower than they are when in the treble clef. But, he added, 'these absurdities are for us to accept; we cannot mend them.' Thus he was, in music, an ultra-conservative, and towards our notation he observed the same attitude. Having once examined some Tonic Sol-fa papers in which the candidates had in their hurry omitted a few octave marks, he formed the impression that the Tonic Sol-fa notation was inaccurate and uncertain, an impression that he repeated in speech and in print ever after. One would fancy that a sightless man would be indifferent to notation. On the contrary, as his pupils so well know, notation was Macfarren's hobby. Whenever, in playing over an exercise or composition, they came to a chromatic note that was susceptible of two interpretations, he would stop and ask how they had written it, and express great satisfaction if the notation fitted in with his theory of harmonics.

The reason why Macfarren so often declared his opinions against Tonic Sol-fa, was that he was so strongly conscientious. Personally, he was a most tender-hearted man; he answered everybody who wrote to him; and was the most graceful maker of compliments that ever existed. But he had a most exalted sense of duty, and could not even be silent about what he considered error. With all his objections to Tonic Sol-fa, he was careful to be just, and he wrote in 1884 to the Burslem Tonic Sol-fa Choir that their singing was the best of any heard during the Eisteddfod week. In almost every letter he addressed to the present writer he took occasion, when the immediate purpose of the letter was fulfilled, (1) to reiterate his views against Tonic Sol-fa, and (2) to add that these views made not the slightest difference to the regard and esteem which—etc., etc. Such a man was naturally very lovable, and the world is richer for his sterling worth."

In confirmation of the allusions at the close of the

above article, these two letters to Mr. J. S. Curwen are very pleasant to read :—

> "7, Hamilton Terrace, N.W.
> "*May 9th*, 1882.

"MY DEAR CURWEN,

"I am told by Mr. Wrigley of your forbearing allusion, at Manchester, to my letter. Regard for your father and yourself, and respect for the zealous work of your colleagues, makes me regret that I cannot approve your system; but while obliged to oppose it, I must feel personal esteem for yourself, and I am indeed gratified to find, as I have always believed, that you entertain like sentiments for me.

> "Yours with friendly regards,
> "G. A. MACFARREN."

> "*October*, 1885.

"MY DEAR CURWEN,

"I accept with pleasure the kind offer of your dedication, because the offer and its acceptance will testify to the world that though, from a sense of duty, I must occasionally appear as your opponent, I entertain a high personal regard for you which you do not reject. I shall be most interested in your new book when it appears."

Of "gracefully made compliments" may be instanced the expression, in a congratulatory marriage letter, written, unavoidably, after the "honeymoon," of the wish that "though the moon was over, the honey might remain!"

On another subject, of vast musical interest, Macfarren has been charged with a change of opinion; no necessary discredit to any man. It has been sagaciously said that no man need be ashamed to own that he has been in the wrong; it is simply to say that he is wiser to-day than he was yesterday. And Macfarren had no stupid reserve in this matter; his was a constantly growing mind, accumulating knowledge,

enlarging its scope and comprehension. And the
subject now referred to, and his progressive, rather
than contradictory, attitudes towards it, furnish a
signal instance of this openness to conviction. It is
the music of Johann Sebastian Bach. At one time
Macfarren seems to have been but little in advance of
other untravelled English Musicians in acquaintance
with, and consequent estimate of, the music of the
matchless old Cantor. When the first volume of the
Leipsic Bach Society reached this country, in 1853,
he wrote a series of articles concerning it, in the
" Musical World," commencing, " Bach is at present
a mystery in England." And then, after alluding to
" the forty-eight Preludes and Fugues, the ' Art of
Fugue,' and a few of the Pedal Fugues," as " the
emulation of organists and the wonder of harmonists,"
and referring to the very few other works by the
Master that were then known in England, he continues:—

" Beyond this, we know that Mendelssohn reverenced
him; that all the world acknowledges his excellence,—it is
not so certain that all the world understands what all the
world acknowledges;—that he is said to have written
much more than any one ever heard; that his music is
remarkable for the profoundity of its contrapuntal elaboration, for the ceaselessness of its continuity, for the strict-
ness of its part-writing, for the occasional most modern
and wonderfully beautiful application of some of the ex-
tremest chromatic harmonies, for the intolerable harshness
of some of its progressions of passing notes, for the
frequency of its false relations, for the absence of rhythm,
and for the abundant employment of the ancient Corales,
or hymn tunes, of the Lutheran Church, as themes for the
various exercise of his powers; that the founder of his
house was a Hungarian miller and baker; that he com-

menced the study of his art at seven years of age; that he defeated Marchand, a celebrated organist, in a trial upon their instruments; that Frederic the Great dismissed a court to receive the first visit of the notable contrapuntist at Potsdam, wrote him the subject for a Fugue, which he improvised; that he wrote a Fugue upon the four letters of his own name; and that he had twenty children, sons and daughters. Knowing all this, we must still admit that Bach is at present a mystery in England—a mystery which the publications of the Bach Society in Leipsic will enable us to solve," etc.

It is hardly necessary to remind the reader of the date at which the above remarks were written, and of the vast change which these thirty-seven years have wrought, by the progressive "solution" of the "mystery." The first volume of the Society's publications contained ten Church Cantatas. After remarks upon the obsolete instruments comprised in the scores, and the impracticability of much that is allotted to certain instruments and voices, as well as the "somewhat extraordinary arrangement of instruments"; Macfarren proceeds (speaking of the first Cantata, for Annunciation Day, on Corale "Wie schön leuchtet der Morgenstern"):—

"It is a conspicuous characteristic of this work, in common with much of the music for full orchestra of Handel, that, both as regards counterpoint and instrumentation, ... each of the parts appears to be written rather with a design to make it independently and individually interesting, than with a comprehensive view to the general effect; thus, we have some of the most irregular and otherwise unaccountable progressions between two or more of the parts, ... [instance given] . . . . and an utter disregard of clearness, which modern experience regards as the highest quality in orchestral writing; but we have not, in common with Handel, the immensely broad, the truly colossal ideas which manifest themselves through all the entanglement of pedantic and useless elaboration, and which make the name of the great author of the ' Messiah' a synonym for sublimity; nor those occasional extremely judicious dispositions of the parts which anticipate the utmost that has been attained in modern times. One might suppose that the habit in composition of the period when this music was produced, must have been to form some general but not very definite purpose as to a progression of harmony, and then to write all the several parts, each without especial reference to the others, the whole process being more or less analogous to the system of Gothic architecture, in which every particular detail is the subject of especial design. In the case of Handel, the analogy may be continued to the massive grandeur of the general effect; in the case of Bach, I greatly question if this would be realized.

Throughout the present work, there is more aim at expression than in anything else of the author, with which I have been previously acquainted. There is also an obviously recognizable form in each of the movements, although this is for the most part somewhat monotonous, and there is, especially in the Arias, a decided, definite, rhythmical phraseology. The art of imitation, I mean the responsive taking up of some particular point from part to part of the score, is so evidently familiar, so obviously natural to the composer, that he plays at elaboration like a game, and treats the most complicate artifices of the musician's repertory as toys invented but to be trifled with. The power of continuity also, the most difficult and the most estimable attainment of the practised artist, is manifested throughout with the most effortless and natural fluency. Upon the whole, the work may be candidly considered as a model to the student of what to avoid, while the accomplished musician may learn from it more that will enrich his utmost acquirements, and enable him to embellish his best ideas, than will ten times repay him for the careful study of the score,—I say careful study, because I am certain that except the utmost care be exerted to discern between the good and the evil, and some considerable knowledge brought to bear, to direct

this discernment, the result of a perusal of such a composition, influenced by such a reverence for the author as
would induce, and therefore accompany it, the result of
such a perusal would be most unquestionable."

In these more recent days of a certain *dilettante*
Bach-worship, such criticism as this, coming from
Macfarren, may awaken surprise. Again, let it be
remembered that even this criticism was at that time
in advance of the prevailing appreciation of Bach in
this country; and, in addition, that even Macfarren
himself seems to have extended his acceptance, as he
enlarged his acquaintance with Bach's works of the
kind, in the course of time; and, to some extent, to
have modified his impressions, although the discrimination evinced in this courageous animadversion
was never laid aside. In further remarks upon the
first movement of this Cantata, he continues:—

"The chief objection to it,—I feel the delicate ground
upon which I tread, in stating objections to the work of
one who is universally, most zealously (it may be in some
cases blindly) reverenced, but I will have the one great
merit of sincerity, whatever be the deficiency of these
remarks, and I can have no such veneration for the reverence of others as to make me disguise my true opinion
of the object of their reverence,—the chief objection to
this movement is the intolerable harshness of many of the
progressions produced by a particular system of passing
notes, which Beethoven has adopted in some of his last
works (for example, in the first movement of the grand
Quartet in B flat), but which even the emulation, the
strongest approval of such a master, cannot justify. No,
until it can be maintained that consecutive fourths, and
consecutive sevenths, and consecutive seconds in the same
parts are euphonious and agreeable, nor Bach, nor Beethoven, nor the reverence of all the world, shall induce me to
admit that they are allowable in harmony, or make me

admire the passages in which they occur. As for such obscurity as is produced by one instrument playing the scale of F major, while another plays the scale of D minor,[1] or such confusion as is created by passages of passing notes being accompanied by passages in arpeggio in the same measure, these are faults that have come down to the writers of our own day, not, I believe, because they are not considered to be faults, but because of the occasional difficulty of avoiding them;—it is much, very much to be regretted, that those who judge by precedent and not by principle, should have such a precedent as Bach for such derelictions."

The series of articles concludes:—

"The publications of the Bach Society in Leipsic are an interesting, perhaps a valuable study for the accomplished musician, but a most dangerous one for the reverential student."

After his animadversions on the "rules broken," "principles violated," and "intolerable things introduced" in the volume, it is curious to recall, as I do, the remark once made to me by a musician, that he knew of no composer who had written more ugly music than Macfarren himself; and it was not unfrequently referred to his "principles" in harmony that he had done so. See, also, the remarks quoted from the "Athenæum," p. 197.

Shortly before the appearance of these articles, when those who were responsible in the matter of the publication of the posthumous compositions of Mendelssohn were generally thought to be too reticent, Macfarren wrote a strong article on the subject in the "Musical World," concluding:—

[1] See p. 224.

"I call upon the parties, be they whom they may, that hold this trust, in the name of the musical public of England, to leave the music of Bach—which will not become any older or more obsolete for remaining a few years longer in obscurity,— .... and to give us, incontinent, all that they possess of what we at least esteem treasure above price," etc.

As time went on, however, more and more of Bach's music was introduced to this country (even as much was unearthed in Germany); mainly through the labours of Sterndale Bennett, who founded the Bach Society here, which did much useful work, and then was dissolved. The *Motets*, the Matthew "Passion-Music," and other works, were performed and published : it became the fashion to accept Bach's Music. Macfarren had the same opportunities as others of enlarging his acquaintance with, and of revising, if not recanting, his expressed opinions. Always open to conviction, always ready to learn, and eager to become acquainted with fine music, he, in no *dilettante* spirit, but from artistic receptiveness, made himself intimate with these—so to speak—"new" works, as they were brought forward, and, one who knew him well has said to me,—"like the good, honest fellow that he was," was not tardy in rendering all homage, as he became, with increasing intelligence, acquainted with the discovered treasures. In February, 1870, in the "Musical Times," he wrote a series of articles on the Matthew "Passion-Music," in which he avows :—

"It is strange, even to wonderful, that the matchless productions of the greatest master of counterpoint should have remained a secret in the land of his birth, and the locality of his activity, for as long again as the whole term of his life, after death had closed his labours. .... It is less remarkable that the fame, the works, nay, the name of Bach, reached not this country. So little did English-men guess at the radiance which would beam from the countenance of the then ' veiled prophet,' that the pon-derous Burney, who devoted four massive volumes to general musical history, and one to his researches in Ger-many, Burney, who was personally familiar with Carl Phillip Emanuel, the most fortunate son of Bach, dismissed the man, the musician, the master, whose now acknow-ledged greatness is the glory of art and of mankind, in a single paragraph ; and this may be regarded as evidence of how little people here knew, how little people here cared, about Bach and his works at the close of the last century. . . . . Bach was assumed to be a profound scholar, and his works within reach were regarded as scholastic exercises, while the character, the variety, and above all, the wondrous expression that specially distinguish them, were to the generality, scarcely more than to the student, impercep-tible. He was supposed, and commonly said to be, a writer of fugues, but of nothing else ; and this brief sum of his capabilities included no acknowledgment of the interest, far beyond the elaboration, that he, of all men, imparted to the fugal form. To this very day the preju-dicial influence of that false estimate clogs our compre-hension of the genius of Bach, and the merit of his music ; and, in spite of growing familiarity with the beauties of his suites, and countless other lighter writings, the habit here is to fancy that Bach is fully represented in his fugues, to regard these but from one narrow aspect, and to expect fugalism in every fresh specimen with which we meet, of his innumerable productions.

" Who looks for this characteristic of the master in his music of the ' Passion ' will look vainly ; and if he be not disappointed at the absence of the fugal element through-out the work, he will be surprised at the poetical beauty of its declamation, the continuity of its melodies, and their truthfulness to the subject they aim to express, at the choral effects, as fine as they are unfamiliar, and at the loving tenderness and intense religious feeling that infuse the whole. The work is indeed a contrapuntal marvel, albeit the device of imitation is almost totally unemployed in it, from first to last. The appliance of the art of counterpoint to the multiplication of melodic interest is shown in the complexity of the writing, and this evidences an unparalleled freedom, which is not more subject for astonishment than for admiration.

*   *   *   *   *

"There is, perhaps, no musical composition extant wherein is embodied so thoroughly as in the present the implicit faith—at once childlike and mature in its simplicity and its depth—of a devout member of the Christian Church. This is said with a full knowledge of Handel's 'Messiah,' of the sublime conception it presents, and of the pre-eminent artistry it evinces. The two works, however, are as different in character as they are unlike in form, and they are as distinct in the nature and means of their expression as the two masters who wrote them were in the constitution of their minds and the habit of their lives. It is not here to compare these masterpieces; and allusion is only made to the English Oratorio in deference to the just position it holds as an illustration of religious feeling in this country. • The music set to St. Matthew's history of the Passion is essentially an unveiling of the personal feelings of the composer, his vivid sense of the truth of the incidents it depicts, and his loving devotion to the divine sufferer, whose relation to himself is shown to be regarded as of the closest intimacy. It relates the facts with the vivacity of an eye-witness, or one, at least, who witnesses them by the second sight of firm belief; and it comments upon them with the affection of a participator in the benefits which have resulted from them, and who feels that his special welfare is due to their enactment."

Later on, when an English edition of Bach's Christmas Oratorio was published, Macfarren prefaced an analytical account of it in the " Musical Times," January, 1874, by avowing :—

" Glad tidings to the world of art are the announcement of this great work in an English garb. The successful production of the Matthew Passion of the same master has made his immortal name familiar to thousands, who, if they had previously heard it, regarded it in the false light of misconception, believing Bach to be the writer of scholastic exercises only, which, because they were wontedly misrepresented in performance, were supposed to be arid and expressionless. The public hearing of the music of the Passion . . . . has convinced, not only those musicians who were formerly unbelievers, but the great mass of the English people, that there was a power cotemporary with the all-accepted Handel, whose influence, though it dawn upon us far later, will affect us as deeply and, in course of time, it is to be expected as universally, as his. . . . . The world must be the better and the wiser for familiarity with this noble music."

This genuine appreciation, however,—more enthusiastic because the result of greater familiarity, more extended knowledge, than he possessed at first,—never interfered with his discriminating judgment. Sixteen years later on, at the Musical Association, in an address on Handel and Bach (when it was my privilege to occupy the chair), he said :—

" With Bach, there was such an exuberance of elaboration, that, save in a few instances, one cannot, without a large amount of intimacy, comprehend the full meaning of the author. Bach had especially the principles of counterpoint at heart in the development of manifold melodies ; but in the entanglement of his melodies there cannot be a question that he introduced often such progressions between parts as are acceptable only because they are Bach's, but would be condemned in the writing of any man who placed not side by side with them such incidents of absolute brilliancy as dazzle our senses, and make us incapable of perceiving the unbeautiful passages. 'From time to time, since musical laws were first inaugurated, there has been forbidden the progression of two parts in perfect intervals, one with another, from fifth to fifth, from eighth to eighth, and fourth to fourth. From eighth to eighth one will not find in Bach's music, but fifths and fourths are not of seldom occurrence, and still worse, and still more often, one finds that his parts proceed in seconds or in sevenths, progressions so hideous that the early law-givers never deemed necessary to prohibit them, believing, one may conjecture, that nobody could be seduced to write what would be repugnant to himself and to everybody else to hear. Will you think from this that I disparage the master? Will you think from this that I slight the genius of the man who, more than any else, proved the capabilities of counterpoint, proved the boundless resources of funda-mental harmony? Oh, no! Let me not so misrepresent the feeling that I have at heart. We should do injustice to even this great master, if blindly (or may I say deafly?) we accepted everything he wrote as a model for our imita-tion. It is only by dissecting the music, and observing what is to be avoided, that we may learn what is to be imitated. To reproduce his beauties is beyond our power, to avoid his faults is within the reach of everyone, and we pay him the greatest homage when we distinguish what is excellent from what is evitable."

To the same effect are his remarks in the " Dic-tionary of Universal Biography," many years pre-viously :—

" He was, perhaps, the most severely conscientious artist that ever devoted himself to music; he deemed that to compromise his art would be to compromise himself, and that to lend himself to anything which did not, to the utmost of his power tend to exalt it, was in the last degree unworthy of him and of music. He was the greatest contrapuntist that has been, and is especially remarkable for the strict integrity of his part-writing, the complexity of which, we must own, often prevents the broad and massive effect that greatly distinguishes the music of Handel from his; his very extensive employment of passing notes induces many harshnesses which will not bear analysis; and his principle of making each part in his score an independent melody, is often carried out at the cost of euphony and the clear-

ness of the whole. These peculiarities were the result of
his never-ending study; his wonderful power of expression evinced in his free movements, in his great choral
works, particularly in his famous 'Passions-Musik,' is
the manifestation of his transcendent genius. As he de-
spised popular applause, so his music is little open to
popular appreciation, and it is, and always, will be,
much more interesting and much more satisfactory to
those who participate in its performance, than to any
passive listener; his music is, beyond that of any other
composer, difficult of comprehension, but its measureless
beauties will ever repay the pains of the student who
unravels them."

Mr. Prout read a most interesting paper on the
"Orchestras of Bach and Handel" before the Musical
Association, December 7th, 1885; after which Macfarren made some remarks, the following being instructive and felicitous:—

"Further, to speak of the groups of instruments which
characterize so very much the scoring of Bach, one may
adduce the custom, in this country, in earlier times, of
assorting the viols together, hautboys together, and shawms
together, and a collection of one class of instruments was
called a ' consort.' Thus, there might be a consort of viols,
or a consort of hautboys, and at that time it was rare, but
not entirely unknown, to have a mixture of one consort with
another consort, and there is a passage of Lord Bacon's
which refers to the mixture of one consort with another
consort, and then it had the name of ' broken music.' A
pretty application of this term occurs in the play of 'Henry
V.,' when the king is courting Princess Katharine, and she
makes very sad havoc of the English pronunciation. The
king says, ' Sweet Katharine, your speech is broken music,
for your voice is music, but your English is broken.' With
reference to the variety of instruments employed by Bach,
I can very often conjecture that some persons in his band
must have had the ability to play on more than one instru-

U

ment, and occasionally left this to go to that. It seems to me extremely probable that such use continued far beyond his time. For example, I cannot suppose it possible that three trombone players would be engaged to play in the 'Messiah,' when Mozart wrote his orchestration, and have parts to play only in the introductory movement in the overture, and in the two small quartets in the last act, which are always sung without any accompaniment. There must have been either some different duty for them in other portions of the work, or there must have been some tradition of these instruments to duplicate the choral voice parts, and I think it is a very possible thing that in Bach's time his horn players or trumpet players, who had no parts perhaps in but a single number in a long work, would play violins throughout the rest of the performance."

Quotations have been made from the " Dictionary of Universal Biography," for which work, in 1857 and following years, Macfarren wrote a number of highly interesting articles concerning musicians. Moreover, at the time of the first Handel Festival at the Crystal Palace, in 1859, the centenary of Handel's death, Macfarren was engaged by the publisher of the Dictionary to prepare a biography of Handel, in pamphlet form, for sale at the festival. The MS. of this biography miscarried in transit by post, and, in order that the publication should be ready in time for the festival, Macfarren dictated it from memory; and, on the subsequent recovery of the original MS., it was found, by comparison, that the differences between the two versions were few and slight—another instance of his marvellously accurate memory !

It may here be recorded that he wrote, on a special commission, for transmission to New York, additional accompaniments and an organ part to "Israel in Egypt;" and for another occasion, parts for four horns (Mozart having only two) for the "Messiah;" also an organ part to Bach's "Magnificat."

Macfarren's acquaintance with Shakespeare was very intimate, enabling him to make apt references such as the one above quoted. Indeed, his literary knowledge generally was somewhat extensive: remarkable, indeed, for a blind man. Of Browning's works, he said to a pupil, a young man: "When you are older, and able to read onwards more than two lines, you will find more interest than you can now feel in his writings." One of the last general conversations that I had with Macfarren was about Mr. Swinburne's poems, which I told him about; he agreeing with me with regard to their wonderful word-power. Writing to Mr. T. J. Dudeney, acknowledging a double gift,—a copy of Aytoun's "Lays of the Scottish Cavaliers" and some violets, he characteristically remarks :—

"The noble Cavaliers of Aytoun's painting set grand example of steadfastness to a purpose : the bunch of sweet violets verify your words on the sweets of spring time, and attest the good wishes of one who has all their modesty."

To the same, acknowledging a copy of Tennyson's poems :—

"The mind that studies his beautiful writing must be enriched, and thus I shall gain strength and pleasure from your gift."

CHAPTER XIII.

Macfarren's Oratorios: St. John the Baptist, 1873;
The Resurrection, 1875; Joseph, 1877; King
David, 1883; St. George's Te Deum, 1884. Method
of Composing and Dictating. Philharmonic Analytical Programmes, 1869-1880.

IN the year 1870 Macfarren renewed his youth and
made a new departure by commencing the composition of the first of the series of works by which, perhaps, apart from his theoretical and critical writings,
he is best known to the general public and the present generation, and by which his name as a composer
is most likely to go down to posterity—namely, his
Oratorios. Notwithstanding the masterly critical
and historical articles that had proceeded from his
comprehensively embraceful mind on the Oratorios of
the great Masters, as well as on Church music as an
allied subject, his antecedents as a composer would
probably have scarcely prepared, or at least suggested
this as the line in which his unquestioned powers
would find their ultimate development or achieve
their most enduring triumphs. Indeed, he himself, as
will be seen, felt this, more or less. But he was
artistically prepared to devote himself energetically,
earnestly, and reverently, to any lofty subject on which
his thoughts were cast, and the result was seen in

the unequivocal, though not uniform, success of the great works of which " St. John the Baptist " was the first.

The oratorio, " St. John the Baptist," of which the " book " was compiled by Dr. E. G. Monk, was originally intended for the Festival of the Three Choirs at Gloucester, and was completed in time for performance thereat, in 1872 ; but, from causes redounding to the composer's honour, it was not then produced. Difficulty was raised, moreover, at Gloucester, to the performance in the cathedral of the florid and blatantly secular song of the daughter of Herodias, " I rejoice in my youth." The honour of the first production of this oratorio is due to the committee of the Bristol Festival, who brought it out in October, 1873.

The choir at Bristol was trained, with great credit to himself, by the late Alfred Stone (1841-78). The conductor at the festival was Mr. Charles Hallé, and the principal singers were Mesdames Lemmens-Sherrington and Patey, and Messrs. Edward Lloyd and Santley. The success was immediate and incontrovertible. At the outset, the dramatic feeling and masterful construction of the overture were apparent, with its trumpet call to represent the " Sohar " summons, and its avoidance of a perfect cadence till the end, indicating the long expectancy concerning unfulfilled prophecy, until the " voice of one crying in the wilderness " proclaimed " The kingdom of heaven is at hand." And not only was this dramatic feeling, together with local colouring, sustained throughout, but innumerable details, some of them too minute to be observable by the superficial, or without repeated hearings or close examination of the score, but nevertheless combinedly maintaining the unity of the work, evidenced the highest order of cultivated musicianship; of which, however, all who knew Macfarren were fully aware, even without this newest manifestation of his artistry. The oratorio was soon performed in London and elsewhere; and, on its first performance in Exeter Hall by the Sacred Harmonic Society, in March, 1874, it was declared by an intelligent critic :—

" Never was success more promptly or more universally acknowledged than that which has bestowed upon Mr. Macfarren the priceless laurel leaf of a great composer. Not a voice has been raised to dispute it, even amid the clashing opiuions and conflicting tastes pre-eminently distinctive of the musical world. Such agreement is wonderful, and more convincingly than any argument or analysis proves that in ' St. John the Baptist ' we have a creation of genius." [1]

And the same critic, probably, wrote in the " Musical Times " of November in the same year, after the oratorio had been performed at the Leeds Festival :—

" It is a really great thing, this English oratorio; one of which we have all a right to be proud; one that will be handed down among the heirlooms of the nation. Speaking thus positively of the future is not rash, because connoisseurs on the one part, and the general public on the other, unite to acclaim ' St. John the Baptist;' and such unanimity has a special significance, as showing that Mr. Macfarren, while labouring in the highest sphere of music, has exerted a power over feelings shared by all. ' St. John the Baptist' is a work of consummate skill, but it is also an epic, to the numbers of which every heart vibrates. Things of this sort do not easily die."

Immediately after the performance of the oratorio

[1] " Daily Telegraph."

at Bristol, so great was the sensation produced, that the committee, feeling justly proud of the lustre shed upon the festival by its being the occasion of the introduction of so fine a work, held an *impromptu* meeting in an ante-room, and, among themselves, without drawing upon the festival funds, subscribed one hundred guineas, which sum was then presented to the composer, in recognition of their obligations.

Shortly afterwards his brother professors at the Royal Academy of Music, "all proud of him," presented him with an address on vellum, with their signatures, the speech on the occasion being made by Sir W. Sterndale Bennett.

With regard to one of the most esteemed numbers in this oratorio, the following statement by Miss Prescott will be read with interest :—

"Another memory lies upon me like a conscience. About his ' St. John the Baptist ' there had been some repetition of the assertion that the setting of the words, ' This is my beloved Son,' was borrowed from the passage in ' Lohengrin,' at the descent of the Grail. I asked him about it, for it troubled me, as I dare say some others of his friends have been troubled. He said, ' I don't know why Wagner should have the monopoly of the harmonies of the violin —for that is the chief resemblance. But as to my borrowing from him, that was impossible : my first possibility of hearing "Lohengrin" was when it was first done in London in such a year (I forget the year), and by that time " St. John" was completed, rejected, and put away in brown paper on the shelf, some time before its first performance. That number, " This is my beloved Son," was the first one of the oratorio that I wrote.' I think he added, ' It was the suggestion or origin of the whole composition.' I asked him if I might put this account in a little book I was then writing, at a point where I considered it might appropriately come in. No ; he would not allow it. ' Not now; when I am dead and gone, you may say as much as you like.' I little thought that in a year or two more he would be 'dead and gone,' as he said, and I free to say as much as I had opportunity for. I am not surprised at a resemblance taking hold of people when they considered the almost horror of Wagner's music that the old Professor had. Then the strange coincidence of *poetic* idea: the descent of the Holy Ghost in the one—of the Holy Grail in the other. But I can't help feeling the extraordinary difference; the complicated harmonies of Wagner's, and the simple diatonic chords of the Englishman's music, coupled with the pure quality of the chorus—all women's voices."

In connection with this Wagner reference may be given a quotation from a letter, which refers to a former communication, oral or verbal, to Mr. T. J. Dudeney of Taunton, though not referring to the oratorio :—

" Much thinking upon your Historical Concerts brings me to withdraw the advice I gave you that pieces by Wagner and Liszt should be included in the series. These writers are working a great evil upon music—the first, most anomalously, by reason of the true beauties that are entangled in his vices. To bring them into notice is to applaud their pretensions, and though your censure or mine, be it pronounced in blame or praise, can have no force against the torrent voice of their upholders, our duty is indeed not to swell their chorus by the whisper of implied assent. A lecturer once expounded at length and with reason what was bad in a piece of music, which was then performed to exemplify his remarks, and the audience encored it with rapture—nay, even spoke with particular pleasure of one point that had been held up for their detestation. This proves the futility of teaching as opposed to the power of appetite. Were you to preach temperance at a gin-shop door, and let your congregation taste the poison sold therein, that they might know its vileness, they would come out drunkards. You must represent the art of now by music of Brahms, perhaps of Bruch, or even of Gounod, but not by the good pieces of men whose habit is ill and whose gleams of light are but misleading."

One of Macfarren's pupils wrote a critical notice of " St. John the Baptist " in a periodical, and this drew from him the following letter — an instance of his tender friendship and humility, as addressed to a pupil :—

"MY DEAR ——,
" I have always avoided acknowledging newspaper notices of my doings in public, under the idea that the writers fulfilled a public duty in stating their good or ill opinions of what was offered to their judgment, and that the subject of their remarks had no right to comment upon the fulfilment of such duty. The strong personal feeling which peers through every line of your beautifully written, most flattering, and most affectionate article on 'St. John the Baptist,' compels me to break my rule, and to assure you that, however little the work merits the opinions you eloquently express, the composer of the work will treasure the affectionate regard thus expressed as one of the richest earnings of his professional life. I know not how much my pleasant intercourse with you may have had to do with the formation of your critical power, but, so far as myself have not influenced it, I am indeed proud of your review of my work, and am impelled by it to try again to accomplish something that may be worthy of some of what you say. I thank you most heartily, and am your sincere friend,   " G. A. MACFARREN."

The reception given to " St. John the Baptist " so re-awakened and extended Macfarren's reputation, that he was recognized yet more widely than heretofore as the foremost representative of English music ; and he was commissioned to compose an oratorio for the Birmingham Festival of 1876. The work pro-

duced was "The Resurrection." This was reflective
rather than dramatic, with a large preponderance of
recitative, and by no means appealed so directly to a
general audience. It met with, at best, a success of
respect, rather than of sympathetic appreciation, on
the part of the press no less than that of the public ;
notwithstanding the advantageous circumstances under
which it was produced. The conductor was Mr.
Walter Macfarren, to whom it was dedicated, and the
principal vocalists were Mesdames Lemmens-Sherrington and Patey, and Messrs. Lloyd and Santley. One
circumstance, however, militated considerably against
its effect, namely, that by some strange misunder-
standing, not necessary to explain here, the pitch of
the organ had been lowered, and did not coincide
with that of the orchestra ; and, as the part of Mr.
Santley as narrator, when speaking for the Saviour,
was accompanied by the organ only, the effect of the
changed pitch was bewildering and depressing. The
composer's own epitome of the oratorio is interesting :—

" The book shows its own argument and the method
wherein this is treated. The latter differs from that of the
early Church, preserved by Luther and exemplified by
Bach, in having the speeches of the personages sung by
him who also narrates the action; in having the texts of
the reflective passages selected from Holy Writ ; and in
having original tunes to the hymns. This last is necessitated by the old practice in England of making Psalm
tunes to metres, not to words, and thus having no tune
and poem identified with each other. One of the rare
exceptions is in the 100th Psalm, and this tune is used as
the *finale* because old versions disperse the sense of the
first prose verse, and neglect the emphatic accentuation of
a primitive and much-liked reading of the tune, a new

version of the first verse of the Psalm is fitted thereto. The musician's beautiful resource, which dates from ' Cosi fan tutte,' in the opera so named, and ' Er ist verstummet ' in 'Fidelio,' at least, not to name the mad scenes in a host of Italian operas (the resource of alluding in an after situation to a phrase which illustrates an earlier, and so associating the two as in one thought, or showing the bearing of each upon the other) is freely employed. Thus when ' the disciples went away again,' the phrase ' Even our faith,' from the preceding chorus, is meant to show the bent of their thoughts on the road to their own homes. ' He is the resurrection ' is quoted in subsequent places to which it is supposed to be pertinent. So are ' They have taken away the Lord,' ' Now is our salvation nearer,' ' For fear of the Jews,' ' Peace be unto you,' Thomas's ' Except I shall see,' ' Blessed are they that have not seen,' &c. The overture is suggested by, but pretends not to depict, the two preceding chapters of St. John's Gospel—at least, this portion of the narrative was evidently in the mind of the composer."

Macfarren's disappointment at the non-success of " The Resurrection " was keen and abiding. He again and again spoke of " my failure in ' The Resurrection.'" Some of his friends say that he loved it more than others of his works, " as a mother loves her sickly child; " others think that " he loved it with justice, as a beautiful work, cast more in the Bach model." To Mr. T. J. Dudeney, who was engaged, in 1880, in rehearsing " St. John the Baptist" with a zealous local society, he wrote :—

" You undertake a troublesome task in ' St. John '—difficult, I will not call it to you, for you know not the word. Some of these days your thoughts perhaps may turn to my still-born Easter Oratorio, which will then indeed have a resurrection."

Much more gratifying is it to record the success, a

year later, of his oratorio " Joseph," composed for the
Leeds Festival, 1877, and produced thereat, September
21st, 1877, under the conductorship of the composer's
brother, Mr. Walter Macfarren, that production being
pronounced " a memorable event in the history of
music." A contemporary critic wrote :—

" Professor Macfarren is not a Handel or a Mendelssohn,
nor does he slavishly imitate them or confine himself to any
particular school of writing. He is simply Macfarren, a
name hereafter to be honoured in musical history, and to
make the Professor's chair at Cambridge memorable for
the two great musicians who have held it in succession. It
will be remembered that at the last Festival the Professor
had a place with ' St. John the Baptist.' This work delighted all who heard it, especially those who appreciate
learned writing. The oratorio yesterday perhaps appeals
to wider sympathies with its beautiful melodies and colour.
At any rate, whether the work is heard many a time again,
or is forgotten (a very unlikely and unreasonable event),
the performance yesterday will mark the present Festival
as an important event in the history of music. . . . The
work is dedicated thus :—' In remembrance of happy hours
spent in its inscription, this Oratorio is dedicated to my
pupil, friend, and amanuensis, Oliveria Louisa Prescott.'
The work is great in design and execution, and seemed to
demand from the audience a front rank in the greatest
musical compositions, or rejection as an over-reaching ambition. The challenge was accepted by the audience, and
at the close the answer might have been heard in the streets
outside, as cheer followed upon cheer. . . . Throughout
the oratorio, Dr. Macfarren has been (with one or two exceptions) above all things original. He tells the beautiful
story of Joseph's life . . . in the most dramatic musical
language. Every phrase must have been the result of intense care and study, arising from a fine artistic sense, an
appreciation of sacred words which would have distinguished the Professor as a theologian of matured experience. From the first bar to the last the work is a sur-

prise—a wonder to those who thought that Music had said all she had to say, and that no resources of novelty were left open. . . . It was a great work, grandly performed, and listened to with eager interest until the last bar. Then followed a scene never to be forgotten. There was a persistent roar until the blind Professor was led into the orchestra, and the cheering was renewed again and again. No need, Professor, to be so overcome with emotion! This is but the first instalment of the tribute of praise which the lovers of the true and good in Art shall pay you in the time to come as you take your just place with the worthies whose names are remembered when the wearers of crowns are forgotten and dynasties have crumbled to dust." [1]

Against this verdict, which has not been in any important way contravened, may be cited, in all fairness, that of another critic :—

"'Joseph' may be a great work, but it is distinctly not a pleasing one . . . dry, if not pedantic." [2]

On the other hand, again, the composer's old fellow-student and friend, the late W. H. Holmes, went to Leeds on purpose to hear the work, and has thus cheerily recorded his impressions in his "Notes upon Notes":—

"I was in the country in a moment, among the shepherds, &c., in the overture to 'Joseph.' And what beautiful pictures Professor Macfarren has presented us with, in his (to my mind) greatest work, 'Joseph.' The glowing sun, in the first chorus, so bright and brilliant and glorious. How one felt the light! What 'music painting!' Then the relation of the dream, with its lovely soul-haunting melody, when one does feel literally to be among the

[1] "Yorkshire Post and Leeds Intelligencer.
[2] "Monthly Musical Record," Oct. 1, 1877.

sheaves. Then the 'hatred scene,' so full of 'bad passion.'
Then the glorious march and chorus of the Ishmaelites,
with their spices and myrrh, so original, almost taking one
into another country; this chorus, with its skilful instrumentation, must, I think, become very popular. . . . And
now, in the really serious parts of the oratorio, how our
friend, the learned Professor, has risen with his work. One
of the greatest contrapuntists, and such a complete master
of instrumentation, he knows when to use his great powers
—often, I believe, rising to the sublime, and, indeed, becoming an eloquent preacher in his work. Happy composer! To illustrate such subjects must be good for the
composer, and to those who intelligently listen. Such music
leads us to think of the far better world. The call for the
composer at the end was overpowering to all. I believe
there were many moist eyes. Outside the hall a big York-
shireman (one of the Ishmaelites) said to me, 'Heigh, but
he's a *fine fellow.*' I then said I had known Professor
Macfarren from his boyhood. You should have seen the
measurement he took of me after that; and I feel sure he
regretted not having any Yorkshire pudding to offer me."

In 1881 Macfarren seems to have been cogitating
concerning another oratorio, though then occupied
with other work—perhaps with the "Ajax" music, to
be hereafter mentioned. He said one day to his indefatigable friend, Miss Prescott, "It is an inspiration
to find a subject fit for musical treatment, of any kind."
She suggested one, and hoped to find words for him.
He himself pencilled a letter to her on the subject—
an occasional feat, to intimate friends, when no amanuensis was at hand—as follows :—

"Bennett's birthday, 1881.—My dearest Oliveria—
I believe in you implicitly, else should I be hopeless of
your valued proposal to find an oratorio theme in the
divine St. John, and even in your hands I more wish for
than expect success. Your intention is however an en-

couragement. With this earnest of good will to begin, I am certain to plant my endeavours in a very hotbed of propagation."

After the suggestion had taken somewhat unwieldy shape, he again wrote :—

"Good Friday, '81.—A thousand thanks and a thank for your interesting budget, which I have heard with eagerness, but cannot yet digest. I will hear it again and again, and in seeking to master all its méaning, hope to do justice to the high subject, and to your conception of its treatment."

After long thinking, he judged the subject impossible, and gave it up as not dramatic. Then Miss Prescott's query, or remonstrance, in return, was answered by this highly interesting letter :—

"7, Hamilton Terrace.
"17th April.

"My dear Oliveria,

"'Why must every Oratorio be dramatic?' My failure in 'The Resurrection' proves that, whatever the case with other writers, my possibility of success is in a dramatic form. 'What is "Israel" and the "Messiah"?' 'Israel' is a narrative, but of most dramatic character; as it has no persons, however, the story is all told by chorus; and no succession of choruses to such extent, save only this, can ever be written again, or would ever be accepted—even this succession was unreceived for a hundred years—the world was coaxed to hear it by the insertion of irrelevant songs, and the perception of its immensity was due to the imperative power of Handel's name. 'Messiah' is dramatic, for though its personages are not named, all its strongest passages are personal; and were they not so, the unique importance of the subject, and the unique mastery of its treatment secure it attention that would be denied to a lesser theme or a small writer. 'The Last Judgment' is, save one scene, not dramatic, and it has succeeded, but this was when Spohr was new here, and when his peculiarities made an almost madness among musicians.[1] 'Lazarus' has been treated by Barnett, and it would be most graceless to tread on the heels of a friend.

" Palm Sunday is in 'The Light of the World,' comparison with which would be as undesirable as with the work last named.

. "'The Mount of Olives' has been handled by Beethoven.

" The trial might indeed be made highly effective, as Mendelssohn has proved in 'Christus ;' but this, which furnishes the only text that could be impressively rendered, you would dismiss in an instrumental movement that could represent nothing, and would interest nobody.

"'The Crucifixion' has been used by Spohr less well than his other theme, and when his great esteem had set. The confiding of the Mother to St. John's care is the only one point in the whole plan that introduces the personality of the hero, and this would lose all its point through English repugnance to the impersonation of the Saviour. To narrate the incident would assimilate it to those in 'The Resurrection,' and though Santley sang them perfectly, professional critics, and the public by their dictation, have denounced those scenes to be ' undramatic,' as if this were the worst stain that could be put on them. This, and the trial scene are given by Bach ; if they are to be treated in his wise, nothing so good as his can be done ; if dramatically, the chief person may not appear ; if narratively, all interest will drop out of them.

" Your 2nd Act is the 'Last Judgment ;' the conditions to which this work owes its success cannot extend to another.

" The objections I have stated, my dear Oliveria, are all as nothing, compared with the enormous one, that St. John appears but once in the whole. He wrote the history, indeed, he commented thereon, and he dreamed the dream, but these facts would not warrant the entitling of the work with his name. To call it ' Oliveria ' would be as pertinent,

[1] See p. 217.

though not so attractive, but then not so disappointing, since not prompting false expectancy.

"I hate saying all this to you who have shown so much love for me and for your subject in the task you undertook. You write diffidently of your own power to make musical rendering of the theme, but I most confidently counsel you not to contemplate such an exercise of your talent, for I am certain, firstly, that it would not reveal the best of your powers; secondly, that general hearers would not give you credit for the good you did. I thank you endlessly, but must seek still for the needful matter.

"Now let me wish you a happy Easter, full enjoyment of this most beautiful day, and a more worthy receiver of your next good offices.

"Affectionately yours,
"G. A. Macfarren."

This letter was followed by yet another letter, probably in reply to further representation,—hardly remonstrances,—on Miss Prescott's part:—

"7, Hamilton Terrace,
"*20th April.*

"More thanks, my dear Oliveria, and more regrets. The more I consider your subject, the more I find it, for me, impracticable. You say St. John may be left out of the title; he does not appear, and cannot, in the whole book; thus we only amuse ourselves by associating it with him, who, if influential as others would be in its arrangement, would be all impersonal in its structure. You cite 'The Woman of Samaria,' which is to my appreciation completely what a book should not be; its wants are that all interest is taken out of the person of our Lord, by the vague confusion between what He says, and what is said of Him, and that the reflective passages so interrupt and overweight the narrative, as to annul its interest. The subterfuge in 'The Light of the World' of prefixing 'solo' to all the passages for the centre figure, rather acknowledges the difficulty than meets it. Your book would best be named also 'The Light of the World,' but it would be less avail-

x

able for my use than its predecessor, because the strongest
points of the action are not in it appropriated, and because
the second act has no action at all. If I am ever to do
anything with it, it must be after manifold discussion,
careful perusal, and long pondering, all of which I may give
to it after the fulfilment of the present commission,—give
to it with regard to a post future work to which I shall not
be committed, but may construct as legacy to my posthumous reputation. Now I must confess that I have lighted
on another theme, and, since my last letter, have made
some advance in its distribution, namely, King David, beginning in Ziklag, and selecting from the subsequent
history. I know me to be the unfittest person to treat a
scripture subject that ever undertook the task; I can only
justify me to myself by the absence of any other task; you
despise critics, I acknowledge but one, namely, myself,
and if his approval be wanting, my attempts will be futile,
and my presumption in treading on sanctified ground will
be many times magnified. All this seems ungrateful for
the pains you have spent, but only seems, for I assure you,
I esteem most highly the interest you take in my doing,
and the help you give to its accomplishment, for it is help
that you have proved to me my inability to work on the
very greatest subject.

" Yours with endless thanks,
" G. A. MACFARREN."

The narrative of King David above alluded to was,
as is well known, adopted by Macfarren, and was the
subject of his fourth and last Oratorio, composed for
the Leeds Festival, 1883. The passages forming the
dramatic story itself were selected by himself, with
Miss Macfarren's aid. Those interspersed as reflective were chosen by Miss Prescott; "that is," she
relates—

" He would tell me, ' I want words for a chorus, or solo,
at this point in the narration, something to this effect,'
and he would give some expression of thought; I would
hunt up various texts or combinations with something of

the meaning, and he chose that which seemed most to his taste; sometimes, may be, a dozen texts were rejected in this way, from his severe, almost fastidious feeling of what was fitting, both to the place in the song, and to be united to music.

" I remember bringing him among others the text, 'Not every one that saith unto me, Lord, Lord, is fit to enter the kingdom of heaven.' I forget the point it was in- tended for, but it seemed to me appropriate. His verdict at once was, 'It is very difficult to make clear any *quoted* words,' alluding to 'Lord, Lord.' Again, I brought the text, 'There is joy in the presence of the angels of God,' etc. He objected, 'This has been set by Sir Arthur Sullivan in a prominent place in his oratorio—it is inviting comparison, or almost stealing his thoughts.' That objec- tion was removed by going to another Gospel for the same thought in different words. It now stands, 'Joy shall be in heaven,' etc.

"Another point gave me a good deal of trouble,—the chorus after David's fall. The beauty of the accompanied recitative which relates the double sin, marks the beauty of the old composer's nature. They say no man can create an artistic work that is greater than himself. Macfarren disputed this assertion, for he said the oratorio 'Messiah' was greater than Handel himself. Surely the reserve, the gentleness, the fire, and the terrible denunciation in this music, tell their story, the story of a good man's horror at the vile deeds of his hero; while his human sympathy and tenderness could feel the undercurrent, 'faithful in unfaithfulness,' which gained forgiveness in the after life of David, and won Solomon his position as king and ancestor of the Messiah. I brought many words for this after-chorus; the texts I could find were not personal enough: he wanted something that should draw thoughts round to present time. His feeling was that in an oratorio, unlike an opera, the chorus (and some of the solos, as *choragus*) take the place of Greek chorus, and thus some- times act as persons in the drama,—sometimes as narrator, sometimes as leaders of the audience's thoughts. In this way he justified the use of a prayer from a modern liturgy. It is not, as a lecturer said at the Musical Association,

that 'we are in Judea, and straightway transported into
an English church,' but rather, we are in England at this
present time, and witnessing by our minds' ears the drama
of past times.   What more fit, and naturally artistic, than
that we of the audience should feel the terror of the evil
deed, and that we are human, and may fall into the same.
'Remember not, Lord, *our* offences, but help us, lest we
also fall like this man David.'

"I do not remember whether it has been written any-
where, but Macfarren's feeling as to the course of the
book of 'King David' was strong ; in this way,—the first
part, beginning with the greatness, works up to the Jewish
idea—*judgment*.   The second part, with all the terrible
consequences,—quarrels and sins among his people and his
sons,—works up to the Christian idea—*mercy*.   Thus the
closing words of the first part are, 'Vengeance is mine,
saith the Lord, I will repay.'   'The Lord shall destroy
them in His displeasure ; He shall consume them.'   Then
the terrified hush ; as he said, 'the greatest terror is silent,
and we can only express silence in music by hushed
sounds.'   (A critic said, without the least appreciation of
this idea, 'What nonsense to put a pianissimo in such a
place !')   The closing words of the second part, on the
contrary, are, 'Joy shall be in heaven over one sinner that
repenteth.'

"At one point in the work, he said he was at a loss how
to set about composition.   It was the parable of Nathan
about the little ewe lamb, 'There were two men in one
city.'   I went home, and thought how to help him.   The
words took root in my own mind and grew up into a
ballad-like song, founded on the idea of the old minstrel
or bard declamation in rhythm, with slight orchestral
accompaniment.   I took it to him ; at least it might set
his thoughts a-going, I thought.   No doubt it did, for,
though he complained to me after hearing it, 'Now I have
a greater difficulty before me ; I have not only to do something worthy of the place, but something that shall be
different to yours,' he soon produced something.   Certainly,
it was about as different to mine as could be imagined ;
though still I feel he had the idea of a ballad-declaimer in
his mind."

As illustrative of Macfarren's readiness to accept criticism, Miss Prescott relates :—

"I was present at the rehearsal of 'King David' in London, before its performance at Leeds; and between the morning and afternoon work, the conductor, passing by me as I sat, remarked 'I wonder where the old man gets such beautiful ideas.' I believe I answered, 'Out of his heart,' for that was my conviction at the time. However, the next remark was, 'That chorus is too long ; it-ought to be cut ; it spoils the oratorio.' I treasured up the criticism, for I knew G. A. M. respected the opinion and valued the kindness of his conductor. As soon as I could, I took the pair of remarks home, both sugar and salt, to its proper owner. No doubt he smiled at the sugar, for he had a sweet tooth, notwithstanding all the bitter he had had in his time, perhaps because of it ; but when I went on to the advice, he asked eagerly, 'Where, where?' and thought over it deeply. By the next rehearsal the cut was made.

"His acceptance of criticism sometimes took the form of humour. When 'King David' had been performed, a critic remarked it was very daring of any composer to set the words, 'Woe, woe, woe,' as he did in one of the songs. When G. A. M. heard it, he only smiled, and capped it : 'I remember when "Ajax" was done at one of the London theatres, it was remarked by some wag that Ajax cried out "Wo, wo, wo," till there wasn't a cab-horse that would budge out of the rank.'

"The second performance of that oratorio was a curious illustration of the questionable truth of some criticisms on his work. Some one had said what nonsense it was to make the chorus repeat the word 'Absolom, Absolom, Absolom;' tossing a single word about hither and thither from voice to voice was 'foolish, nonsensical rubbish,' etc. After the first part of the oratorio was done, there went cries from all parts of the hall, 'Macfarren, Macfarren;' hither and thither the single word was 'tossed about' among the friendly audience, just as in the chorus so blamed. It is said, also, that fugues are dull, uninteresting to any but dry, learned musicians, and incapable of any poetic expression. However, the fugue 'Thy Seed shall be great,' worked up the audience and chorus to a great pitch of excitement."

The Overture to "King David" was written before the rest of the Oratorio, a horn-passage in it, which may be termed the "shepherd-boy theme," being introduced in the course of the work. The "coronation theme," to the words "I will give no slumber," now in the Oratorio, is the second version that was written. The words, "The thing which David had done" are set to an old Church Tone. The Final Chorus is the only one of which Macfarren made sketches before completing it, so far as his amanuensis, Mr. Windeyer Clark, remembers.

At the first performance of this Oratorio, Macfarren was sitting in a convenient, unobserved position, within hearing of the conductor. When the audience interrupted the immediate succession of the numbers, especially in one place, by applause, Macfarren became vexedly excited, and in audible whisper cried out, "Go on, go on," preferring the continuity to the expressed approval. The conductor on this occasion was Sir Arthur Sullivan; the soloists were Mesdames Albani, Edith Wynne, and Patey, and Messrs. Lloyd, Santley, and Foli.

The remaining work of this class to be here mentioned, though not an Oratorio, is the "St. George's Te Deum," composed for the opening of the London International and Universal Exhibition, at the Crystal Palace, 1884, and performed, on the Handel Orchestra, April 23rd. The circumstances of the occasion necessitated, or at least led to, a remarkable construction: two military bands—the Grenadier Guards and Scots

Guards—being employed, in addition to the ordinary orchestral band, chorus, and solo voices ; the principal vocalists being Mesdames Albani and Patey, and Mr. Santley. The first number was a Prelude, termed " The Gathering of the Nations," in which were introduced the Austrian and Russian National Hymns, Danish National Airs, " Die Wacht am Rhein," the " Marsellaise," " Rule Britannia," and " Universal Hymn." In the last chorus, "God Save the Queen " was assigned to the military bands, while a fugue on a totally distinct subject was performed simultaneously by the voices and orchestral band : altogether a marvel of complication to be dictated by a blind man ! The work was treated with small consideration by the musical critics, as a pompous *pièce d'occasion;* but is worthy of more respect than might be supposed, especially in the alternative form which the score supplies, relieved of the meretricious, or, at least, circumstantial accessories.

It may be interesting to give some account of Macfarren's method of procedure in the composition and dictation of his large works, such as the Oratorios which have been enumerated in this chapter; several of which, it may be premised, were transcribed from his already prepared and well-stocked brain, early in the mornings, before breakfast, so as to secure non-interruption and non-interference with the professional business which pressed heavily upon him.

Assuming, then, that he himself was, in the main, prepared with his ideas, on the arrival of his amanuensis he would—for instance, in the case of a chorus— dictate the voice parts first of all, probably of one page, each part separately, not bar by bar, but the whole

page ; and then add the instrumental parts, most usually dictating the first violin part before the other
parts.   In the case of a choral fugue, he would dictate the subject first of all, and then say, " Now let us
get a counterpoint to this," which, it need not be said
to musical adepts, would have to be *double*—that is,
invertible, adapted to accompany the subject either
above or below it.   And then, the subject, answer,
and double-counterpoint being written, the remainder
of the exposition would be completed; this term being
applied to the first series of entries of subject and
answer in all the parts.   In this exposition, his
favourite method, in Oratorios, was to accompany the
voices with the organ only ;   following a precedent to
which he referred in an analysis of Handel's " Israel
in Egypt " :—

" In this ['Egypt was glad'] and several subsequent
movements of the same character, the voices are at first
accompanied with the organ only, the string and brass instruments being introduced considerably later to enforce
some new entry of the subject, which has an admirable
effect, not merely of giving prominence to an important
point, but of giving colour and variety to the tone of the
whole chorus."

Did all inspiration evaporate, meanwhile, and the
whole work become one of mere music-making, without free play for the imagination ?   It might seem inevitably so ; many think that it was so, and that they
can detect a certain " angularity " in the larger works
produced in Macfarren's later years, attributable partly
to this method of production, partly to the theoretical
or grammatical habit of his mind.   His valued aman-

uensis, however, previously quoted, says, with respect to the alleged hindering of inspiration :—

"I think not: in one way it aided it, for it compelled him to concentration of thought; for the separate movement, at all events, if not more, was necessarily complete before a note was written. Thus, one of his most beautiful songs, 'Love is strong as death,' in 'Joseph,' was written in this manner. When I went to him one morning to write what might be ready, he said, 'I thought of this song as I was coming home in the cab from the concert last night, and finding a fire waiting for me at home to sit out, I finished it' (all in his mind, you must remember). Some one has said that hearing music is not conducive to much composition. Rattling over the London streets in a four-wheeled cab might be thought not apposite for composition, and very different to the cosy studies and comfortable chairs, pink satin suits, etc., of some writers. But there is quiet even in the midst of noise, and to him the mere cessation of business was the signal for musical thought, and he had no outside visions to disturb his concentration of that thought. However, thus was the song ready in his mind, waiting for me to write it down. He would sit at the little old square piano in his den, I by his side, so that I could aid my ears by a glance at his fingers,—paper of twenty-four lines and a favourite ink-pot on the piano corner. In this song there are four horns. 'We will write them first, for they have most to play, and will want the longest bars.' I believe he dictated them in C, the key in which they were to be written. This, and other habits he had, shows that he had the score before his mind's eye as it ought to be written. The four horns written for one page only, and the bar lines drawn up and down the rest of the score; the rest of the instruments were filled in for the page, the highest first, and so downwards to the bass. The symphony written line by line, the voice part (words and music) was indicated, because that would take the most space. Then the accompaniment for that was begun at the top line, and so downwards, line by line. When I turned over for a new page, 'Where did we leave off?' would be the question; but before I could refer back, 'Oh, I remember,' and he would play the next bar. Sometimes the voice part would be written for the whole, or a large part of the song—specially this would be the case in choral works,—or in a choral fugue, where the voice parts and words were very much involved. Once only I remember making a pencil 'sketch,' as he called it, of a composition; that was the overture to 'Joseph'; but I believe it was as much out of consideration for my inexperience, as for any wish to help his own work of composition; the ostensible reason being that he might forget the course of the work in the delay of writing score. I have been told he sometimes forgot a composed work before he had opportunity to get it written. In my own work with him, I only recollect one slight forgetfulness; that was a counterpoint he had worked out for a bass part to some chorus. When I went to write, he had forgotten it, much to his distress, and he was obliged to think it out again, bar by bar, as I sat writing. I remember now the warm thanks he gave me for what he called my wonderful patience in writing while he was repairing his error, and 'wasting my time,' as he called it. As a fact, the error was a far greater pain to himself than to me, for it was a real trial to him. I have been told he was impatient with his writers; I always found the impatience was at what he considered his own slowness, not mine, though I was slow enough.

"Never but once have I heard a word of complaint, of fretfulness from him at his blindness—that was only two months before he died, when he must have been suffering keenly from his extreme weak state and effort to keep up. He wrote, urging me, 'Write music, write; you have not the necessity of waiting for other hands; you need scarcely even memory for your writing.'

"Illness did not make him forget his composed work. One day he broke off in the midst of dictating to me, feeling very ill, and he remained ill the rest of the day: before I left the house, however, an arrangement was made that I was to come the next day; then the movement was finished that had been broken off the day before."

During all this productive period of Macfarren's active mind, he had also other work, of most exacting kind. From 1869 to 1880 inclusive, he was retained as annotator of the Philharmonic Society, the analytical programmes supplied by him being of great and permanent interest. One analysis, of singularly sympathetic appreciativeness, may be specially mentioned in this chapter, that of Brahms' "German Requiem," in the programme of the concert, April 6th, 1876. This interesting analysis has been published separately. He reproached himself, however, for writing analytical programmes; but for what reason, does not seem to have been stated by him.

Other labours of the learned musician during this period have yet to be recorded.

CHAPTER XIV.

PRINCIPALSHIP OF THE ROYAL ACADEMY OF MUSIC.
PROFESSORSHIP IN THE UNIVERSITY OF CAMBRIDGE:
LECTURES. UNIVERSITY DEGREES. KNIGHTHOOD.
"AJAX" MUSIC. TERCENTENARY ANTHEM. MACFARREN
AS TEACHER AND EXAMINER. 1875—1887.

ON the 1st of February, 1875, the world of Music sustained an irreparable loss by the death, after a short illness, of Sir William Sterndale Bennett. With characteristic promptitude, on receiving intimation of the deplored event, Macfarren, as one of the committee of the Royal Academy of Music, directed that a meeting of that body should be instantly summoned, so that fitting steps might be taken to indicate the esteem in which their deceased chairman and principal was held, and to determine on the course to be taken for the future management of the institution. Not only was the Academy largely represented at, and concerned with, the funeral of the lamented musician, whose genius had shed upon it such lustre, but, without hesitation, Macfarren was looked to as his proper successor, by reason of his consummate musicianship, long and intimate association with the institution in all its vicissitudes, and sterling mental and moral qualifications; and, with the expectant assent of the entire professoriate, he was appointed to the responsible and onerous office of principal, which, with most important and salutary results, he held until his death.

Shortly afterwards, he delivered a lecture upon the life and works of Sterndale Bennett, at St. John's Wood. And, in the same year, by request of the Philharmonic Society, he composed an "Idyll" in memory of Bennett, which was performed at the final Concert of the 63rd season, July 5th, 1875; the analytical programme by himself giving this account of the work :—

" *Allegro tranquillo,* C.—*Andante,* $\frac{3}{4}$, 'God is a Spirit.'— *Maestoso,* C—(B flat).

"The following are the points in the musician's character and career that have been foremost in the recollection of his friend. His inborn genius; his early orphanhood; the expansion of his powers under kindly nurture; his entry on the active life of the metropolis; his transplantation to a foreign land, where the musical uses and the social surroundings were a new soil and climate for the cultivation of his artistry; the ripening of his strength under these influences; his scholastic offices in England, with their duties; the resumed exercise of his productive ability; his later visit to Germany, when some of his artist friends were no more; his gently falling into the everlasting sleep; the triumphant homage to his manes, when the heart of England beat with pride in her honoured son; the feeling of the mourners that himself was present among them when his own strain was sung; and the glorification of art, in men's acknowledgment of her representative."

Some months later, in writing to Mr. T. J. Dudeney,

he again makes graceful allusion to the departed musician, in a letter which explains itself :—

"*Nov.* 30, 1875.

"MY DEAR SIR,

"The White and the wind and the cold to-day remind me of your pretty setting of Miss Ingelow's poem, and of my remissness in not sooner acknowledging the copy. Let me thank you for it now. I thank you too, and the members of your Society, as a friend of Sir Sterndale Bennett, for the Concert you have given in his memory. Such an artist as he dies but to his friends when he leaves this life; to the world he still lives in his works, and they do themselves as much honour as him in keeping green his memory who study and hear these.

"I am very truly yours,

"G. A. MACFARREN."

And to the same effect, later on, he wrote :—

"Exceat Farm,
"Seaford, Sussex,
"*9th August*, 1880.

"MY DEAR MR. DUDENEY,

"I learn with pleasure that the Washford Musical Society has been giving concerts of Bennett's music, and I congratulate you, as the director and representative of that admirable institution, on the success of these performances. A few such workers with such material would soon Anglicize our musical faith, and, in teaching us to believe in one another, strengthen our reliance on ourselves and trust in the public."

Shortly before the date of this last letter, the Society referred to forwarded the following resolution, passed at the General Meeting :—

"That considering the pleasure and profit the members have derived from their study of some of Dr. G. A. Macfarren's music, and in acknowledgment of the kind advice he has given respecting the formation of their new society, the warmest thanks of the members be due to him, and they also respectfully wish him many happy returns of this his birthday."

It is pleasurable in a high degree to record that, through the enthusiastic appreciation of the works and character of Macfarren, evinced by Mr. Dudeney, the Taunton Philharmonic Association was founded, in his honour, March 2nd, 1875. Macfarren wrote with regard to this and other efforts :—

"It is one thing to produce music, but quite another to have such a partisan as you, who not only gives credit for one's intentions, but infuses his own great interest in the subject into a large circle of surrounders. . . . As much as on my own account I thank you for the partisanship of English music, nay, of music altogether, which you are fulfilling. . . . . If others worked as you do in musical promulgation, they would effect more than is in the power of princes to advance the study and love of art."

Another important office became vacant by the death of Sterndale Bennett,—that of Professor of Music in the University of Cambridge. Immediately after Bennett's funeral, an informal conference was held between a few influential gentlemen connected with the University, to which Macfarren was invited ; and, from that moment, he consenting to stand for the appointment, his election was well-nigh a foregone conclusion. Efforts of an interested kind were indeed made to depreciate his qualification for the duties, on account of his blindness ; but this allegation of unfitness was rebutted by a letter in the "Times," signed by Herr Joachim, Costa, and other influential and competent musicians, in which facts were stated respecting his marvellous and undaunted vanquishment of obstacles which would have unnerved and incapacitated most men. The issue could hardly be uncertain; every other candidate ultimately, though not all promptly, retired; and on March 16th Macfarren was elected in this instance also as successor to his old fellow-student, in the arduous, honourable, and responsible duties attached to the Chair of Music in the University. In his letter of application he said :—

"In the event of your conferring upon me the great honour of appointing me your Professor, I should regard the office not only as an honour but as a trust, and would endeavour to the best of my power to advance the study of Music in the University. I should hope to do this not only by fulfilling the office of Examiner for Musical Degrees, but by delivering Lectures such as I hope might prove useful to resident musical students."

Prior to the election, it had been determined that, in place of a stipend of £100 to the Professor of Music, and certain fees from successful candidates for degrees, as heretofore, the stipend should in future be £200, and "that the Professor be not authorized to receive any fees from persons performing exercises or being examined for degrees in Music." This change was welcome to Macfarren, relieving him from all suspicion of interested motives in passing candidates. And, whereas the delivery of Lectures on Music was not previously obligatory on the Professor, it was enacted "that the Professor be required to give a course of not less than four Lectures in Music annually in the University," etc.

In the following April, the Senate passed the "Grace" "that the degree of Doctor of Music be

conferred on George Alexander Macfarren " ; and on
the occasion of his being presented for that degree, the
Public Orator, Mr. R. C. Jelf, delivered the following
speech :—

"Musicae apud nos regendae clarum praesse virum
Academiae quantum intersit, neminem vestrum opinor
ignorare. Si enim illa vetus artium coniunctio et societas
quam finxit Natura, usus corroboravit ac fecit strictiorem,
nullo tempore nullo loco dissolvi potest, nos certe, qui
litteris studemus Graecis et Latinis, qui nihil liberalis
disciplinae vel apud nos peregrinari credimus vel hinc
patimur exulare, musicen in sede haud infima debemus
collocare. Testimonio sunt veteres, sive philosophos, sive
poetas, sive eloquentiae artifices respecitis, quae videretur
antiquitus esse musices cum ceteris humanioris scientiæ
partibus necessitudo. Summam eruditionem ut auctor est
Tullius, Graeci sitam censebant in nervorum vocumque
cantibus ; quos, ut Epaminondas excoluit, ita Themistocles quod declinaret habitus est indoctior. Quid vero
dicit Marcus Fabius Quintilianus ? Omnium ait in litteris
studiorum, Timagene docente, antiquissimam exstitisse
musicen ; qua imbutus Pythagoras atque eius discipuli
opinionem vulgaverunt, mundum ipum ea ratione esse
compositum quam postea sit lyra imitata. Scimus Pla-
tonem, quom in aliis quibusdam tum praecipue in Timaeo,
ne intelligi quidem posse nisi ab iio qui hanc quoque
partem humanitatis diligenter perceperint : neque frustra
Plato civili viro, quem πολιτικὸν vocat, necessariam musicen
creditit. Immo Lycurgus, duriosimarum auctor legum,
musices studium probavit : musicae subjectam esse gram-
maticen putavit et Archytas et Aristoxenos ; neque cum
Eupolis Hyperbolo demagogo irridere voluit, aliam existi-
mavit graviorem contumeliam quam ut eum innueret
musicen nescire.

" Nostis, academici, vetus illud in Graecia proverbium :
της λανθανούσης μουσικης ουδεισλόγος : quo illi quidem sig-
nificabant, animi dotes, si non proferas, perinde esse
quasi non habeas. Quod tamen nobis propriomagis sensu
accipere licet, musicen rati eo magistruic academiae pro-

futuram quo a viro doceatur clariore. Magna desideria
magnas expetunt consolationes: amisimus insignem virum ;[1] insignem in eius locum esse suffectum nunc merito
nobis gratulamur. Cuius tot opera, tot laudes percensere
neque nostra facile possit oratio neque ipsius verecundia
patiatur: immo est vir eiusmodi quem qui nominat laudat.
Duco ad vos Musicae Professorem, Georgium Alexandrum
Macfarren."

(Free Translation.)

" You are none of you, I think, ignorant how greatly it
concerns the University that a distinguished man should
preside over musical matters amongst us. For if that
ancient alliance and union of arts, which Nature formed
and use has confirmed and made more strict, cannot at
any time or in any place be dissolved, then most assuredly
we who study Greek and Latin literature, and who do not
consider foreign among us, or allow to be driven hence, any
form of liberal learning, ought to place music in by no
means the lowest position. For whether you regard philo-
sophers, poets, or the masters of eloquence, the ancients
testify how close a connexion there was held to be of old
between music and all other kinds of polite learning. The
Greeks, as Cicero tells us, considered that the highest
erudition was found in vocal and instrumental music ;
which Epaminondas cultivated, but Themistocles refused,
and was therefore considered the more ignorant. What
again does Marcus Fabius Quintilianus say ? He says
that, according to Timagenes, music is the most ancient of
all studies. Fully convinced of this, Pythagoras and his
disciples spread the opinion that the world itself was made
by that method and in that proportion which the lyre
afterwards imitated. Plato, we know, in various works,
but especially in the Timæus, could not even be understood except by those who had carefully studied this
branch of learning. Nor is it for nothing that Plato
asserts music to be necessary for the man of his republic
whom he calls πολιτικόν. Nay more, Lycurgus, who
framed laws of such extraordinary severity, approved of

[1] Sir W. Sterndale Bennett.

the study of music. Archytas too, and Aristoxenus, considered that grammar was subject to music; and when Eupolis used to deride Hyperbolus the demagogue, he thought there was no greater insult than to point to his ignorance of music.

"You know the old Greek proverb : ' Hidden music is of no account '; by which they signified that mental gifts, if not brought forth, were as though non-existent. We may apply this to ourselves in a peculiarly appropriate sense, considering that the more eminent the man who teaches, the more beneficial will the art of music be to the University. Great losses require great consolation; we have lost a distinguished man ; we now congratulate ourselves that a distinguished man has been appointed to fill his place. We cannot in this speech enumerate his many works, his many merits; nor would his modesty suffer us to do so ; suffice it to say that he is a man whom to name is to praise.

"I present to you the Professor of Music, George Alexander Macfarren."

In 1876 the University of Oxford also conferred upon him the honorary degree of Doctor of Music ; and, in 1887, the like distinction was accorded him by the University of Dublin.

On May 25th Professor Macfarren was granted the use of the Senate House for his Inaugural Lecture, which he delivered before a distinguished audience, ladies being admitted ; and he began by remarking that—

"He wished to own publicly his sense of the importance of the office which gave him the privilege of addressing that audience that afternoon, an importance which was greatly exalted by the artistic abilities of his distinguished predecessor, whose genius was as a star which shines upon the art he cultivated, the country he honoured, and the offices he administered. He wished to offer the tribute of respect to Sir Sterndale Bennett of one who was his school-fellow and fellow-labourer, however humble, in the work which filled and glorified his life. Bennett, while yet a student, working the exercises set him by his teachers, attained an excellence in pianoforte playing peculiarly his own, and produced some of those compositions for which he would always be best esteemed. The University of Cambridge had a right to expect very much from all functionaries attached to it, but he feared the expectations would be especially great from the successor of this great musician. He (Dr. Macfarren) was not unmindful of Professor Walmisley, who was distinguished for scholastic abilities as well as his musical attainments; nor of Maurice Greene, whose contributions to ecclesiastical music were among the greatest treasures of the Church of England, and whose instrumental pieces, though less known, were of a very high order as works of art; Staggins, Whitfield, Hague, or Randall. They were men who did good honest work, and he would be fortunate who could walk in their footsteps, and gather flowers by the wayside. In the dawn of time truth and beauty were inseparably wedded, 'Spirit of one spirit, and flesh of one flesh,' and as years rolled on, they had three daughters— music, poetry, and painting. These were the arts. The art of form and the art of letters had many able expositors. The art of tone was less generally comprehended, but he looked forward with hope to the time when he might be instrumental in some degree in further extending it. The classic Greeks, who were the filter through which the draughts of Egyptian science have reached our lips, taught that music purified the heart by refining the intellect, and exalted the feelings by reflecting them in ideal forms. What Plato and Aristotle enunciated, Cicero endorsed. In another age, Confucius insisted that the practice of music would be of the highest moral and intellectual advantage; and, to come to our own race, Luther held that the study of music was next in importance after theology. These ancients, however, among whom he included Luther, could have had but a prophetic gleam of music, as we know it. To them it was an exalted declamation; to us it is an embodiment of feeling, for which words can find no utterance; means of expression which no language can compass. It was a vulgar fashion—all fashions are vulgar which step aside from nature—that decried the capacity of English people for music. He had not then time to refute this fallacy. He must ask them to accept his statement until opportunity for proof offered itself. In early days England stood well forward among European nations in respect to her musical abilities. In the beginning of the eleventh century, she was in advance of the whole of the south of Europe ; and was noted by foreigners, who themselves boasted a love of music, for her attainments in the art ; and, from that time downwards, many of the greatest lights that shone in English history in the departments of art had been directed to the illumination of the subject of music. There was no time now to trace the course of the musical history of this country ; but he felt so strongly that the future would come out of what had been in the past, that he believed it would be an encouragement to everybody who strove for the advancement of musical art to know, that whatever might be done in the future would be but a revival, a restoration of the old state of things in England."

He proceeded with historical references such as have appeared in lectures and papers already quoted, to the effect of the Reformation on Church Music, etc.; the works of Tallis and Byrd ; Madrigals, Italian and English ; the choir singing Luca Marenzio's " Lady, see on every side," and John Benet's " Come, Shepherds, follow me," the lecturer pointing out their rhythmical peculiarities.

"Up to Benet's time (1599) bar lines had not been invented to divide music into proper measures. Still, it was necessary that the performers should know whether they were to sing with an accentuation of two or three; and thus the accentuation became distinguished by 'perfect time,' and 'imperfect time.' 'Imperfect time' was when the long notes were divided into two, and 'perfect time' was when they were divided into three.

They justified the term ' perfect time ' on the ground that the Trinity was three and perfect. It was the practice in those days to introduce more frequently than was now done, an intermixture of ' perfect ' and ' imperfect time '; and his audience would notice the happy effect which Benet produced by a change from ' imperfect ' into ' perfect time,' which gave to certain words the particular character they seemed to express. Beautiful as was Marenzio's madrigal, Benet's would bear to stand before it."

After referring to the period of the Commonwealth, he proceeded to consider the life of Henry Purcell, who stood pre-eminently forward in the history of music.

" He was born in 1658, lived from the time of the Restoration, through the reign of James II., up to William, and died in 1695. There was a prodigious advance in the power of expression of his music from the time of Benet. Besides the æsthetic beauty of his music, its technical merit was very important in the history of art, for in his music were anticipated all the most extreme chromatic combinations that signalized the music of the present time. Many of the contrapuntal forms, which have now gone out of use, were practised by him with wonderful success. One anthem of his composition was set to some words of the Litany, and the treatment of these words gave every expression its fullest meaning. It commenced with a most humble deprecation, ' Remember not, Lord, our offences '; it gathered strength when it said, ' Nor the offences of our forefathers '; and then, as if in despair, there was the cry, ' Neither take thou vengeance of our sins.' The whole was tempered with the seeming hope of mercy, ' Spare us, good Lord '; then with most touching tenderness we have, ' Spare Thy people, whom Thou hast redeemed with Thy most precious blood '; and again, ' Be not angry with us for ever.' [The choir here sang the anthem referred to.] It was a remarkable fact that, with the accession of sovereigns in England who could not speak our language, and, therefore, could not take an interest in its expression, music went into disesteem, and painting rose into favour. While the art of painting could show the names of Hogarth, Reynolds, Gainsborough, etc., there was a corresponding blank in the chronicles of the sister art. It would be among the glories of the times of Queen Victoria, that, under her administration, the old musical feeling of former centuries had been revived. It was, indeed, with immense interest that he compared the present with the past condition of music in this country. In the Plantagenet days people sang canons and catches, and delighted one another by such efforts. In the time of Elizabeth, the competency of farm labourers and artisans for service was made dependent on their musical qualification. In the time of Charles II. domestic servants were refused employment because they could not sing their parts in domestic music. In these days it was not domestic servants, artisans, labourers, or the uncultivated people, but the students of a great University who devoted thought and time to the cultivation of music. The organ recital which he had heard in Trinity Chapel, and the concert of last week, were performances such as few artists, even in his young days, could have accomplished. It was quite evident that music here was not a piece of school work, but a work of love among the persons who attained to such merit. Their merit had its influence, their example had its force, but this influence and example would not stay in Cambridge. Every one who learned to love music in Cambridge would carry that love into his own home, which would be as a centre, diffusing its warmth and light on all its surroundings; and when once the love of the art which in former days prevailed among the untutored common people, shone down upon them from above, with the extra radiation which must spring from the culture and refinement of the mind, he could not but believe that the musical character of England would be greatly exalted. He looked forward with fervent hope to the future of music in this country, when the stigmas which we ourselves had taught foreigners to cast upon us for our lack of music culture would be wiped out, and we could show them we could do something more for music than paying for its performance. He particularly wished to urge upon those who had the musical art at heart to carry their pursuit of it into its technical merits. Music was of countless value, but it was of still greater value when the principles upon which it was constructed were apprehended. To hear or practise music, without a knowledge of the principles upon which it was formed, was very much like going to the performance of a play in an unknown language, when one could admire the gesticulation of the actor, but, not knowing the meaning of the words, could do but scant justice to the theme. He was glad that the technical principles of music were studied here; but wished they were studied more; and he was even vain enough to wish that, as a knowledge of music was advancing among us, the authorities of the University might in time consider it to be desirable to make it one of the subjects of special examination. The monuments of the past were as a beacon to the future, but the doings of the present would come still more warmly home to their hearts, by showing the position of the art as practised among themselves, and he would, therefore, close his remarks by offering an extract from the Cantata of the 'May Queen,' by his dear and honoured friend, the greatest English musician of the present period, Sir William Sterndale Bennett, a cantata which, produced at the Leeds Festival in 1858, was characteristic of the season, the country, and the composer. May his memory be as green and balmy as his song!"

The courses of lectures, four in each course, delivered in Cambridge University by Macfarren in his professorial capacity, were as follows:—1876, on "Form or Design in Musical Composition"; 1877, on "The Musical Scales of different ages and nations"; 1878, on "Counterpoint"; 1879, on "Beethoven's 'Eroica' Symphony"; 1880, on "The Growth of the Overture"; 1881, on "Beethoven's Choral Symphony"; 1882, on "Bach's 'Well-tempered Clavier'"; 1883, on "Bach's 24 Preludes and Fugues" (the sequel to the "Well-tempered Clavier"); 1884, on "Mozart's early Symphonies"; 1885, on "Mozart's latest Symphonies";

1886, a first course on "Beethoven's Pianoforte Sonatas"; 1887, a second course on "Beethoven's Pianoforte Sonatas."

Several of these courses were re-delivered at the Royal Academy of Music; those on "Bach's Preludes and Fugues," to the College of Organists; that on "The Growth of the Overture," to the students of the Royal Normal College and Academy of Music for the Blind, Upper Norwood; an institution in which, for obvious reasons, Macfarren felt special interest.

The lectures on "Form or Design" were partly historical, tracing the development of tonality from the old Modes, the origin of Fugue in connection with the Authentic and Plagal Modes, Descant, Counterpoint; the Symphonic or Sonata forms, the Rondo, etc.

The lectures on "Counterpoint" were embodied in his book on that subject, to be referred to later on.

Macfarren objected to the term "the 48" as applied to Bach's Preludes and Fugues, because the first 24, entitled by Bach "Das Wohltemperirte Klavier," were published long before the second set of 24, which were not so termed, and which represent the later development of the composer's mind.

To give an epitome of any of these courses of lectures is quite impracticable in these pages, requiring much space and copious musical examples, which were played on the pianoforte by various students, principally from the Royal Academy, when the lectures were delivered.

In the lectures on the "Well-tempered Clavier," he remarks :—

"When we come to the closest study of this very great master, I must caution you that there are some slight points that are not things for approbation, still less for carrying into practice. To us humble persons who possess not the excellences which appear in Bach—when we see what to our shallow minds appear to be spots in his great distant splendour—let it teach us modesty if we find in one of the greatest men who worked in the art of music that there are some things we cannot account for, and let us know that we also are liable to error. Therefore we must still be the more cautious, the more circumspect, the more careful, to avoid committing errors, since we can by no means flatter ourselves that we shall surround our shortcomings with such a brilliant display of beauty as shall atone for the inaccuracies we may have committed."[1]

But such candid discrimination implies no depreciation, or lack of appreciation, of the great master.

In commenting upon the first Prelude, Macfarren does not neglect an opportunity for illustrating the means furnished by the theory of harmony held by him for accounting for apparently exceptional, and to some unexplainable, progressions. Thus, on bars 20-22 he remarks :—

"Great beauty is in the interrupted resolution of the dominant seventh in the key of F, where the E (leading-note) is retained—fulfilling thus the conditions of a prepared discord, in becoming the seventh of F, but having exceptional treatment in proceeding to E flat, accompanied by F sharp, portions of the chromatic chord of the supertonic minor ninth, and so giving to the preceding harmony, with F natural in the bass, a claim to be regarded as the third inversion of the chord of $\begin{smallmatrix} 13 \\ 11 \\ 9 \\ 7 \end{smallmatrix}$ of G, whose root, third, and fifth, are omitted."

[1] See p. 278, *et seq.*

He proceeds :—

" In the next incident for present notice is an infraction
of one of the most rigid laws.   But when we have learned
all the rules, and are able to apply them, there still is the
fact that art is free ; that it is within the possibility of
great minds even to conceive, and accomplish, beautiful
effects that supersede rules. Do not suppose from this that
inexperienced persons are to abrogate laws and take principles into their own hands.   Let us still believe that our
duty is to learn all that the wisdom of our predecessors has
taught ; and, when we have attained mastery of the whole
code of musical precepts, it is at our own risk we sweep
these long-established laws on one side.   You have heard
of the inflexible rules against false relation—namely, the
having a sharp note in one part of the harmony, together
with or directly after a natural note of the same name in
another part ; notes are related to each other in so far as
they belong to one common key, and this discrepancy of
sharp and natural implies that the two parts are in different keys, and therefore stand in false relation.   Detach
from the rest of the harmony the F sharp and A flat
in the bass of the following, with the A natural and F
natural of the upper part, and observe the almost un-
bearable effect.   Play, however, the two chords as they

are printed, with a change from loud to soft in passin

from one to the next, and I think that in the breach of
this rule against false relation is the means of beauty
which is else unattainable, though beauty that cannot be
reproduced save by quoting the passage before us, which
is but a delicate definition of plagiarism." [1]

It is almost to be wondered at that Macfarren did
not, here, adduce his own cherished (though by others
disputed) theory of a supertonic root for fundamental
discords as applying to the first of these chords, which,
being followed by the dominant minor ninth in the
same key, relieves the succession of any charge of implying two keys. He goes on to relate, with reprobation,
the interpolation of a second inversion of the chord
of C minor between the two chords, by the editor
Schwenke; and then reprobates the " superadding a
cantilena " to this Prelude by "a distinguished musician," and suggests " that our cotemporary would
have exercised his genius to better purpose had he
written a piece entirely his own, than in embroidering
a new fancy upon the complete imagining of another
writer."

In proceeding to analyze the Fugue, Macfarren
once for all defines the principle governing the relation of subject and answer :—

" We must refer to a primitive phase of music for one
of the main elements of the fugue—relation of the subject
to the answer. Greek music consisted of melody alone, of
which there were two chief forms: the authentic, wherein
the dominant—or rather predominant—note stood at the
interval of a fifth above the final; and the plagal, wherein
the dominant stood at a fourth below the final. If, in the

---

[1] See Macfarren's "Rudiments," p. 12.

brief melody that constitutes the subject of a fugue, the dominant be a conspicuous note, the subject is authentic or plagal according to whether that note stand above or below the tonic; and, whichever of these be the melodic form of the subject, the answer has the other form, reversing the interval between tonic and dominant: the fugue is then defined as tonal. If, however, the dominant be not a conspicuous note in the subject, then the answer is the precise transposition of the same melody into the key at a fifth above or a fourth below the primary key; the fugue is then defined as real, for the subject-is then reproduced in its reality instead of being modified to meet the changed tonal relationship of the answer."

In connection with this matter of Fugue subject and answer, a letter to a pupil (in answer to inquiries) may interest students; and possibly occasion some little surprise or discussion with regard to the first example.

"The answer I propose gives always tonic for dominant with reference to implied harmonies, as much as to melody.

"Mozart answers the third of the dominant by the third of the tonic, and then proceeds to the subdominant in the new key."

With reference to the Fugue in C sharp major,
No. 3, Macfarren remarks :—

"Both subject and answer exemplify the ancient use of
diatonic passing-notes as opposed to the modern employment of the chromatic element for notes that are foreign
to the harmony. Ears habituated only to the latter expect,
and are scarcely satisfied without, a semitone instead of a
tone below the G sharp in the first group of semiquavers
of the subject, and below the D sharp in the correspond-

ing place in the answer. Whereas, formerly, long after
chromatic *harmonies* were in use, only the notes of the
diatonic scale were written as passing-notes ; at present,
it is not uncommon to write a semitone below any harmony
note upon which such passing-note has to resolve, and it is
all but imperative when the said harmony note is the root
or fifth of the prevailing chord. The chord of C sharp is
implied, and is naturally supposed to prevail throughout
the first bar of the unaccompanied melody, and even to
continue for a crotchet's length into the ensuing bar ;
hence, the listener regards the G sharp as the fifth of the
implied chord, and if with small experience out of the
idiom of to-day, craves F double sharp as the third note of
the turn. There may be more grace, and more seeming
finish in the use of this minute interval in our phraseology,
but it is bought at the price of simplicity, and of dignity,
too, in passages to which such expression is pertinent. It
is not here to discuss the more or less merit of either
idiom, but to note the distinction, and to be assured that the
chromatic note in this position would be an anachronism,
and quite incompatible with the melodic principle in force
when the theme was written."

Soon after his appointment to the professorship, he
wrote an article in the " Musical World," January 1st,

1876, on " Scholastic Honours "; urging that these were not to be understood as asserting the genius of the recipients.

" A diploma testifies to the knowledge of its holder; his power to apply this knowledge challenges a broader and far different judgment.

" Whatever is fully known is always at command. The value of acquirements consists in their instantaneous applicability. No surrounding circumstances or embarrassing witnesses should be able to dislodge from the mind facts of which it is entirely certain. . . . The frequent reply of a learner, that he understands such or such a thing but cannot explain it, comprises in the latter half a denial of the former, since whatever is clear to our understanding must be ready for our definition."

Then follow remarks on the " requisite proof . . . of a candidate's desert." The article concludes :—

" As to the professor with whom lies the approval or the veto, let it be hoped that he may have a full sense of his grave responsibility, a certainty that his own period for self-improvement is of life-long extent, a ceaseless endeavour to advance his own erudition, and an inflexible will to render justice to them who may submit to the authority which is confided to him."

Many years before his entrance upon his duties at Cambridge, Macfarren had written strongly on the subject of University Professors of Music, in the " Musical World," of March 29th, 1856, just after the election of Bennett to the Cambridge Chair of Music, on the one hand, and on the other, the passing of some new and very important statutes with reference to music at Oxford. He urged, as " part of the original design of the institution of the Music School in Oxford," by King Alfred, "the inclusion of music in the educational course of the University": and commended the recent statutes, viz., "the establishment of a practical school of music in the University": "that any candidate for a degree must attest the genuineness of his exercise by words and signature; that he must pass an examination before a board of three competent judges," such examination including the writing of canons, fugues, etc., in the presence of the examiners; and that "the incumbent of the musical chair must give public lectures in the course of every University term": also, the raising of the professor's stipend.

When he himself succeeded his friend at Cambridge, he was consistently true to his earlier avowed views. He did not, indeed, found a music school in the University. With regard to the stipend of the professor, there was an alteration effected, already referred to, rendering him, most desirably, quite independent of the fees paid by candidates for degrees; and leaving him free in the matter of examinations. A "Board of Musical Studies" was constituted in 1877; and, as it was determined that a literary or arts test should be established, to which candidates must submit in order to pass a musical examination, it was proposed by the Syndicate that the examinations should be conducted "by the Professor, assisted by two or more examiners nominated annually by the Board . . . . and elected by the Senate, of whom one at least shall be a member of the Senate, or a Mus. Doc. of the University." Against this proposal Macfarren protested, though without avail, in the following letter to the Vice-Chancellor:—

"7, Hamilton Terrace,
"London, N.W.

"My dear Mr. Vice-Chancellor,

" Not in the hope of changing the views of the gentlemen I have met on the Syndicate, but to justify my dissent
from one expression in the report, I must trouble you with
my reasons, which are the result of many years' reflection,
and of frequent consultation with musicians. I venture
to wish for the omission of the words 'a member of the
Senate or,' because I am firmly convinced that it is more
than desirable—it is necessary for the honour of the
University and the welfare of music—for every person
who officiates in the musical examinations to be a musician
of proved competency. The words against which I offer a
protest, open the possibility, however improbable, of the
appointment, as examiner, of some physicist, or other man
of extraneous learning, to be subject to whose inquisition
would be painful to any one whose life and best energies
had been devoted to the widely comprehensive study of
music. The distinction between non-professional and professional followers of an art, are very fine, but most
obvious; no book-learning, but the constant habit of producing, can alone make an artist, and the constant habit
of tuition can alone make a teacher. This is because the
daily observing of faults in others sharpens perception of
right and wrong; and the daily working of art problems
is the sole experience of the means of avoiding error. As
little would I trust the life of a friend to a physician
whose knowledge was acquired wholly outside the medical
profession, as I would a score to an examiner whose
musicianship was not his all-absorbing occupation. The
case is different, certainly, in theology, and perhaps in
law, where the subject is finite and changeless, from what
it is in those studies which are constantly enriched by
additions whose truth can but be tested by the continual
habit of practical application. To enlarge upon the uses
of other institutions than Cambridge might be personal,
and would thus be untimely, and far from my purpose;
but I am bound to state the deep-rooted belief that, to
make the Cambridge musical degrees most highly respected,
musicians must be assured against the participation of

z

amateurs in the investigating of their professional pretensions. My sincerity may, I trust, serve as apology, if need
be, for any warmth of expression in the above, which I
must ask you, if you please, to submit to the Council, together with the Syndicate's report.

" I am, my dear Mr. Vice-Chancellor,

" Faithfully yours,

" G. A. MACFARREN.

" THE REV. THE VICE-CHANCELLOR."

At a meeting of the Senate, May 19th, 1877, this
letter, in connection with the report of the Syndicate,
was discussed ; and, the subject of Acoustics having
been recommended, in addition to Harmony and
Counterpoint, that recommendation was supported,
and, together with that support, the objections of the
Professor to the above-mentioned clause were combated by Mr. Sedley Taylor and Mr. Gerard F. Cobb;
and the report was adopted. I look back with
pleasure and pride to the opportunities which I
enjoyed, during certain years, of serving with Professor Macfarren both as an examiner for the Mus.
Bac. degree, and on the Board of Musical Studies.

Although, as an examiner, it has been supposed
that Macfarren was somewhat pedantic, requiring
compliance with rules, especially of his own framing,
rather than manifestation of musical aptitude, on the
part of examinees, yet he was, in reality, very clearly
discriminative as to the nature and purport of
theoretical examinations. He used to say, " I have
tried both ; I have been a candidate, and I have been
an examiner, and I know which is the easier." But
there is no record of his being a " candidate " for
such examinations as those which he conducted.

He determined to inaugurate his entrance upon

office at Cambridge by creating several eminent musicians Doctors of Music, *honoris causâ;* and he named for this purpose Johannes Brahms, Joseph Joachim, and Sir John Goss. The first named, however, declined or was prevented from coming to this country; and, as the degree could not be conferred in his absence, only the other two musicians received the distinction, on March 8th, 1877. The other recipients of the degree, *honoris causâ,* during Macfarren's term of office, were Sir Arthur Sullivan and Mr. Hubert Parry.

Speaking of his, to some eyes, unprepossessing appearance, but, to those knowing him, "his grand forehead," one pupil writes:—

"It was in the Senate-house at Cambridge that I realized this, as I saw him standing in his simple black gown, the centre of a crowd of men and gay dresses, in the fine old hall with its dark oak fittings. The light streamed from the large windows upon him, and singled out from among them all his veiled eyes and large brow. It seemed to point him out—the man who had more than most men of pain to bear—and yet worked harder, and thought deeper, and sympathized more keenly than most men. We who loved him thought him almost beautiful at such moments; we read the sympathy in his heart, through the pity of our own. On that occasion he had to go through the ceremony of presenting some Bachelors of Music to the Vice-Chancellor, to receive their degrees. There were some five or six of them clustering round him; each one was to take hold of his hand—a finger for each was scarcely enough. But he himself must be led, as he led them forward: it seemed a miniature of his life—a leader led, as he was all his life, and therein was his unique influence."

In the year 1878, on May 23rd, the University of

Cambridge conferred upon him the honorary degree of
Master of Arts; on which occasion the following
speech was delivered by the Public Orator, Dr. J. E.
Sandys:—

"Dignissime domine, domine Procancellarie, et tota
Academia:

"Quod anni proximi illo die augurabamur, quo in hac
ipsa domo Orpheum nostrum reducem salutavimus, illud
hodie optimis auspiciis ratum esse vehementer gaudemus.
Studiis musicis in nostra Academia melius ordinandis
novum septemvirorum collegium constituistis: ad summos
in musica honores aditum nemini nisi per scientiarum
portam patere voluistis; musicae ipsi, quae antiquitus
inter septem illas liberales artes erat numerata, novam
lauream baccalaureatus in artibus concessistis; denique
hunc virum, tribus abhinc annis non Regiae modo Academiae Musicae praepositum sed in nostra quoque Academia
et Professorem et Doctorem in musica creatum, senatui
nostro placuit magistratu in artibus ornare, senatorum
nostrorum in numerum asciscere.

"Tanti viri insignia merita in legibus illis quae musicam
moderantur explicandis et ad certam normam revocandis,
non nostrae laudis indigent. Audivistis etiam ipsi carmina
illa nostratium, huius viri arte concinentium vocibus
accommodata; quis 'alaudae cantum' illum non meminit?
quis 'Orphei citharam' non recordatur? quis alia carmina
nostri Shakesperii? Cui non, inter aetatis nostrae, nostrae
Academiae Musas moranti, redeunt in mentem huius
ingenio musicis modis donati lyrici illi versus poetae
laureati, Aluredi Tennyson, necnon viri desideratissimi,
Caroli Kingsley? procul auribus excipio, nisi fallor,
bucinarum longius et longius resonantium concentum;
videor mihi audire trans maris frementis aestum, trans
arenas murmurantes, planctum puellae nequiquam vocantis.
Maias Kalendas (Floralia illa nostra) quas nuper praeteri-
vimus, inter huius viri laudes (hoc praesertim die quo
Floralia aguntur) nemo praeteribit; illud certe carminis
argumentum (ne maiora commemorem) commune habet
cum illo viro, cuius memoriam colit, cuius exemplar aemu-

latur, decessore suo, Wilelmo Sterndale Bennett. Neque
vero neglegenda est nobis nympha illa Caledonici lacus,
quae cum huius Musa consociata ad extremum Britanniae
terminum, 'vel occidentis usque ad ultimum sinum,'
nuperrime penetravit; utque postremo argumenta magis
sacra attingamus, non ignota est vobis huius arte celebrata
'vox illa in deserto clamantis.'

"O utinam hodie inter hanc audientium frequentiam
huius consessus dignitatem pulchritudinemque his oculis
contemplari contingeret: atqui donum illud commune lucis
ereptum donis rarioribus Musa ipsa suo vati compensare
est conata, cui (velut olim Miltono nostro) sub ipsa quasi
'caelestium alarum umbra' tenebris ex ipsis clarius elucet
ingeni lumen. Venit rursus in memoriam vates ille de
quo ipsius Homeri versus inter ultima nostri vatis
praeconia vestro (si placet) praeconi nunc iterum laudare
liceat:—

κῆρυξ ἐγγύθεν ἦλθεν ἄγων ἐρίηρον ἀοιδόν,
τὸν περὶ μοῦσ' ἐφίλησε, δίδου δ'ἀγαθόν τε κακόν τε
'οφθαλμῶν μὲν ἄμερσε δίδου δ'ἡδεῖαν ἀοιδήν.

"Duco ad vos Georgium Alexandrum Macfarren."

(Free Translation.)

"Most worthy Vice-Chancellor and all this University:
"We rejoice to see fulfilled to-day under the happiest
auspices what we foretold last year when we welcomed our
returning Orpheus. You have appointed a new Board of
seven members for the better arranging of musical studies
in our University; you have determined to allow no approach to the highest musical honours except through the
gate of science; you have granted to Music itself, which
was of old reckoned among the seven liberal arts, the new
laurel of a bachelorship in arts; and lastly, it has pleased
the Senate to adorn with a Mastership in Arts and to admit
into the ranks of our Senators him who three years ago
was appointed Principal of the Royal Academy of Music,
and also Doctor and Professor of Music in our University.
"The distinguished skill of so great a man in explaining
and reducing to a settled rule the laws which regulate

music do not need our praise. You have yourselves heard those songs of our land which have been set to vocal harmony by his art. Who does not remember his 'Song of the lark'? Who does not call to mind 'Orpheus with his lute,' and the other songs of our Shakespeare? Who, thinking of the Muses of our own age, of our own University, does not remember the lyrics of the poet-laureate, Alfred Tennyson, and of the greatly regretted Charles Kingsley, that have been graced by his skill. Far away too, unless I am mistaken, I find the harmony of trumpets sound more and more distantly. Across the roaring sea, over the murmuring sand, I seem to hear the complaint of a maiden who calls in vain. Nor can we omit May Day, which we have but lately passed, from among so much deserving praise, especially when May is observed ; a title too (not to mention greater matters) recalling one whose memory he cherishes, and whose example he emulates, his predecessor, William Sterndale Bennett. Nor, again, must we neglect that Lady of the Caledonian lake, who, in union with his Muse, has quite recently penetrated to the extremity of Britain, 'even to the farthest western bay.' And lastly, to approach more sacred matters, it cannot be unknown to you that 'the voice of one crying in the wilderness' has also been celebrated by his art. Oh! would that among this crowded audience *his* eyes could see the worth and beauty of this gathering : but the Muse has attempted to compensate her prophet for the loss of the common gift of light by gifts far rarer. For in him (as before in our Milton), under the very 'shadow of celestial wings' as it were, the light of intellect shines out more clearly from the darkness. Again recurs to our mind that seer, about whom your herald may perhaps be allowed to quote Homer's verses, as the last word of introduction for *our* seer :

> 'And now the herald came, leading with care
> The tuneful bard ; dear to the Muse was he,
> Who yet appointed him both good and ill !
> Took from him sight, but gave him strains divine.' "
>
> W. COWPER.

In virtue of this degree, he might have become a

member of the Senate, provided he kept three terms
by residence in Cambridge; but this his London
duties never permitted him to do.

In the early part of May, 1883, Macfarren received
from Mr. Gladstone a communication proposing, on
behalf of Her Majesty, that he " should receive the
honour of knighthood, in recognition of [his] distinguished talents as a composer and of the services which
[he had] rendered to the promotion of the art of Music
generally in this country." Macfarren was no courtier,
and shrank from honours and publicity which were not
associated with that esteem of his professional brethren
which he did really value. There were circumstantial
reasons, at the time, moreover, which rendered the proposal exceedingly distasteful to him. His answer was :—

" In reply to your favour of the 3rd inst, let me declare
my full sense of the honour you propose in my reception of
the dignity of knighthood from Her Majesty, and allow
me to acknowledge also the gratifying terms in which your
proposal is made. While holding the profoundest respect
for the Queen, I still feel myself unable to accept the proposed distinction; and you will greatly increase my obligation to yourself if you will believe that I say this in
all loyalty, and if you will avert the supposition that I
slight a gracious intention."

Through misunderstandings, announcements and
counter-announcements respecting the alleged acceptance and non-acceptance of the distinction were publicly made; and Macfarren felt himself awkwardly
placed and embarrassed. In reply to a letter from
him to Mr. Gladstone, he was assured, without any
wish to fetter his discretion, " that the acceptance of
the proposed honour would be generally appreciated

and approved"; and that his declining of the offer
"would create considerable disappointment in many
circles." Various friends represented to Macfarren
the duty that he owed to the profession in the matter;
and in the end he yielded; saying in a final letter to
Mr. Gladstone :—

"I own that after your kind words . . . . I cannot still
feel myself unable to accept the proffered honour from Her
Majesty. My expressed inability was on personal grounds,
with which I need not trouble you, and these must give
way to the wishes of others. I shall therefore be obliged
if you will cancel my letter of the 4th inst., if you will
forgive the delay I have occasioned you, and if you will
please to receive my acceptance of the intended honour."

A well-known musician wrote to Macfarren, prior
to the announcement of this changed purpose, con-
gratulating him on his decision, saying, "You are a
trump." Macfarren had to write and disillusionize
him, saying, "Your trump has been taken by the
Queen."

Macfarren hardly forgave himself for his changed
decision; and used to beg his friends not to address
him by his "titular prefix"; though he liked to be
termed "Professor," as indicating an artistically won
distinction.

In November and December, 1882, four performances of Sophocles' "Ajax," in the original language,
were given in St. Andrew's Hall, Cambridge, with
music by Macfarren. The bills supplied the following particulars :—

"The incidental music, written by Professor MACFARREN,
is produced under the direction of C. V. STANFORD, M.A.,
Trinity College. The scenery and proscenium painted by

Mr. JOHN O'CONNOR, from original authorities. The stage-management, costumes, and properties, have been entrusted to CHARLES WALDSTEIN, M.A., King's College. The chorus trained by E. S. THOMPSON, M.A., Christ's College, and C. V. STANFORD, M.A., Trinity College. The dresses, armour, etc., by MM. VINCENT BARTHE and LABHART, of London."

The difficulties of adapting music to the Greek drama were considerable; there were restrictions of compass and difficulty, in the chorus of male voices, and difficulties in the accentuation. The orchestra consisted of one flute, two clarinets, one bassoon, two horns, trumpet, drums, and harp, besides the usual stringed instruments.

The success of Macfarren in the music was acknowledged; "all the more so," said the "Musical Times,"

"that he did not affect the archaic, or any special tone-colouring, and wisely made the music subordinate to the main object—the dramatic representation of the play in the original language. Under those circumstances, the choruses did not sound differently—nor was there any reason that they should—from any chorus in unison in English Opera; except that in many respects the music was more carefully and intelligently given by the Cambridge undergraduates than it would be by a common stage chorus. The orchestration was simple and effective, and all the more pleasurable that it did not remind us of Mendelssohn, whose setting of the 'Antigone' and the 'Œdipus at Colonos' might have invited imitation. Dr. Macfarren seems to have trusted to his own genius and sympathies, and to have employed a vacation in writing the music to 'Ajax' as a *pièce de circonstance*, without intention of affecting the modern-antique, or of making any permanent addition to the musical classics. What Dr. Macfarren can do in the way of tone-colouring, we have heard in the chorus of Ishmaelites in unison, in his oratorio 'Joseph.' Apart from the Oriental character of the instrumental accompaniment to that chorus, the subject, whether accidentally or no, is a remarkable example of the Greek Phrygian mode; and from its commencing in, as it were, the octave mode D, and ending on B flat, the inversion of the final, it remains an historical and theoretical curiosity. There was little in the 'Ajax' to remind us of anything so interesting; but the mellowness of the music was a pleasing feature in these days of tortuous phrasing, even if the 'melos' were more redolent of the London foot-lights of some years ago than of the Athenian stage."

Notwithstanding this account, there is, in the "Ajax" music, one chorus (No. 3) in the Phrygian mode.

This music was again performed at a concert in Queen's College, Cambridge, May 18th, 1883.

In 1884, for the celebration of the tercentenary of the foundation of Immanuel College, June 19th, Macfarren composed an anthem for male voices, "We have heard with our ears."

Though not connected with his Cambridge work, yet to this period belong the setting of the songs in Mr. Lewis Morris's "Gwen," a set of six being published by Messrs. Stanley Lucas, Weber, and Co. Another setting than that published of the "Rose" song was written.

At the Royal Academy of Music, Macfarren's principalship was signalized, not only by the delivery of an annual address at the commencement of each year's work, as already recorded (p. 236), but by a very large amount of personal attention to the details of the work of the institution, the interests of individual students, the wishes of the professors, etc. Moreover, the fortnightly meetings of professors and students were founded by him : these being, in fact, though not in title, semi-public chamber concerts, at which the students, before they essayed the more public appearance at the concerts, might acquire confidence by performing in the presence of academicians and their friends, within the walls of the institution. The social meetings of the professors, likewise, were originated during Macfarren's principalship; but have, virtually, been merged in the meetings of the R. A. M. Club, since established. To the examination work of the Academy Macfarren devoted special attention; both to the annual examinations of the students, and to the local and metropolitan examinations for those not studying in the institution, both these classes of examination having been established under his auspices. In connection with all these, not only did he write all the papers for the theoretical examinations, but also prepared "Seventy Questions on the Elements of Music," with a view to the assistance of examiners and the uniformity of examinations. During the whole period of his principalship, he was the always accessible friend and adviser of students and professors alike: ready of resource in all emergencies, in all difficulties requiring adjustment. He was the staunch upholder of the independence of the Academy as against all schemes for amalgamation with recently established schools, such as would destroy its prestige and usefulness. This reference must here be made, without any reawakening of controversies which have slumbered for some time. The testimony of Macfarren's successor in office to the admirable development of the educational working of the Academy under his management was as unstinted as it was just.

At the time of the controversy above alluded to,

Macfarren contributed an article on the Royal Academy of Music to the " Nineteenth Century " for August, 1882, tracing the history, struggles, and desert of public confidence and State support of the institution, as that which originally, and, according to its means and opportunities, efficiently and successfully, had fostered native talent, and promoted sound musical education in this country. A long letter on the same subject was printed, and extensively circulated, addressed to Mr. Wrigley, of Manchester, formerly a student in the Academy. To another provincial professor who, though not educated in the Academy, entertained good-will towards it, and towards its distinguished principal, and who therefore hesitated whether to accept an invitation and appointment to act as Local Examiner for the Royal College of Music, Macfarren wrote :—

" You are one of several persons who have referred to me on their invitation to examine for the proposed Royal College, and, while I feel the great courtesy of this reference, and perceive in it a regard for the true interest of music, I answer you as them, that the Royal Academy will not allow its friends to make sacrifices on its account, and as it might compromise your professional standing were you to refuse the invitation from your Municipality, this would be a sacrifice that could not be accepted. The case is otherwise as to the canvassing for subscriptions in support of a scheme which, being founded on fallacy, can have no good result, and which appears to be aimed directly against the Academy. I shall have great pleasure in proposing you as Local Examiner, in which I shall be strengthened if you will tell me whether, besides your services to persons wishing to enter the Academy, you may be likely to obtain 12 candidates for the Local Examination of the Spring of 1884."

To speak of Macfarren as a teacher, it is surely
needless to say anything of his artistic and professional equipment, with such encyclopædic knowledge,
and abundant experience. But of the hold that he
possessed on his pupils' confidence and esteem, and of
the manifestation of his personal character in connection with his intercourse with them, a little may be recorded. One pupil says: " I never knew a kinder
or more sympathetic man than the late Professor ; he
was always extremely kind to all his pupils, and in my
own particular case he was the best and truest friend I
ever had." There would be no lack of assent to this
verdict, and self-appropriation of these grateful words,
among other pupils. To this particular pupil he wrote,
after a success :—

" Go on, my good fellow, as you have sped ever since I
first knew you, and you may count on sooner or later success, and on what is better, self-content at having done
your best to deserve it, and you will cause me ever-grow-
ing happiness at having had a share in helping your
studies.—Yours affectionately, G. A. M."

Such genuine, hearty identification of himself with
his pupils' welfare could not fail to enlist trust and
love.

Of the counsel that he gave to students under his
care, these extracts from letters may serve as sam-
ples :—

" You must not deplore as you do the burning of your
music. You speak of having lost your facility—surely
this is a slip ; the value of an exercise is in its working,
which accomplished, the consequent facility remains, and
the paper which led to its attainment is for the future use-

less. Better men and musicians than you or I have voluntarily burned reams of exercises, but maintained the fluency
gained by their means. Things of larger extent which, while
they were a-making, the writers have hoped the world might
regard as works, have proved to be but exercises and been
destroyed to make room for others when the authors have
felt they could shew what profit to their powers had resulted from the composition. Many a painter has painted
out a picture that he might produce another on the same
canvas, and has rejoiced more in his improvement than
lamented his loss. Is there such a great difference between
what is done with the will and what is done against it, that
we should bewail the one and effect the other either to
clear a space or prevent the issue of posthumous attempts
that our own judgment would not sanction ?

"I cannot suppose the time you have spent in studies
other than musical will be fruitless to you as a musician.
I should be proud indeed had I read all the writers you
name, and I am sure from the inkling I have of them I
might then be able to think deeper and express me more
clearly in notes or in words."

"I think you have not considered (because its use occurs
more than once in your Canons) the bad effect of the augmented 4th in melody, or of the two notes of this interval
in consecutive chords. I wish you would consider the
matter. Your Canons are most ingenious, some of them
must have cost immense pains, but this will be repaid by
the fluency which must be its result. Such work is valuable, not for the effect it will produce on the hearer, but
for that upon the writer which is its natural consequence.
"More attractive to others are of course the Anthem
and Organ pieces. Among these I met an old friend in
the Air with Variations. Let me counsel you to exercise
your talent, as far as time and inclination may permit, in
this class of writing. Fancy needs practice as much as
Reason, and one can only acquire the art of freely expressing one's thoughts by frequently experimenting in it. We
must not think however that all we write in a publishable
form is available for printing, and that either for our
credit or money profit all should go before the world, or

that we are slighted if much of it be unaccepted. Remember that Mendelssohn's first published Symphony was the thirteenth he wrote, and believe that every worker in Art produces very many things of which the world never has knowledge. An occasional bonus for a copyright is a pleasant enough accident in a composer's career, but none of us may count on music writing as a means of livelihood."

" . . . . If you still contemplate an University degree, take warmest encouragement as to your likelihood of musical success, but forget not that a musician is an artist and not a schoolman only, and that a work of art must rather shew the application of scholarship than the process of its acquisition. The great men whose works we best love have all wrought as you have been working, but interchangeably with their exercises, strictly so called, they have constantly produced matter of lighter character which in its kind has also been valuable exercise, and to such tasks, and to the pleasure they certainly bring one, I heartily commend you."

A class scene at the Royal Academy is thus described by a former pupil, in the "Tonic Sol-Fa Reporter":—

"The six or eight members of the class show varying talent, and are at every stage of theory work. While one is having his lesson, the others stand about within sight or hearing; they can ask questions as well as hear the remarks made by Sir George upon their companion's work. Sometimes he calls upon them to point out the mistakes in it. Thus all sorts of points crop up, and the conversation is most improving. Sir George unfolds his wonderful stores of musical erudition; his detailed acquaintance with all the great scores; the boundless scope of his observation of classical forms; his familiarity with the capabilities and proper use of every orchestral instrument. The men who enjoy the class and succeed in it are the men who work. The indolent men—clever players, perhaps, who do not like theory, and are seldom in the mood for composition—are evidently a trouble to Sir George. He talks to them with the patience and kindness which in him are never disturbed, and there is the earnestness of affection in his words. He stimulates them by telling of the hard discipline which all great composers have undergone, and of the absolute necessity of study to the musician. Sir George has, however, a cure for idleness, which is, perhaps, more efficacious than even these tenderly worded remonstrances. All readers of his 'Lectures on Harmony' know the fascination which the manifold enharmonic resolutions of the chords of the ninth and thirteenth have for him. If a student has brought no work, he will probably ask him to play a set of these resolutions extempore, or, failing that, he will ask him to manufacture sequences at the key-board. Now the kind of student who scamps his exercises has an intense dislike to this sort of work, and it is probable that the fear of it has a wholesomely bracing effect upon several members of the class. It is interesting to note, as the lessons proceed, that Sir George's knowledge of absolute pitch is perfect. Strike a note at any part of the key-board, and he knows its name ; strike a chord, and his ear discriminates its constituent notes. Rarely, indeed, does a consecutive fifth or octave escape his attentive ears as he sits, with head bent, watching with clear mind's eye the progression of the parts. In the case of six or eight part writing, he will sometimes say, 'I must ask you to play that slowly, as I must confess it needs a little attention,' but that is all. In examining an orchestral score, he asks a few questions as to the apportionment of the tone among the various instruments, and in a few minutes 'sees' the whole thing clearly, and begins to criticize."

Another pupil, writing of these class-meetings, exclaims :—

"Oh, the pathos of that scene! The blind man sitting in reach of the key-board, his head hanging down in the manner so well known, and his face illuminated by the look of attention, patiently listening and marvellously piecing together our work, often so poor and dull!"

Still more detailed and pathetically interesting, as portraying his character in some touching aspects, is this, from another pupil :—

"I first met him when I went to him as a pupil on the 19th September, 1871. That day week, the 26th, his mother died. I remember going to the Academy for my expected second lesson, finding him absent without the cause being known, and hearing the dictum from the governess—'It must be something very important that keeps him, for he *never* breaks an engagement.' In 1878, when I had become intimate, he wrote me, dated September 26th, 'This day seven years I missed your second lesson.' Thus he cherished the memory of those who had gone before him. Seven years more, and when the day came round, I reminded him of 'the day he missed my second lesson.' He thanked me, saying, 'How often it is, when one friend is taken away from our lives, another comes in to fill up the place, or, rather, to make up for the loss.' Then he remained silently thinking for some moments, after a manner he had when deeply touched ; as on the two occasions in his addresses to the Academy, when referring to the death of a professor or student in the previous vacation, he asked for silent meditation for a few moments. (1878 and 1887.) Days of that kind were a sort of saint's day to him, and he kept them holy—not holidays, with a little *i*, for idleness, but holy—to cherish the memory of great and good ones. Part of this sentiment was shown in his habit of dating letters by some favourite's birthday : often have I had a letter dated 'Mozart's birthday,' 'Shelley's birthday,' 'Bennett's birthday'—just as some people will date their letters by a saint's day.

"That first meeting struck the key-note of a friendship that lasted ever afterwards : the same note was in many friendships with him. His great power of helping us, and his great need of help himself, was the link between us and him. There was the half-hour's work with him— playing my very faulty accompaniments to him—his ear bent towards the key-board as I played, and explained

what could not be played: then his dictum—' Don't alter
these ; that will be distressing to you, as they are finished ;
but begin to write something for an exercise; that you
will not mind altering.' Then there were more explanations as to the beginning of the Sonata movement which I
was to do : so he showed his sympathy with my composer's
feelings, inexperienced though I was, and his power to
help me.

" Now came the other side. After other pupils' work was
examined, and lessons were over, he got up to leave; shy,
and not knowing what to do, we watched him ; but once
was enough—once to watch him seek laboriously, by touch,
for the thing that we could see—was to realize the painful
darkness of his life, and from that grew the mental resolve
never to let him grope again, if we were there to guide :
the bond of mutual help and sympathy was sealed in this
way. . . .

" Not only music brought out the sympathy. Once I
spoke of a friend whose struggle for subsistence I could
then only help by kind words. He encouraged me, saying,
words were worth a great deal : he remembered a time
when the one who should have been his greatest helper had
nothing but words of encouragement in his power, and
they were of great help to him.

" He would always encourage, by quoting his own
struggles, and thus draw us into the mystic brotherhood—
make us feel we were of the same kind as he, and worthy
of his consideration as much as the biggest : if *he* could
do it, of course we could. The same was in his teaching.
Many times when he has advised an alteration, he would
add : ' When I was told to put something in, I always
tried to make it as different as possible to what I was
told'; and what he had done before us, he thought we
could do after him. *There* lay a secret of his teaching
power. I don't think he ever forgot his own past difficulties, and that his pupils were going through the same
struggles—whether in learning or in life. Some teachers
work as if they thought their pupils knew as much as they
did. G. A. M. would say, ' If you knew as much as I do,
you would not come to me to teach you.' Generally it
was when we had said we did not know how to do such and

such a thing. 'Of course not; if you knew all about music, you would not come to the Academy to learn it.'

"Another secret of his teaching power was his patience and attention to the smallest things and people. How he would go over and over the difficult point, putting it now this way, now that, till he got a point of view from which we could perceive it and assimilate it. I can see him now, stretching across from his seat beside one at the piano to demonstrate some idea on the key-board. Perhaps it would be the course of some discord, perhaps a suggestion for carrying out some passage in a symphony movement of our own, perhaps an illustration of such a passage by quotation from Beethoven or Mozart. How he would cry out at his bad playing—'Can't I find some right notes? Now, this is the way, or this, how does it go on? this is it,' all the time he was playing."

The same affectionate pupil records :—

"He used to say, somewhat bitterly, it was a mistake to fancy that blind people were quicker in their other senses. *He* could not hear better than other people, he would say. Certainly he was something deaf in the latter years, and required one to speak clearly; but of quickness of hearing, intelligence of hearing, he had no lack. His power of singling out one voice part from another, of analyzing chords as the music was in course, of recognizing one voice from another in speech, or knowing the direction of the voice, was very great. Often in class one pupil would change position; the next remark or answer made, he would turn to the new direction: 'Oh, you are there, are you?' would come with his return answer. His touch, too, was very fine, as one expects from a sightless man. I well remember giving him a snowdrop one day to feel. He held it by the stem with one hand, while with the tips of the fingers of the other hand he felt the blossom. 'How lightly it hangs,' he said, 'and there is a tender fragrance in it.' It was a quick perception which could notice the scent of a snowdrop."

Another devoted student refers to another trait in Macfarren's teaching :—

"His lessons were often tinged with a kind of humorous or racy strain. The—as he thought—intemperate use of extreme discords generally called forth an inquiry if all that was done here, what was going to happen when the hero was going to shoot himself, the heroine was tearing her hair, and all the tragic horrors were heaped up at once? If a pupil said some harshness to which he objected was 'only for a moment,' he rejoined, 'Oh, you don't mind a hansom cab going over your toes, if it goes quickly, then.' He had an odd way of calling a passage 'licentious,' as if it were a moral obliquity. Vague tonality he thought 'an excellent representation of London fog.' A succession of diminished sevenths was 'whining,' and 'like the wind in the chimney.' He never could bear 'the hideous interval' of the diminished third, saying, 'Do it three times in a lifetime, and never let the present be one.'"

His humour was not confined to his pupils, however. About his own appearance in his robes as Doctor of Music,—which some are vain of,—he would say that he was made to look "like first cousin to the Knave of Hearts"! And he made the slyly sarcastic remark

"that Henry VIII. studied music was essential to his youthful preparation for the Archbishop of Canterbury. It was then essential for the Primate, as for all Church ministers under him, thoroughly to understand music; whereas it now suffices that the Archbishop of Canterbury confers musical degrees."

CHAPTER XV.

"ENCYCLOPÆDIA BRITANNICA" ARTICLE : "MUSICAL HIS-
TORY." ADDRESSES AND ARTICLES ON "CORRECT
MUSICAL TASTE," INSTRUMENTATION, FORM, ACOUS-
TICAL DISCOVERY, EISTEDDFODAU, PART-SINGING,
PITCH, ETC. 1878—1885.

DURING the period of his holding these two
honourable offices, at Cambridge and at the
Academy, involving the performance of multifarious
duties, not only did Macfarren produce the important
works enumerated in Chapter XIII., but also prepared
the article " Music " for the 9th edition of the " Encyclopædia Britannica " ; afterwards republished as a
volume, entitled " Musical History briefly narrated
and technically discussed, with a Roll of the Names
of Musicians and the times and places of their births
and deaths " (Edinburgh, 1885) : a most charmingly
readable book.

And he acted as examiner, or adjudicator, for
various schools or colleges, and in various competi-
tions ; and in these capacities, as well as in that of
president or vice-president of societies, he availed himself of any opportunities that presented themselves
to address those concerned, and to enunciate sound
and useful principles concerning Music and its study.

Thus, on distributing the prizes to successful pupils at the Beckenham School of Music, March, 1886, he took the opportunity to reiterate his oft-repeated contention that it is

"a fallacy to suppose that the English nation has no aptitude for music; and that so far from the Puritans having (as has been alleged) blotted music out of the national disposition, they caused a counteraction which brought into effect several of the most important incidents in the musical history of this country. . . . It was in the time of the Commonwealth that the first representation was made for any native musical competition : . . . that there was published for the first time a collection of national melodies which stamped our native musical feeling as of the very highest: . . . that (by the express licence of Cromwell) the first opera was performed in England, which was several years before the performance of an opera in Germany: . . . that the first lady ever appeared in a public performance in this country. . . . The Puritans not only did not prevent the Cavaliers from exercising their musicianship, but they by Cromwell's own act gave them public encouragement. The great interruption to our musical character was due to the Hanoverian accession. . . . But there is rising now a strong and healthy counteraction. The people themselves are now asserting their love for music, and the evidences [he] had heard there that night showed [him] that the true seed of music is taking root in the public heart, and the fruit of this seed will not only do honour to the present time, but will stimulate us to still further exertions in the time to come. Music has a power of expression beyond that of the other arts. For example, a beautiful picture will convey a thought or the impulse of a moment; but music affords means to convey the development of a change of ideas," etc.

On a similar occasion, addressing the students of Aske's School for Girls, Hatcham, Miss Macirone

being the head music-mistress, in December, 1877,
he said :—

"Give me leave to say a few words to you on the subject
of the beautiful art it is the happiness of my life to cultivate. Let one of these words be Love, and another Duty.
Love is not a compelled duty, but the magnetism of the
mind; and to the subject we love, we owe the duty of
advancing it to the utmost. Love will give heart and life,
and promote the work; and Duty will shrink from no toil,
and endure no imperfection. I have been shocked to hear
music called an *amusement*. Music in olden times held a
prominent place in England; and, if since then it has
suffered neglect, it has of late years resumed its position,
and has won the consideration of the greatest educational
institutions of this country. . . . It has been the habit to
call England an unmusical country; and yet this is the
only country in which University degrees are given to
music. We have here Doctors and Bachelors of Music,
and this country is the only one which acknowledges
music amongst the scholastic faculties. Let this, therefore, bear me out when I say that the study of music is
not an *amusement*.

"Music is to be distinguished by the fact that our
musical sounds are the result of the rhythmic movements
of the air, and in the largest sense the old theory of the
'music of the spheres' is the application of this scientific
fact to the movements of the planets of the universe ; it is
a product of the grand laws of rhythmic motion, which
distinguish musical sounds in opposition to accidental
ones, and attention to the rhythmical divisions of the notes
is a matter of great importance," etc.

He examined, annually, the music pupils at the St.
John's Wood Blind School.

As another contribution to the dissemination of
sound views of music among non-professional students,
he wrote an article in the "Girl's Own Magazine,"
on "What is correct Musical Taste?" in which,

enunciating that " taste is the power to perceive the beautiful," he asserts that "the unjust use of the word 'classical' makes the word a scarecrow to many a music lover. Whether a crow or a linnet, he may be frightened by it from fields of beauty where blossoms flourish whose scent and colour may enrich him who perceives them, while their perception impoverishes not the flowers ": and goes on, defining the word as applied to things " classed together" by reason of their enduring beauty: encouraging a "familiarity" with them which does *not* " breed contempt," giving "fitness" for designed purpose as one standard for taste: decrying misapplication, exaggeration, affectation, interest in mere manipulative agility, etc.

When presiding at the Musical Association, on occasion of the reading of a valuable paper by Mr. Prout, "On the Growth of the Modern Orchestra during the past Century," January 6th, 1879, Macfarren, in reply to a question as to the use of valve-trumpets in the orchestra, said :—

" No doubt this was an important subject. In the first place, he believed the valve itself deteriorated the tone of the natural instrument, for he had heard the same player play successively on a hand-horn and a valve-horn, and it appeared to him that the tone of the latter was far inferior. That, however, was of secondary importance; the significant thing was, that by the use of these valves you obtained the entire chromatic scale, and by this enrichment impoverished the orchestra in a lamentable degree. The orchestra was distinguished from the pianoforte by the variety of tones and the prodigious power of colouring which this placed in the hands of the composer. The use of early times, to have complete bands or 'consorts' of one kind of instrument, had now given way to the blending of many qualities of tone one with another. Even this was anticipated in early times, when the expression 'broken music' implied the mixing of several 'consorts,' such as hautboys and viols, and viols or shawms. There were great beauties in the combination, and still more in the contrast of these several qualities of tone. In the scores of Mozart, Beethoven, Weber, and Spohr, it would be found that when trumpets, drums, and horns were used, they gave a characteristic mark to the chords and keys in which they appeared, and when the music modulated from those keys, you either lost those sounds altogether, or else the instruments were employed on peculiar notes of peculiar chords, and thus gave a totally different character to the extraneous keys to that of the normal keys in which the pieces were set; or else when, as in the 'Dona Nobis' of the Mass in D of Beethoven, the piece being in D, the trumpets were pitched in B flat, a totally exceptional effect was produced from the introduction of instruments which were not employed in the normal key. The same was the case with the horns and trumpets in the slow movement in the C minor Symphony. The movement being in A flat, when they came in C, it was a totally new sound, and produced an effect which might be compared with that of the present gathering sitting in that room with the gaslight, and the roof being suddenly thrown open, and the sun streaming in. On the other hand, when these instruments were employed which gave the chromatic scale, the composers who used them were tempted to apply them to any loud chord that was wanted; when they were not used in the degraded sense in which waltz writers used them to play the principal melodies, in order to force out, by manifold duplication of notes through the foggy mass of multitudinous instrumentation, a rampant vulgar tone upon the otherwise imperceptive organs of the hearers. This vulgar use, such as was commonly heard in *entr'actes* in theatres, was a thing quite apart from the beautiful delicacy, from the exquisite feeling, from the heavenly perfection of sound, which you found in those compositions which had been so well described and so warmly eulogized that evening. This employment of valve instruments tended to reduce the orchestra to the level of the pianoforte, which had the power of *piano* and *forte*, but could only have one quality of tone, that quality being only variable by the aid of a different touch. They knew that one player would produce a different effect from another on the same pianoforte, but it would sound a pianoforte all the way through; and the orchestra, with the scarce notes of the incomplete wind instruments, was a far richer power in the composer's hands, than when there was the terrible temptation of writing for cornets like violins, or for horns like violoncellos. There was another instrument besides, which was played mostly in England, for which he believed Mendelssohn intended such a passage as that at the end of the overture to 'Ruy Blas'—a slide-trumpet. A slide did not deteriorate the effect of the instrument as the valve did, just in the same way as a valve-trombone was inferior to a slide-trombone. He would earnestly caution young writers to confine themselves to such trumpets as Beethoven would employ."

A pupil records, as a signal instance of the Professor's fair-mindedness, an incident which bears on the above subject :—

"He was speaking about the trumpet to one of the others, and I struck in in defence of the slide-trumpet, and we had quite an argument, though it was not the first on the subject. . . . I saying that a temperate writer would have sufficient control to deny himself trumpets in chromatic passages, extraneous modulation, and so on, in order to secure the freshness of special effects if they were wanted; whereas in other styles he will have the notes for use if wanted; that he could get all the effects that Mozart, Beethoven, etc., got with them, by ignoring, for the time, the slide, and yet get many more when he wanted them. That was the drift: however, the point is that Macfarren at last, to me, a pupil, in the presence of a class, said, ' Well, I break down ! ' This, of course, drew forth apologies, and he went on to modify his meaning; but I think few men would have had the strength of mind to say such a thing."

The same pupil says :—

" What I remember chiefly of his instrumentation was his dislike of what he thought the modern vice of too much sostenuto bass, his constant recommendation of plenty of unison, and saving a typical tone-colour for prominent keys and passages."

He wrote an Instruction Book for the Clarinet, in the popular series published by Messrs. Chappell and Co.

After the reading of a paper by Mr. C. E. Stephens on " Form in Musical Composition," at the Musical Association, June 2nd, 1879, Macfarren, being in the chair, made the following remarks :—

" The growth of music to its present consistency was but recent, and compared with other arts was entirely new ; but still we might look back two hundred years, and see already the seed from which modern music had grown. The natural law of harmonics, which showed in succession the natural production of sounds, was the basis upon which musical form rested. The most important harmonic after the generator was the fifth, and thus the chord of the fifth was the most important chord, after the chord of the key-note. The key of the dominant in like manner was the most important after the primary key, and their relationships were founded upon harmonic necessity—a necessity because these harmonic sounds were natural existences which, when brought into art use, were only more strongly defined than they are in the slighter and slighter vibrations that are induced whenever a primary note is sounded. When compositions were more concise than at present, this key of the dominant made ample contrast to the primary key of the piece ; but now that movements were more prolonged, another equally certain harmonic relationship, though further advanced in the harmonic series, that of the third, was called into play. . . . . . The thing which most obviously struck the listener was the recurrence of phrases, but in his opinion they were of secondary import compared to the distribution and arrangement of keys.

Tonality should be regarded as furnishing the real substance of musical structure ; and if one were to compare
such a structure with an architectural edifice, the height,
the breadth, and the material of the building were represented by keys, while the pillars, the carvings, the statuary,
and the ornamentation, which more quickly struck the superficial observation, were the themes.   The course which had
been so clearly mapped out by Mr. Stephens of the several
portions of a symphonic movement, constituted a form as
variable as was the human countenance; and when the
outcry arose that musical form had been exhausted by the
great masters, and that some new principles must be sought,
it would be as well to say that the sculptor must seek some
other form than the human face and the human figure.
Every man who looked into the face of a friend knew it
from every other face ; and coincidences were so wonderfully few as to be the subject of comedy, where two persons
were so perfectly alike that one could be mistaken for the
other.   With inconceivable smallness of difference in technical detail, complete variety of effect, of difference of idea,
might be expressed in music." . . . . .

At the Musical Association, Feb. 6, 1882, after a
paper by Rev. Sir F. A. Gore Ouseley (President),
" On Some Italian and Spanish Treatises on Music of
the Seventeenth Century," Macfarren said :—

" I consider it a high privilege to have the opportunity
of joining voice with so eminent an authority on these
highly important and interesting matters.   I can, I think,
fortunately throw a gleam of light on the most interesting
point of our distinguished President's discourse, which I
must refer to the lantern from which I received it, namely,
Mr. William Chappell, that is, the discovery—for one can
hardly call it an invention, since it is the probing of one of
the phenomena of nature, and that phenomenon of all
others which establishes music as one of the natural
sciences, as well as one of the most beautiful arts—the
phenomenon of the chord of the dominant seventh. . . . .

" So far as I can learn in the history of science, no discovery has ever been onefold; it has always been the case
that several explorers in about the same period have divined
the same fact, and, whether simultaneously or in immediate
succession, they have brought it to light ; and their almost
contemporaneous fortune in lighting upon such wonders,
serves not so much to make antagonism between them as
to give confirmation in the works of one, of the views of the
former. Another thing which is of great importance, which
belongs also to the seventeenth century—I think the date
was 1676—is that two Oxford scholars, without communication with each other, lighted on that grand fact which
explains this chord of the dominant seventh, and translates
it from a piece of empiricism into the really natural fact
and wonderful phenomenon that we find it. One was
William Noble, of Merton College, and the other was
Thomas Pigot, of Wadham College. They discovered
that one sound generated others, and that the successively
generated sounds built up the very chord of the dominant
seventh ; and the fact that the notes of this chord are thus
generated is the solution of the contradictory effect of this
to the rules of the earlier contrapuntists—that no discord
could be tolerated except its harshness were mollified by
preparation. As the seventh note is generated harmoni-
cally by the fundamental sound, it is truly prepared in
nature, and our articulating this note in performance by
voice or instrument is only making a little stronger that
sound which already exists where the generator is given to
produce it. Evidently the true basis of the harmonic
theory of the present period is that this is a natural and
not an artificial combination of sounds ; and I think it is a
great glory to our country that that discovery was made
here, and was made all but simultaneously by two persons
who were resident in the same locality, and not in communication with each other. It is one of the many glories of
the University of which our President is the shining orna-
ment of musical light at the present moment, that the discovery was made in Oxford."

On various occasions Macfarren acted as one of

the adjudicators at the Eisteddfodau, and took the
opportunity to give counsel together with criticism.

In a letter to Mr. John Thomas (Pencerdd Gwalia),
anent the Birkenhead Eisteddfod, 1878, Macfarren
thus expresses himself concerning

" the real merits of the festival, and the true good it is
likely to effect. The Eisteddfod as an institution is a
vast moral power, inasmuch as morals are influenced by
intellect, and as intellect is approachable from the two
sides of instruction and amusement. It is an incentive to
cultivate the whole sisterhood of the fine arts,—music,
letters, and painting under its various aspects of the flat
and the round. Inquiry into natural sciences, and application of the knowledge so obtained, is not only prompted
but induced. The investigation of history is stimulated,
and the emulation is encouraged of the honoured deeds of
the past by the nurture of the sense of patriotism. Copious
statistics, which I have had opportunity to examine, prove
that the establishment of choral societies throughout the
country has always been coincident with the diminution of
vice in the district,—that vice which is the greatest stain
upon our national character, the vice of drunkenness. The
choral class-room supplants the tavern, and familiarity
with works of art, which brings insight into the principles
of their construction, refines the mind, and through this
channel reaches the heart of men whose predecessors gave
way to the most sensual excesses. Not alone they who
sing are enriched by the treasures of song; they who listen
participate the profit of this spiritual wealth, and the feeling of thankfulness for pleasure received is in itself a good
that is quite worth the pains of promoting. It is not for
me to intrude speculations on the study of subjects that
are beyond my own province, but it is obvious that the
many means of education on the one hand and entertainment on the other, if more limited in their exercise, since
engaging individuals instead of multitudes, must operate
in the same direction as music, so widely as they reach, with
a like effect. . . . The value of the language of the district

was largely discussed at the meetings, and has been much commented upon, and greatly disputed in reference to the late occasion. Together with this, national egotism has been a lively topic for censure. This word *censure* is here used in its restricted or slang meaning of *blame*, and not in its full or true meaning of *judgment*. Pride of country is the noblest of self-esteem, and is distinct wholly from personal vanity ; the one prompts actions for self-glorification, the other stimulates endeavour for the nation's honour. . . . Our mother's tongue is the mother's milk of feeling ; he who can forget the words in which he has first heard of love, and first owned its force, must have a heart to let, within which love will not occupy the unfurnished apartments. Philologists aver that knowledge of one language is strengthened by insight into another, and that those tongues speak the most purely which have acquired the language of parlance by what may be called artificial rather than natural means, that is, in the schoolroom and not in the nursery. The exercise of the intellect in any of its functions gives greater power to them all. Let, then, the Cymri keep their Cambrian speech, but let them learn the language of their compatriot, Shakspere: his burning thoughts are a lamp, a sun, to illuminate mankind ; but these thoughts are disguised if translated into other syllables, and it is due to his greatness, it is due to our own, that every native of the land which bore the author of " Cymbeline " and " King Lear " worships this greatest of heroes by reading and speaking and understanding the very words he wrote."

In a long letter which Macfarren, as senior adjudicator, at the Eisteddfod at Cardiff, 1883, addressed to the choirs, with the wish that his opinion "may serve a cause which commands the support of every musician," he remarks :—

" The point most to blame in some of the performances was a tendency to force the voices, especially among the boy singers. That boys may sing with beautiful effect is proved daily in our cathedral services, but this effect is produced by an easy emission of tone, without tightening of the throat. The breath should be impelled from the diaphragm, and never influenced by the rising of the shoulders. Disregard of these principles, by female and male adults as much as by boys, induces hardness of tone to the extent of harshness, and causes the rising of the pitch, which, in some instances at Cardiff, proceeded into strange keys, and rendered the singing impossible to in- strumental accompaniment. Noise is not power, and the best quality attained is with the least physical exertion. The fault I have named, and certainly not an incorrect knowledge of the music, was the cause of the singing being out of tune on the occasion. By musicianly phrasing I mean the taking of breath at the natural reading places in the musical sentences, analogous to observing the punctua- tion of words, the giving more or less emphasis to words according to their significance in the musical sense. By just variety of power I mean regard to the directions for loudness and softness, and the gradations between the extremes, avoiding to sink in pitch with the diminution of tone, and beginning every phrase with distinct firmness, whether it be soft or loud. I cannot too strongly set forth my admiration of non-professional musicians such as you, for the ability they have acquired under obvious disadvantage, and for their influence upon those who were fortunate enough to have the benefit of their direction elsewhere, as well as in Cardiff. I have witnessed such proofs of musical aptitude as make me proud of my fellow- countrymen, for so I must and will consider you to be, though my lot be cast on the other side of the mountains that surround, but cannot cut off the Cymric race, and will never part them from the sympathy of music lovers who claim Britain as their native land."

Macfarren's decision of character was illustrated at this Eisteddfod by his admonishing a fussy speaker, who interrupted the proceedings (a choir competition), to desist; and, the admonition taking no effect, even after "Choir No. 5" had been called on, he shouted, in louder voice, " Unless the competition goes on, the adjudicators will retire in a body."

In the first number of the " Part-Song Magazine," May, 1868, an article by Macfarren on " Choral Singing " appeared, in which he enumerates as

"faults most common to untutored singers, and most needful to be overcome :—1. Permitting the musical sound to fade away before the completion of a phrase where there is no requirement for this in the expression of the passage. . . . 2. Prematurely pronouncing the final consonant of a syllable, which should only be articulated at the expiration of a note, instead of continuing the vowel sound throughout the full value of the time. . . . 3. Singing upon L, M, or N, as final letters. . . . 4. Failing to articulate final consonants. . . . 5. Anticipating the sound of the second vowel in a diphthong, as in ' ne-*ar* ' ' fe-*ar* ' de-*ar*,' or in ' da-*y*,' ' sa-*y*,' ' ma-*id*,' ' rema-*in* ' (mispronounced ' da-*ee*,' etc.). . . . The same fault is made with those letters which, though written singly, comprise two vowel sounds, as I or Y, which are composed of the sounds ' ah ' and ' ee '; and O, which is often incorrectly followed by the sound of ' oo,' as in ' home ' (mispronounced ' ho-*oo*m '). 6. Substituting B for M, as in ' home ' (mispronounced ' hobe '); and changing N into D, as in ' chain ' (mispronounced ' chaid ') [surely this fault must be simply the result of a cold in the head !]. 7. Omitting N in words ending with ' ing.' . . . 8. Falsely accentuating unaccented final syllables as in ' lit-*tle*,' ' pret-*ty*,' etc. 9. Sliding up to a note which is approached by leap, instead of attacking it without any preliminary sound to the same syllable. 10. Disregarding a dot after a note, or a quaver when tied to a preceding minim. . . . 11. A tendency to retard the time. . . ." etc.

In July, 1885, Macfarren wrote an " interesting and learned paper "—as it was characterized—for the Musical Congress at Antwerp, on " Musical Pitch," which was read in September. He referred to its constant rise from the earliest period to the present time: the influence of this " on musical composition, vocal performance, instrumental performance, and instrumental structure": its difference in different countries: the important faculty, " almost admitting " of being termed a " sixth sense," of " associating particular sounds with particular names ": the "analogy between sound and colour": the definition of the former being "less easily but not less accurately demonstrable " than that of the latter : the changed effect of musical compositions through change of pitch : with regard to vocalists, "The riddle of Œdipus may be thus paraphrased : What animal ranges in the clouds in the morning, and on the earth in the evening ? Solution: a singer ": reference being made to the early and later years of "this animal": the discrepancy of opinion on the matter among players on bowed instruments, some averring " that the tone of their instruments is attenuated by the elevation of pitch ; others, that their instruments gain in brilliancy thereby : the practical identity of the B flat clarinet of 1812 with the A clarinet of the present day, and the consequent difference of quality of tone from that intended in the music written for the instrument of that period : the importance of uniformity : the appointment of a committee in London to take steps to secure that result, Macfarren being chairman." (See page 269.)

Almost coincidently, however, with the delivery of this address, a communication was received from the Commander-in-Chief, stating that, " owing to financial and other difficulties . . . too great to be overcome, his Royal Highness was unable to support the adoption of the Standard Musical Pitch"; and as its adoption in the bands of the army was essential to the scheme, that scheme had to be abandoned.

Mr. A. J. Ellis, in his translation of Helmholtz's "Sensations of Tone," p. 550, thus refers to some utterances by Macfarren on this subject:—

"In the discussion of my paper 'On the measurement and settlement of Musical Pitch' ('Journal of the Society of Arts,' 25 May, 1877, p. 686), Prof. (now Sir George) Macfarren, Principal of the Royal Academy of Music, spoke of 'the difficulty of representing the compositions of different eras, which had been written for different standards of pitch,' and added, 'it was a marvellous fact, that, while the pitch was felt to be changed, the impression of the character of the keys seemed to remain with reference to the nominal key, not to the number of vibrations of each particular note. Thus the key of D at the present day represented the same effect as was produced by the same key according to one's earliest recollections; it did not sound like the key of E♭ although it might be of the same pitch. If Mozart's Symphony in C were to be played a semitone lower, to bring it to the original pitch, it would not sound at all the same. How far this result was subjective—how much depended on the imagination of the hearer, and how much on the physical facts—was a deep, perhaps an insoluble question; but it was one which really ought to be considered.'"

These extracts must be accepted as specimens of Macfarren's extensive acquaintance with, and readiness to expatiate with more or less premeditation on, the various matters connected with music which have at times claimed the attention of the musical community. In this connection also may be mentioned papers by him in periodicals on "Unity in Dis-

crepancy," on " Musical Criticism," on Mendelssohn's
"Athalie," etc.; also analyses of pianoforte works,
prefixed to a series edited by him for a London firm,
entitled " Macfarren's Universal Library of Pianoforte
Music."

It is difficult to assign the dates and order of publication of many of his compositions. He says, in a
letter to Mr. Dudeney, "There was no *Opus* No.
fixed to anything of mine but the three or four works
printed in Leipsic by Kistner and by Breitkopf and
Härtel." Among works not hitherto mentioned there
are a Trio in A for Flute, Violoncello and Pianoforte;
Three Trifles for Flute and Pianoforte; Recitative and
Air for the same instruments; Andante and Allegro,
also for the same; a Concerto for the Concertina; and,
for the Organ, Larghetto in A minor, Andante con
moto in B flat, and Larghetto espressivo in G minor;
also the following Anthems: "A day in Thy courts,"
" God said, Behold I have given," " Hear me when
I call," " Hosanna to the Son of David," " O Holy
Ghost, into our minds," " The Lord is King," " The
Lord is my Shepherd," " We give Thee thanks,"
"Wherewithal shall a young man," " Blessed be the
poor," " When saw we Thee," " Praised be the Lord,"
" Great and marvellous," " Remember, O Lord,"
" The law of the Lord," " The Lord hath been mind-
ful," " We wait for Thy lovingkindness," " When
all things were in quiet silence," " This day is born."
Also, several Two-part Anthems, besides a " Choral
Service in E flat," a "Morning, Communion, and
Evening Service in G (unison)," " Cantate Domino
and Deus Misereatur " in G, and a similar work in F.

CHAPTER XVI.

MACFARREN'S " COUNTERPOINT." UTTERANCES ON DIA-
PHONY, CONSECUTIVE 5THS, MENDELSSOHN'S FUGUE
IN F MINOR, ETC. 1879—1882.

MACFARREN'S book, " Counterpoint: a Course
of Study" (1879), is in no sense a theoretical
manifesto; it is purely educational and disciplinary,
" edited for the Syndics of the University Press,"
and designed entirely for the use of students, having
their needs always in view. Therefore, its various
rules, directive and prohibitive, must be understood
as indicating, not entirely what is good or bad in
music, but what is desirable or undesirable for students
to do in their course of training. And at the outset,
therefore, as the sure foundation, he bases all upon
Counterpoint in the *strict style*; holding strongly to
the necessity of a course of exercises under its rigid
restrictions, prior to any venture in the region of *Free
Counterpoint* until freedom has been attained within
the narrower limits. Moreover, he rightly characterizes as " dissolute " any lazy, trifling evasions of
strict rules, any availment of *licenses*, until every
effort has been made to comply with stern rules.

The work may therefore be said to be a *manifesto*,
though not theoretical, but educational: a timely
warning against certain tendencies which the writer

discerned, and which he sought, in the interests of soundness and thoroughness, to check; for which effort he was by some regarded, and by one termed, " an obstructive."[1] And he himself says, in the Preface to " Musical History" :—

"He [the author] claims to be a conservative, in the sense in which the first music schools in Italy were, and those in some other Continental States are named, as striving to conserve the pure and beautiful; he claims to be a radical, since seeking the root of truth and founding his convictions accordingly; but he disclaims to be an eclectic, because, believing with Rossini that there are only two classes of music, the good and the bad, he elects the former in all its manifestations."

The distinguishing severities in the book that may be noticed are : (a) the avoidance of modulation, except in the examples of Double Counterpoint; even progression, or diversion, to the so-called *relative* major or minor, being tabooed as " most to be shunned "; the very terms being " denounced as misleading, and consequently dangerous to the composer " : (b) the use of only one harmony in each bar of contrapuntal exercises. " Contrary to the method of some teachers," Macfarren recommends students " to work each Species of Counterpoint successively in two, in three, in four, and perhaps in five parts, before entering on the practice of a next Species." This plan I had myself recommended and adopted years previous to the publication of Macfarren's " Counterpoint."[2] It is possible that I may have heard of Macfarren's practice in

---

[1] See p. 246.
[2] See " Text-Book of Music," H. C. Banister. Preface to 1st edition, 1872. See also my " Musical Art and Study ": paper on " Some Methods of Musical Study," p. 34.

this matter, though I am not conscious of having borrowed the idea.

In the introductory chapter, Macfarren advances the " conjecture " that *Diaphony*, instead of having been, as " alleged . . . . the singing of one melody by two voices, or choirs of voices, at the interval of a 4th, or a 5th, or an 8th asunder, ... may have meant alternation or response, and that the parts which, in ancient copies, stand one over another at the interval of a 5th, a 4th, or an 8th, were sung in succession and not together, their presentation in writing having no analogy to the modern idea of a score." He admits that " this is but a conjecture, whose proof must rest with the antiquary," which, " if . . . . admissible, ... will point to diaphony as the germ of the fugue." Consistently with this conjecture, he remarks, in his " Musical History " (p. 27), that the term " *diaphony* (through the sounds)," is " at least as appropriate to the successive as to the simultaneous singing of a melody at the interval of a 5th above or below."

In the chapter on *Intervals,* he remarks, in a foot-note, that—

" It is strangely remarkable, that, though men of science and musicians have spent elaborate attention upon other philosophical points, which may or may not link acoustical science to musical art, not one has openly discussed the phenomena that separate the 1st [Macfarren's term for the unison] and the 5th, the 8th and the 4th, in character, effect, and treatment, from all other intervals. This is not the place to enlarge upon the very important subject, but the present opportunity may be utilized to suggest its scientific consideration, and to state a belief that any facts bearing upon it, which may be brought to light, will be of the highest possible interest and commensurate value."

It is carrying out the spirit of this remark to give additional currency to the suggestion by its insertion in these pages.

In the chapter on *Scales, Modes, and Keys,* there is an interesting compendium of information respecting the growth of the Scale, the Greek Modes, the Church Modes, etc.

In the chapter on *Progression of Parts,* after giving the rule against consecutive 5ths, he adds this foot-note :—

" The reason of the bad effect of this progression has not been proved, but a speculation respecting it has the sanction of some thoughtful musicians. It rests on the fact that the ear adjusts the fallacy of temperament, and receives what stand for musical intervals on our keyed instruments, as though they were truthfully tuned; and thus, though we have but one C or D, etc., to represent the modification of the note so named in all the keys to which it belongs, the note produces a separate effect upon the hearer in each key-relationship in which it may be involved, so that D sounds as if it were a major tone from C if used in the key of C, but sounds as a minor tone from C if used in the distinctly different key of A minor, while a pianoforte or flute gives but one sound each for C and D. A perfect 5th, more than any other single interval, suggests the complete idea of a key; so, to proceed from one perfect 5th (whose intonation should be peculiar to one key) to another perfect 5th (whose intonation should be peculiar to another key) implies precipitation from one key to another without passing through the harmonic channels that naturally connect the two. The 5th E, for instance, should have 81 vibrations against 27 in the key of A, and but 80 against 27 in the key of C; we have but one A and one E on keyed instruments to serve for both keys, and yet we suppose the 5th to be perfect whenever we hear it; and so, possibly, our shock at approaching this 5th from A, after a 5th peculiar to the key of C, results from the discrepancy that should exist between the two presentations of the chord which are characteristic of the two keys. This speculation is corroborated by the good effect of consecutive 5ths between those notes of the key of which, in truthful intonation, the 5ths are precisely perfect—a good, nay, beautiful effect, however, whose application is limited to the modern, free, or chromatic style of music, and is wholly unavailable in Diatonic Contrapuntal writing."

In a review, evidently by Macfarren, of a certain Anthem, he writes :—

"We protest against the consecutive 7ths . . . . ; how strange it is that composers who would shrink with horror from writing the 5ths in succession in the same two parts, as from a foulest sin, write the infinitely worse sounding progression of two 7ths in cold blood, as if it were quite a matter of indifference, and nobody's heels would suffer from such treading on, or ears from such torture."

These remarks on consecutive perfect intervals are, at all events, logically plausible. But, in reference to the closely allied rule, which he enforces, against similar motion to a perfect interval in the " outside parts " (generally called the extreme parts)—such joint progression often being termed *hidden* or *covered* consecutives, but, by him, an *exposed* 5th, etc.—he inserts the remark, which seems to indicate a failure to understand the sense in which, rightly or wrongly, the term is used,—in fact, altering the term : " By strange contradiction, it is not uncommon to use the term ' hidden ' instead [of exposed], as ' hidden 5th,' ' hidden 8th,' etc. ; but a note can only be hidden by others sounded at once above and below it." Now, it is not desired here to advocate the use of the term objected to ; but Macfarren misrepresents it : the objectionable progression is *not* called, in any book that I know, nor is the one 8th or 5th approached in the objectionable manner, *a hidden* 8th or 5th ; but the manner of progressing to it being considered to *cover* a 5th or 8ve, which is *hidden* by not being sounded, the whole effect is supposed to hide that which, if sounded, would constitute *hidden fifths* or *octaves, hidden consecutives.* The use of the singular or of the plural term makes all the difference in the meaning and consistency of it.[1] It is not a term worth fighting for ; but let it be rightly stated ; not mis-stated, and then opposed. But I have heard Macfarren say, with almost angry vehemence, "No ! it is an exposed 5th."

So far as I am aware, Macfarren is the only writer who forbids, apart from the false relation of the tritone, in two-part counterpoint, all expanding from a 3rd to a perfect 5th.

Treating of successions of harmonies, Macfarren forbids, in the major key, the following of the common chord of the supertonic by the chord of the key-note, " unless both chords be in the first inversion " ; but adding that " the same effect is not produced by a progression from the chord of the submediant to that of the dominant—also a minor and a major chord in consecution." To this he appends a foot-note: " A reason for the difference may be that, from the supertonic to the key-note is the interval of a major tone, but from the submediant to the dominant is the interval of a minor tone." This may hardly seem sufficient justification of the prohibition ; but, rather,

---

[1] See " Text-Book," H. C. B., pp. 50, 51.

an explanation that requires explaining. There is a somewhat more ample statement on the subject in his "Musical History," where, after speaking of the conflict between the followers of Pythagoras and those of Aristoxenus, the latter having "discovered the difference between the major and minor tones, the first having the ratio $\frac{9}{8}$, and the second having that of $\frac{10}{9}$," Macfarren continues (p. 12) :—

"Subsequent theorists disputed whether the major or the minor tone should be above the other, and it was Claudius Ptolemy (c. 150 A.D.) who enunciated that the major tone should be below the minor, which is the principle that directs the intonation of our present scale. This intonation may account for the difference between the effect in proceeding from the minor chord of the supertonic to the major chord of the tonic, and the effect in proceeding from the minor chord of the submediant to the major chord of the dominant, of which the latter, at the interval of a minor tone, is acceptable, and the former, at the interval of a major tone, is repugnant to cultivated ears."

It may be said here that Macfarren has deftly written some of his *Canti Fermi* in such wise as to be quite workable according to his strictest rules, and to exemplify their application; but that observance of some of these rules is well nigh impracticable, in some of the Species, with many *Canti Fermi* not written for such special purpose. Teachers and students will find this out by experiment. This is not the place to enlarge upon or exemplify the statement. Nor must the consideration of disputed points be here entered on: such as the singularly illogical foot-note, p. 29, which does not touch the point at issue; the prohibition of a passing-note occurring simultaneously with the striking of an arpeggio note with which it is dissonant (§§ 54, 243)—which, however, is an excellent disciplinary restriction for students ; some of the restrictions as to cadences, such as § 109, etc. More pleasant is it to notice the emphasizing of the importance of right treatment of passing-notes (§ 148) ; the detailed painstaking in regulating the combination both of two or more moving Counterpoints of the same species (chaps. x., xi., xii., xiii.), and of combined species (chap. xiv.), to which little attention is paid, for the help of students, in other books on Counterpoint; the exposure of the fallacious pretentiousness of much so-called *multi part* writing (§ 275); the suggestive chapter on *Counterpoint in the Modern Free Style,* and other matters in this highly useful work, which has been called a *classic;* and, undoubtedly, is the book which, because founded on definite principles, and not empirical or arbitrary, as so many works on the subject are, takes the highest rank among English treatises, even if its rules and explanations meet not with entire acceptance. Like his other books, it is a practical protest against "slipshod" looseness and indefiniteness in study and in practice. Whether the authority be recognized or not, there is no mistaking what is forbidden and what is allowed, what is rigorous and what is undesirable. The modern spirit is restive, if not lawless, but the wise student will not "ignore or forget," to use Macfarren's own words,

" that discipline is the best warrant of liberty, that he alone can successfully evade rules who is fully capable of obeying them, and that the ancient principles of Counterpoint apply—if practically enlarged in their application—

most stringently to the structure of music in the idiom of
the present day."

Mr. Prout, in his recently published work,
"Counterpoint, Strict and Free," speaking of the
necessity, "if Counterpoint is to be of real use to the
student, to make it conform strictly to the requirements of modern tonality," continues :—

"To the late Sir George Macfarren is due the credit of
being the first to recognize this important fact; unfortunately his treatise on Counterpoint, excellent as it is in
this respect, contains so many of its writer's peculiar ideas,
and prohibits so much that other theorists allow, that the
beginner who studies the subject under its guidance is
hampered and harassed by needless restrictions, until
really *musical* writing becomes all but impossible, and his
exercises sink to the level of mere mathematical problems.
All honour, nevertheless, to Macfarren for first enforcing
the principle that modern tonality should be the basis of
strict Counterpoint ! "

A most remarkable instance of recondite extem-
poraneous speaking is furnished in Macfarren's remarks after an ingenious paper had been read by Dr.
Gladstone, on " Consecutive 5ths," at the Musical
Association, March 6th, 1882 :—

"I should like to venture a speculation on the subject
of diaphony. I thoroughly agree with Mr. Sedley Taylor,
and anybody else who has in any shape the same feeling,
that consecutive fifths are particularly ugly, and that our
dislike to them is not merely from the habit of artificially
trained ears, but from something in the natural fact itself
which makes them repugnant to nature. It is repugnant
to us at the present time, and not in this room alone, not
in this country, but throughout all the civilized world
wherever music is studied, and wherever it has resolved

itself into a language, instead of the barbarous jargon of
savages; everybody shrinks from the sound of consecutive
fifths. I cannot suppose that, as long as the organs of
hearing have been the same, persons can have experienced
pleasure many hundreds of years ago, in progressions
which are entirely offensive to us who hear them now;
that the same acoustical properties, whatever they may be,
which make them offensive in the nineteenth century could
have been absent in the tenth century; and that progressions which through these, as yet undiscovered, properties
are cacophonous to us, can have been acceptable to the
persons who heard them: and I think it is at least worthy
of consideration, whether in those written examples which
come before us, and are quoted now and then in print, it
may not have been intended that the parts should be sung
alternately, and not together. The Greek term 'antiphony'
means, of course, the sounding of notes at once, and
Aristotle expressly forbids, as far as I can understand him
from a good translation, antiphony in the fourth or fifth,
but says that antiphony in the eighth is permissible, and
produces a good effect, namely, that when boys and men
sing the same tune, one is obviously an octave above the
other, and the effect is satisfactory, but that this singing
of the same melody is not allowed in the interval of the
fifth or the fourth. This was then offensive to the classic
Greeks, and can it be possible that in the dark ages a
different constitution of human organs can have prevailed,
and have made that which was formerly, and is now, offensive, agreeable to the listeners? And as our predecessor,
whom patriotically we must honour, John of Dunstable,
said, they were too beautiful; too much beauty could not
be permitted, therefore a succession of these delights was
overpowering to the human sense. In the church, on the
other hand, antiphony does not mean singing in combination, but singing in alternation, and in that sense I appre-
hend the diaphony of the dark ages in music must have
been intended, and that as the parts were written a fifth
asunder, one or the other might be sung by a body of
voices in one key, and then the other part be sung in
response by another body of voices. It appears to me
that such was the original form of the composition of a

fugue—that one side of the choir would sing a passage, say, in the key of F, and that the other side would respond to it, say, in the key of C; then the first choir would continue a counterpoint or descant during the performance of the second choir, and the second choir would return the compliment when the *canto fermo* returned to the original singers; and so, out of that diaphony, our fugue has been developed. Now the bad effect of octaves seems to me to have a very obvious interpretation—namely, that by making two notes particularly prominent, the rest of the score is enfeebled, and that thus the balance of harmony is entirely thwarted. The effect is excellent, of course, for an entire phrase of melody to be sung or played in octaves, whether it be to give prominence to a bass or higher melody. Equivalent to that same effect is the subordinating of an accompaniment to a vocal part. The voice part is intended to be much more forcible than the accompaniment. Whether this is to be so enforced by throwing stronger power into the vocal delivery of the phrase, or whether by playing the passage on two different instruments in octaves, or on a pianoforte duplicating the passage throughout, it is only making that one entire phrase paramount in importance over the accompaniment. But when a passage of harmony in any number of parts has two notes made so very much more prominent than the rest, as is the case in the duplication of those two at the expense of the others, the other portion of the harmony is enfeebled, and the balance is destroyed. I think, with reference to some of the examples we have heard, that from the overture of Mozart, and the sonata of Beethoven, and those two from the oratorio 'St. Paul,' they must be oversights of the composers. I cannot suppose for an instant that the authors intended to write any one of the examples. In the case of Beethoven's sonata and Mozart's overture, the effect is so transient that it leaves little impression; but in the case of the 'St. Paul' choruses, I must own they have checked the pleasure the music has given me. I have noted them in public performance for the first time, not from exploring on paper, as having been conspicuous— not for beauty. There are several things which distinguish perfect fifths from major and minor intervals, and it is of

great importance to teachers and to learners to observe
these distinctions. Perfect intervals have two notes of the
same quality, whereas a major interval may have both
natural, or natural and sharp, or flat and natural. Perfect
intervals, when inverted, produce again perfect intervals,
whereas if we invert a major, we produce a minor; if you
extend a perfect interval by a semitone, you change it from
a concord to a discord, whereas if you extend a minor
interval, you have a major, and if it is a discord in the
first instance, so it is in the second, if a concord in the
first instance, so it is in the second. Then there is this
matter of the consecution of perfect intervals being offensive, whether to cultivated or to barbarous ears, whereas
the succession of sixths and of thirds is accepted as agreeable and euphonious by everybody. Then, again, taking
two notes in the fundamental harmonies, we have, in the
chord of the dominant seventh, a perfect fifth from the
root to its fifth, and we have a diminished fifth from the
third to the seventh. The imperfect interval requires that
both its notes shall have a defined progression under the
term 'resolution,' whereas there is an entire freedom in
the two notes of the perfect interval. We do not stop
there. In the earliest forms of melody, before harmony
was discovered, much more before it was regulated, there
seems always to have been some instinct in men's minds
to characterize these intervals of the fifth and fourth.
The authentic and plagal modes dependent on melodic
forms lying within the interval of the fifth for the conspicuous notes, or the interval of the fourth, were prescribed by Greek rule for melodic arrangement; and that
which prevailed in Greece was received in the church, and
forms one of the particular distinctions in the regulation
of fugal construction as to the subject and answer. Often
and often have I thought it would require the entire knowledge of a physicist to be able to probe this subject to its
foundation; and it would be, I think, of very great interest
to musicians, and possibly of value to the art of music,
if this subject could be scientifically investigated. But
the nearest approximation to a solution that I have made
is the fact, first of all, that consecutive fifths imply consecutive keys, and a very ill effect is produced by the want

of some intervening harmony which shall lead by natural gradation from the one key to the other. That, on a tempered pianoforte, no key is in tune, we all admit in theory; but I am certain the human ear exercises a power of adjusting the sounds which are produced, and of accepting tempered sounds for the true sounds that they are intended to signify. This might be proved, even by examples upon a tempered pianoforte, from the very different effect that the same notes produce when played with a different context. So I believe that if one hears the chord of C, followed by the chord of D, although both C and D harmonies are imperfect in pianoforte tuning, we have an impression of those two keys of C and D, and we want some chord which shall lead by natural course from the first to the second. Now certain fifths are decidedly in tune in the same key, such as the fifth of the tonic and the fifth of the dominant, and the progression of one of these to the other has not the bad effect which other progressions of fifths have. Also the fifth of the tonic and the subdominant may be used, as in the Pastoral Symphony of Beethoven, with beautiful effect. By an extraordinary coincidence the same notes occur in the first chorus of Weber's 'Oberon,' and I think with the same happy effect. . . . . I think the subdominant is a diatonic root in any key, but its influence ceases when, passing upward, the tonic is reached, and then a new derivation of the notes is to be considered. That tonic stands as the natural resting-place between the subdominant and the dominant, and to proceed from the fifth below the tonic to the fifth above the tonic, without the intervention of the tonic itself between, I think, takes us by the boldest, and roughest, and rudest plunge from one key to another. Now, whether we are to follow Helmholtz's theory, and derive the minor key from the major third below its tonic, and suppose that C minor is derived from the key of A flat, counting C as the fifth harmonic, and, to pursue that theory further, to derive the beautiful chromatic chord, the minor second of the key, from the fifth still below that A flat, and so to bring into consideration the subdominant with reference to the key-note; or whether we are to take those two notes, D flat the ninth of the tonic, and A flat the ninth of the dominant; wherever the dominant and the tonic are in tune, their respective ninths must be in tune also; and again, wherever—referring to the other theory—the third below the key-note is perfectly in tune, the perfect fifth below that must be true in the same manner. Thus, I think, is to be accounted for the fact that the progression of fifths by semitones produces the good effect that we sometimes hear. Thus, in the Violoncello Sonata of Beethoven in F, there is an example of the two open strings of the violoncello sustained for some time (C and G), and then a progression to D flat and A flat. With regard to what Dr. Gladstone exemplified, of the resolution of the chord called the German sixth, I think it is from diffidence rather than from real repugnance to the effect, that persons have shrunk from resolving the fifth from the bass A flat to the fifth from the bass G, while there is F sharp proceeding to G in another part. I think many ingenious devices that one finds in melodic progression to elude those two fifths, are rather from diffidence to avoid breaking an established canon, than from shrinking from the bad effect which the progression involves. I think that is not a case of bad effect any more than the case of proceeding from the subdominant to the tonic, or the dominant to the tonic by consecutive fifths, or the instance of the violoncello sonata of which I was just speaking. These are, however, only speculations, but they are not accidental—they are the result of deliberation—and if persons who have the means, from a knowledge of physics, [will] pursue the subject further home, and work to a real explanation of what are these mysterious and yet beautiful elements at the command of musicians, it will be, I think, of very great service."

In an analytical notice of Mendelssohn's Prelude and Fugue in F minor, Macfarren remarks :—

"The art of counterpoint—that is, of combining two or more independent melodies, while maintaining an individual interest in each—is especially exemplified in the composition of the Fugue, throughout which one subject is

always paramount, its variety of effect being entirely dependent on the diversity of the several counter-melodies
that, at different periods, accompany this one principal
theme. No one, since Mozart, has been so completely successful as Mendelssohn in fugal composition ; and the work
[under notice] contains ample justification of this well-
considered remark. . . . A fugue is wont to be considered
as a certainly dull, perhaps ingenious, exercise of scholastic
pedantry; and such, truly enough, it is often its ill fortune
to be ; but a fugue is also, though it may be less frequently, a medium of the manifestation of one of the
greatest qualities of genius—the power, namely, of making
restrictions conducive to the best effects ; and such it has
eminently proved to be in the instance before us, where the
wild passionate outbreak from the pathetic despondency of
the prelude which it embodies, acquires an increased intensity at every fresh entry of the subject, and at each reap-
pearance of the several fragments of this, until the original
expression obtains such an accumulation of power as it
could derive from no other process of development."

Macfarren could be playful, even about such a
matter as fugue. As far back as November 27th,
1843, at a meeting held at 3, Keppel Street (Mr. G. F.
Flowers', Mus. Bac.), for the formation of a "Contrapuntists' Society," it was proposed that the exercise, to qualify for admittance, should be "an *Alla
Capella Fugue,* in not less than four parts—the length
of which shall not be less than eighty bars—the subject of which shall consist of at least three, and at most
four bars ; and, moreover, shall be always heard, in
one or other of the parts, entire and unmutilated."
It was arranged " that a meeting of candidates take
place this day six weeks (Monday, January 7th, 1844) "
. . . ; and the fourth resolution, proposed by Mr. J. W.
Davison, and seconded by Mr. G. A. Macfarren, was,
" That any professor bringing with him, at that meet-

ing, a fugue of his own composition, written according
to the resolution which involves the test of admission,
shall be a member of the Contrapuntists' Society."
Macfarren, in seconding the resolution, said, " As I
understand the matter, anyone who can write such a
fugue is to pay a guinea ! " He hated mere pedantry,
though often considered a pedant. He delighted in
the production of tuneful, light compositions, scholarly
in their finish, though unscholastic in their structure,
such as his innumerable Part-songs ; *e.g.*, six to
Kingsley's words, " The Sands of Dee," etc.: six to
Herrick's words, " Bright Tulips," etc.: six Open-
air Songs, book 4 of " Polyhymnia ": Shakespeare
Songs: several for Men's Voices, " The Arrow and
the Song," " Speed the Plough," " A Legend of the
Avon," besides the Convivial Glees already referred
to : several for Female Voices, " Ye spotted Snakes,"
" The Troubadour," etc. : " The birdès that had left
their nests " ·(Chaucer) : " Ye little birds that sit and
sing ": " Colin and his Phillida " (Madrigal), and
many others: also about twenty-five two-part songs,
such as " Two Merry Gipsies," " The Fairies' Tryste,"
both so popular at one time ; and single songs almost
innumerable, among these being " Lyrics," twelve
or more in number: the songs included in " The
British Vocal Album ": " Songs of the Night Watches "
(three) : " Idylls of the King " (four) : etc., etc.

CHAPTER XVII.

Presentation at the Royal Academy. Various Compositions. Speeches. Failing Health. Last Days, and Death. Memorial Service. Tributes to Macfarren's Memory. Miscellaneous Personal Details. Abiding Influence. 1883—1887.

AS Macfarren advanced in years, the admiration of his life-long consistency and persevering courage, of his great attainments and commanding mental power, no less than of his unfailing kindness, and estimable qualities, which was felt by his professional brethren, sought expression; and it was determined that a purse substantially filled should be presented to him on, or as near as possible to, his seventieth birthday. Well was the secret kept from him, the matter not being made the subject of any advertisement or printed document; and very little, if any, written correspondence taking place in connection with the project. The response was well-nigh world-wide; and the Professor was invited, on a day well remembered by those present, in March, 1883, to come into the concert-room of the Royal Academy, to receive the congratulations of a few friends; he merely expecting verbal congratulations on his reaching that which is spoken of as the "allotted term of human life." But the attendance was overflowing of professors, pupils, and friends, who greeted him, when led in by Mr. Walter Macfarren, with a ringing cheer that seemed to stagger him.

His surprise may be imagined when Sir Julius Benedict, another veteran, after an appropriate speech, presented to him, in the name of those present, and many unavoidably absent, a cheque for 800 guineas. The surprise, and the long-continued applause when Sir George rose to acknowledge the testimonial, overcame him, and for some little time checked his power of utterance.   Thanking, first of all, Sir Julius for his share in the proceedings, he proceeded to speak of himself and his age; saying, among other things, " Having travelled the natural course of human life, I do not feel old, and can only hope that when I have no longer strength to perform the duties which have been to me a loving labour, I may still have the strength to resign."

Speeches by Canon Duckworth, Mr. Randegger, Mr. Eyers, and Mr. Walter Macfarren, followed, and this historical meeting broke up.   The Misses Macirone, who knew him well, were alone with him in his study the day after, when the sightless eyes shed tears at the loved remembrance of so much affection.

But he went on working just as ever: composing, lecturing, teaching, directing.

Among his later compositions mention may be made of an Andante and Rondo for the unusual combination of instruments, organ and violin, written specially for his pupil and amanuensis, Mr. Windeyer Clark, and published in Dr. Spark's " Quarterly Journal," No. 76.   And, in the " Girls' Own Paper," for

November, 1886, appeared a " Romance" for violin and
pianoforte, afterwards included as No. 1 in a set of five,
which were written for Mdlle. Gabrielle Vaillant, and
were engraved and prepared for publication just before
the composer's death, but not issued till after that lamented event. With reference to these, the following
letters to the estimable violinist will be read with
interest :—

" 7, Hamilton Terrace, N.W.
" Dec. 24, '86.

" My dear Gabrielle,
" In the summer I was asked to make a violin piece
for publication, and I thought of you over the making;
and I found the thought so pleasant that I continued the
current through the holiday weeks. This caused me a
singing in the head until I could exorcise the ghost by the
process of transcription, which was not until lately, although
prior to your pretty offer to come and write the new Sonata.
The four afterthoughts are then yours by natural right, if
you will accept them, because they are all about you, and
Christmas is timely for offering them. If you will accept
them, you shall have No. 1 in print when I can get a copy.
We shall have time I trust for the Sonata when we have
laid our dissipations to sleep; and so your ears and fingers
will be as much employed on your next visit as were your
eyes and lips when you last came.
" Affectionately yours,
" G. A. Macfarren."

The Sonata above referred to was for pianoforte and
violin, in E minor, dated June 27th, 1887, and exists
only in MS.

" 7, Hamilton Terrace, N.W.
" 17th February.
[1887 ?]

" My dear Gabrielle,
" What a perfect interval are you that keep your perfection from whichever side one measures you! If you

play, it is delightful, so if you send lilies, and so likewise if you say pretty things, which have infinite charm, whatever their subject. You pretend that my Quintet [1] gave your friends pleasure, and you know that this resulted from the merit of the playing. To feel oneself in the company of that brave and hale and most musical old Sir Frederick Halliday was indeed a treat, and to find age and youth blending to give unity of effect to what they expressed, seemed almost preternatural in the unity of spirit that bound you all. Whatever joy you had in the performance—and to do a kind and clever thing is ever joyous to the doer—I had five times the pleasure of any one of you, since mine was drawn from the efforts of you all.

"Your lilies bring the South of France into the heart of Maida Vale.

"I thank you for the naming of the Romances, and if you play them to your friends as you did to me, the friends must be hard of hearing not to be charmed. I have no present notion of printing other of the pieces than the first, but if occasion arise, will borrow the rest from you and have them copied.

"Yours affectionately,
"G. A. MACFARREN."

Yet another letter to the same :—

"12 *July*, '87.

"MY DEAR GABRIELLE,

"I was indeed sorry to miss your concert, but my examination ended not till half-past five, when of course your performance must have been over. I rejoice to have learned that the music went well, and that many persons were sensible enough, and had sufficient mastery of their time, to go and hear it. I thank you for having the Quintet, for the pains spent on it, and for the good rendering which was the result of it. Further thanks I would send for the new gift of roses that has come to-night. You are indeed the fairy of private life, dispensing flowers and love wherever you pass. . . . .

"Affectionately yours,
"G. A. M."

[1] See p. 99.

During the latter years of his life, moreover, he composed several Sonatas, both for pianoforte alone, and with violin, one of the latter being dedicated to his brother Walter. He also wrote a second Cantata for Female Voices, "Around the hearth," which was performed by the Academy students at a concert shortly before his death. He delighted to "make music" as his great resource, during his vacation-time, which was never "vacant" time with him. One of his Sonatas for Pianoforte, that in G minor, being the third that was published, was written, a considerable time before his death, for his pupil, the distinguished pianist, Miss Agnes Zimmerman. His very latest compositions were a setting of Shelley's "Lines on a faded Violet"; and a theme in F minor for Miss Dora Bright, to which she wrote some thoughtful Variations for Two Pianofortes. The same promising musician performed his last Pianoforte Sonata at a private gathering on the composer's birthday, 1887.

At the distribution of certificates to successful candidates at the Local Examinations in connection with the Royal Academy, in Liverpool, July 28th, 1884, after some remarks of a temporary character, he spoke on the subject of music at large :—

"This is a subject which particularly offers itself to examination by persons who make a life study of its principles. I may refer to some very admirable words of the Mayor of Manchester bearing on this head. In the other subjects of study—mathematical, classical language, or what not—every person may be able, with careful inspection, to note the capabilities of students. It is a very natural, perhaps a very happy fact—but in some respects a somewhat unfortunate one—that friends have peculiar estimates of the merits of their own connections ;

and it is a very hard thing for parents and guardians, and sisters and cousins, to believe that she or he who plays for their entertainment is anything but a mistress of the subject in which she presents herself, or a master, as the case may be. But as a knowledge of the fine arts can only be attained through a life study—to prove the real capacity of a musician or painter, the examination must be made by a specialist. I believe it does not need a master of arts to be able to prove that twice two makes four, or that the deduction of two from four leaves two behind. In this respect, as I have said before, it needs a specialist to see that the education is progressing in the right direction in other subjects, but in the fine arts it does, I assure you, need the test of a professional examination to satisfy the wishes of the friends of musicians that the progress of persons in whom they are interested is such as deserves the success it has met with on this occasion. Music is of very early date in the history of the world, but in the sense in which we know and enjoy it, it is a comparatively very recent institution. I have strong reasons to think that music rests on scientific bases, that it is not the accidental arrangement of sound formed by the almost capricious exercise even of the most powerful genius, but that it rests upon natural principles which are subject to the laws of the universe as much as the other sciences which daily and hourly are adding to the vast amount of knowledge of mankind. I believe that, with this consideration, we may regard music in other than the light of an amusement. Many persons talk of the pleasantry of a musical performance, but it is to be considered that to produce a musical performance many and many scientific facts must be accumulated: the acoustical science, which gives us the very sounds of music; the science of harmony, which teaches us to combine them; the wonderful science which has been from time to time applied to the fabrication of musical instruments; and then those interesting forms of art which are developed in gaining the mastery of those instruments, and acquiring the ability to draw from stretched strings and open tubes, and from that highest of all instruments, the human voice, those sounds which give what is called amusement, and what is often felt as delight. When we consider that the principle of sound itself—the principle which distinguishes musical sound from vague noises—that this fact of periodic vibration is the very same principle that keeps the planets in their orbits and enables them to make the circuit of the universe, and is also that which induces the stirring of the wind, which, falling upon our auditory organs, gives us the pleasure of hearing continuous sounds—we shall see that in this respect our art has a claim to the highest regard as philosophical fact. When we look still further to the lately-proved phenomena that the forms which are made by aërial vibration are identical with some of the primitive forms of shells and plants, and we, by collation of these two phenomena, find that the circumstances which have put substantial creation into the forms in which we behold and teach the facts of the world in which we stand, are the same influences and powers which produce musical sounds, we must feel that we are going in the footsteps of creation by turning those musical sounds to art account."

Macfarren thus showed that he could still think and speak vigorously. Certainly not less interesting, with its antiquarian lore, and personal references, was his speech at the banquet celebrating the second anniversary of the Westminster Orchestral Society, of which he was a Vice-President, March 25th, 1887 :—

"It is a peculiar privilege which is accorded to me to speak in acknowledgment of the toast of ' The Westminster Orchestral Society.' I have to thank the Society, firstly, for the good it has been sowing in promoting the welfare and the culture of music in Westminster, and, secondly, I have to thank the Society, personally, for having conferred upon me what I feel is a great dignity—that of the title of Vice-President—the first function in connection with which post being the present responsive speech. I feel much the value of such an institution as this. Westminster is a city and liberty of very old standing, and its musical importance is a matter of peculiar affection. In the important function of organist of Westminster Abbey some of the most distinguished musicians have had an opportunity of displaying their prowess. Christopher Gibbons, a son of the greater Orlando, was organist of Westminster Abbey, and Purcell, the brightest of them all, was born in Westminster, was bred in Westminster, and, as organist at the Abbey, had the opportunity of producing some of the most remarkable and admirable of his great works. (Cheers.) Then again, there was Dr. Croft, who, whatever the nature of his larger compositions, is well known in every parish and town in this country as the composer of the famous tune to the 104th Psalm. Later than that was Dr. Cooke, whose name stands very high in musical annals, and who owes to Westminster, and Westminster owes to him, mutual fame. But the City and Liberty of Westminster is not confined to the precincts of the Abbey and the parish church of St. Margaret. The first public performance of music that took place in this country was a performance of the oratorio of "Esther" in a public-house now called the Griffin, in the locality of Villiers Street (York Buildings), a site to which I owe my nativity. The success of that performance induced Handel to reproduce his work, which had been written for the Duke of Chandos, at what was then the King's Theatre in the Haymarket; and although the Italian Opera may to some extent have clouded the progress of English music, the King's Theatre was really the nucleus of music in the metropolis for 150 years, and that is within range of this City of Westminster. The time has gone by when Westminster was comprised in the Isle of Thornage—taking its name from the thorny nature of the ground, and its insular character; the river Longditch, which bounded it on one side, entering the Thames somewhere about the locality of the modern Northumberland Avenue, having to turn a water-mill at what is now St. Martin's Lane. As was the case in all great cities of England, Westminster was provided with a safeguard in the city waits, or watchmen, who used to parade the streets, playing on the hautboy. King Charles the First granted a peculiar charter to this company of waits, which remained in operation as late as the year 1820. It

is curious, indeed, that the king, who did so valuable a
service as to assist the hautboy players in Westminster,
should, in that very locality, have been considered too
tall, and have been shortened to the dimensions of popular
esteem by having his head taken off. Such, however, was
his fate.

" Let us now leave the great men of Westminster, and
the important locality which has given birth to some of
them, to consider the musical condition of the community
in Westminster. There has been for some few, but only
recent years, an Abbey Glee Club, which in the department of vocal music has doubtless exercised very good
influence among its members. But its members are
limited. This new Orchestral Society, which has reached
the second year of its existence, aims to gather into its
fold any and every Westminsterian who has a love for
music, and a desire to indulge his love therein. The
Westminster Orchestral Society has been cradled in a firm
which shall be nameless—but which all here well know
and recognize. Two years ago, a knot of about a dozen
members congregated together for the practice of orchestral
music, and with the utmost liberality of spirit—not wishing
to confine or concentrate whatever good they might be
able to accomplish within their own special circle—instituted the Westminster Orchestral Society, and it is a great
pleasure to me to know that many students of the Royal
Academy have had the gratification and felt the advantage
of co-operating with the original circle from which the
Society sprang. These have been joined by amateurs of
the City and Liberty of Westminster, and it is fair to
believe that the Society, which is still in its infancy, will
expand, and from the excellent beginning it has made,
will grow into an institution of great importance in the
subsequent history of our art.

" Nothing in the world is so remarkable for its power of
unification as is the phenomenon of music. In its performance is pleasure which no listener can comprehend;
to take part in the interpretation of musical works produces a peculiar satisfaction and delight, which one must
experience to know how to enjoy and appreciate. It is an
acknowledged fact in science, that our coal, in rendering the

heat which emanates from its combustion, but gives to the world again the warmth which it drew from the sunshine when growing as ferns upon the earth. I would not compare musicians nominally with coal. But the musical composer draws in his warmth, and gives it out again in the performance in the enthusiasm which it generates.

" I must not close my remarks upon the Westminster Orchestral Society without an allusion to its Conductor. Mr. Charles Stewart Macpherson was a student of the Royal Academy of Music. He entered under circumstances of peculiar honour in gaining a scholarship at a very arduous competition. In the course of his studentship he gained every distinction that could be conferred on a student, and with as much credit to the Academy as to himself. Many of the performances that have been brought before the public here attest to his efficiency for the post which has been entrusted to him, and the fact that he and the members of the Orchestral Society have mutual confidence in each other, will enable them to do credit to each other's exertions.

" The phenomena of music have often been described. They are eloquently exemplified in the colossal performances which have taken place at the Crystal Palace. One sees the beat of the conductor some seconds of time previous to hearing the sound of the voices, and four or five thousand executants with one accord utter the same thought of the same great composer. Now, in no other instance than music is that possible. I have stood beside one on the slope of a hill who noticed the march of a company of infantry, and observed that when the right foot of the first soldier went down, the left foot of the last touched the ground. Therefore, you see that from person to person, in an infinitesimal period of time, the pace has been slacker, until there was this difference between the first and the last man who marched. But musicians instantaneously and at once join in the utterance of the one word which joins all their hearts and all their feelings. May there be throughout the world among lovers of music the same unanimity of feeling, not only in the Westminster Orchestral Society, but among the whole community of musicians; and may the excellent work which has been begun by this

Society extend its influence and gather votaries from all parts of Westminster, and even from all quarters of the metropolis!"

He accepted the Presidentship of the Sunday Society, in the latter years of his life.

Notwithstanding, however, all the determination to work, and the still manifest mental vigour, Macfarren's friends could not fail to observe the unmistakable signs of physical decline, as evidenced by cough, weakened voice, less upright gait, and other symptoms of advanced age. At the dinner of the Academy Professors, in July, 1887, in acknowledging the toast of his health, he begged his friends that, should they observe that health failing so as to render his performance of his duties inefficient, they would intimate the fact to him. Inefficiency, however, was not that which was in the minds of those present with regard to the indefatigable worker presiding over them. They were as glad to see him back among them, after the Vacation, as he was to welcome them, when, on the 24th of September, he delivered his annual inaugural address; commencing by a touching tribute to the memory of Francis Ralph, a violin professor, who had passed away, amid general regret, on the 8th of that month. A most thoughtful address followed, dealing with the necessity of a life's devotion to art, the career of a student, the pursuit of truth, and other pertinent matters; ending:—

"In this large Universe we have the songs of the nightingale and the songs of the lark, but do they more ascend to the skies than the song of the sparrow? No. Believe me, that in working with the idea that your progress is your prize, you do justice to yourselves, you may do credit to the Academy, you may do honour to your country, and you will glorify the art of music. I wish you a successful course of study in the coming year." (Warm applause.)

The last warm applause from his beloved academicians! The last earnest counsel to them from his revered lips!

A month later, I received the following letter from Lady Macfarren (with an invitation card for "at home" evenings):—

> .   "7, Hamilton Terrace.
> "*October* 24*th.*
>
> "DEAR MR. BANISTER,
>   "I fear that the Professor may not be able to go out much during the winter months, and so I hope his friends will kindly call on him, and make him some pleasant hours.
>   "The evenings are intended to be entirely informal, and I trust we may have sometimes the pleasure of seeing you. . . . ."

Most gladly did I (as, I doubt not, many others) accept this invitation, and look forward to "pleasant hours" for myself, in conjunction with solace to the Nestor among musicians. Alas!

On Sunday, October 30th, though weak, and far from well, he went out with his attendant to pay a visit to his brother John. Lady Macfarren urged upon him the necessity of riding the greater part, at least, of the distance, to which admonition he seemed to give heedful assent. He walked some distance, however, though compelled, most unusually, to slacken his pace, checking his companion, and saying "My dear boy, I am afraid that I cannot walk quite so fast." The lad observed that the Professor leaned forward considerably; and, at last, almost doubling, fell. A cab was procured, in which he proceeded to his brother's house, Rochester Square; during the ride, however, giving evidence of suffering from the effects of the fall. After resting at the house, he was taken home, very prostrate; though he, and those around him, hoped that he would soon rally. On the Monday, however, he was quite unable to leave home; and, indeed, was not able to proceed with work that he had planned for the early morning. He put out, ready for completing, papers for an approaching Cambridge University Examination; and sent round to his amanuensis, Mr. Windeyer Clark, asking him to come in the afternoon to finish them, not doubting, apparently, that he himself would be well enough to attend to them. He dictated the following letter to his valued assistant at the Royal Academy of Music, Mr. T. B. Knott :—

> "*Oct.* 31, 1887.
>
> "MY DEAR KNOTT,
>
> "I have a sprain which renders walking impossible, and movement of any kind extremely painful. Hence I cannot be with you to-day, and shall be glad if you will tell this to those who have appointments to meet me.
>
> "Please also to send cards to [here follow several names of pupils], saying that I will make up Wednesday's lesson on the first Saturday when I am well enough. . . . If you pass here on the way home to-night, I shall be glad of your calling to tell me whether there be any news. But you must not do this at an inconvenience.
>
> "Yours with best regards,
>
> "G. A. MACFARREN."

Considerate of others to the very last! as the concluding sentence shows.

Alas! there were to be no more invaluable lessons; no Saturday " well enough."

Mr. Gill, the then Secretary of the Academy, had an interview with him, and received the dictation, from a perfectly clear brain, of one or two somewhat complicated letters. His brother Walter, also, conversed with him. Neither of them apprehended an imminent end. But as Lady Macfarren and a faithful attendant who was attached to her master were, shortly afterwards, applying some remedial alleviative, his head sank gently, and, at about three o'clock, he passed away!

Tributes to his memory, for the most part rendering more or less adequate acknowledgment of his great and diverse merits, were abundant. A requisition, signed by a number of distinguished musicians, by the Earl of Aberdeen, the Marquis of Lorne, and others, was presented to the Very Rev. the Dean of Westminster, representing that his interment in the Abbey " would be a fitting tribute to this gifted English musician ; and on more public grounds a just recognition of the art of which he was so distinguished a member." The reply of the Dean was that " such a course was impossible, from the fact that there was no available space in Westminster Abbey; but, as he was anxious to do honour to the art of music, he would be pleased to hold a Memorial Service there on the day of the funeral, at three o'clock." Accordingly, the interment took place at Hampstead Cemetery, on November 5th. Besides the family of the deceased, the Directors and Committee of Management of the Royal Academy of Music, the staff of that institution, deputations from the College of Organists, the Phil-

harmonic Society, the Royal Society of Musicians of
Great Britain, the Sacred Harmonic Society, the Royal
College of Music, the Guildhall School of Music, the
Musical Artists' Society, the National Society of Pro-
fessional Musicians, the Liverpool Musical Club, the
Liverpool Sunday Society, the Derby School of Music,
the Westminster Orchestral Society, and a large num-
ber of private carriages, formed the procession. The
service at the grave was conducted by the Rev. Canon
Duckworth, assisted by the Rev. W. Sterndale Steg-
gall. The pall-bearers were Dr. E. G. Monk, Messrs.
G. T. Rose, P. Sainton, Gerard F. Cobb, G. A. Osborne,
W. Dorrell, J. F. H. Read, J.P., and H. R. Eyers.
The inscription on the coffin was—

"GEORGE ALEXANDER MACFARREN,
BORN 2ND MARCH, 1813,
DIED 31ST OCTOBER, 1887."

A wreath of violets was laid, specially prepared by
a lady who had been tenderly interested in him latterly,
which, by Lady Macfarren's special desire, was designated "A Crown of Humility"; appropriately testify-
ing to his character. Many other floral tokens were
sent by numerous friends and societies.

At the Memorial Service in the Abbey, the music
performed consisted of Sir G. A. Macfarren's Obse-
quial March ("Ajax"), his anthem, "The Lord is my
Shepherd," the "Nunc Dimittis" from his Service in
E flat, Sir John Goss's "Brother, thou art gone before
us," and the hymn, "Now the labourer's task is o'er."

Before pronouncing the Benediction, Dean Bradley
said that

"they had arranged the service that day in order to show their sympathy for those who met there in sorrow, and to show their honour for him whose loss they all deplored. There were some present who had only just left the grave-side of one who, from early youth to old age of a long and honoured life, had devoted all his talents to the study and to the furtherance of that great Art whose mysterious power over the human soul was so great, but which he (the Dean) need not dwell on. Their departed friend had achieved much, as they well knew, and he had followed steadily a high ideal. They remembered him with gratitude at an hour like that. He had set them all an example, not only of kindness and of gentleness, but of industry and perseverance in the use which he had made of the great talents which God had lent him, and in the heroic manner in which he met one of the very worst of all deprivations and trials. They also thought of him as a leader in that Art to which all who worshipped in that edifice were so deeply indebted. They reverenced him as a brother, in the true sense of the word, of the many masters of music who lay in the Abbey."

The " Dead March " in " Saul " was performed by Dr. Bridge at the conclusion of the service.

At a Memorial Service, held on January 29th, 1888, at the Oratory, Brompton, the musical portion being under the able direction of Mr. Thomas Wingham, Macfarren's Trio in E,[1] Andante and Rondo, violin and organ,[2] and several vocal pieces from " St. John the Baptist" and " Joseph," were performed by Master Hawkins and Messrs. Russon, Pearson, Musgrove Tufnail, Kiver, Szczepanowski, D'Evry, and White-house.

An organ piece was composed in his memory by Dr. C. W. Pearce.

At the rehearsal of the Westminster Orchestral

[1] See p. 100.　　　　[2] See p. 3?0.

Society, November 2nd, the proceedings, "in consequence of the death of Sir G. A. Macfarren," were of a special character. The Secretary of the Council announced, so soon as the members had assembled, that the proceedings would be as follows :—

Overture . . "In Memoriam " . . *Sullivan.*
Short Address by the Conductor.
"Dead March" in "Saul " . . . . . *Handel.*

Sir Arthur Sullivan's overture having been played, Mr. Charles Stewart Macpherson said :—

"We meet to-night drawn in sympathy one towards another by the consciousness of a common loss. Since our last coming together, the world is the poorer by the death of a great and good man, Sir George Alexander Macfarren, our revered vice-president, who breathed his last at three o'clock on Monday afternoon. He had won the respect and admiration of all by his marvellous capacities as a musician and didactic writer, by his vast knowledge, and by his most extraordinary versatility. Yet more than this, he had endeared himself both by word and deed to an immense circle of devoted friends and disciples, among whom I count myself as one of the most attached. No one who came into contact with the deceased gentleman felt otherwise than impressed by his charm of manner, and by that indescribable faculty, peculiarly his own, of making one immediately regard him as a friend ; but it was reserved for his pupils and his most intimate acquaintances to experience to the full that large-hearted kindness and unselfish regard for the welfare of others, which were Sir George's chief characteristics. Needless is it to say that the Westminster Orchestral Society has indeed lost a true and staunch supporter, and more than one of its members a dear, personal friend. Sad is it to think that the beloved voice, recently heard on the platform of the Royal Academy of Music, sympathizing so touchingly with the sorrows of

another bereaved family, should now be silent for ever, and
that those lips which have so often uttered words of affectionate encouragement to many a youthful and aspiring
musician, should now be cold and lifeless.   Such, however,
is the sad fate we have to lament ; and I now beg you for
a moment's silence ere we proceed to the remainder of our
evening's duties."

After a short pause, the "Dead March" was performed, and the members, before separating, gazed at
the handsome wreath to be sent that evening, in the
name of the Society, to the house of the departed
Professor.

Within a few days of the death of the Professor, I
was honoured by a request from the College of Organists, of which he had only recently been elected President for the year, to deliver an address to its members on his life and work.   With this request I felt
bound to comply, and in the following month read, to
a large and sympathetic gathering, including many
who did not belong to the College, a paper, which was
received with the interest inspired by the subject.   With
some variations, to suit changed surroundings and
listeners, I, by special request, re-read this paper, subsequently, before the Streatham Choral Society, the
Musical Association, the Royal Academy of Music,[1]
and the Royal Normal College and Academy of Music
for the Blind.

At the Royal College of Music an extra concert was
given in his memory, November 10th, when his String
Quartet in G (MS., 1878), Quintet in G minor [2] (piano
and strings), and the two songs, "A widow bird" and
"Pack clouds away"[3] (but with violin obbligato instead

---

[1] See p. 120.   [2] See p. 99.   [3] See p. 267.

of clarinet), were performed, as well as Beethoven's Quartet in F minor (Op. 95).

Little remains to be said in addition to the detailed account that has been given in these pages of the diversified and multifarious labours of the hard-working, high-minded musician whose career has been traced. All has not been recorded, indeed, concerning his works. A very large number of compositions, both printed and in manuscript, of all kinds, have not been mentioned. It is not pretended that these were of equal interest. Even with the acknowledgment of his great merits which was, on various occasions, rendered, and which, in his later years, few indeed would have withheld, it can hardly be said that Macfarren reaped the personal reward of his unweariedly staunch advocacy of English music. The day of its more general recognition seems to have dawned just as his day was declining. But all these his labours, and his earnestness respecting theoretical study, must continue to bear fruit, in spite of all cavils, or non-recognition of the source of the influences which are now working. A vocalist writes : " I do not believe the dear old man's influence was, or ever will be, thoroughly appreciated. To see that patient, concentrated face, was a lesson in itself." A pupil writes: " Some writer in a newspaper seems to hint that he was too much addicted to the love of fugue, and was too learned, to have done much to raise music in England ! " A strange combination of superficiality and misapprehension, surely ! " I believe nobody knows the vast progress made in music in England during late years, simply owing to his steady, quiet, and earnest influence."

Miscellaneous incidents, from various sources, may be mentioned that illustrate different points in his character.

As illustrating his undauntedness : he would not begin a work that he did not feel able to finish ; and, having begun it, he would complete it, whether with prospect of performance or publication, or not. This was an article of artistic faith with him : he would say to his pupils : "The French say it is the first step which *costs,* but I am sure it is the last step which *pays.*" He would also say that, although it was ill waiting for a posthumous fame, it was yet a duty to one's own talents to leave works in a complete state. So, everything of his was completed, not relinquished, though with no immediate prospect but to put it away. This was the case with "Kenilworth," even when he knew that it was not to be performed during the season for which it was commissioned.[1] He took minute pains with it. He availed himself gladly of the opportunity of an interview with three ladies who were familiar with Cumnor Place, the form of the house, the lie of the passages, etc., that being the scene of a good deal of the Opera; and he was pleased to accept a model of part of the house, that he might feel over the form of it. Though merely a cardboard box or two, cut up and sewn together, he treasured it in his little study, because "given in kindness": "such things he valued; they must be taken care of." "He was not afraid of undertaking this Opera in Italian, for he always thought that the best language for singing," notwithstanding all that he had written about its "evil influence": "English

[1] See p. 198.

came next,—very close behind Italian; German and French, a long way behind."

Although the "books" of his Operas and Oratorios are, rightly, ascribed to John Oxenford, etc., yet the construction was in most cases—probably in all, except those written by his father—Macfarren's own : the lyrics, etc., of the Operas, and the selection of the illustrative and reflective passages in the Oratorios, being the work of those whose names are attached to the respective *libretti*.

His memory and his sense of locality seem to have gone hand in hand. When in Swanage, walking with a pupil, he knew, notwithstanding his blindness, how they were proceeding, and pointed out Corfe Castle, at one place; and, at another, said, "Now, look on your left, and you will see the house occupied by John Wesley."

He was hurt by even a kindly intentioned advantage being taken of his blindness; as when a gentleman called on him to inquire various particulars, and seek advice, respecting candidateship for a Cambridge degree; and, thinking that he had occupied the Professor's valuable time, left a fee on the table. When Macfarren discovered it, he was sorely offended.

Family affection was a strong trait in his character, with all the tenderness therein involved. One best qualified to attest this tells how, when a little granddaughter was staying in his house,

" he used to arrange special times for her to read her History (a baby affair), and other tasks, to him; she lying on a sofa because of weakness, he sitting by her side, explaining and enlarging on the text. Nothing ever seemed small or unimportant to him : he had the happy gift of raising all things into an intellectual atmosphere, where the appearances of life range themselves in unfading types."

It is hoped that the insertion of the following letter may be accepted on account of the artistic friendliness which it evinces, rather than as an intrusion of personal vanity: let it rather be charitably called pardonable pride. The letter has reference to the biographer's "Fantasia tanto patetica quanto appassionata," for the pianoforte, dedicated to Professor Macfarren.

"7, Hamilton Terrace, N.W.
"6th Feb.

" MY DEAR BANISTER,

"I could not fitly thank you for your Fantasia till I had heard it, and I could not hear it till to-day. The publication of such a work is most highly to your credit, expressing, as the music does, the best aspirations of an artist, and taking no aim at pecuniary profit, or popularity. I feel its dedication to be the greatest compliment you could pay me, and I can but wish the circulation of the piece may help to make known our friendly relationship.

"Yours with kind regards,
"G. A. MACFARREN."

He was interested in the culture, and even in the amusement of a less exalted, if not debasing, kind, of the people at large. He related to a highly esteemed professor how a wealthy man had engaged Drury Lane Theatre, on two occasions, for the purpose of giving free entry to a mass of poor persons of all ages to witness the pantomime. "Oh! that I might have been there to see," he said, with great emotion.

Some poor pupils at a benevolent institution, to

whom he had shown kindness, desirous of expressing their gratitude, subscribed to present him with a ticket for a musical performance of special interest to himself. The admission was to an upper gallery, where they themselves also sat. Though persuaded to go to the higher priced seats, where he might have had the *entrée,* he insisted on going into the same place as the humble, well-meaning friends who had testified their regard. In small incidents such as these, he ever exhibited the delicate feeling and true humility which so constantly characterized him.

No peroration of panegyric seems necessary to this memoir. Macfarren's position as a composer, time must determine. "The old order changeth," and there is much in current musical thought which is transitional if not revolutionary. But of Macfarren's wide-reaching influence, by his earnest thinking, and persistent teaching, spoken and written, there can be little question among unprejudiced observers. While the marvellous attainments, memory, and achievements, under such depressing circumstances, and in the face of such apparently unconquerable obstacles, must surely command the lasting admiration of all who can appreciate stedfast energy and undaunted determination, affording an example such as may well furnish encouragement and stimulus to all aspiring students, who can hardly be weighted as he was, who, nevertheless, so succeeded in leaving his mark upon Musical Art.

No more fitting conclusion to this record can be made than these touching words by his intimate and appreciative friend and pupil, who has already been so frequently and freely referred to :—

" A few years ago we used to hear from his critics, even among his friends,—' a master of musical resources,'—' the first contrapuntist in Europe,'—' his strength is in dramatic writing,' etc., etc. Now that he is gone, we hear hushed whispers of the tenderness and pathos of his music. One says, ' Nothing more lovely than his anthem, " The Lord is my Shepherd " ' ; another speaks of the tender beauty of an introit, 'When all things were in quiet silence ' ; others mention the pathos of a melody written for a pupil to set with variations, a touching song, ' I arise to seek the light.' Not till his death comes to open their eyes to it, do men see what his nearest and dearest have long seen— that his finest characteristic was the tenderness of his heart, the depth and strength of his feeling, the quickness and sincerity of his sympathy ; for all of this comes out in his music. We who knew him closest· feel how much his great sorrow—those fifty years of first twilight, and then total darkness—made his character what it was ; that he could never have been the man he was, the friend he was, nor the artist he was, without it. Doubtless the story of that half-century of effort to live usefully and bravely under what would have been to most men a crushing weight; and the culminating ten months' struggle for life and duty, has shown what otherwise men could not know. All now can realize what he felt, when he wrote all that is touching in his music, and the verdict comes to all hearts, ' He felt this, and we can feel with him.' "

INDEX.

CHISWICK PRESS :—C. WHITTINGHAM AND CO., TOOKS COURT,
CHANCERY LANE.

WORKS BY PROFESSOR H. C. BANISTER.

Professor of Harmony, Counterpoint, and Composition (and of the Pianoforte) in the Royal Normal College and Academy of Music for the Blind, in the Guildhall School of Music, and in the Royal Academy of Music.

Fcap. 8vo, cloth, 5s.

TEXT BOOK OF MUSIC. Fourteenth Edition.

Thirty-fifth Thousand. This Manual contains chapters on Notation, Harmony, and Counterpoint; Modulation, Rhythm, Canon, Fugue, Voices, and Instruments; together with exercises on Harmony, an Appendix of Examination Papers, and a copious Index and Glossary of Musical Terms.

". . . . The neat, clear, and concise language in which it is written makes it a refreshing and agreeable study for musical students. The fact that an eleventh edition has been called for is a sufficient witness to its importance and widespread popularity among musicians."—From the *Biographical Dictionary of Musicians*, by JAMES D. BROWN, Glasgow, 1886.

Second Edition, revised. Crown 8vo, 7s. 6d.

LECTURES ON MUSICAL ANALYSIS, embrac-
ing Sonata-form, Fugue, &c. Illustrated by the Works of the Classical Masters.

"It is beyond comparison the best work on the subject in our language."—*Athenæum.*

"The excessive care with which extracts have been made from the best classical models in illustration of the plan thus explained, is deserving of the warmest commendation; and we are certain that any pupil who attentively reads these chapters will derive a very large amount both of pleasure and profit from the study."—*Musical Times.*

Second Edition with an additional Paper. Fcap. 8vo, cloth, 2s.

MUSICAL ART AND STUDY : Papers for Musi-
cians. Printed on hand-made paper.

"The volume contains three papers . . . . all of which exhibit a commendable desire to elevate the art in public estimation, and a keen perception as to the best method of effecting this object. We cordially commend both Mr. Banister's works as most valuable aids to the true appreciation of the imperishable creations of musical art."—*Musical Times.*

"The book is full of material for thought, and should be widely read."—*Musical Standard.*

LONDON : GEORGE BELL AND SONS.

MESSRS. BELLS' BOOKS.

Sixth and Popular Edition. Crown 8vo, 2s. 6d.

MEMORIALS OF THE HON. ION KEITH-FALCONER,
late Lord Almoner's Professor of Arabic in the University of Cambridge, and
Missionary to the Mahommedans of Southern Arabia. By the Rev. Robert
Sinker, D.D., Librarian of Trinity College, Cambridge. With new Portrait.
"We can warmly recommend the book as a faithful record of a really remarkable career, and of a character which possessed all the elements of nobility,
strength, devotion, unselfishness, faith."—*Guardian.*

A MEMOIR OF EDWARD STEERE, D.D., LL.D. (Third
Missionary Bishop in Central Africa). By the Rev. R. M. Heanley, M.A. Oxon.
With Portrait, Four Illustrations, and Map. Second Edition, Revised. Crown
8vo, 5s.
"Strong sense, clear vision, a firm grasp of truth, a wide charity, and breadth
of view which recognized true work under any outward form, as well as unsparing
devotion and lively sympathy, are qualities which may be seen in every page of
this memoir."—*Guardian.*

SCHUMANN (ROBERT): His Life and Works. By August
Reissmann. Translated from the third German edition by A. L. Alger. 3s. 6d.
"Herr Reissman's Life of Schumann stands very high among the biographies
of the masters. The translator has done his work, on the whole, with very great
skill."—*Musical World.*
"As a concise guide to Schumann's musical works, we do not know a more
convenient little volume."—*Saturday Review.*

SCHUMANN'S EARLY LETTERS. Originally published by
his Wife. Translated by May Herbert. With a Preface by Sir George Grove,
D.C.L. 3s. 6d.
"A fascinating little volume."—*Athenæum.*

FURIOSO: or, Passages from the Life of Ludwig van
Beethoven. From the German. Crown 8vo, 6s.

Two volumes, demy 8vo, 32s.

THE EARLY DIARY OF FRANCES BURNEY. 1768–
1778. With a selection from her Correspondence, and from the Journals of her
sisters, Susan and Charlotte Burney. Edited by Annie Raine Ellis, Editor of
"Evelina" and of "Cecilia," by Frances Burney.
"Mrs. Ellis has done the editing admirably, and she must have brought infinite
care and patience to an extremely laborious task."—*Times.*
"We have not for a long time come across such a land of pure delight in the
book sense as the volumes which Mrs. Ellis has here been enabled to put before
the public."—*Saturday Review.*

NORTH'S LIVES OF THE NORTHS. Right Hon. Francis
North, Baron Guilford, the Hon. Sir Dudley North, and the Hon. and Rev.
Dr. John North. Edited by A. Jessopp, D.D. With Three Portraits. 3 vols.,
3s. 6d. each.
"Dr. Jessopp has added a reprint of the autobiography of the author, which
was published by him in a limited and now scarce edition a few years ago. . . .
Lovers of good literature will rejoice at the appearance of a new, handy, and
complete edition of so justly a famous book, and will congratulate themselves
that it has found so competent and skilful an editor as Dr. Jessopp."—*Times.*

COOPER'S BIOGRAPHICAL DICTIONARY. Containing
concise Notices (upwards of 15,000 of Eminent Persons of all Ages and Countries,
and more particularly of Distinguished Natives of Great Britain and Ireland).
By Thompson Cooper, F.S.A., Editor of "Men of the Time." With a Supplement, bringing the work down to 1883. 2 vols., 5s. each.
"The mass of information which it contains, especially as regards a number of
authors, more or less obscure, is simply astonishing."—*Spectator.*

LONDON : GEORGE BELL AND SONS.

New and cheaper re-issue in **fortnightly volumes**
2*s*. 6*d*. each (*formerly* 5*s*.).

The Aldine Edition

OF THE

British Poets.

THE Editors of the various Authors in this Series have in all cases endeavoured to make the collections of Poems as complete as possible, and in many instances copyright Poems are to be found in these Editions which are not in any other. The volumes are carefully edited, in most cases with Notes and a Memoir. A steel Engraving also is added in all cases where an authentic Portrait is accessible. The volumes are printed on toned paper at the Chiswick Press, in fcap. 8vo. size, and tastefully bound in cloth by Messrs. Burn and Co.

The volumes will be issued in the following order :—

1. BLAKE. With a Memoir by W. M. ROSSETTI, and *Portrait.* *Sept.* 1.

2. KEATS. With a Memoir by the late Lord HOUGHTON, and *Portrait.* *Sept.* 15.

3. CAMPBELL. Edited by his Son-in-law, the Rev. A. W. HILL. With Memoir by W. ALLINGHAM, and *Portrait.* *Oct.* 1.

4 and 5. COLERIDGE. With Introduction and Notes by T. ASHE, B.A., St. John's College, Cambridge. *With Portrait and an Engraving of Greta Hall.* 2 vols. *Oct.* 15, and *Nov.* 1.

6 and 7. CHATTERTON. Edited by Rev. W. W. SKEAT, M.A. Including the acknowledged Poems and Satires, the Rowley Poems, with an Essay proving their authorship, a Memoir of the Poet, and Selections from his Prose Writings. 2 vols. *Nov.* 15, and *Dec.* 1.

8. VAUGHAN. Sacred Poems and Pious Ejaculations. With Memoir by Rev. H. LYTE. *Dec.* 15.

9. ROGERS. With Memoir by EDWARD BELL, M.A., and *Portrait*. *Jan.* 1.

10. RALEIGH AND WOTTON. With Selections from the Writings of other COURTLY POETS from 1540 to 1650. Edited by Ven. Archd. HANNAH, D.C.L. *With Portrait of Raleigh.* *Jan.* 15.

11. HERBERT. Edited, with Memoir, by Rev. A. B. GROSART, and *Portrait*. *Feb.* 2.

12. GRAY. With Life, additional Notes, and Bibliography by J. BRADSHAW, M.A., LL.D., and *Portrait*. *Feb.* 16.

13. GOLDSMITH. With Life, additional Notes, and Bibliography by J. BRADSHAW, M.A., LL.D., and *Portrait*. *March* 2.

Other volumes will be announced shortly.

"This excellent edition of the English classics, with their complete texts and scholarly introductions, are something very different from the cheap volumes of extracts which are just now so much too common. . . . . We have nothing but praise for this new re-issue of the Aldine Poets, on the whole, as regards form and outward appearance, to say nothing of intrinsic attractions."—*St. James's Gazette.*

"An excellent series. Small, handy, and complete."—*Saturday Review.*

"The strong and handsome binding of this series deserves a word of commendation."—*Guardian.*

LONDON: GEORGE BELL AND SONS.

www.ingramcontent.com/pod-product-compliance
Lightning Source LLC
Chambersburg PA
CBHW030950110726
47900CB00004B/1202